Taken
Liberty

A Tale From The Arbiter Chronicles

by

Steven H. Wilson

TAKEN LIBERTY
copyright © 2005, Steven H. Wilson

This is a work of fiction. All the characters and events portrayed in this book are fictitious, and any resemblance to real people or events is purely coincidental.

Published by
    Firebringer Press
    6101 Hunt Club Road
    Elkridge, MD 21075

ISBN: 0-9773851-0-8

February, 2006

Printed in the United States of America

The Arbiter Chronicles is a Trademark of Steven H. Wilson

Cover photo by Renée D. Wilson

For the Contact Crowd, the Farpoint Committee and the Usual Suspects

And for Renée, Ethan and Christian, always.

Audio Dramas written by Steven H. Wilson

The Arbiter Chronicles:

Mutiny Springs Eternal

A Man Walks Into A Bar

Man of Letters

The White Lady

Playing Politics (February, 2006)

Granny, a Ghost Story of the North Carolina Mountains

Available from Prometheus Radio Theatre

www.prometheusradiotheatre.com

Acknowledgments

I couldn't have gotten this book finished without the support and encouragement of an incredible group of people. Scott Farquhar, Renfield, June Swords, my wife Renée and my mother-in-law, the late Beverly Volker, suffered through the early drafts.

Eli Senter, Howie Weinstein and Cindy Woods were my readers for the final (almost, anyway) version, and gave me the confidence to believe someone might actually enjoy reading the thing. Howie, additionally, provided maddeningly good suggestions on how to *fix* what he thought was wrong.

Dr. Yoji Kondo ("You *are* writing, aren't you, Steve?") answered endless pesky questions on interstellar travel. His daughter, the brilliant evolutionary biologist Beatrice Kondo, told me where my ideas on genetic engineering were all wet. (Scientists with brilliant scientist daughters. You'd think they were characters in a Heinlein novel. You'd be right. They were, at times.)

Sandy Zier-Teitler performed the arduous editing and proofreading tasks. Paige Senter endured damp and dust and bright lights in her eyes to pose for the cover.

And the cast of Prometheus Radio Theatre brought the characters to life for me, on stage and in the studio. What more rewarding experience can a writer have?

Wondering what's hot this week in Quintopolis? Just ask any of the young men bathing on the beaches of the Confederacy's tropical paradise planet. You'll recognize the ones we mean – their skin is just *that* shade of bronze, their hair blond almost to whiteness, their eyes dyed to that particular shade of ice blue, their naked bodies painted to resemble the miliary regalia of a Confederate Navy captain. Not just any Confederate Navy captain, mind you. We're talking about *the* Captain's Captain, Jan Atal.

And if you don't know who *he* is, gentlebeing, get out from under that rock! (Unless your health or chosen lifestyle depends on that beautiful rock, and no offense meant by your humble editors.)

That's right, Atal's back, fresh from the wars – almost. That is why the rage among the young and beautiful is to be as beautiful and harshly masculine as Atal himself. The scion and heir apparent to the Atal Industrial fortune, the leader who led our boys and girls to victory over the Qraitians in more battles than little Brand Greer has styles of nipple rings, the bad boy and plague of the Admiralty, is back. He's been away on patrol of the Qraitian Border, guarding us against threats and incursions we don't *even* want to know about!

Eyebrows were raised when he was sent away on *that* little mission, as we're sure you know. Say what you want about our need to have the best resources out there where the Qraitian Empire lurks, those in the know know that everyone would be more comfortable with the keystone of our military right here among us. So why did he go away? You may remember, a few years back, this journal chronicling how our intrepid Captain, just back from the Qraitian War that nearly ended it all for little humanity, was placed in charge of reclaiming our worlds that those nastiest of nasties had taken from us in battle. We told you further how, learning that some Confederate military governors were skimming profits off the top for themselves on those beleaguered worlds, Atal dragged their scurvy hindsides out into daylight and saw them busted for their trouble.

Well, guess what? Some of those embezzling crooks had friends and relatives in high places. We won't name names, but one had an uncle in the Admiralty itself. Any coincidence, then, that they made Atal a lowly teacher at the Naval Academy on Hestia?

We don't think so either. Nor was it a coincidence when, not long after, the man who should have made Admiral before he was fifty was shipped off to the Border when he stood in defense of one of his cadets at a court martial. He won the case, but he was shipped off to the armpit of space in the tiny ship *Arbiter*. Boo! say we to the Admiralty!

But our hero is back to protect us. Okay, sure, he won his battles twenty years ago. But a hero's a hero. And one fine piece of hero he is! Touted as a masterpiece of genetic engineering, it's rumored two genius designers spent six years apiece just mapping out his penis! (And we're still working on getting you exclusive holos of *that* work of art. Sorry, lads and ladies, those "authentic" replicas you've been buying in the curio shoppes just ain't even close.)

And best of all? Public pressure has finally caused the Admiralty to get something right! Atal will be taking command of that grand old lady herself, the *CNV Titan*, flagship of our fleet and pride of the stars. And do you admirers of real bravery think our boy will stay out of trouble this time? Time will tell, but we think the answer's a big, fat, "no."

Chapter One
The Trouble with Aer'La

"She's not human!"

Dr. Romney Flynn's nostrils flared, and his face reddened. That was unusual. The genetically engineered citizens of the Inner Worlds usually had more control over physical manifestations of emotion.

Unusual or not, Flynn's new Captain, Jan Atal, did not bother to mention it. He was intent on studying a readout on the efficiency of his ship's engines.

"Eh?" asked Atal. "How's that?"

"The one called Aer'La."

"What about her?"

"She's not – Captain, are you listening?"

Atal turned to study the man. Flynn was out of shape, soft in all the wrong places. Lack of fitness was also unusual in the Inner Worlds. He'd probably been handsome once, due to good genetic design. Now, his general air of irritable superiority nullified anything naturally pleasant about his looks.

"I warned you, Doctor, that I was very busy," said Atal. "*Titan* launches in less than a day, and I would not call her spaceworthy... even if the Navy would."

"It is my job," Flynn said testily as Atal punched up a more detailed readout on engine performance, "to ensure that the crew is spaceworthy."

"Surely you'd done the bulk of that work before I arrived. There's been very little crew turnover, with the exception of – "

" – With the exception of yourself, Captain," Flynn finished for him, "and the officers you transferred with you from border patrol. I was hard-pressed to examine them all in time."

"Their medical records were transferred," said Atal, crawling under a console as he spoke. He cursed to himself as he discovered dust. The automatic cleaning systems must have been disengaged.

"Captain!" Flynn prompted, as Atal went silent for too long.

"Still here, Doctor. I was about to say that my personal physician has kept very close tabs on the health of all the officers who came with me from the *Arbiter*. I'm sure you could consult with Dr. Faulkner – "

"Your personal physician," Flynn interrupted, "is little more than a faith healer! I can hardly place any stock in the medical opinion of someone who would rather appeal to the goddess to realign the body's energy than perform surgery!"

Atal came out from under the console and could not help but grin.

"My personal physician is standing right behind you. Hello, Celia!"

Celia Faulkner grinned acerbically. She was over one hundred years old, but she didn't look it. At least half her short-cropped hair was still its original fiery red, her face bore only the lines it needed to display character, and she stood straight. She didn't stand tall, for she wasn't; but she stood straight.

"Good morning, Captain," she said.

"You're too late," said Flynn. "I've already come to tell him."

"And I'm waiting patiently – with more patience than you've shown me – to hear what you have to tell me," said Atal.

"He thinks Bos'n Aer'La isn't human," said Celia.

"She's not," insisted Flynn. "I've just completed my examination of her." He snapped his fingers. A holo appeared. Flynn gave it a shove in Atal's direction. It chased its way down to where the Captain still sat on his haunches and stopped inches from his nose. Unable to actually see it as it bobbled noiselessly before him, Atal shushed it to a viewable distance with one finger. As the interface programmer intended, the three-dimensional image obediently shifted two feet away from the finger which had broken its containment envelope.

Atal grimaced at the cluster of glowing numerals before him.

"Those," Flynn continued, "are the results of standard bloodwork. On Aer'La's blood. Note the count of 3x27-tagged proteins."

Biology was not the Captain's forte. He asked, "Something wrong with her diet?"

"They're antibodies, captain. The result of exposure to the Varthan Flu virus. It's an exceedingly common illness in Varthan Freespace. Humans do not develop Varthan flu, but they do develop Bergstrom's Syndrome as a result of exposure."

"So?"

"So, Aer'La doesn't have Bergstrom's syndrome. Has never had it. And her story about picking up the virus as a child, living on New Bedford – "

"Well, she is from New Bedford," said Celia.

Flynn hmphed at her. "New Bedford is a convenient birthplace. Most of the records were destroyed when the colony was lost to famine. After the food riots and the mass executions, anyone attempting to cover her tracks might claim to be a Bedford refugee."

"Why are you so convinced she's trying to 'cover her tracks,' Physician?" Atal asked.

"Because, Captain Atal, while there were numerous ills suffered by New Bedford during its final days, its quarantine against Varthan Flu remained intact. There was not one, single case." He sniffed again. "I did my doctoral thesis on disease on failing worlds – New Bedford, being recent, was one I researched in depth. I therefore examined Aer'La's bloodwork personally. There's no question in my mind – the little bitch is a Varthan Feral."

Celia Faulkner's eyes narrowed, and she opened her mouth to speak. Atal gestured for her to hold her peace.

"It's not appropriate to speak of a fellow officer that way, Doctor."

He snorted in disbelief. "A fellow — !"

Atal cut him off. "Aer'La is field-commissioned, but an officer nonetheless." He added. "Until proven otherwise."

"Well, I believe I've proven – "

"And, even if she is proven to be of Varthan descent, I will tolerate no demeaning racial slurs being applied to any person on this ship, while I'm its Captain. Is that clear?"

Flynn nodded quickly. "Of course, sir."

"Good. Now, as to Bos'n Aer'La... What do you propose I do, if your claims are borne out?"

"Take her into custody, of course!"

"I don't believe you've convinced me of her crime."

"She posed as a human!"

Atal raised an eyebrow. "Is that a crime?"

Flynn considered it. "It is proof of extreme dishonesty."

"Dishonesty – motivated by an impulse to survive – is no crime."

"Oh, don't be dramatic, Captain!"

"Romney, have you been to Varthan Freespace?" Celia Faulkner demanded. "Do you know the conditions the ferals have to live in? The children are raised to be nothing but sexual servitors. They're kept drugged nearly all the time – "

"Because most female Varthan ferals can tear a human male in half with their bare hands!" Flynn shot back.

"Superior strength is no excuse for slavery," Celia maintained. "And do you know what Varthan slavers do to escapees? The Captain is hardly being dramatic when he says that an escaped feral's very survival would depend on going undiscovered."

"Then you admit she is a feral?" Flynn countered. "I would be surprised if that fact escaped even your medical abilities."

"That's enough, Dr. Flynn," Atal said loudly, cutting off Celia's reply. "And I'm not prepared to discuss the matter until we've investigated further."

"That is your prerogative," said Flynn, "But there's no doubt as to what she is. Surely, Captain, you know enough about ferals to know we can't have one running loose on the ship. With the pheromones they secrete and their... training... Just think of the effect on the men aboard! A Varthan female, unrestrained among human males, will entice as many as necessary to satisfy herself. At the height of their sexual fever, the females have been known to rape and kill!"

Atal held out a hand for quiet. "All right, Doctor Flynn. I'm familiar with the nature of Varthan ferals." He sighed. "And granted, a female Varthan can be dangerous. But if — and I do stress if — Bos'n Aer'La is a Varthan, why did I have no incidents on *Arbiter*? She served with me for a year, and with Captain Miles for some time before that."

"I — I wouldn't know, sir." Flynn said disingenuously.

Atal raised an eyebrow and fired off a mildly dangerous sneer. "You were about to say something else?"

"I believe you are aware, sir, that a feral attached to a human master can be controlled. The psychological bond formed, ferals being pack animals — "

"Aer'La is not an animal, Doctor," said Celia, her voice so sharp and tight it might have sheered steel.

"Nonetheless, Doctor, you understand my point. Like canines, ferals bond with a leadership figure, will not challenge him, will remain monogamous with that leader, if that leader is using them sexually." He looked pointedly at Atal.

"Are you suggesting that I was keeping my Boatswain... as a slave?"

"It would explain — " Flynn began.

Atal stood, looming over Flynn. The Captain had never considered it fair to use his considerable height as a weapon, but sometimes it was damned effective. "You'd better worry about explaining your insubordination to a court martial board if you try to take that story any farther, mister!"

The Doctor flushed, and, for a change, looked a trifle intimidated. "I — no offense meant, sir. I'm merely considering all possibilities."

"Then consider that your judgment may be in error."

Atal turned and mounted a gangway, moving to leave the engine room. He did not look to see if Flynn would follow, but assumed he would. Atal reached the bounce tube before Flynn caught up with him, Celia close on his heels. Celia never was one to miss a good fight.

"Captain," Flynn called after him, his breath coming unevenly as he hurried, "I am well aware that you would prefer – "

Atal seized the handholds at the entrance to the bounce tube, lifted his feet into it, and dropped. He plummeted down through several levels of *Titan's* huge superstructure, gliding gently along, as force fields caught him automatically and supported his mass. He emerged, quickly, on one of many gangways leading to the ship's stores. Flynn and Celia emerged soon after.

"I said, sir, that I am well aware you would prefer another officer as your ship's physician." Flynn gave Celia a withering glare and added, "Any other officer."

"I never said that," said Atal. "I am an officer in the Navy like any other – my assignment as Captain of the flagship notwithstanding. I work with the people I'm assigned."

"That's a little hard to swallow," said Flynn, "coming from a man who managed to have so many of his proteges brought aboard as midshipmen. No one who can secure prime slots for two Terrans is an innocent pawn of the Admiralty."

"You have a problem with Terrans, Flynn?" asked Atal.

"Many Inworlders have a problem with Terrans. Many think you included them in the crew to make a point."

"I included Metcalfe and Carson in the crew," said Atal tightly, "because they are outstanding examples of naval officers. If that offends those who believe that only the genetically engineered are capable of excellence, I do not have time to be concerned."

"You need to be concerned, sir, that you have developed a reputation for giving preference to non-Inworlders in your everyday decision-making. That is a sign of prejudice, don't you think?"

They'd reached the food storage area, and Atal stopped at its entrance, turning on Flynn. "If you have a complaint to make about my treatment of you, Doctor – "

"I do, sir!" interrupted Flynn. "Beginning with your failure to address my concern that a dangerous alien may be loose aboard this ship!"

"And how would you have me address it?" asked Atal. "I've already told you that being an alien isn't a crime. The girl has a spotless record. You tell me she's a Varthan. What if she is?"

Flynn's mouth hung open. "What if she – ?"

A young man in a coverall matching Atal's rounded a corner, heading for the door they were currently blocking. Atal flagged him down.

"Sir?" the young man asked.

"Are you one of the quartermaster staff?"

"Yes sir. My name's Kendall, sir."

"Good to have you aboard, Mister Kendall." Atal jabbed a thumb at the door. "I came to check out this hold. It's rations for the casual crew, is it not?"

"That's correct, Captain."

Atal nodded. "And the manifests that came across my desk this morning said it contains grade-K nutrient packs."

"That's right, sir."

"That's wrong, Mister Kendall," Atal frowned. "I ordered that rations for the casual crew match the rations for my officers and the marine contingent."

Kendall shifted on his feet. Atal knew the poor boy was trapped between a rock and a hard place. "Sir... respectfully... the quartermaster's mate felt we didn't have the storage for all those supplies."

"Is the quartermaster's mate suggesting that I don't know the storage specs for my own ship?" Atal asked pleasantly.

"Oh, no sir! At least... I don't think so. It's just... well, Captain, it's customary to feed the casuals..." Kendall's face indicated he was searching for the words.

"Garbage?" supplied Atal.

"Storage efficient foodstuffs," finished Kendall.

Atal put his hand gently on Kendall's shoulder. "Mister Kendall, would you pass a message to the quartermaster's mate for me? Tell him that I ate grade K nutrient packs for sixteen straight months during the war with the Qraitian Empire. Tell him they taste like human excrement, and look worse. Tell him I won't ask anyone working for me to dine on excrement, unless he cares to volunteer to do so himself."

Kendall swallowed.

"Can you tell him that for me? And tell him to feel free to bring any questions he may have to my attention."

Kendall nodded.   "Yes sir," he muttered, and began to walk away.

"Sir," said Flynn, "I believe – "

Atal held up his hand and called after Kendall. "Mister Kendall? Also tell your boss to check his personal inbox. There'll be a commendation there for you from the Captain, for exemplary conduct in dealing with a very demanding superior officer."

Kendall grinned and blushed. "Thank you, sir."

Atal turned back to Flynn. "You were saying?"

"You were saying," Celia reminded Atal. "You were saying 'what if Aer'La is a feral?' I believe you've shocked Romney."

"Have I shocked you?" asked Atal.

"Are you seriously proposing that no action be taken against her?" asked Flynn. His tone was shrill.

Atal shrugged. "She's committed no crime."

"She's stolen property!" cried Flynn.

"How do you figure?" asked Atal. "Who stole her?"

"A Varthan feral is legally the property of her owner, just as an animal would be. If she escapes custody, well... it's the same as if you'd picked up someone's pet. If you keep her here, knowing her real, legal status, Captain... you've stolen her."

"You really believe that?" demanded Celia.

"It's not a question of what I believe," said Flynn. "It's a question of law."

"By Confederate law," said Atal, "no sentient being may own another."

"By Confederate law," Flynn reminded him, "the laws of member worlds take precedence, provided they do not threaten the safety of other member worlds. Varthan law allows the ownership of ferals."

"But we're not in Varthan Freespace," said Atal. "We're in the Quintil system. The seat of the Confederacy, and bastion of human freedom."

"The Admiralty will not see it that way, Captain. The Varthan trade lobby is powerful – "

"The Admiralty won't know," said Atal.

Flynn drew himself up to his full height. "I'm afraid they will, sir. As I have discovered the girl's origins, it is ultimately my responsibility to alert the Admiralty of a possible interstellar incident."

"You need only alert me," said Atal.

"No sir. I need only alert you if you're willing to report my discovery. If you don't report it, the responsibility falls, again, to me. I will not risk court martial to protect this feral of yours."

"And if I order you to keep it quiet?" asked Atal.

"You would stand trial yourself," said Flynn levelly, "for obstruction of justice."

"Flynn, you bastard," hissed Celia Faulkner. "You know what the Admiralty will do, in the name of 'interstellar harmony.' They'll hand Aer'La over to the Varthans! She'll be killed, or worse!"

"If she's a feral," Flynn said smugly.

"And if she's not," said Atal, "she'll have been replaced aboard *Titan* while the investigation was conducted. She'll lose her rank." He paused, considering the implications for his Bos'n. "You're taking a pretty big chance with someone's future, Flynn."

"It's my duty, Captain," said Flynn gravely.

"And your economic interest, no doubt," Celia observed. "Tell me, Romney, how many of your investments depend on slave labor?"

Flynn ignored her, and said to the Captain, "Remember, if you don't report it to the Admiralty. I will."

He walked away.

"Detestable man," said Celia Faulkner. "If I weren't a white witch, there are a dozen ways I could drop him in his tracks."

"Well," sighed Atal. "It looks like the jig is up. I suppose Aer'La was going to be found out, sooner or later. I just thought I could keep her secret until we were better prepared to defend her."

"I tried to keep her secret from you, back on *Arbiter*," said Celia. "We know how that turned out."

Arbiter...

Atal had always thought it one of the great ironies of the Confederate Naval history that the ship named for the highest office in that part of space, the elected office of Arbiter, was one of the humblest, if not indeed the most squalid, in the service. An Arbiter of the Confederacy was one of a handful of individuals who made law which influenced countless worlds. The CNV *Arbiter*, on the other hand, did the kind of dirty work (with the kind of dirty people) that genteel folk didn't like to hear about. It was a great atmosphere for keeping secrets.

Atal, when he'd assumed command, had guessed right away that his new Bos'n was keeping secrets. He'd attempted to learn more from the only other seasoned officer aboard *Arbiter*, Celia Faulkner. The attempt had not gone as he'd hoped...

* * *

"I'm afraid I don't understand what you're getting at, Captain," Celia Faulkner said politely. "You think there's something wrong with Bos'n Aer'La?"

"Not wrong, exactly – "

" – there's nothing wrong with her. She's very good at her job, and she's a delightful girl."

"I agree with you," said Atal, stifling his impulse to be too placating with this woman who was twice his age. "But she doesn't look like anyone's idea of a Bos'n. And that's my first problem – she's too young and pretty."

"I wasn't aware that that was a problem, Captain."

"It's just out of place, that's all. Bos'ns are supposed to be big, gruff, intimidating characters."

"She's more than she appears to be."

"I'll say she is," agreed Atal. "The first time she opened her mouth in front of me, the only non-profane words she uttered were 'the' and 'is.' Some of the curses she bandied about were words I'd never heard."

"Yes, Aer'La swears like a sailor. Did you ever meet a bos'n who didn't? A Border crew is composed largely of undesirables, Captain. Hard cases and malcontents. The malcontents are those who stand a chance of getting out. The hard cases actually like it here. The hardest cases are the former malcontents."

Atal smiled. "Which are you, Doctor?"

She blinked. "I'm sorry?"

"It's unusual for someone born and raised on Hecate to leave home for more than a short trip. I believe you've been on *Arbiter* for quite a few years. Why would a follower of Wicca choose to live out here among the gentiles? Aren't you normally a pretty cloistered lot?"

"Yes, we are. The rest is none of your damned business, Captain."

"Fair enough."

"And, if you'll pardon my bluntness, Aer'La's secrets – if she has any – are her business as well, not yours."

Atal sighed. "Doctor, I learned a long time ago to trust my instincts. Despite living in a culture that urges us to not judge a book by its cover, I've lived enough years to realize that, when I sniff something wrong about a person, there usually is something wrong. And I sniff something wrong about Aer'La. Or maybe I should say something too right. She's like a little china doll, enhanced with a foulmouthed talk unit. So why are the casuals so afraid of her?"

Celia shrugged.

"Do you deny they are afraid of her?"

"I don't deny the obvious, Captain. Neither do I question it too intensely. People on border patrol distrust outsiders. I've learned not to ask too many questions."

"One might say you're being defensive, Doctor. Are you hiding something you know about Aer'La?"

"I – "

"Like, perhaps, her age? How old is she?"

"That is a matter of record, Captain. Why ask me? Consult her records. For that matter, consult your predecessor's logs."

"I've checked the records," said Atal. "And Miles's logs. They tell me she's an orphan from New Bedford, her childhood records destroyed. She was pressed into service at age fifteen – "

" – 'Pressed into service,' Captain? I don't believe I've ever heard a career officer utter the phrase."

"You'll find I'm plain spoken, Doctor. Whether the Admiralty wants to admit it or not, the majority of the casual crew are blackmailed or otherwise forced into serving aboard our ships by paid recruiters. Sometimes they come here to avoid jail time they fully deserve. Sometimes they're framed. Either way, the process stinks, and I will not attempt to perfume its stench."

For the first time, Celia Faulkner actually smiled. It softened a face which otherwise seemed to be carved in granite. "The legendary Atal pragmatism rears its head."

"I make no claims to being a legend."

"You don't have to. You are. Trust me, I've been a legend for some decades."

"I know," said Atal, relaxing for the first time in her presence. "The Old Witch of the Navy."

"Accurate on all three counts, though the stories of my mystical powers are largely exaggerated. I've never turned a crewman into a toad, for instance."

"But they're never sure you can't," said Atal. "And that, Doctor, makes you an excellent candidate to keep secrets for someone who has something to hide."

"Back to business. For a moment there, we almost managed to be civil."

"I'm rarely uncivil, Doctor; but I do insist on cooperation. If the girl is underage to serve here – "

"Captain, age is no guarantee of maturity. Some very old people can be exceedingly childish, as I'm frequently reminded by my children and grandchildren. And my younger husbands."

"Agreed. Still, I have no tolerance for the militarization of children. Soldiery is a necessary profession, but not a game to which the immature should be indoctrinated. I've found mature-looking twelve-year-olds in my crew before. I sent them home, or at least to a place of safety where they could get an education other than the harsh one of non-commissioned service."

She regarded him impassively. "How nice. Shall I commission a medal for you?"

"Why are you fighting me, Doctor?"

"I'm not, Captain, not really. I'm just suggesting you get the lay of the land before you take any action."

"I always do. And I'm a quick study, I hope. For instance, I take your suggestion to mean that Aer'La is underage?"

"Not any more."

"Hmph. Okay. Thanks for being honest. I suppose there's no need to ship her out retroactively. She's extraordinarily young for the job she's doing, but... she is doing it well. I never imagined a Border crew could be managed so tightly. How did my predecessor ever think to put her in as Bos'n?"

"She... displayed a knack," Celia said carefully. "Against a couple of skulls, when two of the casuals tried to rape her the first week she was here. Miles made her bos'n's mate. Then the bos'n left – "

"A mate usually follows her Master."

"Aer'La... let's just say her loyalty was to Captain Miles. He took care of her. In exchange..."

"Oh. Oh. It's like that."

"Some of us don't have the luxury of following the conventional path to promotion, Captain. It doesn't make us less valuable as officers. Or people." Her tone was hard, icy, even. Atal felt as if he'd failed a very critical test, given by a very demanding teacher.

"Doctor, I don't – "

"Just give the girl a chance, Captain. Not all questions deserve answers – not even the Captain's." She stood and smoothed the physician's smock she wore. "Excuse me. I need to get back to work."

* * *

Celia's defensiveness about Aer'La had only intensified Atal's curiosity. He'd kept a close eye on her. He was not alone. Most of the male (and a few of the female) members of the crew kept a close eye on her as well. He suspected their motives were less pure than his own. One could not help but be aware of one's self as a sexual being in her presence. He noted that she rarely returned to her quarters alone at shift's end.

He also noted that Aer'La wore strong perfume, and used it liberally. This was unusual in the Confederacy, where such a high level of control over the human body's functions had been achieved. Body odor was self-regulated, not masked by perfumes and colognes. It was true that some, especially those in the sex industry, spent a great deal of money having their body chemistry tailored to produce a certain scent, but cosmetic perfumes were common now only on Terra and other worlds with non-engineered populations.

Ship's gossip had it that she slept around, that she was sexually insatiable. No one gossiped to the captain, of course, nor did Atal place much stock in ship's gossip. Still, he'd long made a point of hearing it whenever he could. Just as the mythology of a culture can be as important to an understanding of its identity as is its recorded history, so can the bits of slander and bile that make the gossip circuit be a telling indicator of the state of mind of a group. Atal consequently kept his ears open when rounding corners, and he walked softly. He'd heard some interesting things in the course of his career.

In Aer'La's case, what he heard was hardly unusual: a pretty young girl, assigned to a ship crewed by misfits with questionable morals, was seeing a lot of sexual action.

The question nagging Atal was, amongst these jaded sensualists, why were Aer'La's exploits the stuff of conversation? Fortunately for his curiosity, he had an available spy for all matters sexual: Kevin Carson. While not outwardly interested in life itself, the boy was fiercely attractive to the majority of those his own age. Unlike the serious Metcalfe, whose intensity discouraged those who might otherwise approach him, Carson's lack of emotional involvement (an attribute which, in Atal's experience, cloaked a great deal of pain) was a magnet to sexual partners.

It was inevitable that Carson and Aer'La would at least entertain the idea of a liaison. He had only to wait. He kept his ears open, and soon the murmurings about the Boatswain and the "new kid" drifted into them.

And he called the "new kid" to his cabin.

* * *

"Sir, I... 'scuse me, but I'm not precisely sure what you're asking me."

Atal had given Carson permission to speak freely, made a little small talk, complimented him on his handling of L-space transmissions and monitoring during his first week. Then he'd stepped through the invisible wall between captain and crewman, teacher and pupil: he'd asked Carson to explain his relationship with Aer'La.

Kevin Carson didn't like to admit he had feelings. Beyond a certain level of machismo regarding his sexual conquests, and his continual irritation with Metcalfe, whom he nevertheless continued to shadow, he wanted it believed that he simply cared about nothing. Consequently, he didn't mention to anyone the names of sexual partners, and would never confess to being in "a relationship."

"I want to know," Atal said evenly, "if the rumors I'm hearing have any basis in fact."

Carson bit his lip thoughtfully. "I trust you have a very good reason to ask, sir."

With the wrong tone, it could have been a very impertinent question. It could have been downright insulting. Carson didn't use the wrong tone, however. He wasn't telling Atal to mind his own damned business; he was acknowledging his trust in his captain, that he would not ask a prying question without good reason. They both knew that Carson wouldn't have answered if were not for that trust. "I do have good reasons. And to protect Aer'La's privacy, I'm not going to share them with you. Suffice it to say that I need to know as much about her as possible."

"She's a bit of an enigma, isn't she?" he grinned. "Yes, Captain, she and I have..."

"I understand," Atal interrupted. "Have you noticed anything... out of the ordinary?"

"You mean like, 'she's hiding the fact that she's really a man?'"

"Well, I don't suspect she's a man."

"No, she's emphatically not," he said. "But I haven't noticed anything other than..."

"Yes?"

"She's very... competent."

"Sexually?"

"Yes, sir. It's as if she studied or something."

Atal allowed himself the briefest smile. At the same time, Carson's words caught him and stayed with him. 'As if she studied...'

"Did you notice her perfume?"

"Yeah. Cheap stuff, too. I asked her why she wears so much. She just said she likes to – never had it on her home world. But she never lets it wear off. Never."

"Do you know if she has any trouble with the rest of the crew?"

"Never. She says they're all afraid of her."

"Did she say why?"

"No, sir. She just admits she knows they are. Is she in trouble, sir?"

Atal didn't answer. He was assembling the pieces of the puzzle in his mind, and formulating a plan of action.

Finally, dismissively, he said, "Thank you, Carson, I think you've told me exactly what I need to know."

*   *   *

Atal hated secrets. He didn't like keeping them, and he despised having them kept from him. He was accustomed to being up front with people, and expected them to be so in return. To his thinking, any organization in which the majority of relevant operational discussions were held behind closed doors was an organization in grave trouble.

He knocked at the door of Aer'La's cabin. *Arbiter* was an old ship. It had once had the same announcement systems that all ships in the fleet had. Once upon a time on this vessel, he would have pressed his thumb against an indentation in the door frame, his print would have been read, and a voice inside the cabin would have announced him. If necessary, that same voice would have informed him if there was no response, or if the cabin's occupant had instructed that he not be admitted. Or it might have told him to carry out an impossible reproductive act. The system was passive when it came to accepting instructions. It made no attempt to edit or interpret.

Those systems on *Arbiter* had been disabled long ago. Border officers didn't believe in letting machinery substitute itself for etiquette, and they didn't want a disembodied voice chasing them all over the ship, letting them know someone was looking for them. They'd opted to be left alone.

Having checked the water usage to her cabin before coming, Atal knocked, knowing Aer'La was in the shower and, therefore, wouldn't hear him. He had timed his visit carefully. He entered the cabin, giving himself some time before Aer'La finished in the shower.

The room was typical of a Border officer's in that it was atypical. In this case, the cabin testified that its occupant was a slob. There were clothes discarded on the floor and entertainment cartridges scattered all over. In an unusual tribute to luxury on such a vessel, the bed (unmade) hosted a tangle of exotic fur comforters and satin sheets. Atal noted bottles of massage oil and lubricants and averted his eyes, which then caught the true oddity of the place: a hologram of a teenaged Quintillian musician. Larger than life, the boy's nude body stood slick with the sweat of an exhausting performance, his only attire a guitar (which he probably didn't know how to play.) A spray of tiny stars shot from his eyes, and he smiled, innocently and lewdly all at once, at his adoring onlookers.

Such holos were expensive, and designed to adorn the rooms of the impressionable and immature. A Captain hardly expected to see one in the cabin of his bos'n. Where the young singer fit into the equation he would divine later. For now, he had a suspicion to confirm. He sat down on the bed and waited patiently for Aer'La to emerge... without her perfume.

In the interior chamber the sound of running water ceased. He heard the muffled sounds of her coming out of the shower cubicle. She emerged moments later, clad as many women are following a shower, in two towels. One was wrapped around her body for warmth, the other draped over her head as she massaged her hair dry with it.

Without sensing the presence of an intruder, she reached for the bottle of perfume on her dressing table.

"Bos'n," Atal said quietly.

She didn't jump. She was neither a coward nor a victim of overactive nerves. She turned to regard him cooly. "Captain," she said, an eyebrow arched. "I wasn't expecting you."

"I didn't intend for you to expect me," he smiled. "I wanted to catch you without the perfume, so I could confirm my suspicions."

"And they are?" she asked quietly.

"You're a feral."

She did not answer, nor did her face register the sick horror of a fugitive discovered. She returned his gaze, as if assessing him. Then, carelessly, almost mechanically, she untucked the secured corners of towel from above her full, exquisite breasts, and dropped it, standing naked before him. When he said nothing, she began to advance on him slowly. There was no threat in her manner, though he knew, since she was a feral, that she could easily have killed him bare-handed. As she drew near, his arousal struck him like a gust of hurricane wind.

He caught her wrists and stopped her. She didn't fight. Strong as a Varthan woman is, he couldn't have held her off if she had fought.

"What are you doing?" he asked.

She shrugged. "Giving you what you came for."

There was no trace of bitterness in her voice, no suggestion that she resented the demands she must now expect him to make. Nor was there any enthusiasm evident. There was only resignation to the inevitable.

She was beautiful. Naked, the evidence that her skin was dyed was clearer – traces of darker blue in the creases and crevices of her flesh, around her nipples, at the smooth mound of her pubic region. "It would be worth having," he said quietly. "But it isn't what I came for. I don't take liberties with my crew."

"Why not?" she asked, in a tone that added, 'everyone else does.'

"It's bad for crew morale. It's bad for my ego. I never know if the attention is being given to me or this damned star on my belt."

She considered that. "That's... smart."

"Thank you."

"What the hell is someone smart doing out here?"

NCOs don't usually speak the master of a vessel that way; but this was the Border, Atal had entered the cabin without permission, and Aer'La was naked. The conference thus qualified as informal.

"I like to vary my experience."

"I hear you pissed off the old men."

"I hear I'm not really human, but an android sent to infiltrate a Qraitian vessel and detonate myself near the Home world." At this declaration, Aer'La looked confused. Atal clarified. "Be careful about rumors."

"I'm always careful. It's why I'm still alive. Why did you come here? To find me out?"

"To make certain I was correct, yes."

"And now you're gonna turn me in?" She asked. Then she reconsidered. "No, you're not that by-the-book. Think maybe you'll sell me? Escapees don't fetch much at auction. I'm good at gettin' away, too."

"And you're very honest, apart from disguising your race."

"Yeah, Captain, I am. I got no reason to lie to you now."

"I'm glad. That means you can tell me how you came to be here, and I'll be able to believe what I'm hearing."

She crossed her arms over her breasts – not for cover, just a thoughtful gesture, indicating she was baffled. "You're a strange one," she said.

"Really?"

"You're not here for sex. You don't wanna sell me – "

"I have no such intention. I just want to hear your story."

"I'm not sure I trust a man who doesn't want sex or money."

Atal laughed. "Neither do I. I assure you, Bos'n, I'm strongly interested in both. They're just not my first concern."

"What is?"

"My career – and thus my vessel and crew. I won't take any action – or allow any situation – which jeopardizes the people under my command."

She smiled without humor. "Like Varthan ferals running loose?"

"I'll reserve judgment until I know more about you."

"Okay," she said. She sat down, crossed-legged, on her bed, and gestured to a chair.

Atal cleared his throat, and, despite lifelong exposure to both nudity and public sexuality, averted his eyes. Aer'La, clothed, could have given a corpse an erection. Aer'La, naked, was far more than even a disciplined Naval officer could easily resist.

"Wouldn't you like to put some clothes on?" he asked.

"Not really. Would it make you more comfortable, Captain?"

"It would allow me to concentrate."

Chapter Two
Raised in Captivity

Haltingly at first, but with growing confidence as Atal listened attentively, Aer'La told her story...

I guess the first thing I remember is pain between my legs. I think I was about four years old. I don't really know. Inihu weren't taught to count. I was naked. We were always naked. I was on my back, on a table, and a big man's face was above me. I still have nightmares about that face. He had greasy black hair, and a beard. His breath stank. I wanted to hold my nose, but something, or someone, was holding my arms behind me, pinned down. Most of all, I remember he had a scar that ran up and down over his left eye. Even his eyelid had the scar, like someone had sliced a knife down it. His eye was okay, so I guess maybe he'd had a new one put in.

Something way too big shoved itself into my body down there. I felt something, some part of me, rip. I tried to scream, but they stuffed a cloth in my mouth. All I could do was lie there and cry. Now I know it was the man's dick – his penis, sorry – inside me. That was the first time. They did it to all the girls, at about that age. The man with the scar did most of us. He really enjoyed doing the first one to a girl.

I guess, after that, he wasn't much interested. They trained us – stuck something in us – all the time, but it was usually the old women who did it. They'd use fake ones, different sizes and shapes, and make us learn to hold them in. They didn't only put them where the man with the scar had put them, either. Some of the girls learned to like it. At least, they pretended they liked it. I guess I don't know. Maybe they thought I liked it, too. You learned to keep quiet, anyway. The whippings weren't as bad if you kept quiet while they stuck you. I learned to hold my breath, not to yell, not to let my eyes tear up.

I remember one little girl – younger than me – that didn't like it. She couldn't learn to take it like a big girl. The first time the scar man stuck her, she screamed and kicked and bit so hard she made herself bleed. I think she kicked him in the balls, too. I didn't see, but I heard, later. When she came back, she had bruises on her face and all over her body, where he must have beaten her. They laid her on the bed, and she cried herself to sleep. No one helped her. I thought about going to her, saying something to try to make it easier. I didn't. I was afraid.

I guess it's a good thing I was.

That night – the night after the little girl's first time – I remember waking up to screams and the sound of a fight. Some of the older girls had gotten up and pulled that little girl out of bed, the one who'd cried. They beat her. They threw her on the floor and kicked and punched her. She screamed and begged, but they kept it up. Then she stopped screaming, and they still kept it up.

I pulled my blanket over my head and pretended to be asleep. I wondered why none of the teachers came in. They were always right outside the door. There were three or four whippings a night for girls who got up, or talked, or just weren't asleep. Why weren't they coming in now?

Once, I opened my eyes just a crack. The little girl was on the floor, not moving. The other girls had finally stopped beating her, and were just looking at her. A few of them smiled. One spit on her. There was blood on her face, all purple, and a pool of it on the floor, under her head. I didn't know what death was then. I don't know, even now, if she was dead. "Think you're better than the rest of us?" one of them asked the little girl. I thought that was pretty stupid, 'cause I was pretty sure the little girl couldn't hear her, or say anything.

The teacher came in then. There weren't any whippings. She just told the girls to go to bed. They carried the little girl out of the room. That was the last time I ever saw her. After that, I knew you didn't dare tell anyone that it hurt. You didn't dare let on that you didn't like something they did to you. The teachers would only whip you, but the other girls were likely to kill you. That was the way it was.

* * *

I must have been eight or nine when that happened. It wasn't long after that that I first heard the 'F' word. By then, I didn't sleep alone as much any more. I was usually warming the bed of one of the masters, or one of their customers. But this was a night I got to sleep in a bed by myself, back in the barracks. That's where the Ini-hu stayed, when we weren't in use.

One of the other girls, Jin was her name, was in the room with me. I asked her what she thought might have happened to that little girl, the one that got beat almost to death. Had she died? Or had the masters killed her? Or what? How come we never saw her again? How come we were never told anything?

"Y'ain't s'posed to ask them questions, Aer'La," Jin said. She didn't sound mad. She wasn't one of the mean girls. That's why I felt like I could ask her about it.

"I know," I said. "I just wondered, is all."

Jin was quiet for a while. I figured I'd scared her, but then she whispered, "I bet she went to Freedom."

"Freedom?" I asked, "Where's that?"

Jin shushed me. "Don't say it out loud! It's not a place we're s'-posed to know about."

"What kinda place is it?"

"Well," she said slowly, "I reckon it's warm there. And bright and pretty."

After I got away, I found out that my home planet was a lot colder than most planets where people lived. That it was farther from its sun than most planets. I didn't know there were real places where you never got cold, or where you could even find a place to get completely warm. At home, the cold seemed to hang on, even when you sat right by the fire. And the sun wasn't as bright as the moonlight I've seen on some planets since.

"Where is it?" I asked.

"I don't know. I just heard of it. I heard it's a place where no one touches you, 'less you want them to."

"How do I get there?" I asked. A place where no one touched you... I wanted to go there.

See, I hated it. The sex, I mean. I wanted to scream and cry, too, every time. I'd seen what would happen, though, so I took it. I kept taking it. I even smiled and cooed and pretended it was exactly what I wanted. But I didn't want any of them near me. The things they did made me feel dirty, even when they didn't hurt. They usually hurt.

"I don't know," Jin answered. "I guess... I guess you gotta..." She whispered the last word. She was afraid of it. "Ex-scape."

I let out a yelp. You didn't say that word! No one escaped. No one talked about it, ever. It was a sin. No one had a right to say no, or to try to leave this place. We were made to be what we were. Anyone who wanted to be something else was a freak, and deserved to die. And I wanted to say no. And I wanted to leave. And I wanted to be something else. I deserved to die. So when Jin said the bad word out loud, I yelped, because it was all my sins come to light.

"Shut up!" Jin hissed at me. "You're gonna get us caught! Don't you tell no one I told you any of this!"

We didn't talk about it again. I didn't talk to anyone about it. I didn't dare. I might be found out, and punished worse than anything I'd been through yet.

But after that, when I was alone, or when the man or men I was with would roll off me and start to snore, I'd dream about that place Jin had told me about. That warm, bright place where no one ever touched you. That place called Freedom.

* * *

I got older. By ten or eleven, I'd grown big breasts, and my body didn't look like a little girl's. We Inihu grow up fast. I was called to serve the masters more often. I kept dreaming about going to Freedom, and hating the touch of a man's flesh on mine.

Then, one night, I was taken to the bed of Master Hix. He was one of the masters who didn't only keep Inihu girls for company. He kept a boy Inihu, too.

I knew there were boys of my kind, but I'd never met one. He was there alone in the master's bed chamber when they brought me in. I'll never forget the first sight of him. He was beautiful. He was small – smaller than me, though he was probably my age. He was lying on the bed silks, naked, and completely unashamed of it. All the men I'd ever met pretty much kept their clothes on, even during sex. They didn't show their bodies to mere Inihu. We only saw the parts we needed to deal with. This boy didn't bother to hide anything.

He had greyish skin, like mine. It was smooth and perfect, like a girl's, if she's been treated okay. The only hair on his body was on his head, and it was gold like honey. He had green eyes. He looked like a statue someone had made out of silver and gold, with emeralds set in the face. A pretty, sweet little statue. He was drinking from a gold cup, and playing with some kind of bone pieces on the bed silks. I later found out that they were pieces from a game. I didn't know what games or toys were. Inihu girls weren't given anything to play with. This was the first time I saw that Inihu boys were treated differently.

After my first glimpse of him, I made myself look away. He was like me, but he was a male. I'd been taught not to look at a male unless he wanted me to. I was supposed to be respectful and obedient, unless, in bed, I thought he wanted me wild. Then I could kick and claw and bite. Some of them liked that. If they didn't, they'd beat us for doing it. Of course, they were likely to beat us even if they liked everything we did.

He got up from the bed and walked towards me. I figured he was going to hit me for looking at him. I wondered if I was allowed to hit back at a boy Inihu like I was at a girl. The masters liked it when girls fought each other, but boys were the special property of just one master. This one might not want his boy damaged. I figured I should probably just let him hit me and leave it at that.

He didn't hit me, though. He smiled at me, a friendly smile. "I'm Druberj," he said. "Who're you?"

I didn't answer. Inihu didn't introduce themselves to each other. Or to anyone. No one cared what our names were. We only had them so the teachers could call us out to punishment.

"It's okay," he said. "We're alone. You can talk. The master won't be here for a while. Anyway, I know you're not afraid of me. I'm not strong enough to hurt you."

He was right. Female Inihu were designed a lot stronger than their brothers. It made us more exciting to the masters. It made us good fighters against each other, and it made us wild in bed. Boy Inihus were designed to be weak, so they didn't stand a chance of overpowering the masters. Girls could be controlled a little more easily, I guess.

"I'm Aer'La," I mumbled.

"Would you like something to drink?" he asked. He pointed to the goblet in his hand, and walked over to a sideboard, where there were more like it. He poured wine into one from a fancy, crystal bottle.

"Don't" I snapped at him. "That's the master's!"

He laughed. It was a good laugh. I'd never heard a laugh that wasn't harsh, or mocking, or brought on by someone else's pain. It was a playful laugh.

"So? I'm the master's, too. He likes for me to have wine," He grinned. "He says it loosens me up."

He held the cup out to me. I shook my head. "He'll whip us."

"He won't whip me," said the boy. "He wouldn't take the chance. Any scars would lower my value, in case he loses a big bet, and has to sell me off." He ran the backs of his fingertips over the curve of one smooth buttock. "Boys are rated on their skin. I don't get anything but spankings." He rolled his eyes. "But I get a lot of them. My master likes it. Last week, he bruised me, and he had to have the healer fix it."

I had been to the healer a few times, too, when the cuts from a whipping bled too much. My own back and buttocks were not perfect, like this boy's. They didn't care if a girl was perfect.

"That's nice for you," I said.

He knew I was mad. He bit his lip and pouted. "I'm sorry. I know how they treat you. But you're lucky, though. You're strong."

"So?" I asked.

"You can take care of yourself," he said, and I really got the feeling he admired me for it. "I'm the weakest kind of person there is. Always will be."

He was right. He wouldn't have lasted a day in the girl's barracks. I said we didn't have any toys, but we did. We had the weaker girls. Beating on them was our play, and we played for keeps. This little creature wouldn't have stood a chance against the smallest girl in my clan.

"At least you're allowed to have wine... and they care what happens to you," I said. "I don't think you'd want to be like me."

He thought about that. "I guess," he said. "I guess it would be better... if there were some place where neither one of us had to worry about getting hurt."

There was another difference between us. He said that with no fear. No Inihu girl would've dared speak so plainly. I wondered if he'd heard of Freedom, the place I dreamed of every night.

He held the goblet out again. "Please take it," he said. "The Master does like to use the whip, and... it'll hurt less, if you drink it."

It was a pretty sad offering. He knew I'd be whipped, knew there was nothing he could do to stop it, knew I'd probably leave with the beginnings of a new set of scars. But he offered me something to make it a little better. It was the first time in my life that anyone had ever shown that they gave a damn what happened to me.

I took the cup, and drank it right down. We finished the whole bottle, before Master Hix got there that night.

* * *

Druberj was telling the truth. His master did like to use the whip. When the fat, old bastard had finally had his fill of both of us, and passed out in his bed, I was sore and bleeding. Nothing new for me. What was new was that Druberj was there. He got up from the bed and left the room. A girl wouldn't have dared to do that. When he came back, he had a little bottle of something, and a soft cloth. He cleaned the cuts on my legs and backside. Whatever it was in the bottle stung for a minute, but then made the original stinging from the whip fade away.

"Thanks," I said when he had finished. I guess I was amazed. No one had ever shown any concern for my pain.

"Sure," he said. "It always helps me. I don't know why they have to be so rough on the girls."

I shrugged. "We're worth less. There are more of us."

He looked a little pained.

"What's wrong?" I asked.

"You know why there are more of you, don't you?" he asked.

I didn't. Druberj explained. "They want us small and weak. That's what we're designed to be."

"And pretty," I said. He smiled, and we were both a little embarrassed. "Well you are."

"I have to be." His smile faded away again. "The engineers... well, I guess they're not very good at their jobs. Some of us – the boys, I mean – they grow up a little too strong. Maybe their faces are a little rough, or their bodies too stocky or too skinny. They're not... usable."

"What happens to them?" I asked. I felt a lump in my throat. I knew what happened.

"They're killed. Maybe as many as half of us, maybe more...before they're two or three. The ones who are left are rare."

"So that's why they treat you so much better than us."

"I cost the master about three times what it would cost him to buy you."

I didn't have an owner. I was part of the stable of girls that the masters kept to rent out. Very few of the girls were actually sold to one person, and most of those left the planet.

"Guess I'm lucky to be a girl," I said. "I'm one of the strongest, and I bet I'm not nearly the prettiest – "

"Bet you are," he muttered. Then we were embarrassed again.

"Are all the boys as nice as you?" I asked him.

"We're supposed to be nice. Make our masters feel big and important."

"I mean... to the other Inihu. The girls all treat each other like shit."

"I haven't seen one of the other boys for a long time. Some of them are real little bastards, though. The really pretty ones, the ones whose masters spoil them. Buy them clothes."

"Clothes!"

He nodded. "Some get them. They know how special they are, and they act it. I'm just as happy not to see any of them."

"Who do you see?"

He nodded at the snoring mountain of flesh behind him. "That's about it. Sometimes he has a girl or two brought in. They don't talk much. Most of them I think would kill me as soon as look at me."

"You're right. So why try to talk to me?"

"You looked... different. Smarter, maybe. The other girls, their eyes are all dead."

"It's the grog," I said.

"Grog?"

"I don't know what it is. They give it to us to drink. It's supposed to calm us down. They let us have as much as we want. Some of the girls drink it until they get sick. I take as little as they let me get away with. It makes you stupid."

"Like the wine?" he asked.

I shook my head. "Worse. There's something else in it. I don't know what. They say, without it, some of the girls would tear apart everyone in sight, and have to be put down. Killed."

"I guess that's why I thought I could talk to you. You looked more with it."

"Be careful," I said. "The girls are also more violent when they're not on much grog. They could hurt you." It suddenly occurred to me that I didn't want to see this boy hurt. I didn't know why. Pain was part of our lives. You tried like hell not to care if someone hurt you. You didn't even show any interest if someone hurt someone else. The idea that anyone would ever hurt Druberj, though, that just seemed wrong. An image from before came into my head, of Druberj, squirming and kicking as his master struck his naked backside. It had excited the fat man, spanking the boy. I'd seen the proof of that between his puffy, stubby legs. I wished now I'd torn his arm from its socket, so he could never hurt Druberj again.

He was watching me. I wondered if he could tell how mad I'd gotten.

"Why are you staring at me?" I asked.

"Sorry," he said, looking away.

"No, it's all right. Really. I just wondered."

"I've never really had a chance to look at a girl before. You're... different."

I laughed and stretched out on the bed to give him a better look at me. Normally I couldn't stand the looks men gave me. Maybe it was the wine, relaxing me. "Yeah, I am," I said. "Is that good?"

He nodded, looking me up and down. It wasn't the kind of look the masters gave me. It was the kind of look you gave something special. Something that was better than it had any right to be. I can't describe how it made me feel. I'd never felt that way before.

"Does it hurt?" he asked. "When they put their dicks in there?" He pointed between my legs.

"Not usually," I said.

"It hurts me, when the master puts it in me. I'm used to it but... I read that that hole isn't really meant to be used that way."

"You can read?"

"Some," he admitted. "The master taught me, so I wouldn't be bored when I'm alone. I read better than he does, I think."

"What do you read about?"

"Whatever I can. There aren't many books here, but... Mostly books on how to have sex. He likes it when I learn new tricks. Some of the tricks won't work unless you have... what you have between your legs."

He went on staring.

"I'd let you borrow it if I could," I said, and we both collapsed, laughing.

Master Hix snorted in his sleep, and his arm flailed out, nearly hitting me in the face. I was afraid he'd wake up and start using us again, or have me whipped for bothering his precious boy toy.

Druberj crawled up and kissed the old monster, whispering little words of love into his ear to quiet him. The old man rolled over and snored regularly again.

Druberj came back down and lay next to me. He went back to watching my body, studying it like he was trying to memorize it. He traced the outlines of my curves in the air with his finger.

"You can touch me," I said. "If you want."

He reached out and laid the fingers of one of his hands on my skin, starting with my cheek. He was gentle, just brushing me with the very tips. His touch gave me chills. It was so different from anything I'd ever felt before. Slowly, real slowly, he followed the line of my cheekbone, down to my throat and collarbone. His fingers slowed when they came to my breast, wandering in circles, playing with my nipple until it stood out from the rest.

That wasn't all that was standing out.

"Look at you," I laughed. "All big and hard, like one of the masters."

He looked between his legs, then turned purple as he blushed. "Sorry. It doesn't usually do that when I'm with someone else."

"Does it do that a lot?" I asked. I was surprised I could look at it and stay so calm. It was a thing that meant pain and fear for me. On Druberj, though, it didn't bother me. I was fascinated.

"Pretty often," he said. "But only when I'm alone, reading some of the books, usually. I guess it must like you."

"You mean you can't tell it when to go up and down?"

He laughed. "Of course not! It's a reflex."

"Oh." I didn't know what a reflex was. "I thought the masters just kind of... turned them on... when they were ready to hurt someone."

"They turn themselves on," he giggled.

"Have you... you know..." I hesitated. The thought of Druberj doing what the masters did was stupid, and yet he had the parts that were needed.

"What?" he asked, "Put it in someone? No. I just take care of it myself."

"How?"

He didn't seem to know how to answer my question. "I... just... I dunno... Watch."

He wrapped his hand around his dick, making a fist. He started to move it up and down, massaging it. The skin of it grew more purple than before, and it looked like it got harder. He moved his hand faster.

"What are you doing, choking it?"

"You wanted to know. It feels good."

"And... how long do you do that?"

"Till it's... done. Y'know... till it shoots... stuff."

"Oh."

"What do you do?"

"About what?"

"When you get... excited."

"I think you already noticed I don't have one of those between my legs."

"No, but... girls can do it, too."

"Do what?"

"The books call it an 'orgasm.'"

"What's that?"

"It's like... when a man shoots from his dick."

"A woman doesn't do that."

"No."

"Then what does she do?"

"I... I have no idea. But she does something. You mean... you've never?"

"I don't think so."

"I think you'd know."

"How would I do it?"

"You'd touch yourself. There. Or," he took a very deep breath. "You'd let someone else do it."

Very slowly, I took his hand from between his legs, and put it between mine. It felt strange, at first. He didn't know anything about girl parts, except what he'd read in books. I started to get the idea, though, and I started to enjoy what Druberj's fingers were doing to me. I arched my back and my hips lifted up off the bed. I felt like maybe my body might explode.

And then he stopped.

"No!" I cried out.

Druberj smiled. "There's something I do for the master some-times. I think it works on girls too, kinda. Can I try?"

I didn't care what he tried, as long as he kept bringing me closer to... wherever it was my body was going. I nodded impatiently. Druberj climbed between my legs and lowered his head. When his tongue touched me, I yelped so loud that he had to stop and quiet the master again. But he came back.

He was right. I'd never. Not until then. Druberj showed me, that night, that even a lowly slave girl could feel good about some-thing.

* * *

For the next few weeks, I didn't see Druberj or his master. I was glad not to have to share the bed of a sick bastard who gets off on hurting people, but I really wanted to see Druberj again. Inihu don't look forward to things. I don't think any of them, other than me, even think about what the next day might bring. It won't be good, so why waste your time? I looked forward to the day I might see my new friend – my only friend – again. While I waited, I practiced the things he'd taught me. It was exciting to have a secret pleasure, to do something when the lights were out and the others were sleep-ing. To do something they couldn't share. They shared my bed, my food and my misery, but they didn't share this. Orgasms didn't seem to be as much fun alone as they had been with Druberj, but I wasn't about to invite one of my clan to join me.

When we weren't being used for sex, the Inihu were kept busy cleaning the compound. I don't remember much about the place I grew up in, but it was called "the compound." It was in a city. It was fenced off, of course, because slaves were kept there. It wasn't too far from a section of town where a lot of rich men, like Master Hix, lived. When we were taken to their homes to service them, we were carried in the back of a delivery truck with no windows. The rides were never long, though, and then we were in the bedrooms of some huge mansion or another. The compound also had a brothel, with rooms and girls for rent to men who didn't live in the area.

Anyway, I was weeding the flowers. I don't think our customers gave a damn about flowers, but the owners – whoever they were – wanted the place to look classy. They had had gardens planted all over the compound, making a lot of work for us. I was in one of the courtyard gardens, where customers liked to act out fantasy scenes. Just dressed up rapes, really.

There was a rustle in the hedge beside me. It was tall and thick, a green, flowery wall that cut off the garden from the rest of the world. And I heard my name whispered urgently. I looked up, but I didn't move. Leaving my work would get me in big trouble. The girls were always playing tricks on each other. It was a big joke to get one of your sisters whipped.

I didn't see anything. I went back to my weeding.

"Aer'La!" the voice whispered again, a little louder. This time I recognized it.

"Druberj?"

"Shhhhh!"

"Where are you?" I whispered to the hedge.

A clump of leaves shook, letting me know where he was hiding.

"Are you crazy?" I asked.

"Just make sure no one's looking, and come in here."

I looked all around. I was alone. I'd been ordered to work here until someone came and got me. There was nowhere I could go, and I wasn't considered a troublemaker, so I wasn't watched closely when I worked outside. There didn't seem to be anyone to notice if I got up. I was afraid, though; so I kept weeding, and worked my way close to the patch where Druberj had shaken the branches. I guess he knew what I was doing, 'cause he kept quiet.

When I got to the spot, I peered in through the leaves. I could just make out some gray patches of his skin showing through. He held out his hand.

"Come on in!" He said.

I looked around again. It looked safe. On my hands and knees, I crawled between the branches, and into the dark hollow that was formed by the bushes. I was naked, of course, and the branches weren't soft. They itched as they scraped against me. This wasn't the best hiding place in the world.

Druberj sat on his haunches, grinning at me.

"What are you doing here?" I demanded.

He shrugged. "I wanted to see you."

I wanted to see him too, but I was more scared than I'd ever been. "We're gonna get caught!"

"I don't think so," he said. "I hide here all the time. No one ever finds me."

"Doesn't your master notice you're gone?"

"He doesn't worry. He knows I always come back. He just thinks I'm off playing."

"Don't you have work to do?"

He laughed. "I do my work at night. Days are mine."

He reached out and took my hand. My skin tingled when he touched me. I felt ashamed that my hands had dirt caked all over them, when his were so soft and clean. "Look, I didn't come here to make you mad. I... I wanted to see you. I missed you."

I glared at him for a minute, but then I said, "I missed you, too. I just don't want us to get in trouble."

"Don't worry," he said. "I know these gardens pretty well. My master's house is only on the next street."

"You're allowed out in the street?"

"Yeah. All the boys are, unless they ever tried to run away." He was quiet for a minute. He just looked at me and smiled. "I'm really glad to see you."

"But I can't stay long."

"I know. I'll come back whenever I can. I'm here almost every day."

"Every day? Have you been... waiting to see me?"

He nodded, proud of himself. "Yep. For a while now. I've sat for hours and watched you, from a distance. I was starting to think they'd never send you to work this part of the yard. But it helped just to see you."

I didn't know what to say. Someone – a boy! – had sat and waited for me. Just for a glimpse of me.

"You are crazy," I said.

He just laughed. Then he crawled over to me and took my face in his hands and kissed me. No biting. No jerking my head around by the hair. No forcing his tongue in, the way the masters did. Just a kiss. Then he wrapped his arms around me and held me close against him. It was warm, and I felt safe. I know now that was crazy, but I did. I never wanted to leave that place.

"Are you mad at me for coming?" he asked.

"No. I've been... thinking about you. A lot."

"Me too. You're all I think about."

"When I think about you, I do the things you taught me."

"You do? Does it feel good?"

"Some. But it makes me miss you more."

He kissed the top of my head.

"When I'm with men now," I went on, "I think about you. It makes it easier. Makes the time go quicker. I pretend..." I stopped. I was embarrassed.

"What?" he asked, his warm breath tickling my hair against my forehead.

"It's stupid."

"I want to know. I want to know everything about you."

"I... I pretend it's you, doing those things to me. I pretend it's your dick inside me. Even when it hurts. It makes it a little better."

"But I wouldn't hurt you," he said.

"I know. That's what makes it better."

He kissed me again. He ran his little hands over my naked back. I felt the tingling warmth that came at night, when I touched myself, come over me now. He shifted, pressing his body against me, and I felt the hardness between his legs. I reached down and took hold of it, gently. He moaned against my lips.

Laying my hand against his ear, I drew his face back a little, so I could look into his emerald eyes. "Could you put it inside me now?"

* * *

Druberj and I saw each other whenever we could. It wasn't every day, 'cause I wasn't in the garden every day, and I wasn't always alone. It was only ever for a few minutes at a time. We didn't have sex every time, either, but most times.

When Druberj would come and wait for me in the hedge, he'd bring a book, 'cause he'd often have a long wait. He was the kind of person whose mind had to always be doing something, so he'd read. Times we didn't have sex, for whatever reason, or, after we did, if I just didn't want to leave him yet, I'd ask him to read to me.

I think I even liked the reading better than the sex, and I really liked the sex. Just hearing his voice, soft and gentle, and speaking only for me. Only to tell me whatever stories there were to be told from his books. He'd found one book of stories called "Fairy Tales." They had the funniest people in them, doing the strangest things. They climbed magic beanstalks, and killed giants. They met talking animals, and changed into other kinds of people. Some of them were talking animals. Some of them were only as big as your thumb. Some of them lived cruel lives, like we did; but a lot of them found a way out. An escape. I started to think maybe I had found an escape, right here among the Inihu. I'd found an escape in Druberj, and in the incredible stories he read to me.

I wanted to ask him to teach me to read. I planned to. I never got the chance.

* * *

It was the middle of the night, and I was in the barracks, sound asleep. At first, when a pair of hands yanked me bodily to a standing position, I didn't know where I was, or what was happening. As I came around, I realized that two of the teachers had me in their grasp. One held both my arms. The other had hold of my hair, and used it to yank my head back, so I could look up at her.

"Don't make a sound," she spat at me. They dragged me from the room. I was taken to the teachers' room – a little, windowless closet just outside the barracks. My blood ran cold when they led me into the room. It wasn't empty. Jin was there, for one. She wouldn't look at me. The other person in the room had no trouble looking me in the eye. It was him that made my blood run cold: the man with the scar over his eye. The scar I could never forget, or keep out of my nightmares. The scar that had loomed over me as this man had raped me for the first time.

"They call you Aer'La?" he asked.

I nodded. The teacher who had had me by the hair slapped me hard.

"Speak when you're spoken to, bitch!"

I swallowed blood and said, "Yes, Master."

"I'm Master Harl, girl. I'm in charge, here. Do you know why you're here?"

I looked at Jin, wondering why she was here. Were we both in trouble, or – ?

Master Harl slapped the cheek the teacher had left untouched.

"Look at me, girl! Not at anything else!"

"I haven't done anything..." I muttered.

The teacher raised her arm to cuff me again, but Master Harl stopped her. "Never mind that. We're going to whip her thoroughly enough later." He put his face in mine. His breath stank as much as I remembered it had years before. It mixed with my own stink of fear. "And we'll add extra for lying."

"Please... " I whispered.

"Please?" Master Harl demanded. "Please what? Please don't whip you? Be glad you're getting a whipping, girl. Be thankful you're about to receive the worst whipping of your life. A whipping means we're going to let you live."

He looked at me, waiting for an answer. I said nothing. A sick feeling was overtaking me. There was only one thing that they could have found out to make them this mad.

He paced a few steps back and forth in front of me. "You're very lucky, really, that I found out first." He gestured at Jin. "That your sister wanted t'be good to ya, and let us handle this... in the family."

I looked to Jin, whose dead eyes wouldn't meet mine. "What did you tell them?" I pleaded.

"It was wrong what you did," she said coldly.

Harl reached out and cupped the back of her head with his hand, fondly stroking her pale hair. "That's right. Little Jin saw wrongdoing happening in our house. She did what any good girl would do. She told her teachers." He reached into his pocket, and pulled out a white glob. It had been a cube once. I recognized it. It had been a sugar cube. The teachers gave them to us as special rewards. I'd had one in my life. I wouldn't have wanted this one. It looked like it had been in his pocket since the coat was made. Its corners had worn down, and it was dirty and wrapped in lint.

He held it out to Jin. "There's your reward, my good girl."

She clawed it greedily from his hand and shoved it into her mouth. Then she looked at me and smiled in a way that made me wish I could rip her face from her skull.

"If you had been found out by others, I couldn't have kept you safe, my girl," Master Harl went on. "Not given what damage you've done. You see, a girl who commits perversion... she can be salvaged. With enough whippings and grog, a girl whose sinful nature leads her to want to choose her own partners for sexual deviance can be made to behave herself again. But a boy..." His face darkened. He turned murderous eyes on me. "A boy cannot be fixed. His nature is changed. Once he's had a girl, or a boy he's picked himself, he can never be brought back to the same desirable level of compliance." He shook his head, mockingly. "It's very sad. If Master Hix had discovered you, ruining his prize boy, he'd have killed you outright."

Master Hix! My worst fears were confirmed. They knew. But

did Master Hix know? Had he been told that...? But Harl wasn't shutting up.

"For you see, little Aer'La, a boy in such a state is no use to anyone. A boy who's worth five of your miserable kind, once ruined, must be disposed of...

Master Harl opened the door. Someone was standing just outside. "Come in," Harl said. "Come in, and show her."

Master Hix entered, carrying something draped in a stained sheet. Something about the size of a small human body. I shook my head violently. I knew what was under the sheet, but I didn't want it to be true. Somehow, I had to be wrong...

Tears were running down the fat old man's face as he held the body in his arms, cradling it. "You filthy little bitch," he sobbed. "You filthy..." He buried his head against the covered bundle.

Harl clapped Hix on the shoulder. "Steady now, Master," he said. "You know how I regret your loss, but the law is the law. And the law says that a ruined boy must be destroyed."

He ripped away the sheet. I screamed and dropped to my knees. The purple blood which had stained the sheet was all over the naked chest and arms, all over the perfect face. The perfect, dead face, with its emerald eyes still open, wide in shock. Blood trickled from the lips that had kissed every inch of my body.

I screamed and screamed. Vomit rose in my throat, and I choked it out on the floor, and over my legs. All the while I told myself I was wrong. They were just trying to scare me. This was some other boy they'd butchered. My Druberj wasn't dead!

My eyes met those of Master Hix, both flooded with tears. "You killed him," I sobbed. "He never was anything but good to you, and – "

Harl grabbed the back of my neck. "The law is the law!" he roared. Then he made his voice gentle again. "And don't insult good Master Hix, girl. He loved his boy. He'd never have harmed him. It was I who was forced to do what needed doing."

He smiled. He'd killed Druberj. He'd slit that perfect throat, and he smiled.

I can't tell you exactly what happened next. It happened fast, and, for me, the world seemed to be spinning at lightning speed. I do know that, as I lowered my head, as the horror in front of me sank in, my eyes locked on Harl, on the bit of him that was directly in front of my face as I knelt. My eyes locked on his crotch, covered in rough fabric in front of me.

I hurled myself forward and bit, snapping like a wild animal. I grabbed his legs and dug my nails in, raking through the fabric to tear the skin underneath. I sank my teeth in hard and butted my head forward. If the cloth kept me from biting off his dick or balls, I'd sure as hell smash them with my skull.

Harl screamed. The teachers both scrambled to tear me from him. I splayed my arms and legs out and spun my body. I'd lost my mind entirely. I wanted to kill everything in sight. I wanted to rip out their souls and stuff them into Druberj's dead body, to trade with the gods for his life. I wanted, more than anything, to kill as many of them as I could, before they killed me.

And, oh, I wanted them to kill me. Yes, I wanted to die. I wanted to go wherever they'd sent my Druberj. If that was hell, I'd march in, singing.

I broke one teacher's nose with the back of my hand. The other got hold of my ankle, but I pulled her off balance and her head cracked on the stone floor. I saw blood ooze out, but I didn't hold still to see more. Shoving aside the woman with the broken nose, I hurled myself across the room, ducking low to avoid Harl's arms as they grabbed for me.

Frantically, I looked around for a weapon. Something light enough to swing but heavy enough to break bones. Instead, I saw Jin, huddled in the corner, the sugar still caked around the edges of her mouth and trickling down her chin in a stream of drool. She wasn't smiling anymore. She was babbling in terror. She was terrified. Of me.

I pounced, landing on top of her, our naked bodies tangling up in a heap on the floor. She didn't even scream. She just moaned stupidly. No words came out. She didn't even really fight back. When I grabbed her head in my hands, she just sobbed; and when I twisted her neck, and it snapped like a twig, she didn't even give a cry of surprise.

Killing Jin drained a little of my anger, and it slowed me down. I wasted a second looking at the first person I'd ever killed. It was a second too long. Harl had me. He wrapped his hands around my throat and catapulted me to the floor, landing on top of me and bringing a heavy knee down hard against my pelvis. I didn't have enough breath to scream in pain.

"Kill her!" shrieked Master Hix.

Harl looked down at me, still gasping out his breaths. His eyes, again, were black and murderous. "You deserve to die, bitch," he said. He spat, hitting me in the face. I shut my eyes. I was ready. Please, I begged whatever god would listen, just let me die. Let it only hurt a little. Harl tightened his grip around my throat.

Then he sighed. "No. No, Master Hix, I shan't kill her. You may, if you like. I won't stop you."

There was silence. Hix was thinking about it. Good! Let him kill me! Let someone else who'd touched Druberj, someone who, in his own twisted way, also mourned, let him kill me! That was right.

"But," Harl cautioned him, "I will take her price out of what I owe you."

Hix sobbed again. "You're right. I can't afford the loss."

"Good," said Harl gently. "I do regret what my house has cost you, good Master Hix. We'll sell this animal off planet, and that will help me pay you the price of the boy."

I opened my eyes. I was not to die, then.

"When you awaken," Harl said to me, "I believe I'll whip you myself. Yes. I'll enjoy doing that, in return for all you've cost me. But that will come when you awaken."

He tightened his grip on my throat again, until I couldn't breathe in or out at all. Everything went black.

* * *

The naked girl on the bed hugged her knees and sobbed as the memories overwhelmed her. Atal kept silent, allowing her a moment with her feelings. When she lifted her head again, she brushed the hair from her eyes and said, "I'm sorry, Captain. It's just hard to remember it all. A-after that – "

"Aer'La," Atal said quietly, "that's enough."

"I'm telling you the truth!" she protested.

"Yes," he agreed, "I think you are. He stood, and, fighting his own reaction to the pheromone which had only intensified with the telling of her emotional tale, he crossed to lift her off the bed and into his arms. She melted into him, sobbing hard.

"I don't need to hear anymore. I hadn't meant to bring back painful memories."

"But now you know. I'm an animal. A killer."

"Welcome to the human race," he said. She looked up, bewilderment

showing through the tears. "No offense meant. I mean, 'welcome to the race of sentient beings.' We all strike out when we've been hurt. You've been hurt more than most."

"If you let me stay, Captain, I promise I won't hurt anyone... much. I'm good at my job."

"I'll be the judge of that," he said gently.

This time, her eyes clouded over with fear. Not the fear of a creature who recognizes a more powerful force, but the fear of someone who stands to lose something precious. Atal brushed the hair from her eyes and rocked her gently.

"But I'll give you time to let me be the judge of that," he said gently. "And I promise you, Aer'La, that I won't send you away. If you can't be part of my crew, you won't have to leave this ship until we find a safe place for you to go."

And she hadn't left, until Atal had left *Arbiter*, and brought her with him. And that was how they'd come to this place, this day...

And this very large problem.

Chapter Three
Departure

At the moment her superior officers were pondering her fate, Aer'La herself was downing her second "Atal's Stout" of the evening.

The tavern owner had quickly renamed his signature brew upon receiving the news of the famed Captain's return. His place of business, after all, was situated on Quintil L-5, in orbit between Quintil and its moon, Hestia. The station was the jumping-off point for all major military and commercial transport in the Rigel System. Civilian travelers who dined and drank with him would be very cognizant right now of the fact that *Titan* was docked just beyond the titanium skin of the station, and of the more stirring fact that Atal was her new captain.

Civilians wanted to feel good. Atal's return made them feel good. Buying a beer named for him would remind them how good they felt, or so the barkeep hoped. The question was, would the tourists have enough money left for his beer, after they'd spent heavily on official *Titan* pressure suits, *Titan* zero-grav shoes, and Jan Atal collectible action dolls? (Especially if they bought the good ones, which still walked and talked hours after they'd left the system?)

Most members of the military weren't impressed by such frippery, but the former crew of the *Arbiter* had bought the first round of Atal Stouts (not a flattering name, when you thought about it) out of loyalty to their Captain. They'd bought the second round because it was actually damned drinkable.

"Honey," asked the waitress as she placed mugs before Aer'La's companions, "D'ya mind if I ask where ya got your skin done?"

Aer'La looked down at the iridescent blue of her flesh, little covered by a brief tunic and shorts. (It was warm on the station, and spacers strove for comfort above all.) "Did it myself," she told the girl. "It's not blotchy, or anything, is it?"

"No, it's perfect. The color's you. Goes with your hair." The girl gestured to her own much-exposed flesh, a shocking, magenta-and-yellow domino pattern. "I'm just a little tired of mine, is all. Had it for almost two weeks. I don't suppose you work for cash on the side? Only – "

Across the bar, a customer called gruffly for service, and the girl rushed away. Aer'La returned to her beer.

"Your heart just skipped two beats," a voice next to her said.

It was Cernaq, her Phaetonian shipmate. Like all of his people, the young midshipman was of light build, with white-blond hair and eyes strikingly pale – a yellowish green that almost seemed to glow. Aer'La had heard them referred to as "cat's eyes." She had to take that comparison on faith. She had never seen a cat.

He was right. Of course he was right. He was a telepath – a telepath so skilled that he could read, in the minds of others, signals their own bodies sent to their brains. Aer'La didn't know her heart had stopped, but some piece of her brain did; so Cernaq did.

"I thought for a minute she knew what my makeup job was hiding. I guess she was just making small talk." said Aer'La.

"And there was no hint of suspicion in her mind," Cernaq assured her. "You need to relax."

"You don't know what it's like, Cernaq. Looking over your shoulder every minute, to see if someone's recognized you. Wondering if every stranger who gives you a passing glance is really a bounty hunter, or someone who's seen your face on a police holo."

"I know exactly what it's like," he said. "I've been in your head, remember?" He grinned. "Among other places."

She couldn't help but laugh at his attempt to be suggestive. It was so unlike a Phaetonian, and so new to him.

"Besides," Cernaq said, "why would you be in a police holo?"

Aer'La looked away. "You never know what they might try. I can't trust anyone.."

"You can trust me," he said sincerely. Much of what Cernaq said had a note of sincerity, of course. Coming from a world where spoken language was rarely used, as the natives communicated telepathically, his speaking voice was slow and deliberate, as if he'd only just learned to use it. That quality added to his air of openness. Well, on a world of mind-readers, what would be the point of learning to lie?

She took his hand across the table. "I do trust you. You're one of the few I trust."

He didn't respond. He often didn't. Cernaq didn't use excess words.

Aer'La liked quiet people. She wasn't one herself, particularly, but she enjoyed being in their company. They were less taxing on her mental resources, and they gave her less reason to punch them in the jaw.

Right now, Cernaq was quietly enjoying what was often referred to as 'local color.' At the bar, two couples – one pair of females and one male and female – were vying for the attention of the crowd with some particularly acrobatic feats of sexual intercourse. This sort of performance was common on Quintil and its outposts. Quintil was reputed to be the most sensual of human worlds. Displays of sexuality – live and depicted artistically – were everywhere. Any Quintil would have laughed – or become furiously indignant – at the suggestion that such displays were indecent or harmful to those who viewed them.

"See something you like, Cernaq?" Aer'La asked.

He looked appraisingly at the man astride the woman on the bar. "I would think that would be uncomfortable for the female," he said blandly. "His... equipment... is misshapen."

Aer'La nodded. "Gotta be an enhancement."

"His rhythm is erratic," Cernaq went on. He tilted his head and squinted thoughtfully, as if studying a blueprint. "The irregularity of motion is not conducive to – why are you laughing, Aer'La?"

She covered her mouth. She hadn't meant to be rude to him. "It's just so damned funny. Cernaq, the Phaetonian sex expert. You've come a long way."

"I suppose I am somewhat unique," he said. "My people value the mind, to the exclusion of all else. Anything of the body is suspect. Since we reproduce artificially, we don't need sex. And it's caused a lot of grief throughout history – via jealousy, prudery and disease – "

"You're lecturing again."

"Sorry."

"I just think it's funny to see you being so open about it. When you came on board *Arbiter*, I'd have sworn you had no interest in sex. My crewmen told me you had no balls."

"A common misconception about my people. We don't use them, so we've lost them." He turned up one corner of his mouth in a smile. "You know the truth, of course."

Aer'La nodded at the copulators on the bar. "Yep. So, maybe you should go show him how it's done," she said.

Cernaq appeared to consider that. His pale brow wrinkled, and he studied the copulating pair more closely. Finally, he announced, "I don't think so. While engaging in this act, the young lady is contemplating the purchase of a new type of urinary absorbent for a small mammal she keeps at home. I'd rather have a partner with more interest in the process. Besides, I don't know her. I'm not that comfortable with sexuality."

Aer'La reached forward and brushed a blonde curl from his forehead with her fingertips, letting the fingers trail lazily across the skin of his face. "Comfortable enough for me," she teased. "Maybe," she added, with a wicked glance at the public display on the bar, "we should clear this table and show everyone what good technique looks like."

"I..." Cernaq stammered, "I don't think..."

"C'mon, Cernaq," Aer'La chided. "As a public service. Think of all the lousy lays you could prevent." She began unfastening her tunic, exposing magnificent cleavage.

"I owe the public nothing," replied Cernaq, no doubt devoting some mental energy to the task of canceling the involuntary reflex which the sight of Aer'La's breasts brought on. "And... my sex life, like the rest of my life, is private."

"What did I just walk in on?" asked Terry Metcalfe, their Terran shipmate, as he plunked three overflowing mugs on the table.

"Aer'La wants me to have sex in public."

"With her?" wondered Metcalfe.

Cernaq eyed the girl. "Not necessarily."

"A little encouragement here, Navy," Aer'La said to Metcalfe. "You'd do it, wouldn't you?"

Metcalfe sat down and hefted one of the mugs. "You forget, my people are almost as backward as Cernaq's."

"More backward," said Cernaq. "Since your people actually believe in sex, but feel ashamed of it." He shook his head. "Why is that?"

"Control," said Metcalfe carefully. Unlike Cernaq, he could not prevent the alcohol they were consuming from affecting him. His speech was starting to become slurred. "It's all about keeping us in line. We're supposed to believe that the Church of Terra is more important to us than anything else. If we get caught up in our own sex lives, we're being selfish."

"Freedom of sexual expression leads people to feel ownership in their own bodies," agreed Cernaq.

"And thus in their own souls," finished Metcalfe. "We're supposed to remember that the gods own us, body and soul. The Church speaks for the gods, so..."

"So it must control all forms of expression," said Cernaq.

Metcalfe nodded. "For the good of the people." He took a large swallow of his beer, frowned at it. "Ah, anyway. Sex is a damned nuisance. I wonder if the Phaetonians don't have the right idea. Maybe it is time to train the race to live without it."

"Because you're not getting any?" wondered Aer'La.

"Who said I wanted any?"

Aer'La laughed. "Your face does, every time you look at Kaya." She nodded to where Captain Atal's daughter, their fellow midshipman, sat a few tables away.

"Not just your face," added Cernaq. "Don't ask me to enumerate all the physical symptoms you experience in her presence."

Metcalfe made a rude gesture. "Kaya and I are over, all right? Done."

"Wasn't it fun while it lasted?" asked Aer'La.

Metcalfe rolled his eyes. "It was great while it lasted. I just wanted more."

She gestured around the bar. "Lotsa willing partners, Navy. No waiting."

"I wanted more from Kaya," Metcalfe said, too loudly. He lowered his voice. "It's not just about being horny, I... never mind."

"You're in love with her," said Cernaq.

"I was," said Metcalfe. "Maybe I still am. It doesn't matter. She's moved on. I guess I... crowded her."

Aer'La smiled, feeling genuinely sorry for him. There was a time when she hadn't liked Metcalfe. He was too young and eager and by the book for her. Then she'd come to admire his courage and stubbornness. "Hey," she said, "you can crowd me anytime."

He nodded at her gallant offer, but didn't seem to cheer up. "I guess," he said, "I'm a hopeless romantic."

"Hopeless," echoed Cernaq.

"It's just... when I was growing up and going to Sunday School, I heard all these stories where the hero gets the girl... because he's been good, and true and... I thought life would be like that for me. Like Abraham and Sarah, or Odysseus and Penelope... The Vision and the Scarlet Witch."

"I hate it when he gets religious," muttered Aer'La.

"Sorry," said Metcalfe.

"Navy, your church's teachings were crap! You said so yourself!"

Metcalfe colored. "Not all of them," he said quietly. "I still believe..."

"Okay," said Aer'La, "but lighten up! Have some fun! Get laid!"

Metcalfe slumped his shoulders, and his dark eyes seemed somehow darker. "As a matter of fact, I tried. Last night."

Aer'La grinned and pounded the table. "Details, details!"

Metcalfe leaned back in his chair. "Attempting to shed my annoying, backwater attitudes and romantic inclinations, I came here, in fact. I came looking for a girl and an evening of empty, erotic bliss."

Possibly realizing that his voice was growing loud again, he stopped and looked around. "I found what must have been the only girl on Quintil who was looking for a husband. After agreeing to my proposition to spend the night, she begged me to marry her, to begin planning our children, to take her with me on my next assignment – "

"No!" countered Aer'La.

"Yes. I sure can pick 'em! Every man in the Navy – except me! – is capable of finding a loose, shallow woman for a night."

"What did you do?" asked Cernaq.

"I..." Metcalfe inhaled dramatically. "I told her about the accident."

"Wait," said Aer'La. "What accident?"

Metcalfe ignored her and went on. "I told her how a quirk of my unplanned, Terran genetics caused my body to reject cloned tissue, so bionics was the only answer. The doctors were confident that – eventually – the appliance would be sophisticated enough for something like normal sexual activity; but a bionic penis is still a bionic penis – "

At the word 'penis,' Aer'La laughed so hard that she sprayed beer all over the table in front of her and choked. After a few coughs, she recovered and said to Cernaq, "Hey! How about a slap on the back for a choking person here?"

"Slapping the back does not aid a choking victim," he said calmly. "I did send signals to your nervous system to relax the smooth muscles of – "

"Yeah yeah yeah," Aer'La said, waving him off. "So, Navy. What happened to your wife-to-be?"

"She excused herself to the restroom," he replied. He looked nervously at the doors to the public facilities. "For all I know, she's still hiding in there."

It was just as Aer'La was about to offer to go and investigate that the very fat drunk sat on Metcalfe.

Two tables away, the former object of Metcalfe's affections was attempting to drink an admirer under the table. Kayan'na Atal had learned to drink hard liquor as a very young girl, living with her father aboard a series Naval ships, on occupied worlds, and at the Academy. As attentive as Jan Atal had been, he couldn't prevent the pretty, precocious girl from associating with the younger members of his staff, and from picking up their vices.

Kaya's drink of choice was Quintillian Rum. She preferred its sweetness and smoothness to the harsh, wooden bite of whiskey. Her fellows aboard *Arbiter* had been whiskey drinkers, however, so she knew how to handle the stuff. She was winning her battle with the admirer, who also preferred whiskey to rum.

She didn't need Cernaq's telepathy to tell her that the man seated across from her had one goal: to get a pretty girl drunk and take her home – or take her right there on the table. "Take her" was the important part of the operation.

He was one of those career good-looking types. Someone had spent a small fortune having his appearance engineered, and he was obviously spending another keeping it up. His teeth were too white and too straight, his eyes too blue, his skin too smooth and tinted too deep a hue of the currently fashionable color, which was a reddish bronze. He wore a white silk shirt, open to the navel, exposing hard pectorals and a sharply defined abdomen. The opening of the shirt formed an arrow, pointing to a cloth-wrapped package which Kaya was confident included a significant volume of excelsior. She had no intention of finding out, one way or another.

She was actually surprised that he'd invited her to have a drink (or twelve) with him. Kaya had no illusions about her looks. She was pretty, with skin that had a natural golden cast, and had never felt the gentle sting of color alteration. She had eyes a few shades either side of violet on one end and magenta on the other. They were perfect genetic duplicates, she was told, of her mother's. Her father had paid the designer a hefty bonus for them. She was not tall, but slender and athletic, with small but elegant breasts. Her hair showered around a pixie-like face in dark copper ringlets. Men liked her. Women liked her. She'd had her share of both, but she knew she was no Aer'La. She was surprised this predator had chosen her over her more flamboyantly well-endowed friend.

She had agreed to join him at his table, though. She was tired of watching Metcalfe try so hard to pretend she hadn't broken his heart. She thought it would be fun to have a distraction.

Sadly, the man was as stupid as he was good-looking. His sole topics of interest seemed to be professional zero-G wrestling and, well, amateur zero-G wrestling. The latter, pseudo-wrestling, being the kind he wanted Kaya to join him in practicing.

"Shall we have another?" he asked her, raising the whiskey bottle and pouring several ounces of it on the table, with a few drops accidentally landing in his glass. It would not be long now, Kaya thought. She'd have to pay for the bottle when he dropped from his chair to the floor, but she'd have the satisfaction of knowing she could outlast a pretty fool.

She took the bottle from him. "Why not? I think I'll pour mine."

"Careful," he giggled. "You've had quite a few, and you might spill it. Aren't you worried that I'll take advantage of you, while you're this drunk?"

Kaya smiled. "You wouldn't take advantage of an innocent little thing like me, would you?" she asked sweetly. She knew the answer was no, of course. Whether he would like to take advantage or not, she hadn't met the man she couldn't physically incapacitate, if necessary. Again, she was no Aer'La, but she held her own.

As it happened, Kaya did wind up spilling as she attempted to pour a shot. This was not the result of inebriation, but of a body flying across the table, on a course for the opposite side of the room.

This unexpected human missile not only interrupted the flow of conversation, it caused Kaya to realize that her friends, as usual, were in trouble.

Upon finding himself reclassified as furniture, Metcalfe had objected. At least, he had objected as much as he could from beneath the very fat drunk's bulk. The drunk, noticing him for the first time, had advised him to move elsewhere. He, the very fat drunk, had business to transact with the charming lady whom he had just witnessed exposing her charming breasts.

In his best clipped, military manner, Metcalfe had instructed the very fat drunk to move along. The very fat drunk had found this amusing, and had informed Metcalfe of same.

There had followed two unpleasant, crunching sounds, and a blur of motion. Then the very fat drunk was on the floor, cradling one injured arm in the other, his mouth open in a silent scream as Metcalfe stood over him, smiling pleasantly. Metcalfe had then advised the very fat drunk that he might should have his hearing checked at the next opportunity. He had then attempted to return to his seat. It was at this point that he learned that the very fat drunk had five very drunken friends. Those friends had taken the opportunity to make their displeasure known.

By the time Kaya reached her friends, the battle was in full swing. Metcalfe struggled in the grip of a man twice his size, who held him in a half-Nelson. Nearby, one man screamed as Aer'La lifted him over her head, begging that she not hurl him to join the broken bodies of two of his friends, on the wrong side of a shattered glass window of the tavern, where Aer'La had already thrown them. The first one had shattered the window with his impact, and suffered the worst injuries. The second had fared somewhat better, but the third had no wish to join him.

He joined him anyway.

In front of Cernaq, a prospective assailant was slowly lowering his raised fist, a blank expression in his eyes and drool trickling from the corner of his mouth. Cernaq had obviously paralyzed a few nerve centers.

Kaya decided that Metcalfe needed the most help, and pounced to his aid. An earth woman would have known that it was dangerous business to save her ex-lover from injury at the hands of a man twice his size. An earth woman would have grown up in a misogynistic culture, riddled with double standards, and well-versed in the care and feeding of the male ego. Kaya was not an earth woman. She was one of the highest-ranked intellects on Quintil, and had grown up in a sexually liberated world where men and women were political and social equals.

Sometimes the very intelligent and well-adjusted suffer when attempting to deal with those from less fortunate backgrounds. They break rules they didn't know existed, and they are often mystified at the results. So Kaya would be completely bewildered when Metcalfe, for the next forty-eight hours, would be unable to look at her without feeling an outburst of unbridled rage which would cause Cernaq, if he and his empathic abilities were nearby, to wince in physical pain.

Across the barroom, seated on a stool with a nude young woman in his lap, and another draped around his shoulders, Kevin Carson watched the developing brawl with clinical detachment. He didn't tend to worry about his friends in a fight, if Aer'La was there.

He was an attractive young man, with bright, blue eyes and dirty blonde hair, which spilled over his collar. He dressed and groomed in a manner which said he noticed his own appearance, and wanted others to notice it. They did notice it, especially in settings such as this tavern, where all ages and genders came seeking a sexual thrill. The two nubile beauties with him, whose names he hadn't learned and probably wouldn't, were typical of an evening's entertainment for him. Quintil had always suited him well, providing plenty of sex, and almost no danger of serious entanglement. It was a vapid culture, but it was always exciting. Barroom brawls were rare on Quintil proper, but this was an orbital station, hosting primarily foreign guests. Their diverse cultures often clashed... violently.

As Carson watched the fight, he occasionally shouted advice, or proudly claimed that he had taught Aer'La everything she knew. This was, of course, for the benefit of his young, naked admirers. (He only assumed they were young. One had two children older than he.) He was so engrossed that he failed to notice as a small figure flashed into existence by his elbow.

Though a normally proportioned human male, it was six inches in height, clad in the full dress uniform of the Confederate Navy. Had he been looking, Carson would have recognized the small hologram as the image of Scutley, the holographic herald of the Confederate Naval Vessel *Titan*. No one knew for sure whether Scutley was modeled on a real human, perhaps a crewman from *Titan's* past, or if he was the fancy of some forgotten designer.

Scutley had been the voice of *Titan* for as long as anyone could remember. He was one of the voices, anyway. *Titan's* A.I. was massive in scope and capacity, and could interact with its human customers via thousands of personality models at once. The Scutley program was the one reserved for public announcements, particularly calls ashore to officers and crewmen on leave. Scutley's appearance was rarely welcomed, for it signaled the end of the party. Scutley's personality was suited to his task. He might have been called "rat-faced," but for the happy fact that few of the genetically engineered residents of the Inner Worlds had ever seen a Terran rat. He had all the personality traits classically associated with a scavenging rodent.

"Midshipmen of the CNV *Titan*," Scutley called out from his position beside Carson's empty beer mug. "Deputy Captain Phyn Darby hereby orders you to – "

A fragment of a chair passed through Scutley's mid-section, continuing in its flight until it came to rest, with a tremendous crash of broken glass. Shards rained upon the floor behind the bar, shards of bottles which once had held very expensive liquors. More recently, and until that moment, they had held the cheapest substitute for their former contents which the tavern proprietor could acquire. Now they held nothing, for now they were a starscape of glistening fragments on the midnight black of the floor. A robot sweeper scurried from beneath the bar to collect them before the wait staff, whose skimpy outfits did not include shoes, could step on them.

Scutley, being a hologram, was not injured by the chair leg penetrating his form. He was, nonetheless, quite annoyed by it. Scutley was a sensitive and complex program, and his algorithm included a quite sophisticated system for processing and responding to insults.

In other words, Scutley got angry. "Excuse me!" He cried out across the chaos of the barroom.

The brawlers enthusiastically continued their brawling.

"Hey!" Scutley called out, more loudly. "I'm talking here!"

The large elbow beside him knocked the large glass beside him off the bar, as the large person to whom the large elbow belonged jumped in surprise at Scutley's outburst.

"Oh, shit," said Carson. "What lousy timing!"

"Who's the funny little guy?" asked one of the nudes.

"My name, madame, is Scutley," the hologram said with quiet indignation. "And I am here on official military business. And," he added, "I am not funny."

The nude's giggle was interrupted as Carson leapt to his feet, unceremoniously dumping her on the now-littered floor. As she muttered obscenities and crawled away, ducking kicks and blows and flying objects, Carson turned to the hologram.

"What's up?" he asked.

"Your leave, Mister Carson."

Carson snapped his fingers, engaging his personal data implant. The time appeared in front of him as a set of glowing, holographic numerals. "We've got two hours left," he argued.

"Wrong," said Scutley. "You're late. The Deputy Captain has shortened your leave."

"He can't do that!"

"He's the Deputy Captain. He can do anything. And, if you don't report to *Titan* on the double, 'anything' will include time in the brig for all of you."

"Dammit," said Carson. He turned back to the brawl and called out, "Hey!" This was followed by "Quiet!" and "Yo!" and "Fire!" None elicited any reaction. He picked up a handy (and miraculously unbroken) liquor bottle and smashed it, dramatically, against the edge of the bar. The sound was drowned out by the other sounds of breaking furniture. "They're not listening," he said finally.

"I'll handle this," said Scutley, adding a contemptuous, "Humans!" under his breath.

The Scutley program had been designed for communicating information in a variety of scenarios, while confronted with all manner of interference. It was not daunted by the open warfare which surrounded its holographic personification now. It cycled its audio signal volume up by a factor of one hundred. At the same time, it magnified its visual aspect over 800 per cent, and increased its luminance to a painful threshold.

A 25-foot Scutley appeared in the center of the combat, shining with an aura nearly as blinding as a naked sun. Its obscenely large mouth opened, and a foghorn-like bellow shook the room.

"Knock it off!"

The brawlers ceased, craning their necks to see the head of the giant figure as it scraped the arched supports of the tavern ceiling. There were mutters of astonishment, followed by a pervasive quiet, which seemed to please Scutley. He surveyed the small human figures with satisfaction.

"Thank you," he said, clearly not meaning it. "Now, as I was saying: Midshipmen of the CNV *Titan*, Deputy Captain Phyn Darby hereby orders you to report to him forthwith aboard ship. No extensions. No excuses. That is all."

Carson, who had joined his fellows when Scutley had stifled his viewing pleasure, said quietly, "Damn. I was hoping to lay some money on the big guy."

"Thanks," said Metcalfe, massaging a strained shoulder. "Your support means so much." He sighed. "Well, I guess we'd better jump a shuttle."

"You had better," said Aer'La. "The order was to the midshipmen. I didn't hear a word about the ship's master. I'm not really an officer, so I can stay and fight." She scanned the remaining brawlers. "Fellas? Anyone still up for a workout?"

Suddenly, no one in the bar wanted to make eye contact with the slight, blue-skinned teenager who had, in the last two minutes, broken more bones than there are in a single human body. Aer'La appeared supremely disappointed.

"Guess I'll head over with you guys," she said glumly. She started for the door.

"Hold it," a voice squeaked from behind the bar. Then the same voice cleared its throat, and said more confidently, "Just a minute." The bartender stepped out, advancing on the small party of officers. "Don't think you're walking out of here without paying for this mess."

"Paying?" Aer'La demanded. "You expect us to pay, when those idiots," she pointed, indicating essentially everyone in the room who hadn't come to the tavern with her, "started this?" She advanced on the barkeep.

Metcalfe's hand shot out and caught her shoulder. Physically, he could never have actually restrained her, but the gesture did seem to get her attention.

"Never mind, Aer'La," said Metcalfe, and, to the barkeep, "We'll cover it." He tapped his palm, activating his own data implant. His credit account number appeared in front of the man's nose. "Charge it to me."

The man nodded, and seemed to relax. He'd clearly been expecting more resistance. "Uh... Right." Then he scanned the information presented and, upon realizing the identities of his guests, his face tinged with embarrassment. "I should have expected, of course, that officers under Captain Atal would pay their debts... as well as," he added, now glowering at the non-military contingent of the brawlers, "those of others. Couldn't you – "

"I'm afraid we have to go," said Metcalfe. He indicated the area where the Scutley image, having completed its programmed assignment, no longer stood gazing down at the dregs of humanity.

The proprietor nodded sadly, and gazed after them as they exited. No doubt he was promising himself that, in future, he would check the celebrity status of his guests immediately upon their arrival in his humble place of business.

* * *

"No, I'm very sorry, Mister... Metcalfe," said the dockmaster. "There are no other shuttles available."

Metcalfe blew out a heavy breath, ruffling chestnut bangs not yet trimmed to a style appropriate away from the Border. They'd been waiting for fifteen minutes. After they'd asked to have their shuttle readied for boarding, the dockmaster had said he had to "check something." He'd returned with this baffling answer.

"I didn't ask about other shuttles," said Metcalfe tersely. "I asked about ours. The one we arrived in. The one we left with you."

"Ah. Well, of course, that one was taken."

"Taken?" Metcalfe demanded. "You mean stolen?"

"Commandeered, actually."

"Commandeered," Metcalfe repeated calmly.

"That's right."

"Not many people have the authority to commandeer the XO's shuttle."

"Executive officer?" the dockmaster asked with polite embarrassment. "I wasn't aware, sir. Your shuttle was taken by your fellow midshipman, Mister Blaurich."

"Mister who?"

Kaya wrinkled her nose as if a very large mammal had farted nearby. "Sestus Blaurich," she explained. "Dad didn't tell me he was on *Titan*, though I should have guessed. This is the kind of stunt he and his family would pull. Just to prove they can."

Metcalfe turned back to the dockmaster. "We have orders to report immediately to *Titan*," he said. "And we need our ship."

"I understand. I wish I could provide it. Unfortunately, as I've already told you, it is gone, and there are no others. You'll have to wait for the crew transport in three hours. Again, I'm sorry for the inconvenience. Now, if you'll excuse me," the dockmaster turned his back and left the counter, returning to his office.

"Great," said Metcalfe. "He's sorry for the inconvenience."

"He isn't actually," said Cernaq. "This Blaurich character tipped him rather handsomely to hand over our shuttle."

"Who the hell is this jerk?" Metcalfe demanded.

"Apparently," said Cernaq, "he's the other midshipman. *Titan* has an allotment of five."

"And Mister... Five... obviously has connections. Or his family does."

"Important connections," Cernaq observed. "He's the heir to an extremely wealthy family corporation on Quintil. His father and two of his uncles also serve in key positions in the Quintil government. It's speculated that he'll complete his tour of duty in the Navy in three years, and then assume control of a segment of the family business. That's assuming he doesn't single-handedly defeat the Qraitians and become the Navy's youngest admiral. He's widely considered to be the 'next Jan Atal.'"

"That'll be the day," said Metcalfe. "How do you know so much about him?"

"I didn't," said Cernaq. "The dockmaster did. The information was foremost in his mind, since he just met Blaurich."

"Oh. Well, that –

"He also has a hot, tight little ass," Cernaq added.

Metcalfe grimaced. "You disturb me, Cernaq."

"It was the dockmaster's opinion, not mine."

"He does have a nice ass," Kaya said matter-of-factly. "A very good body in general, though he doesn't have a clue what to do with it."

At Metcalfe's mildly surprised glance, she added, "I screwed him once. It was forgettable. He's very pretty but very pompous."

"Just your type," said Carson.

"Shut up, Carson," said Kaya. "No, he's not my type. It was at a party, the liquor was poorly selected, the guests were all insipid and boorish. I was just trying to pass the time." A pixieish twinkle appeared in her eye. "Besides, there were news cameras everywhere, and I knew they couldn't resist seeing the son and daughter of industry go at it on the banquet table."

"And you were mad at your father," finished Metcalfe.

"I was not."

"Like hell."

She sighed, caught out. "I was mildly annoyed. He had just told me he wouldn't recommend me to the Academy. I wanted to get his attention."

"By getting laid? I thought Quintils were indifferent to their children's sexual exploits."

"But I was on every holo player for the next two days, being clumsily speared by a boy Daddy detests, right on top of the salmon mousse, which he also detests." She grinned in her former lover's face. "And no one could be indifferent to my sexual exploits, Yank."

Yank. It was Kaya's pseudo-affectionate nickname for him, adopted at the academy. In fact, it was a derogatory epithet for a person from Terra. It implied stupidity, ill health, birth defects, genetic uncleanliness. Anyone else who applied the term to him would be asking for a fight. From Kaya, however, he tolerated it.

Metcalfe shook his head. "I think we should focus on getting to the ship. I doubt the Deputy Captain will accept theft of our shuttle as an excuse."

"I'm on it," said Kaya. She tapped out a pattern on her left palm. Her implant activated, and a stylized logo appeared in hologram in front of her. It was quickly replaced by the disembodied head of a very polite woman. She recognized Kaya immediately and asked what service she required.

"Just hang on a sec," Kaya told her. She crossed to the dockmaster's office window, hologram in tow, and tapped on the plastiglass. After two rounds of finger-drumming, the man appeared in the door, looking harassed.

"Midshipman, I believe I already told you – " he began.

"Oh, I don't need a ship," Kaya said sweetly. "Could you just tell my dispatcher the ring number of this dock, and the available slips? I'm so stupid about these things, and – "

"I don't understand," said the dockmaster. "What dispatcher? Who are you?" he demanded of the hologram.

The woman informed him she represented Atal Holdings Transportation Division, and that she was responsible for getting company officers and their guests anywhere they needed to go.

"Since you couldn't help us," Kaya explained, "I'm having one of my grandfather's private yachts sent round. The pilot will need to know where to meet us, and – "

"Oh no!" said the dockmaster. "That won't do!"

"But we have to get to our ship," said Kaya. "Daddy would be very upset if we were late."

"Daddy?" asked the dockmaster, his face now the color of sunbleached bone.

"Captain Atal of the *Titan*," said Kaya. "He's my father."

The dockmaster swallowed hard. "Mistress Atal."

"Midshipman Atal, actually. Also of the *Titan*.." She stopped and assumed a wistful expression. "I suppose I really shouldn't arrive in company transport."

"No."

"It would look improper."

"Yes."

"It would be talked about on the news."

"Yes."

"It would embarrass the Navy."

"Yes."

"It would cause the Admiralty's Public Information Officer to speak to Internal Affairs, who would investigate the circumstances which led to the Executive Officer's party being deprived of their shuttle – "

"As it happens, I've just found you a shuttle," said the dockmaster.

"I thought you might," said Kaya.

Five minutes later, four midshipman of the *Titan*, as well as its Boatswain, were shuttling to the great ship in a vessel which the dockmaster at ring seven, slips one through forty-six, reserved – quite illegally – for his own private use. As they cleared the slip, the dockmaster helped himself to a generous portion from a bottle he kept – also quite illegally – in his desk drawer, and swore to himself that he would be unavailable the next time rich Navy brats came to his sandbox to play.

* * *

Titan's boat deck – not a 'landing deck,' as some incorrectly called it, for shuttles did not land as much as light on the skin of the great ship's passenger sphere like bloodsucking insects – was writhing with unwelcome guests when Metcalfe and his party's shuttle arrived. The concourse, which occupied a 90-degree arc at the equator of the sphere, was larger than most enclosed buildings on any planet in the Confederacy. There was still no place for them to stand and breathe comfortably at the same time.

Atal, having been informed of their arrival, made sure he was on hand to steer them clear of the press of reporters who hovered like vultures around each new arrival. He quickly and quietly shunted them, bewildered, into an ante-room meant for temporary storage of mail.

"Hello, children," he grinned at them.

"Dad," demanded Kaya, "what in the world – ?"

"We received orders to report back early – " began Metcalfe.

Aer'La was muttering something about breaking up the bodies on the concourse for more efficient storage when Atal held up his hand.

"Wait," he snapped. They waited. "I apologize for the abrupt termination of your leaves. In fact, it was my fault."

Their eyebrows shot up, but they remained silent.

Atal went on, "Plans were made – without my knowledge – to hold this ceremony a day out from launch."

"Ceremony?" asked Kaya.

"A launching ceremony," Atal explained.

"But you didn't want – " began Metcalfe.

"I didn't, no. Others... did. It seems we're wanted to parade ourselves before the cameras and look heroic. I have my own opinions on the matter of the ceremony being planned before your leave was over. I will not share them. Suffice to say that I could not delay or cancel the launch ceremony, but I could make damned sure my officers were here to accept their dubious honors along with me."

"That is very considerate of you, Captain," said Cernaq.

Atal laughed bitterly. "We'll see if you still hold that opinion when you've come out the other end of this ordeal, Mister Cernaq."

* * *

When Atal and his young officers had last embarked on a mission, they'd gone to meet *Arbiter* at the Border. There had been no moments of ceremony. They'd left the Rigel system in a cramped shuttle, departing a dimly lit, dusty docking bay usually reserved for freight. Even the dockmaster had been asleep, and thus not available to wish them well on their journey.

Today, for all they could tell, the entire population of Quintil was on the concourse. A large contingent of the press and dignitaries would stay with them for the first day or so of the voyage. It was a posh vacation for them. *Titan* boasted a five-star hotel, after all. Those not actually riding the ship to its next port of call or rendezvous with a commercial liner, numbering in the millions, watched on holo or from the observation decks of the orbital station.

There was a clamor from the audience when Jan Atal, accompanied by his officers, mounted the patriotically draped dais which Phyn Darby had ordered assembled for the occasion. Atal, flanked by Darby, stepped to the fore. The five midshipmen, Doctors Flynn and Faulkner, and Aer'La lined up behind them with a dozen or so minor officers.

It was a small cadre of officers, for *Titan* was a heavily departmentalized ship. While Atal theoretically commanded all of it, he and his officers were really only directly in charge of the command module and engineering. A separate corps of marines, who would join the ship in three days, staffed the gun decks and handled torpedoes, space to surface missiles, and the like. They theoretically were answerable to the Naval command crew, but a wise captain knew they had their own culture, and generally left them to do their jobs. He also did not blur the boundaries by inviting their officers to stand with his at public appearances.

As he allowed the applause to reach its crescendo, Atal gestured for the midshipmen to come forward and stand with him. Darby's face was immediately at his ear.

"Don't you think it would be sufficient, Captain, to let Mr. Blaurich represent the junior officers?"

Atal smiled politely. "I do not, Mr. Darby. If I did, I would have invited him alone." Adding insult to injury, he was well aware, Atal motioned Aer'La forward as well. Darby made a complete blank of his expression and stared straight out, above the audience.

Atal lifted his hands, looking as though he were offering a blessing upon those gathered before him. He wasn't aware that he looked this way, nor was the majority of his audience. Religion was a dead concept in most of the civilized galaxy. Those pockets where it continued, like Terra, like Hecate, kept it to themselves. Still, the gesture had the benefit of quieting the heathen assemblage.

"Thank you all for being here," he said, clearly and strongly. He had an excellent voice for public speaking, as little as he chose to make use of it. No doubt that detail had been carefully planned. "And thank you for the many good wishes you've expressed, and the gifts you've sent. I plan to feed and clothe two or three planets with them, later in the mission."

Light chuckling.

"I'll make this a brief address. Those of you who know anything about me probably know that I'm here to do a job, not a stand-up act. Besides, the hotel and taverns have a great number of launch-day specials I'm sure they want to advertise, so I really need to make room on the stage for some representatives of *Titan's* Chamber of Commerce. Quickly, though, I'll introduce my officers..."

He did so, as if he needed to. *Titan's* crew consisted of the most biographed humans living, at that given moment. Still, the audience made appreciative grunts. They applauded Sestus Blaurich, and there were many wolf whistles, from both males and females, when he stepped forward. Kaya fared almost as well. The rest were received politely, except for a certain measure of fearful silence which greeted Celia Faulkner.

"How do your officers feel about the *Titan's* curse?" called out a reporter near the front.

Atal slouched his shoulders disgustedly. "Oh, must we?"

"It's their favorite story," said Sestus Blaurich, through his teeth.

"Ladies and gentlemen," said Atal, "I believe *Titan* has established itself as very much *not* a cursed ship. If you don't count my arrival today as her captain."

Again, light chuckling.

Atal continued. "Seriously, decades of service, all without a major incident or significant loss of lives, should put this matter to rest. Frankly, I'm not sure I understand why there's even talk of 'a curse' in our technologically advanced culture."

The reporter pressed on, "Very good point, Captain, but could you explain, for the audience – "

Applause and cries of assent drowned out the rest of the request, but its meaning was clear to all.

Terry Metcalfe grinned and whispered to his Captain, "Tell us a *story*, Uncle Jan."

Atal made an unhappy face, and then became thoughtful for a moment. He gestured for silence again, and said, "I suppose a bit of foolishness is called for on any festive occasion." He smiled a crooked smile. "My executive officer, Mr. Metcalfe, will be happy to supply the necessary background for you."

Metcalfe gave Atal a panicked glance. Silence fell over the crowd. Atal stepped back.

Metcalfe cleared his throat, and began the tale he had learned as a child, enriched with more accurate details he'd picked up as a cadet. "Uh, as you know, *Titan* was designed by the great Lindstrom Douglas, the developer of the process of L-Mapping, which allows us to take shortcuts through the fabric of space without becoming lost forever." He stopped and surveyed his listeners to see if they were registering. Learning nothing, he plunged forward.

"The name of the ship was a point of contention. Throughout the history of sea and then space travel, only one ship, to that time, had been named for the race of elder gods of my planet's Mediterranean region. That ship, the *Royal Mail Steamer Titanic*, sank on her maiden voyage."

"Sank?" asked the reporter.

"In water," said Metcalfe. "It was a sea-going ship, the largest built, to that date. Anyway, although the *Titanic* incident was centuries ago, the general public found it in questionable taste to similarly name a ship. *Titanic* was considered unlucky, and cursed by the gods. You see... to build so large a ship was considered arrogant on humanity's part. Her destruction so early said to many people that the gods were unhappy with humanity's attempts to become too godlike themselves. That the gods had taken their revenge, by sending an iceberg to destroy the ship and kill two thirds of its passengers.

"They felt *Titan* was, similarly, ambitious, prone to failure. In fact, Douglas gave her the name to challenge directly the attitude that humankind's destiny is one of meek acceptance of nature's dictates. He intended *Titan* to be a monument to our refusal to submit to the whims of fate."

"Mr. Metcalfe, as a Terran, do you feel our conquest of space is also seen as arrogance by the gods?"

"If I did," Metcalfe asked, "would I be here?"

Undaunted, the reporter said, "There are those who suggest that a Terran agent might join the Navy with an agenda. That he or she might wish to be on the inside, as part of a plot to help fulfill religious prophecies about human arrogance."

"So... " said Metcalfe thoughtfully. "You think that I'm the curse of the *Titan*?"

Atal stepped forward. No doubt he was afraid Metcalfe would lose his temper. It was a reasonable fear.

"I wouldn't say that you, personally – " the reporter began.

"I am not aboard *Titan* as a Terran," Metcalfe cut her off. "I am aboard as an officer in the Navy. An officer goes through a rigorous battery of physical and emotional tests. If I'm here to sabotage the ship in the name of superstitious fear of technology, then either I'm a very clever lunatic, or the psych jockeys haven't done a very good job of screening me."

The reporter was silent now.

"I'll only add to that that the story of *Titan's* curse has been perpetuated by inworlders, not Terrans. Even though *Titanic's* story is chronicled in the *Book of Heroes*, it is not we who made the original comparisons between this, Lindy Douglas's greatest design, and the Terran steam vessel."

"And I will add," said Atal, "that I have the utmost faith in the officers I've chosen to serve on my ship. I find any questions about their loyalty – especially when based on the ethnic heritage – patently offensive." He looked to his officers. "Now I believe we're done here."

* * *

As they dispersed, Aer'La moved to catch up to her fellow Arbiters. She was glad no one had asked her to speak. She could have done without that question about the curse. The Inihu were strong believers in curses. She had heard many grisly tales of demons and angry gods while a child in the barracks. Nothing in her experience had convinced her that there were not dangerous, otherworldly forces. Such stories made her nervous.

She was so focused on thoughts of impending doom that she jumped a bit when Dr. Flynn suddenly spoke in her ear. He'd followed her off the stage and into the corridor.

"Well, Bos'n," he said, "very generous of the Captain to ask you to stand with the other officers."

"The Captain is a very generous man," said Aer'La tightly.

"Oh, I don't doubt that fact," agreed Flynn. "But perhaps he's a little reckless, given the circumstances, don't you think?"

"What are you talking about?"

Flynn shrugged. "Only that it will likely prove quite an embarrassment when the public learns who and what you are."

Aer'La froze. Blind fear and an impulse to lash out at the man combined in her, resulting in an inability to react to him at all.

He smiled, clearly savoring her reaction.

"Surely you didn't expect to fool competent medical personnel? Or that your friends Faulkner and Atal could protect you forever?"

"Leave them out of this!" Aer'La hissed, clenching her fists.

He took a step back from her, but kept his composure.

"I'm afraid I can't do that, my dear. You see, they've implicated themselves. When my report goes in to the Admiralty – "

"Report?" Aer'La demanded, damning herself for the fear in her voice. "Captain Atal won't let you – "

"Captain Atal has no choice," he cut her off. "Nor will the Admiralty, for that matter. According to all precedent of law – and all common sense – you belong back in Varthan Freespace. I suggest you start packing, young lady. You're going home."

He strode away, casually. Watching after him, Aer'La reflected that perhaps a curse could manifest itself in a very human form.

* * *

"It was all my fault, Captain."

Atal reached out and took Aer'La's hand, holding it gently. He was not a touchy person, normally, nor was Aer'La prone to let people touch her in such a way. Still, the gesture fit the moment for them both.

"Don't be ridiculous," Atal said. "Is it your fault that your people are abused throughout the galaxy? That you have to masquerade as a member of another race just to be left alone?"

"No, but... I panicked. When Flynn started asking questions about growing up on New Bedford – where I lived, who I knew .... I just froze up. I couldn't think of a story and I just... blabbed."

"There's no sin in finding it hard to lie, Aer'La. Lies are difficult things to construct and keep consistent. That's main reason to avoid telling them."

She shook her head. There were tears in her eyes. Atal had rarely seen them there. He was confident no one else had, either. "It's just that no one's ever really questioned the story before, not since you and the Doc made it up for me."

"If it's anyone's fault, it's mine," Atal said. "I'd intended to get this matter settled once *Titan* was underway. I'd intended to contact a few friends in the right places and have enough background evidence established to make your claim unshakable. I didn't count on someone like Flynn, with nothing better to do than put his nose where it doesn't belong." He sighed. "But that's no excuse. I should have moved faster. All that time on the Border must have made me forget what it's like to swim with the sharks."

If she agreed with him, her expression didn't reflect the fact, nor did it reflect anger at his perceived failure. In fact, she looked puzzled. "Sharks?"

"Predatory sea creatures, with very sharp teeth. They hunt the oceans for the taste of blood. The expression refers to how quick everyone is to pounce on weakness and profit by it here in the Inner Worlds."

"I think that happens everywhere," said Aer'La.

"So it does," agreed Atal. "Well, Flynn's discovering you may be for the best, in the long run."

"How can you say that?" she demanded. "He's going to report me! They're going to send me back!"

"Not if I can help it," Atal assured her.

"And what if you can't?" she asked, without a trace of sarcasm.

After a moment, he said, "I'll put in a call to Admiral Fournier this shift."

Aer'La frowned. Fournier was Secretary of the Navy, Atal's superior. He despised the Captain, and the feeling was mutual. "Not exactly a friend you can count on for a favor, is he?"

"Not by any definition of the words, no. But, if I can convince him that helping you will keep him in office, or increase his prestige, he'll be with us."

She looked at him and swallowed. "You know I don't scare easy, Captain."

He nodded.

"I'd follow you into a hot reactor, if you asked me to. I know you'd bring us out alive. But I was told all my life... no one escapes them. No one beats them. If my people want me back..." She covered her face.

Atal felt a stab of pity. Since she'd escaped her home, he wondered, had anyone seen her so vulnerable and afraid? He stepped forward and gently clasped her wrists, moving her hands so he could look her in the eye.

"They won't get you."

"No," she said with resolve. She raised a hand to brush tears from her eyes, and sniffed back those that still threatened to fall. "No, they won't. I'll die before I go back there."

She pulled free of him and went to the door.

"Aer'La – " he called after her.

But she was gone.

* * *

"What the *hell* were you thinking?"

Flynn, still at attention by the door to Atal's cabin, looked on impassively as the Captain shouted at him.

"I want an answer, Flynn!"

"I felt it only fair to warn the girl – " Flynn began.

"Fair? You don't know the first thing about fairness, Flynn! You saw the chance to bully someone, and you took it! I bet you tortured small animals as a child, too!"

Flynn was silent, but his expression suggested for a moment that Atal had struck a nerve. "I don't see the relevance."

"And I don't see the relevance in terrorizing an innocent – "

"I would hardly call the Bos'n innocent, Captain! Further, I would point out that you have taken no action in this matter since I informed you – "

"You don't know what actions I've taken."

"Well, then, you haven't informed me – "

Atal smiled as coldly as he knew how. "I'm not answerable to you, Flynn. I don't have to inform you of my actions."

"Then you leave me no choice but to assume that you have not reported Aer'La's illegal status. I informed you, Captain, that I considered it my duty to submit my report to Admiral Fournier. I have done so. I estimate it will be in his hands by 1400 hours tomorrow."

Simmering, Atal said "I could have you removed from this ship, Flynn."

"You have no grounds!"

"Do you think that will stop me?" asked Atal.

Flynn clenched his teeth. "I am only doing my duty, Captain."

"Has it occurred to you," Atal asked, his weariness coming through in his tone, "that your duty might include exercising some discretion?"

"What do you mean?"

"I mean, Flynn, that Aer'La was here less than an hour ago; and it was clear that your little... warning... had frightened her more than I've ever seen her frightened. She told me she'd rather die than go back home. I believe she meant it." He sighed. "You can talk all you like about doing your duty, Doctor. But, when doing it might drive a young woman to suicide, doesn't it give you pause?"

Flynn was silent a moment, then said quietly, "Perhaps you haven't considered, Captain, that the girl's suicide might solve a lot of problems."

Atal counted to ten. He quietly dismissed the ship's physician. He counted to ten again, not registering whether or not the man had followed his orders. Then he pummeled the computer console on his desk with his fist until, three times, he had heard the satisfying sound of strained plastic fiber cracking and breaking.

He summoned Dr. Faulkner to tend his bleeding hand, promising himself that he would, someday soon, sign up for a seminar on controlling anger.

Chapter Four
The Fifth Midshipman

Following the launch, Metcalfe and his fellow midshipmen attempted to report to the Deputy Captain, as ordered. Darby had disappeared amidst a throng of reporters, seemingly lost in his natural element. Metcalfe led them to the logical place to wait for him: Darby's office. Darby wasn't in.

"For someone in such a colossal hurry to see us," said Kevin Carson, "he's sure hard to locate."

"*He* wasn't in a colossal hurry," Kaya reminded him. "Dad ordered us back. Darby just took the credit."

"I hope that isn't going to be a pattern," muttered Metcalfe.

"That would be unfortunate," agreed Cernaq.

"Speaking of unfortunate," said Kaya, nodding toward the opposite end of the corridor, "here comes our shuttle thief."

Metcalfe recognized Sestus Blaurich from the ceremony, although they hadn't been introduced. Blaurich was close in age to the other midshipmen, but hadn't attended the Naval Academy with them. He was handsome, as all Inworlders tended to be, with a boyish face, a confident (if arrogant) smile, and tousled, blond hair. His teeth gleamed so when he displayed them that Metcalfe wondered if a radioactive veneer had been applied to them. He also moved too gracefully for Metcalfe's liking.

Like the orbital station they'd just departed, the passenger sphere of *Titan* was rotated on its axis at a speed which maintained, via centrifugal force, one full G. Even short-time spacers hated the feeling of full gravity on a spaceship. *Arbiter's* passenger module, to which they'd grown accustomed, was kept at .5 G. Moving around on *Titan*, while its gravity approximated that of their home planets, made them feel like they were wearing lead weights on all their limbs.

Still, Sestus Blaurich walked toward them with a practiced grace. He stopped a few paces short of them and grimaced disapprovingly.

"Captain Darby is waiting for us in the officers' lounge. I trust you all know the way?"

"We just got here," said Carson.

"That's unacceptable," Blaurich shot back. "It's an officer's responsibility to arrive at a new posting early, and familiarize himself with the area."

Carson began to reply, but Metcalfe cut him off. "We haven't met, Blaurich. I'm – "

"I know who you are, Metcalfe. I studied the dossiers on all the new officers. I'd be lying if I said I didn't have some concerns, but I'll proceed from the assumption that Captain Atal knows what he's doing bringing you all here. I think, with my guidance, you'll all be able to stay out of trouble."

Metcalfe stopped in his tracks. "Any guidance we require we'll take from the Captain, Mister Blaurich."

Blaurich's careful smile turned up sharply on one corner, forming a bit of a sneer. "This isn't the Border, Metcalfe. There's a chain of command here. Midshipmen report to the Deputy Captain. As senior midshipman, I – "

"Hold a moment, Blaurich. You may have seniority on this ship. You may have it in the service, I don't know; but Captain Atal has appointed me his executive officer. You'll find I don't take kindly to peers who try to bark orders at everyone because they were the first to pee on the ground where we're standing."

Blaurich looked blankly at Metcalfe. "'Pee?' As in urinate?"

"As in the way wild animals mark their territory," Metcalfe said.

"I wouldn't know. My travels haven't exposed me to wild animals. Present company excepted." He sniffed. "I'm pleased to see, at least, that you didn't bring that dreadful Bos'n along."

"I'd appreciate it if you'd accord Bos'n Aer'La the respect her rank and experience deserve," said Metcalfe tightly.

"It doesn't pay to be sentimental about the casuals, Metcalfe. Though I understand, given your background, why you might be more drawn to the working class. You'd better adjust to the world you've come into. Isn't that right, Kaya?"

"I wouldn't know, Sestus. I never adjusted to our world."

He slipped a proprietary arm about her shoulders. "Well, now that you're back in civilization, I think you'll rediscover the benefits of being around people... more like yourself." He added quietly, "I look forward to renewing our... special relationship."

Kaya sighed thinly. "We didn't have a special relationship, Sestus. We had sex. Once. I had sex before I met you, and I've had it since. Most of the time it was better. Occasionally," she said, removing his arm from around her, and going to recline against Metcalfe's shoulder, "it was even an experience worth repeating."

For a moment, Blaurich's facade cracked. Kaya leered in a predatory fashion, reveling in his vulnerability. His confident air quickly returned, however. "Well," he said with amusement, "good for you, Metcalfe. I suppose, given your knowledge of animal husbandry, that you do have certain... primitive advantages."

Metcalfe opened his mouth, but Kaya was not relinquishing her place in the battle. "His 'primitive advantage' does have a few inches on yours, Sestus. That's one stereotype about Terrans to which Yank conforms. But he also knows how to use his primitive advantages. Maybe you should ask him for lessons."

With that, she turned and, patting Sestus lightly on the cheek, entered the officers' lounge without them.

* * *

Leftenant Phyn Darby looked old. By the standards of the Confederacy, where human life expectancy exceeded century, he actually wasn't. He was just one of those people who *looked* old. No doubt he had looked old since he was a teenager. For one thing, his forest-sandy hair was thin. No one in the Inner Worlds went bald unintentionally. Male pattern baldness had been conquered, genetically, before the first humans left Earth. Terrans were still bald or balding, but that was only because they did not avail themselves of the benefits of scientific progress.

Still, Phyn Darby's hair looked as if it needed only the gentlest of breezes to free it from his head and cast it, lost forever, on the solar winds of some forgotten star system. He also had a thin, pinched nose, which sat a bit higher on his face than it should have. His black eyes were beady. His jowls drew his mouth permanently into an expression which was half shock, half disapproval.

Sestus Blaurich strode up to the Deputy Captain, who was helping himself to coffee from a well-appointed buffet table. "The midshipmen, reporting as ordered, Captain."

"Very good, Mister Blaurich, thank you."

Blaurich nodded curtly, giving the impression that Darby should, indeed, be grateful for any service he offered, and also helped himself to coffee. Darby's gaze lingered, approvingly.

"Wow," muttered Carson. "Someone has a hard-on for Five."

"He does not have an erection, Carson," Cernaq whispered.

"I didn't mean it literally."

"I know that. I can explain what you meant better than you can."

"It's bad manners to read my mind."

"Yes, but in your case, it's necessary, since your ability to frame your thoughts into spoken language is so lacking that you're in danger of being declared non-responsive and placed on life support."

"Gentlemen," said Darby loudly, obviously annoyed at the private exchange in his presence. He looked to Kaya and added, with a smile that was too conscious of her parentage, "And *lady*. I am *Titan's* Deputy Captain, Phyn Darby."

"Excuse me, Leftenant," said Metcalfe.

Darby cleared his throat loudly, and waited, expectantly. Whatever he was expecting didn't happen.

Blaurich looked at Metcalfe pointedly. "It is considered polite to refer to the Deputy Captain by his acting rank. Thus, we should address our superior as 'Captain Darby.'"

Metcalfe blinked, digesting this.

"Did you have a question, Mister...?"

"Metcalfe. Yes, I had a question. Why – "

"Sir."

"Sir?"

"Sir. 'Yes, I had a question, *Sir*.'"

"You had a question, Mister Darby?"

"*Captain* Darby."

"You had a question, Captain Darby?"

"Yes, I – No! Dammit, Mister Metcalfe, *you* had a question! And it is expected that, when asking a question of a superior officer, you append 'Sir' to the end of said question. Is that quite clear?"

"I believe so, sir."

"Good. What is your question?"

"What was the emergency? Sir?"

"Eh? What emergency?"

"Captain Darby... sir... you sent Scutley to retrieve us several hours before our leave ended," said Kaya. "We assumed there was an emergency situation."

Darby sniffed. "An urgent situation, yes. I activated the Scutley program because members of the press were aboard *Titan*... and four of my five midshipmen were not. It looked quite bad."

"It is a matter for grave concern, Captain" agreed Cernaq. "Were you expecting us aboard before the end of our leave?"

"I damned well was, Mister Cernaq. This isn't Border Patrol, dammit! It's the Inner Worlds! And in the Inner Worlds, we do not go gallivanting about, drinking and carousing, until the last minute!"

"Shit!" Carson whispered urgently to Metcalfe. "We were supposed to carouse! We forgot to carouse!"

"Mister Metcalfe!" Darby roared.

"He's Mister Carson, Captain."

"Yes, but I don't know his name."

"May I introduce Midshipman Carson, sir?"

"No, you may not! Now, if we may maintain some sense of the decorum befitting officers, let me make a few things clear. While you are on shore leave, on any world, but particularly in our home port, you are expected to be always available to me. Is that clear?"

"We came as soon as you called, Captain," said Cernaq.

"Yes, but you should have checked in with me before I called you."

"Why, sir?" asked Metcalfe.

"Because the press was here! Didn't you expect the media to want to cover the launch of the Navy's flagship?"

"Of course we did, sir," said Cernaq. "But we didn't expect the media to be allowed aboard until all officers were present. And we expected all officers were only expected to be present at the end of their assigned leaves."

"Well, the media arrived early," said Darby. "And you should have anticipated that, as well."

"If I may, sir, why were the media allowed aboard ahead of schedule?" asked Metcalfe.

"Because it doesn't do to make enemies among the press, Mister Metcalfe!" Darby shot back.

"So... you let the media aboard early... and that's our fault?"

"Do not take that tone with me, Metcalfe! It is not unreasonable of a captain to expect his crew to anticipate his orders and his wishes. You will all consider yourselves so advised. Now..." He stopped to sip his coffee, and gave an unpleasant expression when he tasted it. "We don't have time to waste. I must be available to lead tours of the ship for our guests, and all of you must be available to assist me. First, you will review your pre-departure orders, filed in your personal in-boxes."

Each of them triggered his or her data implant, and reviewed the orders according to their established preferences. Cernaq, already accustomed to bypassing his five senses, allowed the data to flow directly to his cerebral cortex. The others used either a visual display, the words appearing as holograms before their eyes, or audio, with a quietly regenerated waveform playing just by their ears.

None of them had used the data implants aboard *Arbiter*, although they all had experience with them. Atal was not enamored of them, and they were controversial for the potential they offered for violation of privacy, even though they could be nominally switched off by the user. Those stationed close to the Inner Worlds, however, used implants almost exclusively for communication. Pragmatism had forced the former *Arbiter* crew members to re-adopt the abandoned technology.

After giving them insufficient time to study the orders, Darby said, "In future, you will remember that midshipmen report directly to the Deputy Captain. You work for me, and laxness in the chain of command will not be tolerated. Those of you accustomed to more... informal arrangements will need to bear in mind that this means direct access to the Captain is strictly limited to those occasions when I grant such access."

"Excuse me, sir," said Metcalfe, "I don't believe you have the authority – "

"Once again, Mister Metcalfe, this is not Border duty!" Darby hissed. "Here the Captain has important matters to attend to, and cannot be bothered with the type of petty concerns that more junior officers are apt to raise. This is a very prominent job – "

"And we can't have filthy Terrans soiling the Captain's promenade," Carson muttered.

"Mister Carson, I'm well aware that you space lawyers specialize in claiming discrimination," snapped Darby. "You may avail yourself of all of your legal options, but you will not find me easily intimidated. Is that clear?"

"Pretty transparent, sir."

"Mister Darby," said Metcalfe, "to begin with, regulations allow all officers access to the captain – "

" – Upon notification of the captain's deputy or executive officer," Darby finished for him. "But you will find me... displeased... if I am too frequently disturbed with such matters. Now," he stopped and smiled at Blaurich. "Since I am eager to engender a spirit of coopera-tion between us, I am allowing Mister Blaurich the discretion to speak to the Captain without notification or prior approval. Since he is the senior midshipman – "

"Sir," Metcalfe said, unable to keep the exasperation from his voice.

"Mister Metcalfe, you have a decidedly irritating tendency to in-terrupt! I do hope we can expect this to improve from this day for-ward."

"It's just that the... Deputy Captain... seems to be unaware of cer-tain portions of my orders."

"What?" Darby demanded. "I assure you, I reviewed the orders thoroughly!"

"Then you know that I am Captain Atal's executive officer, and thus am empowered – "

"What?" Darby demanded. "This is impossible!"

"It's in my orders, sir," said Metcalfe. "If you'd like to check."

Darby checked, then sniffed with great displeasure.

"I see," he said quietly. "Surely I missed it because it's so... un-precedented. An executive officer, on a ship of *Titan's* size, is usual-ly a leftenant."

"A midshipman can act as a leftenant," said Kaya. "Just as," she added with a small grin, "a leftenant can act as a captain."

Darby swallowed and squared his shoulders definitively. "Very well. We have our orders, and, as officers, must follow them. Mis-ter Metcalfe, you are the Captain's executive, whatever I may think of the arrangement. But you will await the Captain's pleasure, and speak when spoken to." He glared at Metcalfe, who glared back.

"But," Darby went on, "one's official title is not the measure of one's character. I think you will find Mr. Blaurich a valuable re-source. Indeed, were I a young midshipman, I would consider my-self privileged indeed to serve with someone of his caliber. I would attempt to learn all that I could from him. Now, if you will – "

The door opened, and Dr. Flynn strode in purposefully. Not noticing the midshipmen, he came up to Darby.

"Phyn, I'm going to need your strong support against that – "

"I wonder," Darby interrupted too loudly, "if the midshipmen have met Doctor Flynn."

"We have," said Metcalfe coldly.

Flynn regarded them with equal chill. "Ah. Yes. Sorry, Phyn, I didn't know you were... meeting." He lowered his voice. "I've just come from the Captain. We must act, and act decisively."

Darby looked pained but interested at the interruption. "Quite," he said. "The midshipmen are dismissed. You all know your orders."

As they filed out, Metcalfe listened closely to the mutterings behind them. Apparently, Flynn was too agitated to wait until the door closed to speak.

"I told Atal I'd submitted the report. He's threatening – "

"You submitted it?" Darby demanded. "You should have come to me first! I might have limited your exposure to – "

" – Well, whatever you can do, do it now. He's threatening to have me transferred!"

"We'll see who's – "

The door closed, obscuring the remainder of the exchange.

When Blaurich was out of earshot, Metcalfe asked Cernaq, "What the hell was that about?"

"I attempted not to pry," said the young Phaetonian.

"Dammit, Cern – "

" – But I couldn't help picking up that it was about Aer'La."

* * *

Titan had several cargo holds. Some were squeezed into spaces left unclaimed by other ship's functions. Some – particularly the largest hold – had been planned from the outset. Cargo space could be supplemented by coupling cargo containment along the ship's exterior, since *Titan* need not be aerodynamic. In cases of extraordinary need, the ship was capable of towing barges.

Most space cargo was indifferent to gravity, and thus the largest holds were in the zero-G sections of the ship, outside the passenger sphere and its spin. There were holds inside the sphere, and consequently, they were at full G. It was in one of these small holds that Aer'La had been ordered to meet with her new crew for the first time.

The fact that she was ordered to meet them in full-G concerned her. Experienced spacers were more comfortable in reduced or zero-G. They avoided full-G whenever possible, beyond the minimum exposure necessary to prevent their bodies from becoming permanently acclimated to lower-G environs. Once that happened, returning planetside was no longer an option. The fact that they awaited her in a full-G area suggested that these were not experienced spacers.

Aer'La tried hard to focus on that concern. It was all she could do not to think of Flynn's smug face as he'd taunted her, of the horrors his threats brought to her mind...

She knew she wasn't in prime form to do her job, but she reminded herself that she could count on Atal. She also tried to remember that he must be able to count on her. She had to stay calm.

"How many of you have worked the hours needed for your zero-G badge?" Aer'La asked as she walked in front of the multi-layered lineup of her new crew. Introductions, extremely brief, were out of the way. That is, she had introduced herself to the men and women who would be working for her.

Only about half those in front of her raised a hand. Aer'La swore under her breath. "All right," she said, "how many of the rest of you know how many hours in zero-G you need to get your badge?"

Two other hands went up. Aer'La swore again, out loud this time.

"What the hell are you doing here, if you don't know anything about the job?" she demanded.

No one answered. Aer'La wouldn't have known anything new if they had. She'd already been told that the game was played differently in the Inner Worlds. On the Border, casual crew were fairly hard to come by. The result was that Border crews were belligerent and stupid, but they knew something about taking care of themselves. Even though they didn't know the job at hand, she'd found most of them could be taught.

On *Titan*, however, the job of casual crew member was actually sought after by many. At least two-thirds of the available slots could be filled with volunteers. Most of these were young people, bereft of financial support of any other kind, looking for a way to get into space. They could be counted on to desert the ship at any of the nicer ports of call. They were more intelligent than the rabble that border patrol brought in, but they were less blessed with survival skills, less interested in the job, and, Aer'La was warned, were not willing to learn. They also did not mix well with those who filled the other third of the openings, who were a lot like what Aer'La was used to on the Border.

An important difference between the two groups was that most people on the Border were accustomed to the real rigors of space. It was the Border, after all. Nice people didn't live there. There were no comfortable, clean cities on Border worlds. If you lived on the Border, you didn't sit still for long. That meant you'd been in space a good deal. Since few on the Border were rich enough to afford passage on fancy liners, being in space meant riding in ships that did not have passenger spheres with planet-like gravity. Border people were pretty much born knowing zero-G.

In the Inner Worlds, even the scum of most planets was comfortable enough to be able to stay on a planet, sometimes all their lives. Consequently, they didn't tend to know much about space.

"All right," she sighed. "We'll have to set up zero-G training for the rest of you. You can't do this job otherwise. I'll arrange for an instructor – "

"Bos'n?" a woman in the front row said, quietly, and even politely.

"Yeah?"

"I'm a certified zero-G instructor. I'll be happy to handle the classes."

Aer'La looked the woman over. She was middle-aged, a little heavyset. Too old to be one of those with the yearning to explore. Too clean, with too much awareness in her eyes to be one of the cons. They usually had a dull look, sly and defeated, all at the same time. This woman's expression was more open, if cautious.

"What's your name?" Aer'La asked.

"Smith, Bos'n. Ceres Smith."

"Smith..." Aer'La looked down her crew roster. "Here you are. Your cert's not listed."

"No one asked," Ceres Smith replied.

"When did you last teach?"

"A year or so ago. On the *Titmouse*. One of Atal line."

Aer'La nodded. Atal Holdings' fleet was nearly as big as the Navy's. "Okay. I'll check out your references. If it looks good, the duty's yours."

"Instructor bonus?" the woman asked.

Aer'La approved. She didn't like people who offered something for nothing. They reminded her too much of her sisters in the barracks.

The barracks... where, all too soon, she might return... if she lived...

"A bonus, of course," she said. Aer'La made a note to speak to the woman later. There had to be a good reason that someone with credentials and obvious education was signed on as casual crew. She knew from experience, though, that people with secrets didn't like to be asked about them in public.

She turned back to the rest of the crew. "Those of you who aren't trained in zero-G will handle cleaning and maintenance in the sphere until you are trained. You won't be eligible for bonuses until – "

"That's not fair!" cried a young woman halfway down the line.

Aer'La walked down to her. She was only a little older than the Bos'n herself, though considerably taller. Pretty, but with a pouty expression about her that put Aer'La off. A spoiled child, perhaps, or just someone looking for a fight because she felt the universe hadn't treated her the way it should.

"Crewman...?" Aer'La asked.

"Shan. Felicity Shan."

"You have a problem?"

"You can't withhold bonuses, just because we haven't been trained! Some of us have debts to pay, and – "

"What you do with your pay is your business, Shan," Aer'La interrupted. "I don't care whether you have debts or not. The Navy didn't agree to pay your debts for you when it hired you on. It agreed to pay you a fair amount for the work you did. If you're not prepared to do your best work, you're not worth as much to us. It's that simple."

"But some of us have never had an opportunity to train in zero-G!"

"And I'm giving you one. On the Navy's dime. Now that I think about it, that's pretty unfair to the people who got their training on their own time, isn't it?" She set her jaw hard and glared up at the taller girl. "Any other questions?"

Aer'La knew she was being harsh. She couldn't help it. She didn't like Felicity Shan. She carried herself wrong. She looked too soft. She smelled wrong. She'd never known what it was to suffer hunger, violence or loss.

Aer'La stopped herself. Was she treating Shan unfairly because she envied her the easy childhood of an inworlder?

No! Aer'La had always trusted her instincts and her first impressions. Unless Shan did something to prove herself otherwise, Aer'La would consider her a liability and treat her as such.

The inner hatch at the far end of the hold opened. With considerable difficulty, a man hefted his body inside. He was tremendously overweight, and the standard-issue blue coverall he wore strained to the point of splitting its seams at his waist and buttocks. Having completed the improbable task of entering the room, he began to waddle toward the crew in their formation.

Aer'La suppressed a gasp. She knew this man. She wondered if he would recognize her, or if he had struck his head too hard when Metcalfe had thrown him to the floor in the tavern. As he made his way to her, she checked his arm. She had thought Metcalfe might have broken it. It seemed all right now, so perhaps he'd found the time to see a doctor before reporting aboard.

The man stopped in front of her and saluted sloppily. "Sorry I'm late, Bos'n. Volster's my name, I – " He had been looking at the deck while muttering his apologies. When he'd raised his eyes, he'd recognized the Bos'n, although she, too, had changed into a coverall while en route to *Titan*, covering her more obvious assets.

"Volster?" Aer'La asked politely. She checked her roster for his name.

Volster stuttered over a few profane, if quiet, words of surprise.

"Something wrong, Volster?"

"N-n-no, ma'am. It's just – "

"It's just that you're late reporting. Got an explanation?"

"I was injured, ma'am."

"You were fighting."

"I was just havin' a few before we shipped out, Ma'am," he protested. Then he added, very quietly. "I didn't know who you was, Ma'am. I wouldn't a – "

Aer'La smiled, wondering if she was enjoying this too much. "You assaulted an officer."

"Aw, Ma'am, be fair, now! He broke my bleedin' arm!"

"After you damned near crushed the life out of him. What do you weigh, Volster?"

"A - about two... eighty.... ma'am."

"Try something that begins with a three. I don't think you're in shape for this work. Has the doc seen you?"

"He has, Ma'am. He did say I should drop a few pounds. But my weight's no trouble to me in zero-G."

"You're... checked out in zero-G?"

"Seventeen years in space, Ma'am. Fourteen of 'em right here on *Titan*."

"Amazing," said Aer'La. "All right, Volster, get in line. I'm docking your pay two hours – "

"What?!" the man demanded.

"Be glad Mister Metcalfe isn't pressing charges! Your behavior station-side was a disgrace to the ship."

"But, Ma'am, I didn't know you was the Bos'n! I thought you was – "

"I know damned well what you thought I was, Volster!"

"I thought those... gentlemen... was harassin' ya!"

Aer'La laughed out loud. "Believe me, Volster, I'll let you know if I need you to rescue me. In the meantime, try not to sit on any more officers."

Volster, properly chastised, made his way into the line. As he did, Felicity Shan stepped forward. "'Scuse me, but you can't do that."

"Sorry?" said Aer'La.

"You can't dock our pay without the Deputy Captain's approval," Shan explained smugly. "This is a Union crew, see, and there are regs which govern pay. You have to cite grounds clearly defined in the M.O.U., and, furthermore, something like this requires a third offense – "

"Shan," said Aer'La, "I'll ask for advice if I need it, and I won't ask you."

"It's not me, Bos'n. It's the Union you have to – "

"Get back in line."

"I'm just saying – "

"Crewman Shan, get back in line!" Aer'La barked.

The girl stood her ground, pointing her chin upward in defiance.

Her defiance vanished, replaced by outrage and a surprised yelp as Aer'La picked her up by the elbows and set her, not gently, back in line.

"What the hell – ?" Shan demanded.

"Quiet!" Aer'La shot back at her. "Under my command, you will follow orders, or I will make you follow orders. Is that clear?"

Shan only glared back at her.

Shaking her head, Aer'La called out, "Duty assignments will be posted after launch. I'll be selecting a team of Bos'n's mates by the end of the week. Those of you who need zero-G training, report here at oh-six-hundred next cycle. *Dismissed.*"

They filed away, Shan and Volster, clearly old friends, muttering to each other. Aer'La heard Volster urging Shan to go to the Deputy Captain.

"Those two are going to be trouble," said a quiet voice by her ear.

Aer'La turned to see Ceres Smith standing beside her. She nodded agreement. "I'll deal with them. I've handled worse cases."

"I know," said Smith. "I pulled your public record. Hope you don't mind."

"No. You do your homework. That's good."

"You need to watch yourself here, if you don't mind my saying so, Bos'n. It's not like the Border. A lot of these idiots have been here a long time, and plan to be here a long time after you're gone. They know how to work the system, and they'll work it against you."

Aer'La laughed, happy to feel comfortable in the older woman's presence. "The system's been against me all my life, Smith."

"Call me Ceres, if you will."

"I will. Thanks. And I'm Aer'La, in private, anyway." She looked after the departing crew, particularly Volster and Shan.

"Ceres? Was I too harsh?"

Ceres Smith chuckled. "By your rep, I'd say that's not a question you ask."

"Maybe not," Aer'La agreed.

"Aer'La," said the older woman, "I don't happen to think it's possible to be too harsh to rabble like that. I wouldn't think someone like you would either. Is something bothering you?"

Aer'La considered the question, and the implied offer of friendship behind it. She decided she wasn't ready to open up yet. Besides, new friends would just be more people who could get hurt.

"Nothing I can't handle," she lied. "See ya 'round, Ceres."

* * *

"Hey, earth-trash, where's your master?"

Metcalfe was climbing the arch – the passageway through one of the massive arms which encircled *Titan's* passenger, gently tugging it along with the rest of the ship. The sphere was not, in fact, physically anchored to the rest of the ship's structure. Rather it was held captive within a cage formed by the arms, and prevented from colliding with them, during changes in acceleration, by a system of force fields and buffers. These same force fields maintained the spin of the sphere, and minimized the impact of sudden course changes on those who lived within.

The arch was a zero-G space, generally, and Metcalfe was relieved to be in this more comfortable environment again. The hurled insult, and the presence of those who issued it, ended any blessed sense of relief or privacy that he'd hoped to find by traveling this little-used passage.

"Hello, Five," Metcalfe said, although the taunt had come from the other, Blaurich's companion. This second man was, like all inworlders, a healthy and handsome specimen, though his attitude was decidedly ugly.

"My name is Blaurich. Mister Blaurich to you."

"Whatever you say, Five. But while you're giving lessons in manners, it seems your friend could use some. Who is he, anyway?"

The other, older, taller, wore the plain coverall of one of the casual crew. Of course, so might an officer, when on duty away from the command deck or public areas. Metcalfe knew he wasn't a midshipman.

"I asked you a question, wog," the stranger blurted, kicking off from a support strut and drifting toward his intended victim. "I said, where's your master?" He punctuated his question with a jab of his palm to Metcalfe's solar plexus.

Five watched, amused.

Metcalfe resisted the urge to strike back at the oaf. Clearly, they were thrilled to catch him alone. It wasn't the first time he'd met up with their kind in some dark corner. He hadn't had to contend with this kind of ambush since the academy, but he should have been expecting it. Inworlders resented his presence, because he was Terran. Young, male inworlders tended to be more demonstrative and aggressive about it. It hardly surprised him that Five, for all of his obvious political savvy, was just a schoolyard bully when the cameras were pointed somewhere else.

He decided to try the high road, or at least the military equivalent. "I'm on business for the Captain, and you just shoved a superior."

"Superior? You'll never be superior to one of us, mongrel."

Metcalfe's anger was creeping up his neck, turning his face, he knew, bright red. He wondered if they'd notice, in this dim light, and comment on his lack of bio-control.

He tried to keep his voice even, and speak clearly, though his mouth was drying out, as it did in these situations. "The Navy disagrees with you. You understand that my authority comes from them... or was enabling that particular synapse left unchecked on your carefully researched genetic blueprint?"

"Watch your mouth, wog... There are laws against your kind taking shots at us, just because we're engineered."

And there were laws, passed long ago, when the genetically engineered could still remember the oppression they'd suffered before leaving earth. Inner World laws made it a hate crime to denigrate a person based on any aspect of his genetic heritage, but the laws only applied to the genetically engineered, in practice.

From Metcalfe's perspective, it seemed that inworlders could say whatever they liked about the earth-born "mongrels." And they did. They said Terrans had children by impulse and sex drives like savages. Their very existence wasn't screened and approved by an almighty genetic council, and so they were inferior. Because they were inferior, they harbored ill feelings towards the genetically excellent beings of the outer worlds. That made Terrans bigots. So, even though inworlders had better living conditions, higher incomes, more advancement potential in the interstellar employment arena, Terrans were legally forbidden to dislike them.

Metcalfe was used to the situation by now, and tried not to let it hold him back.

"The only shot I'm taking," he said, " is a shot at keeping you off report, mister. I am your superior officer. If you don't believe me, ask your silent partner here."

Five shrugged. "I didn't even see you here, Metcalfe. I'm not here at the moment. I'm in my cabin. I have witnesses who will say so."

"And I am on business for the Captain," said Metcalfe again. "You are in my way. Move aside. Now."

They didn't move. Five's companion said, "Why do some Terrans get so damned uppity? Doesn't he know that the only reason any Terran gets into the Academy is that they have to fill a quota? If

you had to get in according to your abilities, like we do, you would-
n't make the first cut."

"It's an excellent point," said Five. "What quality makes you fit to
lead your betters?"

"The same quality that keeps me from loosening your friend's
teeth right now," Metcalfe said. "I'm not interested in what you
think of me personally. In fact, I'd rather not be liked by either of
you. I have a job to do, and I intend to do it."

"As long as the Captain keeps finding jobs to suit your limited
talents," observed Five.

"Blaurich," Metcalfe said evenly, "I didn't come here looking for a
fight. But if you don't get out of my way – "

"Is there a problem here, gentlemen?"

It was Darby, floating several yards away from them, having
come up behind Metcalfe.

Metcalfe opened his mouth to speak, and intended to tell Darby
that he was handling the situation. Five cut him off.

"Mister Metcalfe saw fit to accost us. It seems he's insecure in his
position as executive officer, and wanted to secure it via threats
against our persons."

"Mister Metcalfe! What do you have to say for yourself, sir?"

"Nothing you'd believe, Mister Darby. Your protege is lying, of
course."

"Mind your tongue, sir!"

"Very well, sir. I respectfully request that we drop the matter.
Mister Blaurich's complaints against me are unfounded."

"He would seem to have a witness," said Darby.

Metcalfe bit his cheek and counted to ten silently. "So he would,
sir. I stand by my account."

"And I stand by my conviction that officers will be treated with
the proper respect aboard this ship. Consider yourself on report,
Mister Metcalfe."

"Yes sir. I will, naturally, appeal to the Captain."

Darby stiffened. "I am in charge of discipline on this ship, mister! You may appeal every decision of mine to the Captain, but – "

"I will, Mister Darby," Metcalfe promised.

"Officers who abuse the appeal process often find themselves
transferred to... disadvantageous posts," Darby said quietly.

"Often they do," agreed Metcalfe. "But that will be the Captain's
decision."

Darby cast a sideways glance at his two fellow inworlders. No doubt he was keenly aware that he stood to lose face in this encounter.

"Very well," he said finally. "I will discuss this matter with the Captain. But do not gloat, Mr. Metcalfe. I believe you will find that your days on this ship may be numbered."

Historian's Note:

The following passage from Midshipman Metcalfe's Prayer Journal is included for purposes of historical completeness. It may or may not have any bearing on the events chronicled in the balance of this account, but it is material from a contemporary source, written by one of the participants, while the actual events were occurring. It is therefore deemed to be of value to the student of history.

Further passages from this same source are incorporated later in this text.

For those students unfamiliar with the (principally Terran) practice of prayer, a brief explanation is fitting. Prayer is the Terran term for a one-way communication with a deity or deities. No evidence suggests that such deities exist or ever existed, yet prayer has continued for centuries.

Prayer has manifested itself in many ways throughout Terran history, and it is not surprising that it has been brought into space. Early Terrans burned animals or even humans, or slaughtered them with knives, in order to attract the attention of the gods. Thus they hoped to make their prayers – their requests for favor and assistance – heard. As civilization took hold on Terra, the abuse of other creatures became less prevalent, and prayer became a matter of simply calling out one's requests to the gods. Sometimes this was done in a public forum, out loud. Sometimes it was done silently, and in private, as a form of meditation. Various sects at various times used drugs, alcohol, or the infliction of pain upon the body to alter the state of consciousness and find the spirit drawn closer to the gods.

In the early days of interstellar travel, it became a fad to broadcast prayers via L-Space radio, in the hopes that the gods might actually occupy L-Space, and receive the messages broadcast. To date, none of the broadcasts thus directed have been answered by anyone.

Metcalfe's prayers take on a more benign form, though one not employed as often as the spoken or silent prayer in Terran history. He recorded his communications to his deity in data storage. They do give fascinating insight into the character of this important historical figure, into his philosophies and their evolution, and into the environments in which he lived.

Why did you send me here?
Did you send me here?
Do you send us places? Do you intervene in our lives? People at

home believed you did. I remember the old women on the farm telling us that all we had to do was listen, and you would tell us what we should do. Nothing we do is our own choice, or anybody else's but yours, they said, as long as we obey you.

Does it offend you to be told that I don't believe that? Why would you give us the ability to make decisions, and then expect us to let you make the decisions instead? Is it a test? Some kind of trick question? Do you tempt us with the power of our own minds, give us free reign to use them, wanting us all along to discover that we can tap into the power of your mind instead, so ours really don't need to be used?

Would you create a whole intellect just as a test device? That doesn't ring true. Oh, I suppose I could consider how crude and limited our intellects are compared to yours. Looked at that way, I suppose you might say they're a dime a dozen.

But don't our intellects live forever? And don't our immortal souls join you when our bodies pass away? So you don't consider us disposable, do you?

Then – why? Why create thinking beings, give them the ability to reason and develop a moral code, to invent and discover, put them in a testing ground and let them suffer hardships and learn lessons, and then give them the job of, essentially, L-space transmitters, broadcasting a pre-written message for the real intellect?

Perhaps, lacking your wisdom, I don't understand the point. Perhaps there's a wonderful reason for doing just that.

But lacking your wisdom, I have to say, I don't understand it, I don't believe it, and I don't like it. If that's truly the way things work, if you created me to be a worshiper and a follower and nothing else... well... you screwed up. No offense. That's not what I'm apparently designed to do. And if you gave free will and intelligence to trillions of humans and other sentient species, only to declare that every decision we make ourselves is inherently sinful, well... I don't guess you and I would get along. I mean... I suppose I just wouldn't like you.

Sorry. Guess I can't say 'no offense' to that one, can I?

What I really don't like is this assignment, surprisingly. I want to know if it was your idea to send me here, and I want to know why. I'm not asking to be arrogant and demanding; I'm asking because, if there is good to be derived from my time (read imprisonment) here, I want to move on to the good stuff. I want to know what to be looking for.

Open my eyes.

Show me the way.

Or at least get me off the *Titan*!

Arbiter was tough, but it was also somehow comfortable. There was bigotry. I got called 'terp' by the crew; but I was never directly challenged. Those who were supposed to obey my orders did. The others left me alone. Maybe that was Aer'La's doing. She kept the crew in line on *Arbiter*. They were afraid of her. Here... well, maybe they'll be afraid of her here, too, in time. But it doesn't work that way when you're not on patrol. This is home space. We're near the Admiralty and serving on the flagship of the fleet. Decorum is expected.

So why are all of us who came with the Captain being treated so indecorously?

I thought, I really did, that when I left poor, backward, rural Terra that everything would be different. I knew I was surrounded by ignorance, illiteracy, bigotry and fear. I guess I thought as little of Terrans as the inworlders do. I was ashamed of my people and the condition they allowed themselves to live in, and I vowed to get out. I thought that's what you wanted of me.

I came to Hestia expecting to find a center of knowledge, enlightenment and opportunity. I expected to see everyone reading all the time, debating lofty principles, discovering and inventing and expanding the frontiers of science. That's what I thought people did out here. I guess I expected to find a galaxy full of people just like me, only more educated, and willing to help me be like them.

It was a big shock to me, learning that the enlightened people I thought would welcome me and make me whole considered me a joke, an embarrassment, an example of all that was wrong with humanity. They assumed that I hated them, because I was Terran. Why? Why didn't they bother to find out? Why didn't they ask me what I thought?

I would have told them, I only wanted to be like them. I would have given anything to have the gifts they possessed as a birthright.

I suppose that was the naivete of youth. I can say that now, at the ripe old age of twenty Terran years. I came out here and learned that, though rich and educated, these people are just as eaten up by hate and fear as my own people were. What a disappointment, to find I'm not welcome out here...

So where am I welcome?

And if I don't want to be a Terran, and I don't want to be an in-worlder, what am I to be?

Got any answers?

Just checking.

Duty calls.

Amen.

was forced to raise his voice as she tried to object. She let him finish. She was getting better. "Point two, it was never established to be an apple tree; and point three, must you continue to use that distasteful term to refer to him, now that we're back home?"

"Yank? It's his nickname. He says he's proud of it."

"I could as easily see a Phaetonian being proud of 'gelding,' or an Hispanic of 'spic.'"

"What's an Hispanic?"

"You are – twenty-eight-point two per cent. I can't believe he lets anyone call him that."

"Well he does. He says he'd rather carry an offensive name and be Terran than be one of us."

"That I do believe. I – and I did *not* tell you this! – received a memo from Darby, saying that there was some 'unpleasantness' with Sestus Blaurich."

"You mean 'Five.'"

"'Five?' Another nickname?"

"Yank gave it to him. It's appropriate. It indicates his mental age, his IQ, his – "

"Don't you dare talk about his penis size."

"Penis size? Who said anything about penis size?"

"You were about to."

"Daddy, you spend too much time thinking about penises. It's unhealthy."

"Just tell me... Metcalfe hasn't been fighting again, has he?"

"I wouldn't tell the Captain, Captain."

"And the Captain is a bore for asking," Atal agreed. "I just don't want Metcalfe to get in trouble."

"Then you should have let them drum him out when he was court martialled. The only place he'll stay out of trouble is down on the mountains of Terra. As long as he stays in space, he'll be in trouble, and so will the rest of the Confederacy."

"As long as you stay out of trouble."

"I can handle Terry Metcalfe."

"If so, you're quite unique."

"Never wanted to be anything else."

"He's in love with you, you know."

"That's a damned lie!"

"Young woman, you are addressing your commanding officer," Atal said archly.

"That's a damned lie, *sir!*"

"That's better. But he is."

She took a breath before she said casually, "People our age are too young to fall in love."

"Tell that to the Bard of Avon."

"Who?"

"William Shakespeare – a celebrated playwright of Terra's past. One of the few included in the library at New Genesis. If you don't know Shakespeare, you've been rather scatter-shot in you attempt to verse yourself in his planet's history."

"Whose planet's history?"

"This boy who's not in love with you. In whom you have no interest."

In her eyes, Atal was fairly certain he saw every offensive monosyllable invented by humanity since the first caveman hit himself on the toe with his new invention, the hammer. To her credit, she uttered none of them aloud. Instead, she brightened, smiled sweetly and said, "Captain Daddy, you're a tease."

"Guilty as charged. Well, whatever your feelings about him, be aware of his feelings for you. Males are fragile creatures, you know. And Metcalfe shows a great deal of promise, despite the chip on his shoulder."

She shook her head. "Of course he does, but... will he ever fit in?"

"Never," He replied. "And that's part of his advantage. Kaya, the human race is not pulled forward towards destiny by the well-adjusted. It wasn't a well-adjusted amphibian that took to living on dry land, or a well-adjusted primate that abandoned his family and moved out of the trees. Historically, humans have been at their best when the odds were against them. The odds are against Terry."

"Seems to me the odds have been pretty well in his favor," she said. "How many Terrans make it into the Academy each year. Two? Three? He had to be better than any of us to win one of those coveted slots."

"But most of our people don't look at it that way. They see only a mongrel, someone not carefully designed, like themselves. To most inners, Terry is just a savage, uncultured package of bigotries, rages and primal fears. For all of our grand talk about universal brotherhood and our laws preventing a man from even thinking that someone from another world might be in any way objectionable, we still harbor a great deal of contempt for the humans from which we sprang."

"Because they drove us off earth."

"*They* didn't drive anyone, and *we* weren't driven anywhere, daughter. You and I grew up in comfort and affluence on a planet that's the seat of human power. While you were refusing your vegetables, Terry was standing in a line with a hundred or so orphan children, wondering if there'd be a drop of soup left when it was his turn. Half his people die before age fifteen. Terrans don't have time to sit around hating us. Their time and energy are devoted to survival."

"But they don't like us."

"And we don't like them. The universe is and always has been made up of those we call the *haves* and the considerably larger contingent of *have-nots*. We, darling child, are the *haves*. It's unreasonable of us to expect those who don't enjoy our wealth and comfort to like us."

"Don't kid me, Daddy. You know as well as I do that the vast majority of have-nots, as you call them, stay that way because they have no initiative."

"How did I breed such a cynical child? Was it your diet? I know no such thing. It can't be proven as fact, so I can't claim to 'know' it."

"But – "

"Hush! Father is expostulating. I happen to believe that most people who are poor are so because they refuse to correct the condition. They sit around waiting for someone to make the universe 'fair' so that they can get ahead. They miss the point. The universe is not fair and never will be. Not everyone can be above average, or average would have no meaning. I just as strongly believe that most of the wealthy are as lacking in initiative as the majority of the poor, and are just coasting along on their influence and their advantages – and usually the wealth their families earned before they were designed. Most people are subject to inertia and have no qualms about it.

"What they don't like are people who are not subject to that same inertia. The rich can't abide a self-made individual, who rises from poverty by his brains and the skin of his teeth. There are many old terms to describe such people – 'upstarts,' 'nouveau riche,' 'gold-diggers.' What it comes down to is that those with power and status know they could lose it at any moment in a fair contest, so they make the contest as unfair as possible. A lot of our new shipmates

call Terry Metcalfe 'yank' and 'mongrel' and worse, but I think a little piece of them recognizes that they're afraid of him. Well, they
should be afraid. He can outperform any ten of them on his worst
day. They'll do anything they can to keep him at the bottom of the
pile, or get him out of the Navy, if possible."

"Well he's doing everything he can to help them," Kaya said rue-
fully. "I think he would have beaten the tar out of Five up in the
Arch, if Darby hadn't – "

"*Who* wouldn't tell the Captain?"

"I didn't tell the Captain, I told my doting father." She lowered
her voice to a conspiratorial whisper. "If you see the Captain, don't
tell him a thing."

"What happened in the arch?"

"Five and one of his cronies tried to jump Yank. Darby broke it
up."

"Rather barbaric behavior for Blaurich."

"At heart, he's just a little ruffian, Daddy. He didn't even say
'Thank you' when I let him – "

"I see I should have paddled that bottom while the Salmon
Mousse was still fresh," Atal interrupted. Then, annoyed, he asked,
"Why didn't he come to me if he was attacked?"

"He wants to fight his own battles. He's pigheaded that way."

"Reminds me of one of my children."

"You only have one."

"So I do."

"I'm nothing like him."

"If you say so."

"I'm not that hot-headed." She paused a moment, then stopped,
turning to face her father. "What's your fascination with him anyway?"

"I think that's obvious. He's my student. He shows great
promise. He's in love with my daughter."

"Who's not in love with him."

"Mmmm."

"What's that supposed to mean?"

"Nothing. That's why I only grunted. If I'd meant to say anything, I would have used words."

"I think you don't believe me."

"Don't try to read my mind, daughter. You're not Phaetonian. If
I haven't said it plainly, it can't be attributed to me. I haven't said I

don't believe you, and until I do – "

"Which you don't – "

"Very well, I believe you are in love with him." Atal wasn't sure he believed anything of the kind, but Kaya had that effect on him. She wheedled him into making decisions he wasn't ready for.

"I'm not." She said.

"Mmmmm," He replied.

* * *

Mors was a senior member of the faculty at Hestia. He was not the kind of dried out academician who achieved seniority simply by outliving his colleagues. Such relics were universally viewed with scorn, while Mors was respected by just about everyone who met him. His intellect was huge. For Phaetonians, the intellect nearly always was. Contrary to the stereotype of the arrogant intellectual, however, he had the gentlest of personalities. It ensured that even his criticism of others was not offensive, but taken as a genuine display of concern for their welfare. His classes were both popular and educational, and his students had included Atal himself, many years gone, as well as all of Atal's midshipmen and officers.

Mors was also something of a celebrity. He was, after all, the only living person who had actually been a close friend of Lindstrom Douglas, the controversial father of real interstellar travel. It was Douglas who developed the process by which L-Space could be mapped. L-Space – so named because Lindy Douglas had blazed trails through it – was an extra-dimensional space outside the known universe. Douglas's mapping process plotted a network of interdimensional shortcuts through L-Space, the entry ports to which are conjugate points. The locations of the conjugate points – and the way they interconnect – was in constant flux due to the constant expansion of the universe. In order to travel L-Space reliably – and therefore be able to travel between stars in a timely manner – one needed a reliable map. Guessing could be fatal.

And much guessing had been done, prior to Douglas. Many of the colony worlds had, in fact, been settled and well established when L-space had been first mapped. On some, humans had traveled on generation ships to reach their destination, taking decades to reach a nearby star. On others, as was the case with the original settlers of Quintil, a ship had entered a known conjugate point, gambling that the pathway they'd chosen still ended where it used to. In Quintil's case, they'd guessed wrong. The colony bound elsewhere had wound up at Rigel, nearly a thousand light years from Terra. It was, perhaps, one of the happiest accidents in human history, for the Rigel system's fifth planet had proved uniquely hospitable. Very few Quintils, however, would have welcomed the prospect of traveling through unpredictable L-space again. They'd fallen down a well and hit deep water once. The odds were against it happening again.

Then Lindy Douglas had taken the guesswork out of long distance travel.

Douglas had made the Inner Worlds' current prosperous way of life possible, and so was a hero to many, a demon to many others. To all, he was somebody important, and Mors had known him, spoken with him, traveled with him, eaten meals with him. Mors was what was left of Lindstrom Douglas, his living memory.

So, without holding any public office, Mors had considerable influence. A quiet word from him helped put Atal back on the *Titan*, consequently easing Georg Fournier's latest headaches of public disapproval. That was why Mors was coming to *Titan* now. Fournier wanted his personal assurance that Atal wouldn't "pull any fast ones." Mors was here as a watchdog. Atal resented the implication from Fournier, but never the presence of the Professor aboard his ship.

Metcalfe was there when they arrived on the boat deck. Having dismissed the usual dockmaster, he was orchestrating the approach and docking maneuvers himself. He informed the Captain that Mors' small ship had emerged from the conjugate gateway and was matching speed with *Titan*, in preparation for gently clipping onto her docking rings with mechanical waldoes.

Kaya moved to stand at Metcalfe's shoulder, and began to offer helpful suggestions, which he enthusiastically declined to employ.

Atal wondered if this would be a good time to remind Kaya that she was not in love with Metcalfe. He also took the time to wonder, once again, why he found himself interested in her relationship with his executive officer.

Most fathers of the Inner Worlds had no more interest in their children's potential sex partners than in their favorite flavor of ice cream. On Quintil, children received sexual instruction when their psych evals indicated they were ready. A child's first partner was generally another child close to his or her own age, but with at least a year's sexual experience. Inexperienced sex partners could inadvertently cause a virgin initiate pain, and that was to be avoided. Initiates generally picked their training partner after reviewing the files of five or six candidates and being given a chance to view their images, hear them speak, smell their scent, and even taste simulated saliva and caress simulated flesh, if desired. All this happened before the initiate met his or her partner in person, to avoid awkwardness or hurt feelings.

Usually, the field of candidates was divided into an equal number from each gender, and studies showed that this practice resulted in a fifty-fifty split between initiates having a heterosexual or homosexual first encounter. This distribution was, according to conventional wisdom, proof positive that the human animal was naturally bisexual, and that all gender preferences were programmed by environment. This claim did not take into account that initiates spent their lives, up to that point, being told it was healthy to be evenly bisexual, of course.

Those who were not naturally bisexual – Atal himself had been such a child – were put through special training. If an aversion to (or disinterest in) homosexual contact was deep-rooted, an initiate's candidate field was populated only by partners of the opposite sex. This gave the initiate a pleasant and encouraging introduction to the mysteries. The initiate would then be required to participate in homosexual sex to prove that he was wired correctly.

Perhaps it was an artificial practice, all this teacher-supervised sex. Then again, Atal had often thought, perhaps it made too pedestrian an act which should have emotional tension and mystery interwoven in its fabric. He had often thought Kaya too disinterested in the subject. She'd taken little notice of other boys or girls growing up. She was more interested in Atal's career. She'd had sex when the doctor told her to, and when, such as with Blaurich, she thought it would create a scandal or annoy her father.

Metcalfe was the first male she'd noticed was a male. Possibly it was his alien origins – the attraction the primitive beast holds for some. Anyway, they looked well together. She was small, lean and dark, with laughing eyes and a fierce intensity. He was likewise on the small side, with a trim body he held like a coiled spring. Surprisingly, to those who had only the stereotypical image of Terrans by which to judge, he was also quite handsome. They seemed a matched set. Certainly, Metcalfe had always seemed to think so.

The red warning light which indicated zero pressure without the airlock warmed to amber, indicating that a docking seal had been completed, and pressure was equalizing between *Titan* and another vessel. In complete silence, for the airlock was too well sealed and shielded for the hiss of atmospheric gases flooding its inner chamber to be heard, the light cooled to green. Then the inner airlock hatch cycled. Metcalfe's eyes left the Captain's daughter, possibly never to return thence, for it was not the aged Professor Mors who emerged first.

Atal had met Dr. Pallas, the Professor's assistant, before. Metcalfe and Kaya had not. Although he was no gawking teenager, the Terran's dark eyes widened visibly as the Phaetonian woman's lithe, sculpted form, seemingly undaunted by gravity heavier than that of her native world, emerged. Atal didn't need Phaetonian telepathy to know that Metcalfe was immediately smitten, nor that his daughter, while also aware of the other woman's beauty, was aware of her fellow midshipman's reaction, and was not completely comfortable with it.

And Pallas was beautiful. Phaetonians could tend to look unhealthy, focused as their culture was on developing the mind. Professor Mors himself looked frail. Cernaq, while certainly not ugly, look somewhat like an elf out of Tolkein. They all had an ethereal quality to them, with their delicate bone structure, milky pale skin and white blond hair. Some compared them to the mythical Terran angels.

Pallas was all of the good physical qualities of a Phaetonian personified, and more. She did not look as though she might break. With a simple, black coverall stretched over her tall form, she looked, rather, like a toned and healthy black panther. The yellow cat's eyes of the Phaetonian only added to this image.

She smiled as she recognized Atal. "Hello, Captain." Her voice was quiet, low and cool. It didn't suggest disinterest or dry amusement, as Cernaq's did, merely reserve. Its reserve also hinted that, perhaps, there was a passionate core beneath the surface. Atal couldn't help but admit to himself that this woman fascinated him. He could understand the reaction of Metcalfe, who had yet to stop staring.

"Doctor Pallas. Welcome aboard."

She did not take his hand. Phaetonians didn't. Often, they kept their hands clasped behind their backs when they met new people, to make it clear they didn't want to touch. The resulting enhanced mental contact could be uncomfortable for them.

"Thank you. Mors is directly behind me. He's... " She quirked one corner of her mouth in a wry smile. "Signing an autograph for the pilot."

Atal chuckled. "Some things never change. I told him to use military transport."

"He says it's wrong for the government to take business away from the private sector."

"Some things really never change."

Mors emerged at that moment. Atal's old friend and mentor was strong and tall as ever, a commanding presence, though he looked as old as time. Unlike his young assistant, he took Atal's hand and pumped it happily. He did this often, and Atal had never been sure if it conveyed a measure of comfort with the individual in question, or simply a measure of the greater power of Mors's psychic shields, when compared with those of his countrymen.

"Well, Jan! The Border doesn't seem to have done you any harm, you look well. Settled in yet?"

"Hardly. How are you, Professor?"

"Old. Old as hell." He gestured at the girl. "If it weren't for Pallas, I might forget to keep breathing between sentences, or I might wander out the airlock."

Pallas assured Atal that this was far from the truth, while Kaya and Metcalfe, their argument over the docking console completed, came over to greet their former teacher. Metcalfe's eyes were still riveted on Pallas.

Mors smiled broadly when he saw them, grasping one of their shoulders in each hand firmly. "Mr. Metcalfe, and Ms. Atal. I trust you're both pleased with your new assignments?"

"It's a step up from *Arbiter*, Professor," admitted Metcalfe.

"Don't underestimate the benefit of any assignment, my young friend. All of life is a learning experience, and even the unpleasant parts eventually contribute to the good. In my case, the displeasure of growing infirm is balanced by the joy of watching all of you grow into your own. And, in Pallas's case, a dull business trip will afford her the opportunity of associating with people closer to her own age."

"I've looked forward to this trip, Professor. And I hardly find your companionship lacking."

"Still, child, you've spent too much time listening to an old fool philosophize. My standing order on this trip is for you to acquaint yourself with Jan's officers. They're some of the best the Inner Worlds have to offer."

"I'm sure they have better things to do than serve as my personal escorts," said Pallas, favoring Metcalfe, for the first time, with her gaze.

Metcalfe blushed, though the assembled company was polite enough to ignore it. He knew an answer was expected, however, and attempted to give it. "Um... no. I mean yes. That is, Doctor, any friend of Mors's..." He looked to his companion. "Right Kaya?"

"Right what? You didn't say anything." She laughed quietly, and said to Pallas. "But I'm sure, in your case, it's the thought that counts, isn't it, Doctor?"

"Call me Pallas, please."

"Pallas. I think we'll be quite happy to show you..." She looked meaningfully at Metcalfe. "...anything you want to see."

Atal cleared his throat. "Mr. Metcalfe has arranged quarters for you both, of course. He'll be happy to escort you – "

Mors shrugged. "I know my way around this ship pretty well. I think I'll remain with you for a bit, Jan. Pallas, you'll be all right?"

"We'll take good care of her, Professor," said Kaya cheerfully.

Then he took Atal's arm in the manner of the frail old man he wasn't, and led the Captain away from the young people. "Then, come, Mr. Atal. Let's see this Captain's promenade that had the tax-payers in an uproar."

This exchange told Atal something new about Pallas. Phaetonians were known to be naive. Most of them, off their planet, avoided the company of humans who might be sexually interested in them. The old Phaetons tended to make sure any chance of their juniors being alone with a human in such a situation was avoided. Mors, the old spy, had to be well aware of Metcalfe's attraction to his assistant. The fact that he not only allowed but encouraged her to be alone with the boy said that he trusted her to take care of herself. And that said that Pallas was a very special young Phaeton. Mors's trust was never known to be misplaced.

"I sense," Mors continued, "that something is distracting you, Jan. I'd like to hear about it, if it's not prying."

"Are you reading my mind, Professor?"

He smiled. "No, son. Only your face. I do know how to mind my manners. Besides, if you make a habit of reading every mind around you, too often you read something you wish you hadn't."

* * *

Twenty minutes into their tour of *Titan*, an urgent page summoned Kaya to engineering. Amid much grousing about her subordinates' and co-workers' utter lack of competence, she left to straighten out what ever needed straightening. This left Metcalfe alone with Pallas, and an awkward silence ensued, broken only by Metcalfe's occasional terse explanations of some aspect of the ship, its care, its feeding and its relevance.

The silence was not to last. As they rounded a bend in the gently curving corridor, they encountered Aer'La, hurrying toward the main cargo holds. Despite his very real desire to make Pallas like him, Metcalfe was relieved to see a familiar face.

"Aer'La! I'm glad we bumped into you. I'm showing Professor Mors's assistant around, and – "

He stopped as he noticed that Aer'La's own welcoming smile had vanished as she looked at Pallas. Her eyes narrowed. Her lip curled. Her fists clenched.

"Hello, Bos'n," Pallas said coolly.

"You two know each other..." Metcalfe began. "Where – "

Aer'La cut him off with a hiss of pure hatred. "Blondie. What the hell are you doing here?"

"Mr. Metcalfe is showing me the *Titan*."

Aer'La considered that, and looked at Metcalfe. He got the distinct impression that she didn't think he was safe with Pallas, and that Aer'La was trying to decide if she needed to kill the other woman to protect him. Fortunately, she didn't seem to decide that drastic action was necessary. If she had, he wondered if he could have stopped her.

"Just stay out of my way," she said finally. She took a step closer to Metcalfe. "I hear you had some trouble earlier."

Had everyone heard? Metcalfe wondered. "Nothing I couldn't handle."

Aer'La nodded. "Still, if they're willing to double up on you on the first day, I'd watch it. I'd be happy to... discourage them for you."

"I don't need a bodyguard, Aer'La," he said, his irritation throttled up by the presence of a beautiful woman during this exchange.

"Okay... but be careful. These pedigreed lapdog types fight mean." She looked pointedly at Pallas as she said this, then went on her way.

"I'm... sorry," said Metcalfe when she was gone. "I can't say I haven't seen Aer'La behave that way before, but – I think something's bothering her."

"She dislikes me intensely," Pallas replied. "She has since the moment we met."

"Where did you meet?"

"On *Arbiter*, last year."

"Where was I?"

"I believe you and the others were on an assignment off ship."

"She really doesn't like you."

"No. And I'm not sure why. I can only gather that she resents my level of education, or the fact that I've had better opportunities than she has. It's a pity she lets her feelings descend into envy. She should allow the accomplishments of others to motivate her to improve."

"Spoken like a true Phaetonian," said Metcalfe. "Your deity would be proud."

"We have no deities," Pallas said. "Blind faith is irrational."

"I was referring to Ayn Rand."

"She is not a deity. She is merely one of the philosophers whose work was instrumental to the development of Phaetonian culture. We value her application of Reason. We don't worship her."

"Maybe we can debate that later. And maybe you and Aer'La will give each other another chance. She's a good person, really."

Pallas looked critically down the corridor where Aer'La had gone. "Goodness is a relative term, but most systems of measuring personal worth recognize that violent behavior is detrimental to the individual and to society. Your friend's thoughts are... extremely violent. Chaotic, even. There's less rational organization of her thought processes than in most human minds."

Metcalfe said nothing, although the word 'human' had caused him a mental shudder. Pallas looked at him as if he had spoken.

"She isn't human?"

He shook his head. "I suppose there's no point trying to deny it. We... don't talk about it."

Pallas was silent for a moment, and Metcalfe realized she was probing his thoughts.

"You're supposed to ask before you do that," he said.

"Sorry," she said, though she didn't look sorry. "I have a habit of assuming that free-floating thoughts are being offered up to be read."

"Free-floating thoughts?"

"It's a telepathy thing."

"I wouldn't understand."

She nodded agreement. "So, Aer'La's a Varthan feral."

"Shhh!" Metcalfe hissed involuntarily. "I mean... we keep that quiet."

"A secret?" She wondered, then, answering her own question, added, "Because she could be repatriated if discovered." At his look of annoyance, she added, "And I'll try to stop reading your mind."

"Thanks."

"It's just that it's an easy mind to read."

Metcalfe stammered, then gave a bewildered laugh. "I'm... not sure how to take that."

"Oh," Pallas said, genuinely surprised at his offense, "it's a compliment. It means you know your own thoughts well, and they're organized clearly. It's the sign of an adept, analytical mind."

"Well... then thank you."

"Unlike Aer'La's," Pallas went on, "which is really quite a mess. I didn't pick up much of her background from her mind, because it would require great concentration to find useful information amongst all the emotional impulses she emits. That may be partly the result of her lack of education."

"Trust me," said Metcalfe, "Aer'La had an education."

"I'm sure. As a sexual servitor. Hardly what I'd call consciousness-raising. Hardly what I'd call an 'education.' More of an indoctrination. She's been raised in a de-humanizing manner. I suppose that's why the signal to noise ratio in her brain is so very poor."

"So... emotions are 'noise?'"

"From the standpoint of gathering useful information, yes. That's not to say they can't be beneficial. Tell me," she said, abruptly changing the subject, "can Aer'La read minds?"

"Not that I know of. Why?"

"I detected some measure of jealousy in her, brought about by the fact that you and I were here together."

"Aer'La? Jealous? I doubt it. Especially of me."

"But you've had sex with her," Pallas said evenly.

Metcalfe felt his face go very hot. "Uh... yes."

"Sorry. That's very clear in your mind... and becoming clearer as I speak."

Pallas's eyes widened.

"You have very vivid sense memories of your encounters with her."

"Could we change the subject, please?" asked Metcalfe. "Like maybe back to why you thought Aer'La could read minds."

"Oh," said Pallas, as if it were obvious, "because it would explain her jealousy. She sees you already as a sexual partner. If she could also see in your mind how very much you'd like to be my sexual partner, it would explain a reaction of jealousy." As an afterthought, she added, "In so primitive a mind."

Metcalfe was both speechless and unable to look Pallas in the eye.

"Weren't we going to finish the tour?" she asked innocently.

* * *

The captain's promenade was located on the outer skin of *Titan's* life globe, adjacent the captain's cabin and office. The point of the private promenade, like its larger cousins, the passenger and officers' promenades, was to allow human beings to see something other than walls and monitor screens and holograms. The captain's promenade served the additional purpose of letting the captain separate himself from his crew while relaxing. To some captains, this was a necessity of command. To others, it was merely a status symbol.

Titan was an old ship, nearly as old as her current captain. She'd been refit and refurbished many times, to keep her at the cutting edge of speed, safety, defensive capability, and luxury.

The most recent refitting of the *Titan*, unfortunately, was initially proposed by a member of the Confederacy's Council of Arbiters. This particular gentleman had never been to space, had never toured a space ship, and had never held a job in his life, other than a political one. He had no training for anything, outside of a few degrees in fields in which he'd never practiced; but he was from the right families, and so was pushed forward, by those who "knew people," as a political candidate. Successful candidates, after all, don't just up and declare one day. They are 'sponsored' by someone. That someone usually smells an attempt to gain wealth and power.

This young man, picked to lead others because he could do nothing else, was wont to find projects to undertake which made him look busy and gave him lines to add to his resume. One project he conceived was to give the Navy a truly grand flagship, designed for more than just tawdry functionality. He wanted something worthy of bearing the flag of the Confederacy, something elegant, something beautiful.

"We are the rulers of the stars," he said in Council. "We should have a vessel at the fore of our fleet which says so, and says so grandly." They stood and applauded him.

So this young arbiter, driven by the momentary adulation of his fellows, sat down with the plans of the *Titan* as she was laid out by Lindstrom Douglas, and began to make revisions. According to some experienced spacers who saw the plans, he damn near revised poor old *Titan* right out of space. His initial design wouldn't have held atmosphere, much less moved.

He began by writing a poem.

Now, most people in the Inner Worlds would have agreed that a well-designed ship is a thing of beauty. That the accomplishments of human minds and human hands are – when a modicum of reason has gone into their design – monuments to be celebrated. Those officers who thought *Titan* one of the most beautiful objects in the universe, however, those who were downright religious about the old girl, felt that way about her long before this young Arbiter put quill to parchment.

Lindy Douglas, Jan Atal had told all his students at the academy, was a genius, tested, certified, recorded for posterity. *Titan* was the capstone of an ingenious career, a career which may have affected human progress more than any career in our history, for Lindy led humanity to the stars. Or it might be more accurate to say he led humanity home from the stars. Many had attempted shortcuts through hyperspace before Lindy Douglas. Most had become hopelessly lost and died in space as well. Lindy's mapping of L-Space made long-distance travel safe and practical. *Titan* was his living, breathing monument.

But *Titan* wasn't built by a poet. It was designed by engineers

and scientists, built by craftspeople.   There was solid scientific
thought behind its development, and solid philosophical thought
behind the use to which it would be put – the exploration of space
and the protection of human society.   One doesn't arrive at the successful conclusion to a project like *Titan* by vomiting chaotic emotions onto paper, or into data storage.

This young Arbiter didn't understand that. He was one of those
to whom feelings – raw, ungoverned, unexamined emotions – were
the be-all and the end-all. He believed science should take a back-
seat to compassionate sociology, that scientists and all whose work
derived from rational thought, as opposed to directionless emotional reaction to the infinite, were, essentially, retarded.   Perhaps it
would be better to say he thought they were blind. They were unable to see or to understand the irrational, the nonsensical, the 'cosmic,' as Terrans had once called it. Others would say these rational-
ists functioned in a world that made sense, in which life had a purpose, in which right and wrong had definitions, in which you believed in what you could see, and withheld judgment on things you
couldn't.

This kind of mind-set, he maintained, prevented one from
glimpsing the eternal. Since the universe made no sense, since humanity was at the whim of higher forces it could neither appease
nor understand, it was ludicrous – nay, blasphemous – to attempt to
understand the framework of reality.   One should merely leave
one's mind open to experience, not attempt to draw conclusions
based on facts, for the human mind is feeble and all facts are really
matters of opinion.   One should understand that right and wrong
had no definitions, and it was sacrilege to say otherwise.

Since it was the mind-set of rationality which had designed *Titan,*
it was necessary, in his eyes, for someone whose mind was unclut-
tered with the conditioning of reason to propose the new design.

So he wrote a poem. The poem described how the ship should
feel.

He then contacted some friends who were some sorts of engineers – it didn't matter what kind, for all technicians were of the
same, dumb, blind ilk – and they, under his tutelage, molded a new
design from his poetic direction.

And one "petty detail" he was too busy to notice was that the glo-
rious promenades he had designed had windows in the floor. The
life sphere's gravity is supplied by its rotation, which results in cen-

trifugal force. That force attracts objects inside the sphere toward its outer perimeter, not toward its center. So the floor of, say, the captain's cabin is on the outer wall of the ship. It took one of those 'tawdry engineers' to point out this failing to the designer, and to propose that a system of mirrors below the floor and within the bulkheads could be used to project the view of space outside onto a wall, where it was less prone to induce vertigo than it would be beneath the occupants' feet.

The young Arbiter wasn't happy. Having never been in space, he couldn't visualize it. It was 'artificial,' since passengers wouldn't be looking right out a window at space. Several people tried to explain to him that all vision is just reflection and refraction anyway, but he never understood the point. He tried to insist that they come up with another system for supplying gravity, so his child could have windows. A lot of people quit the project. The Arbiter broke down crying in the Council room, bemoaning that no one around him understood his emotional genius.

While he was in therapy, one of his staff took over the refit. The project was completed five years overdue and nearly 300 per cent over budget. And the promenades – which had scandalized many taxpayers as an unnecessary luxury – had "windows" in the walls, extending into the ceilings, which were actually mirrored images, reflected from under the floor. No one could tell the difference.

* * *

"Brilliant!"

Mors was shaking his head, examining the dregs of the Quintil coffee in his mug as he gently swirled them. Mors loved to drink coffee. His doctor had insisted for a period of sixty years that he quit. Then the doctor had died and no one had bothered him about it since.

"I'm sorry?" Atal said.

"How do you do it, Atal? Your ability to find new ways of getting into trouble is exceeded only by... Ah well, never mind."

He set the mug on the table between them. They were seating in that very controversial captain's promenade. Atal's predecessor had furnished it with antiques – glass and whitewashed wood – to give the appearance of being on a cruise ship's promenade on the seas of Quintil. The effect was convincing. Only the absolute blackness of space in place of the ocean on the other side of the huge windows was a giveaway.

"No, tell me, Professor. What exceeds my ability to get into trouble?"

"I was going to say your ability to get out of it. But, my boy, I don't see that happening this time. You've wound so many hot political threads into this one problem – "

"I walked in in the middle of the problem, sir. If my predecessor on *Arbiter* hadn't adopted Aer'La – "

"Adopted? Interesting euphemism for making the child his sex slave."

"Professor – such language! My virgin ears – "

"Only one of them, boy. I know, I've seen the vids. Amazing. And yes, this old Phaeton has loosened up a bit on the subject of what young Metcalfe's people call 'original sin.'"

"Do they *really?*" Atal didn't know which astounded him more. Mors speaking openly of sex – which his people deemed a dangerous luxury – or learning that Metcalfe's people actually believed in sin, and considered sexual intercourse to be one. People who allowed themselves no other way than copulation to continue their race would logically consider copulation a sacrament... but human mores were rarely logical.

"Oh yes," Mors replied. "For millennia now. It's quite a taboo for them, too. I've always found that fascinating. At least, when my people declared it a taboo we stopped doing it."

"And mine made it a party game. Useless, from an earth perspective – "

"Hardly useless! I'd call some Quintil erotica a high art form."

"You've viewed erotica? Professor, you *have* loosened up."

"Part of my latest research, actually."

"I'll be interested in hearing about it. Later. But sir – "

"Yes, back to the poor child. Jan, this is exactly the kind of thing Fournier is expecting."

"You mean that I might try to apply the principles of the Confederacy?"

"That you might create a political hornet's nest for him during your first week on the job. You know how the Varthan alliance will react if this gets out. The girl is one of their nationals. They'll demand her immediate release to their authorities."

"So that they can put her back in chains."

"Precisely. Think of the black eye this gives them, the hope it might engender in other slaves in Freespace."

"That's exactly what I'm thinking about. Why the hell don't we take a stand against these bastards? Our entire alliance is founded on the principles of freedom – "

"Our alliance is founded on the principles of safety and convenience, and you damned well know it, Jan."

"You're an old cynic."

"To the core. The Confederate Charter has lots of lofty words in it, written by a few idealists who remembered the oppression they'd suffered on old Terra. But the reason most worlds bought into it is that we're nearby each other, and we have to watch each other's backs. Terra's not a superpower anymore, but the Qraitians are. If we don't stand together, we'll be conquered, the Varthans among us; but that doesn't mean we all share the same beliefs or even that we like each other. You'd be surprised how many people condone Varthan slavery, and how many more just don't care about it. We're held together by stellar geography, not brotherhood."

"You're lecturing."

"Sorry. Old habits."

Mors sipped his coffee for a thoughtful moment. "I suppose I should blame myself as much as you. I knew about the girl's past."

"You did?"

"From Cernaq."

"Of course. And I guess you couldn't have missed it, having met Aer'La."

"Interesting that you say that, though, Jan. I was surprised, when I met her, at her behavior. I wouldn't have guessed her for a feral, were I not a telepath."

"No? What makes you say so?"

"As I said, her behavior. Ferals – I know from the few I've encountered, and I gather from what I've read – are usually either in a state of extreme agitation, or they're... I believe the best word would be 'dopey.' When one is agitated, I quite believe that a human male in her clutches would be in grave danger."

"Aer'La can become extremely agitated. I've never seen her dopey. As to the rest, she can be very dangerous. I also assume she can be gentle, since I believe all of my male midshipmen have been intimate with her."

"I gather she doesn't use the traditional drugs?"

"Which traditional drugs?"

"The ones used to manage them by their masters. Here." Mors activated his data implant. "I just recently came across this article about the practice."

Holographic words appeared in the air before Mors, forming a shape roughly akin to a large, printed page. He gently shoved the glowing rectangle toward Atal. Responding to its programming to react so to an encounter between human flesh and its holo matrix, the page shushed its way forward in the direction Mors had pushed.

Atal scanned it, a piece from a news service's health section titled, "Hope for treating sociopaths from an unlikely source."

Physicians working in the Confederacy's penal system believe they may have an alternative to incarceration for some of the truly violent cases in their care. It's an alternative coming from an unlikely source: The Varthan Slave Trade.

Dr. Arvenius Frook, chief physician of the Confederate Cometary Detention Center in the Rigel System, points to promising research on a compound known to Varthans simply as "grog."

"Varthan Ferals are, of course, the most violently natured species in the known galaxy," Frook explained in an exclusive interview last week. "Many, if not most of them will kill for no reason whatsoever. This compound has been used for generations by the Varthans to take the edge off the ferals' killer impulse. According to interviews I've conducted with people in the, ah, industry, it provides clarity of thinking and a sense of well-being to the ferals thus treated. And, apparently, they love the stuff. If these reports are true, they're probably better off under its influence. Of course, I don't condone slavery."

Frook went on to discuss possible applications for serial murderers and hate criminals.

"While many behavioral aberrations of days gone by are prevented by careful genetic screening, there's still a lot we don't understand about violent behavior," said Frook.

Civil rights groups, meanwhile, have protested...

"Hmm," Atal said, snapping his fingers to dissolve the image. "Aer'La did mention grog. She didn't say anything about clarity or a sense of well being, though. She said it made them stupid."

"Doubtful something the Varthans would admit, if they think they've found a way to expand the market for the stuff."

A chime sounded in the air, and Carson's holo, ten inches tall, appeared on Atal's shoulder. Atal wondered if he would soon be accustomed again to the niceties of Inner Worlds technology.

"Request from the Admiralty, Captain," said Carson's image. "Admiral Fournier requests the pleasure of a conference with you."

"Send him through," Atal sighed.

As if the man himself had, in fact, been transmitted into the room, Admiral Fournier appeared in front of them. Nor was he, like Carson's avatar, ten inches tall. Conferences with the Admiralty demanded full size holo. In fact, Atal suspected the oily bastard had himself enlarged a little in transmission.

The technique was called compressed interactive communication: A hologram was crunched down into a tiny data stream and transmitted in packets, the signal following its own path through Lindstrom space. The technology was highly unstable, since an actual probe had to be sent into L-Space to transmit and receive. The probes tended to get lost, since they were on automatic. It took a human or a very sophisticated navigational computer to process the ever-changing data of what was where in L-Space.

It wasn't a cheap way to communicate, but Fournier didn't have much regard for economy. Appearing thus allowed him a chance at virtual intimidation, as well as a peek into the goings on on Atal's promenade. Today, however, he didn't seem interested in peeking. His eyes stayed glued to his terminal screen, reading some report or other.

"I'll get right to the point, Atal," he said. "I've no time for pleasantries."

"I'm sure my guest would appreciate that, Admiral."

Now he looked up. He was a good politician. His face brightened politely. "Professor Mors. Good to see you."

"And you, Admiral," said Mors. "And thank you for that bit of pleasantry amidst your busy schedule."

Fournier didn't reply. He really couldn't. Highly placed as he was, he couldn't be Mors's enemy. No one in the Navy could.

"I hope the Captain isn't burdening you with this embarrassing situation, sir."

"On the contrary, I insisted on hearing about it. I am here as an advisor, Georg."

Fournier nodded curtly. "Very well, then. As you've no doubt surmised, Atal, I've received a transmission from Dr. Flynn. I'm disappointed, though not surprised, that you didn't see fit to contact me personally."

"I am still investigating the matter, Admiral. The physician's call to you was premature, and against my orders."

"The physician was carrying out his responsibilities as an officer."

"Be that as it may, he's second-guessed me for the last time. At the earliest opportunity, I want him off this ship."

"We'll discuss that later. Now, because of the sensitive political nature of this matter, and considering the importance of our trade relations with the Varthan free state, I've already contacted their representatives. The Confederacy can't afford to be accused of harboring Varthan fugitives. It could cause an embargo and millions could starve."

He looked pointedly at Atal. "Or weren't you aware that seventy-eight per cent of our grain is imported from Freespace?"

"Seventy six point four eight nine," The Captain said quietly.

"Don't spar with me, Atal!" the Admiral snapped. "I know you think you're acting the hero, but you've caused great difficulty for the Confederacy by trying to hide this. The Varthans will never believe you were ignorant of the situation for two years."

"I didn't claim to be."

"No, but the only way to keep you innocent is to make that claim *for* you! And believe me, I have no desire to keep you innocent. But to let you swing in the breeze would create greater problems for the Navy than you're worth. You have therefore protested your innocence. The Varthans won't believe you, but so what? We're cooperating now."

"And how are we cooperating?" Atal asked.

"The Varthans are sending an investigator, who will determine the girl's worth and circumstances of escape, and decide what's to be done. It may be that you could purchase the girl away from Vartha," he added with the wry, self-satisfied grin of one who considered himself a supreme wit. "But either way she's to be stripped of rank immediately. To show their benevolence, the Admiralty won't charge her with impersonating an officer. We... understand her desperation."

"How kind of you."

"It *is* kind of us, Atal, and don't forget: that kindness covers your posterior as well!"

"But doesn't protect human rights?"

Fournier shook his head. "Grow up, Atal. Human rights are for the human. And you're not paid to be a cosmic Harriet Jefferson."

"Tubman."

"All right, dammit, *Tubman*. You knew who I meant – the black abolitionist who was Jefferson's slave and lover. I could care less. Terran history is nothing but a collection of trashy scandal anyway, and best forgotten. And now, Captain, Professor," he added a deferential nod for Mors, "I must attend to other crises of the ego. Goodbye."

He vanished, as the other party always did. Atal envisioned his disappearance being the result of a blaster fired from his own hand, and smiled, as he always did.

Mors leaned back in his chair and shrugged. "I don't see any legal way out of this mess, Jan. He's wrong, but he's got you. And you realize," he said carefully, inclining his head and narrowing his eyes, "that his little invitation to you to purchase the girl is nothing but entrapment."

"I'm a veteran of his entrapment schemes. He'd appease the slavers with one hand and have me court martialled for trafficking in slavery with the other. If I stand against this 'investigator,' he's invited, I'm bucking Varthan law and probably violating treaty. Meanwhile, all I'm doing is abiding by my oath as an officer and the principles of the Confederacy. 'All sentient creatures are of equal standing.'"

"Unfortunately, every republic which has ever incorporated such a statement into its laws has also, somewhere along the line, legalized some form of slavery. Would you believe some societies actually mandated it as part of an educational curriculum? At any rate, there will never be a cure for the disease which makes some humans wish to possess and control others."

"Ah, but she's not human, by our definition."

"Nor are you, by that of many Terrans."

"Says the mind-reader with the disabled reproductive system."

"Slander, sir! My reproductive capacity is merely *untried*... thus far."

"Stop it, professor, you're shaking my faith in my own sanity."

"Then my work here is done... except for one more pointed question: what are you going to do now, Jan?"

He didn't need to ask. He knew Atal too well to need to ask. He was just employing one of the tricks from his teacher's arsenal: make the student put his thoughts into words, to be certain the student understood them.

"If the law can't be used to do what I know must be done, then I'm going to find a way around the law..." Atal grinned. "Or through it."

Chapter Six
The Arbiters' Society

Terry Metcalfe believed in God – several of them, in fact. This made him something of an oddity in the community of the Inner Worlds, for few of its people had what would traditionally be called religion. (Those who did, like the Hecatians, usually came from colonies founded specifically to provide a haven for people of a given faith. Also like the Hecatians, such people tended to stay away from mainstream Confederate civilization. It wasn't a comfortable environment for the religious.) The core of faith for the Church of Terra, in which he'd been raised, was *The Book of Heroes*. It was filled with tales of deities coming to walk among humanity, where they accomplished wonderful feats. The jaded among the Terran population pointed out that it was odd that the gods only visited in long ago times, and couldn't be troubled to appear now. This had never troubled Metcalfe. He'd always been secure in his faith that the gods were there, and that, if it suited their purposes, they would once again walk among their children.

He was pretty sure that was happening today, for, if Pallas wasn't a goddess, then Terry Metcalfe didn't know a goddess when he saw one. To Metcalfe's eye, she was too inhumanly beautiful to be classed among mere mortals. All Confederate woman were beautiful, save those odd few whose design had been focused on achieving some other end. Surely, though, human genetic planning was too flawed to design such perfection. There had to be a divine source for her radiance.

When they'd completed their tour, she'd asked him if he'd have some off-duty time to spend with her later. Terrans, she explained, were of particular interest to her in her studies. Until today, she hadn't actually met one. Though only partly recovered from his awkward inability to speak when in her presence, Metcalfe had been more than happy to assist her in her research.

"What made you want to leave, to come out here?" she now asked. They were on the public concourse, where she'd refused to allow him to pay for her dinner. They'd found a seat in one of the many carefully manicured indoor gardens that dotted its length.

"You mean among the hostiles?" He asked.

She smiled. "We're not all hostile."

"No, but I haven't exactly been popular."

"With whom?"

He shrugged. "Inworlders."

"All of us?"

"Only ninety per cent of those I've encountered. To be honest, I've mostly encountered those in the Navy."

"And me."

"And you. You don't seem hostile."

"I don't see any reason to be. Actually, I'm curious."

"To find out how savage I really am?"

"I didn't expect you to be savage. I don't believe every racist slur I hear."

"Thank you."

"For what?"

"For admitting that knee-jerk hatred of my people *is* racist. Most people believe that we're a special group they're entitled to hate, because their stereotype of us is that we're narrow minded, uncultured bigots."

"And of course that's racism. That's simple logic. Racism is the application of an unproven assumption, based on limited observation, to all the members of one genetically similar group. It results in actively hostile treatment of members of that group by people who know nothing about them. That certainly describes the way you were treated at Hestia."

"So you know how I was treated on Hestia?"

"Of course. Dr. Mors has told me quite a bit about you."

"And do you believe all of that?"

"Naturally. Dr. Mors wouldn't lie unless it served a higher purpose. And I doubt he could lie to me if he wanted to. He's far more experienced, but I'm a more powerful natural telepath than he is."

"I'm impressed."

"Why?" She asked. "It's just a fact. I was designed that way. Anyway, I questioned him extensively about you."

"About me?"

"Of course. I needed anecdotal data to guide my research."

"So... any unconfirmed hypotheses I can address for you?"

"Quite a few. Dr. Mors and I have particularly been studying myths and taboos of human reproduction."

"I thought your people weren't interested."

"Those are some of the taboos we're investigating – those of our own culture. Many of them stem from yours, so we're very interested in learning more about Terran attitudes and particulars."

"And I'm the first Terran you met. How lucky for me. What can I tell you?"

"Would you be willing to spend some time with me on my project?" She seemed genuinely excited. "It would be a great opportunity to get some real personal feedback from a Terran native. I mean, I realize you're just one person, but you could give me valuable insight. There are a lot of misconceptions I'd like to clear up, a lot of stereotypes I'd like to investigate."

"I feel like a lab rat. Are you going to stick electrodes into me?"

She looked surprised, hurt even. "No, why would I do that? That would be painful."

"I'm kidding."

"Oh, good. I'm relieved. But do you mind if I measure your penis?"

"Excuse me?" He blurted.

She had said it with such a straight face. Metcalfe gathered she was serious. "For my records. I have to start somewhere."

"Start with what, might I ask?"

"Collecting data on penis size. There's a long-standing perceived correlation between male sexual performance and the size of the erection. That, too, seems to come from your world, where the males are purported to have very large penises."

Metcalfe cleared his throat and wondered absently if something was wrong with the ship's cooling system.

Looking at him, Pallas's eyes widened. "Are you doing that intentionally?"

"Doing what?" He demanded.

"Causing your skin color to change like that. A minute ago you were as pale as I was. Now you're... well, you're red. Bright red."

"Don't they blush on Phaeton?"

"Blush – oh, I think I remember! Wasn't it a symptom of a plague, or – " She took a small step back.

"It was not," He said, too emphatically. "It's a simple, biological reaction to – "

" – sharp emotional reactions, of course!" she said. "I knew I'd read about it. It's brought on by anger or – "

" – embarrassment."

"Yes. I'm sorry, did I cause that? Are you angry? It's because I've repeated a stereotype, isn't it?"

"I'm not angry."

"But you're... oh." She asked in a small voice, "did I embarrass you?"

"You... would have embarrassed most Terran males."

"How?"

"By talking about my..."

She waited patiently, encouragingly.

"...about the size of my..."

"Your *penis*!" She looked delighted for a moment at solving the mystery, then she became puzzled. "Why?"

"I – well, it's – I don't think I can explain."

She thought quietly for a moment. "I suppose I've broached a taboo subject," she said slowly. "But I really can't understand. You've been away from your world for several years, and you seem quite intelligent. Why should a taboo subject evoke such a profound emotional reaction?"

"Because it's *my*... taboo."

"What?"

"Men – Terran men, anyway – don't like having their penises discussed. Especially in public, by women."

"But we're alone."

"But I just met you."

"Oh. Can we discuss your penis tomorrow?"

"No. I mean... "

"Are there any other parts of your body I shouldn't mention? Just so I can be prepared? Your ears?"

"What's wrong with my ears?"

"Well, they sort of stick out, too, and I thought maybe – "

"Can we stop talking about this?"

"I just want to understand."

"I guess it's a Terran taboo. We don't like to be... that is, we consider that a private part."

"Private part?"

"Of our bodies."

"You have public parts? In what sense?"

"I – oh, god! – a private part is one we don't... display."

"So your ears are public," she thought out loud. "That's funny."

"Would you please leave my damn ears out of this?"

"Are you angry?"

"No. Maybe."

"Why aren't you turning red?"

"I – Would you like to go somewhere and get a drink?"

"No."

"Well, I sure would."

* * *

They called themselves "The Arbiters' Society," or, more formally, "The High Order of the Sublime Arbiters." The name had been coined – no one remembered by whom – while they were still at the academy. "They," in this case, being Metcalfe, Kaya, Cernaq and Carson. The four of them were already a recognized group of misfits when they'd learned that they would share a posting after graduation, and that that posting would be *CNV Arbiter*. The habit of referring to themselves as "The Arbiters" had stuck, through and beyond their assignment to that ship.

Best of all, the name, which was now more or less public knowledge, really irked people like Phyn Darby and Georg Fournier. To these worthies, the title "Arbiter" referred to an official elected to the governing body of the Confederacy, a representative of an entire planet's population. It was an honored title, a solemn title. The very idea that it should be used to describe a gathering of young officers intent on over-imbibing alcohol and encouraging each other to lewd acts was repulsive to anyone who had a genuine respect for the Confederate government.

Consequently, since coming to the Inner Worlds, Metcalfe, Kaya, Cernaq, Carson and their later inductee, Aer'La, had taken to using the title more often.

On *Arbiter*, meetings of "the Society" had been their only social outlet. There were others their own age among *Arbiter's* crew, but these were casual crewmen with rough backgrounds. They tended to look with scorn on the midshipmen. Even Aer'La had done so, at first. Somehow, though, she'd gravitated away from her enlisted companions (whom she saw only as sexual playthings, anyway) and toward this group of young upstarts from the Academy.

On *Arbiter*, they'd gathered at least weekly – more, if the duty was slow and boring – and debated the evils of the universe, and how they might be solved. They also drank, told sexually oriented jokes, and sometimes went to bed in twos and threes to finish off the evening.

On *Titan*, it was already clear, their meetings were going to be more frequent. They were going to be needing each other's support, as well as an emotional outlet.

Tonight's was a scheduled meeting. Metcalfe, now approaching the cabin door, could already hear Carson expostulating on some subject with the loudness he attained after tossing back a few. Metcalfe hadn't really wanted to be there. Although she'd made him exceedingly uncomfortable several times during the course of the day, he'd wanted to stay with Pallas. There was an unspoken pledge, however, that you didn't stand up the Society on grounds of sex or romance. You wouldn't find romance anyway, someone (probably Carson) had cynically declared, and there was always time for sex. Sometimes that time was during the gathering itself.

Besides, hosting was the obligation of the holder of the largest cabin, which Metcalfe had shared with Carson on *Arbiter*, and which he now occupied himself on *Titan*, as senior-most midshipman. If he didn't show up, they would still use his cabin, and confronting its state upon his return would most likely be an unpleasant experience.

So here he was, come to drink and laugh with his friends. Tonight, however, while potential conquests were a popular topic of conversation, he would keep silent about his infatuation with Pallas. It was just possible that something very serious could develop between the two of them. He'd never felt this... longing... before, for anyone, not even Kaya. And right from the start, too. It had taken him weeks to really even notice that the sharp-tongued younger Atal was even female, she'd put him off so when they'd met.

This could just be, he thought, the oft-rumored love at first sight. He would not endanger its growth by discussing it with his friends. With a sense of resolve and peace of mind, he opened the door to his cabin.

"Holy shit, Metcalfe's in love!"

Peace of mind fled with all speed and astonishing fanfare. Peace of mind had always been a fleeting commodity, for Metcalfe. The exclamation which had cruelly murdered this particular instance of peace came from Carson. He was kicked back on Metcalfe's bed, quite at home, Metcalfe's best bottle of whiskey in one hand, an empty glass in the other.

"I am not," said Metcalfe. Then quickly, "Don't drink all of that. You'll just vomit it all back up anyway, and I'll be out two days' pay."

"Don't change the subject," said Kaya. "And why shouldn't you be in love? She's beautiful... if you like the tall type. And, if she's... open minded, Phaetonians are incredible lovers." She ran her nails gently through the hair at the back of Cernaq's head.

"Are they?" Cernaq asked, with only the faintest smile. "And when have you had the opportunity to have sex with a Phaetonian, Kaya?"

She removed her hand and lightly slapped the area she'd only just been caressing. "Louse! Denying me in front of our friends... Oh, the shame!" She coughed out several sobs.

Carson applauded. "Ah, the theatre! Did you really do her, Cern? She any good?"

"I refuse to answer on the grounds that it might incriminate me." His dignity intact, he sipped his own glass of scotch. After a swallow, he added, "Besides, Carson, you have no reason to ask. You've had every female on this ship."

"Not every!" Kaya corrected. "There's a few engineered wildebeests in the livestock pen that I think he's missed."

"I am so *there!*" He leapt up from the bed, lost his footing, and landed again. By some miracle, the bottle survived intact and unspilled.

And thus was the meeting called to order.

While Metcalfe repossessed his whiskey bottle from Carson and poured himself a drink, Cernaq drifted up to him. There was an amused twinkle in the Phaetonian's golden eyes. "So, you're... impressed with Pallas."

"You're old friends, aren't you?"

"Yes. She's only about my age. When I chose to leave Phaeton, she chose to enter a rigorous program of study as a fellow of the

University. I expected her to be entombed in the Hall of Wisdom by now."

"That would have been a waste."

Cernaq nodded agreement. "So... you want to have sex with her?"

"Jesus, Cern!"

"What?"

"Well, that's just a little... blatant."

"You don't want to have sex with her?"

"No."

"You find her repulsive?"

"God, no!"

He shook his head. "I'm sorry, I don't mean to pry, but I sense definite sexual desire in you. Unless you've newfound lust for me, I believe – "

"I just meant... It's not just about sex! I think... She's just..."

"What is it with all of you?" Cernaq demanded, loudly, "Do you want to fuck the girl or don't you?"

The others turned and looked at Cernaq in disbelief. He didn't often speak so crudely. Metcalfe glared at him.

Meeting his gaze, Cernaq asked, "Why do you want to do that?"

"Do what?"

"'Deck me,' as you so quaintly put it?"

"Asks Mr. 'I-don't-read-minds-it's-beneath-me.'"

"My dear Metcalfe, sensing that thought could hardly be called 'reading.'Why did you feel an impulse to hit me?"

"Because that was such a vulgar thing to say about..."

"A goddess?"

"Stop it!"

"I can't help it! Turn down the volume!"

"How?"

"Someday, perhaps, I'll take you to Phaeton for training in the telepathic arts. I can just imagine you at the University, learning telepathy." Cernaq began to laugh quietly.

"Think I wouldn't cut it?"

"With your overwhelming volume, I think you'd probably shout everyone down and take over. You'd be the universe's first tele-pathic school bully."

Looking around for some reason to change the subject, Metcalfe noticed Aer'La. She sat at his desk, absent-mindedly playing a game on his terminal. Her glass, full, sweated onto the desktop.

"Well, since I'm not a mind-reader yet, what's up with our Bos'n?"

Cernaq followed Metcalfe's gaze to Aer'La and frowned. "I don't know, actually. She does seem preoccupied – "

"And, being her best friend, you're entitled to do a little thought surfing – "

"But she threatened me with grievous bodily harm if I tried."

Metcalfe's eyes widened. "She is in a funk. No idea why?"

"She's becoming better at blocking my casual readings."

"Well, I can't let her sit there and play games all night. I'll – "

"It's your funeral," warned Cernaq. "Do you prefer flowers, or donations to charity?"

Metcalfe waved him off and went to kneel beside Aer'La.

"If you're trying to hide, I suggest the bathroom. It's where I always hid from Carson, when he lived with me."

She forced a smile. He didn't buy it.

"What's wrong?" he asked.

She looked up briefly from her game, started to say something, then shrugged. "Nothing."

"All right," sighed Metcalfe. "You clearly don't want to talk about this, but you haven't left, either. So you don't want to be alone. Which means – "

"I don't know what the hell it means, all right?" Aer'La hissed. "Just drop it, Navy!"

Metcalfe swallowed and considered the situation. He didn't look back to see if the others were watching. He was sure they were. Aer'La's outburst had not been as quiet as she'd meant it to be. "No," he whispered. "No, I may be taking my life in my hands, but I think something's wrong. If it's none of my business – "

Aer'La sighed and, in one swipe, picked up her glass and downed its contents. "No," she announced when she was finished. "I guess you need to know, even if there's not a damn thing you can do about it. You'll find out tomorrow, anyway."

"What will we find out tomorrow?"

"What's up?" Kaya asked, admitting that she was listening in. Cernaq sat quietly, his eyes trained on Aer'La with an expression of infinite patience. On the bed, Carson, already drunk, cast a bleary eye toward them.

Aer'La stood. "I... I talked to the Captain earlier. You all know who – what – I am."

"You're our friend," said Kaya, her voice gaining a dangerous edge.

"Thanks, Kaya, but... I'm afraid you can't help. See, Dr. Flynn didn't buy my cover story, about being born on Bergstrom's world. He did some checking... he figured everything out."

"So Dad orders him to keep his mouth shut," said Kaya.

"He probably did, but... Flynn already told the Admiralty. They've contacted the Varthan government and... they're sending an investigator."

"What?" Metcalfe demanded. "I mean... why? So one person got away, so – "

"You don't understand, Metcalfe. No one gets away. No one escapes. That's how we're brought up. If they let me go, and others find out – "

"Then their whole, evil system starts to come apart!" Kaya spat.

"And they won't let that happen," said Aer'La.

"Wait, wait," said Metcalfe. "Can't you demand asylum?"

"The Captain and Professor Mors are both trying everything. But Mors said... he said there may be nothing they can do. The Admiralty doesn't want to endanger their trade relationship – "

"That's bullshit!" Carson slurred.

"That's politics," said Aer'La.

"Aer'La... we'll figure out some way to help you." Metcalfe said, knowing how weak it sounded

She shook her head. "No, Navy, you won't. It's done. They're coming to take me back." She silently reached for the whiskey bottle and, very deliberately, poured herself another drink. She held the glass and the bottle, not looking at them, and stared straight ahead of her at nothing.

"I've had a few good years. That's more than most of my people get. If it's going to come to an end now, I don't want to waste the last few hours of it arguing or being angry. I just want to say... " For a moment, her face crumpled, tears came to her eyes. Then she recovered. "I'm glad you were all a part of it."

She held up her glass and proclaimed, "To the Arbiters! Let the universe tremble in fear!" She then downed the contents of the glass in one swallow, and threw it behind her into a corner, where it shattered.

Nobody moved. For a moment, no one said anything. Aer'La,

now showing the effects of two fast glasses of whiskey, considered the bottle.

"I... I think... I think I need to be alone now." She started for the door.

"Aer'La – " Metcalfe began.

"Don't say it, Navy. I don't think I could stand it."

They were still silent as she opened the hatch and left them.

"I think I'm going to cry," Kaya announced quietly.

"You don't cry," said Metcalfe with no expression. "I've known you for four years, and I've never seen you cry."

"You're right," said Kaya. "And I'll be damned if I'll cry in front of a bunch of drunken men. Excuse me." And she, too, left them.

"Shit," said Carson, his mouth hanging open sloppily as he slouched on the edge of the bed. He stood clumsily, staggered to the desk, where Aer'La had left the whiskey bottle, and lifted it. He looked at Metcalfe and Cernaq, as if seeking an opinion. Neither said a word. With permission implied, Carson drained half the remaining contents of the bottle. Then he set it down, missing the edge of the desk, and the bottle fell to the floor, where the remaining liquor flowed onto the deck.

Carson looked defiantly at his two friends. He appeared on the verge of saying something extremely profound. Sadly, when he spoke, all that came out was, "Gotta go to the bathroom." He then stumbled into the bathroom and closed the door.

Metcalfe sighed. "Well, he's done. I may just let him sleep in there."

Cernaq nodded silently. Throughout the entire exchange, he'd remained seated in a chair against the bulkhead, saying nothing. Metcalfe dropped to the floor and stretched out opposite him, his back against the edge of the bed.

"You must have known," said Metcalfe, "that what was bothering her was more serious than just a bad day at work."

"I did."

"Then why – ?"

"It was her story to tell."

"So what do we do?"

"I honestly don't know," said Cernaq. "And I'm... concerned."

"About what? I mean, apart from the obvious?"

"About what she... might do."

"What might she do?"

"I don't know."

"Then read her mind!" said Metcalfe.

"It would be... improper."

"Dammit, Cernaq! This is serious!"

"So are the ethics of mindreading. Aer'La has a right to privacy."

"Aer'La's about to lose all her rights."

Cernaq slumped. He looked confused, beaten, even. It wasn't often that his face and body showed so much expression. "I know," he admitted, "and I want to help. I just... she hasn't talked to me about it. I don't have the right to pry."

"Cernaq," Metcalfe said gently, "sometimes, with friends, you have to overstep the bounds of propriety. You have to push. Look at Carson and me. Have we ever given the slightest indication that we respect each other's privacy?"

Cernaq smiled. "But you do."

"That's not the point."

"I know. I'm just... having trouble deciding what I should do. For all that I've changed in my years among you, I'm still Phaetoni-an. We're... contemplative. We don't act rashly."

"Sometimes you have to."

"I know." Cernaq leaned back in his chair and stared at the ceiling. "I want to go to her," he said. "I want... I want to help her. She's... she's important to me."

Metcalfe knew that, of course. Cernaq had lost his virginity to Aer'La. They had spent many nights together. They weren't any sort of formal couple, but they were closer to each other, in many ways, than either was to anyone else.

"Terry," said Cernaq. "You've... seen someone die."

Metcalfe looked away for a moment. Cernaq knew he'd seen someone die. His sister, Lydia, had died of influenza seven years earlier. Metcalfe had been at her side to the last.

"Yes," he said quietly.

"When death is near, the mind often accepts the inevitable. A deep calm descends."

"I suppose so."

"Did you not see such a look in Aer'La's eyes tonight? A look of resignation? As if her life was over?"

Metcalfe shrugged. "Are slavery and death really that different? When you take someone's freedom, aren't you taking away their very life?"

"I'm afraid Aer'La agrees with you. I'm afraid she might..."

"... try to finish things before the Varthans can get to her?"

"Yes."

"But you still didn't... check?"

"My people believe we each have a right to decide when our life ends."

"Dammit, Cernaq!"

"Are you going to tell me this isn't about rights?"

"No!"

"You were thinking it."

Metcalfe raised his hands, giving the momentary appearance that he might strangle Cernaq. Then, frustrated, he drove a fist into the opposite palm. "Okay! I was thinking it."

"A little ironic, don't you – "

"Yes! Yes, damn you, it's a little ironic! That's why I didn't say it!"

"I'm sorry I made you angry."

"It's... not your fault. You're right. This is all about rights. But Aer'La shouldn't be driven to suicide by fear of something that shouldn't be allowed to happen in the first place. We should be able to prevent these bastards taking her away."

"And how do you suggest we do that?"

"I don't know. Do you really think she might try to kill herself?"

"It's... possible. Her level of desperation – "

"Cernaq, you've got to find out. Go see her. Read her damn mind whether she likes it or not. And... maybe you can keep her from doing something stupid long enough to let us find an answer."

"'Maybe I can keep her from it?' Say it plainly, Terry."

"I just meant – "

Cernaq interrupted, his voice hard. "You just meant that I have the power to force her not to commit suicide."

"I... I guess."

"And you're right, I do. As strong as she is, she couldn't make a move, if I chose for her not to. I could hold her under my control for hours. Then what? What if we can't find an answer? I'll be keeping her from exercising her only alternative to slavery."

Metcalfe was silent for a moment, daunted by the forcefulness behind Cernaq's argument. "Sometimes your rationality is... over-whelming."

"It's the only way I know of to deal with things. I still believe it's the only approach that really works. I believe that all problems – including emotional ones – can, eventually, all be solved by the power of the human mind. If all people took such an attitude, slavery wouldn't exist, for it would be seen to be irrational for one human being to own another."

"The problem is," said Metcalfe, "that the Varthans don't agree with you. And the Confederacy, irrationally, is willing to go along with them."

"You see, then, how irrationality creates artificial mandates, which are foolish when viewed objectively, but which seem inescapable to those caught up – "

"Oh, shove your analysis up your ass, Cernaq! Your artificial mandates may cause Aer'La to kill herself!"

"I know," Cernaq admitted helplessly.

Metcalfe stood. "Well, dammit, if you won't do anything, I'll go and – "

"And what? Sit on her?"

"If I have to!"

"Has it occurred to you," Cernaq asked slowly, "that, in addition to killing herself, Aer'La might also be willing to kill anyone who tries to interfere?"

"She wouldn't!"

"She might."

Metcalfe slumped back to the deck, defeated. "So you really are the only one who can stop her. And you're hidebound by your damned rational analysis!"

"All right," said Cernaq, "what do you do, when you have trouble making a decision. ?"

"I pray."

"To whom?"

"My god."

"And that is?"

"I'm... not sure."

"How many gods are there?"

"Now, how would I know that?"

"How do you know there are any?"

"I... I just believe."

"So... how do you know... to whom to address a prayer?"

"There are many gods. Each of them has different powers and different interests. A mortal can establish a rapport with one, usually does, even as a child."

"But... how do you know to whom to pray?"

"You don't. You just... pray."

"How do you begin your prayer? 'To whom it may concern?'"

"Okay, make fun!"

"No, seriously. You pray to... whoever will listen?"

"Right. And there is at least one god who will listen to you."

"Do they answer you?"

"I... Sometimes. Yes."

"*You've* been answered?"

"I... think so. Sometimes I get answers in prayer to questions I couldn't answer by myself."

"But you don't know which god is answering?"

"No."

"Have you asked?"

"Yes."

"But you have an obtuse god?"

"Or maybe I'm not listening correctly."

"What do you call your god?"

"I told you, I don't know – "

"I mean, how do you refer to him?"

"Her."

"Excuse me?"

"I'm pretty sure it's a female."

"What has led you to that conclusion? Does it have a feminine voice? Does it speak out loud?"

"No."

"Have you seen it?"

"No."

"Then on what evidence do you base the conclusion that it's female?"

"She... it... just *feels* female."

"Perhaps... unfulfilled sexual fantasies are – "

"Okay, I *don't* want to talk about it anymore."

"I apologize," he said softly.

"It's okay."

Cernaq sat back. "I still don't know what I should do."

"What does you heart tell you?"

"My heart," said Cernaq irritably, "is a mechanism for distributing oxygen into my blood stream and maintaining pressure in my circulatory system. It is a mechanism. It has no sentience, so it can't tell me – "

Metcalfe sighed. "Cernaq... do you love Aer'La?"

"I don't know."

"Yes you do."

"I – I don't even know if I know what love is. Ayn Rand said that – "

"Fuck Ayn Rand!"

"I can't. She's been dead for five centuries."

"Cernaq, what happens when Aer'La's close to you?"

"My blood pressure rises. My pulse quickens. In public, I must suppress the involuntary erectile reflex which – "

"She makes you horny."

"Fine."

"And would you ever hurt her?"

"Of course not."

"And would you let anyone else hurt her?"

"Not if I could prevent it."

"And what would you do if she died?"

"I... "

"Don't think! Just answer! What would you do if she died?"

"I don't – "

"You do! You do know!" Metcalfe jumped to his feet and leaned over his friend, placing his hands on the arms of the chair in which Cernaq was sitting. "What if she died, Cernaq? How would you feel?"

Cernaq pulled away from Metcalfe as much as he could. "Terry, your level of emotion is hurting me."

"How would you feel?" Metcalfe demanded again.

"Stop it," Cernaq said quietly. He looked away from the black eyes boring into his.

Metcalfe took hold of his chin and forced him to hold his gaze. "What if she dies, Cernaq?"

"I said stop it," said Cernaq. His voice was beginning to shake.

"No! I won't!" spat Metcalfe. "I want you to tell me – "

"I don't know!" Cernaq shouted.

"Yes you do!"

Cernaq rocked his upper body back and, using his legs to give him leverage, shoved Metcalfe with all the force he could muster. "Leave me alone!" he almost screamed, as Metcalfe stumbled backwards and fell against his bed.

Cernaq stood for a moment, clearly amazed at his own response.

"You made me angry," he said, his voice raw from shouting.

"It's one of my talents," said Metcalfe. "I can piss off damn near anyone."

"Did... did I hurt you?"

Metcalfe shook his head.

"I'm sorry, Terry."

"I'm not. We got your feelings unstuck." He stood and came to place his hands on Cernaq's shoulders. "Now tell me," he said evenly, "how you would feel if we did nothing tonight, and Aer'La died?"

"I... I can't imagine anything that painful."

Metcalfe raised one hand and clapped it on Cernaq's neck, catching his fingers in the blond curls and squeezing affectionately. "Then do whatever it takes to keep her alive."

Chapter Seven
Den of Thieves

After he had knocked several times, for she had disabled the A.I.'s receptionist function, Aer'La opened the hatch of her cabin to Cernaq. She was still dressed in the coverall she'd worn the previous shift. She didn't look like she'd been sleeping. In fact, she looked as though she hadn't slept in days. He knew that wasn't the case, but knowing didn't lessen the effect.

She wouldn't look at him. "What do you want?" she asked.

"I want to come in."

"I'm not... " she began, and then didn't seem to know what she wanted to say. "Not right now, huh?"

"I think it's very important that I talk to you... right now."

"I'm tired."

"Yes, you are, but you have no intention of sleeping, do you?"

She glared at him, as if holding his gaze could make him back down. It couldn't. "No. But I want to be alone."

"What you want and what's good for you may be two different things."

"Cernaq – "

"Aer'La, you're afraid."

"I don't want to talk about it." She started to close the hatch.

Cernaq put his hand out and held it open. She could have overcome his resistance and closed it anyway, of course. She didn't. The gesture, from someone who so rarely showed active resistance to anyone, was enough.

"Fear keeps you from thinking clearly," he said gently.

She rolled her eyes. "Cernaq, I don't want to be analyzed! Just – "

"It's clear that you don't know what you want. Why don't you let me come in?"

She sighed and opened the door. Without waiting for him to enter, she walked back into the cabin and threw herself down on the bed.

Cernaq closed the hatch and stood just inside it, leveling his eyes at her. "You're not treating your friends very well. You know that, don't you?"

"Excuse me," she said. "I guess I'm just a real bitch when it comes to being put in chains."

Cernaq considered his reply carefully. He agreed that she was being a real bitch, but he didn't think it healthy to agree with her. "It's natural to be upset. Just remember that this will be hard on the people who care about you, too."

"They'll get over it. Their lives will go on."

"And yours won't?"

She looked at him, and the expression in her eyes went from anger to desperation.

"Suicide is not the answer, Aer'La."

She shook her head. "You don't understand, Cernaq. You don't know what it's like."

"No, I don't. But you mustn't give up hope."

"There's none to give up," she sighed, getting up from the bed and crossing to him. She rested her hands lightly on his shoulders. "Look, Cern, I appreciate what you're doing. I guess I should have figured that you, of all people, would come here. I just don't think there's any point..."

He brought his hands up, gently moving the hair away from her face and cradling it. "Let us help you," he said.

Her head sank to his shoulder. Her body melted into his, and her arms drew him close and tight. "What does someone like you see in me?" she wondered. She moved her hands up and down his back, and began, softly and teasingly, to kiss the exposed flesh of his neck. Her lips were soft and wet, promising, offering...

Cernaq took Aer'La firmly by the shoulders and pushed her away, holding her at arm's length. "No," he said.

"I was just – " she began.

"You were trying to distract me. Get me into bed, physically exhaust me, and then, once I'm asleep – "

She ripped herself out of his grasp. "You don't understand!" she cried.

"Then help me understand."

"Why? Fournier has already agreed to send me back."

"Fournier will back off if we can turn public opinion against him. If people know what's happened to you and the others – "

"But they won't *know!*" she insisted. "Don't you get it, Cernaq? The Varthan slavers are experts at confusing people! They're trained liars, the best in the business! Look at all that bullshit in the press – people here think slavery is over with in Varthan Freespace."

"Then let's show them that it isn't."

"How?" she demanded. "How, when they're shown nothing but holos of slavers with their arms around some important admiral or arbiter, saying everything's all right! Why would the media want to show my side of the story, when they can have all those pretty people on camera?"

"You'll be heard. Captain Atal and Professor Mors will back you up."

"No," she sat down hard on the bed, covering her face with he hands. "It won't make any difference. They'll just say that Atal and Mors haven't been there and don't really know. That I've made up a clever story."

"People will know that Mors can't be fooled. Telepaths can serve as third party witnesses in some cases. He can vouch for the truth of what you're saying."

"But I won't be saying anything. First chance they get, they'll feed me grog."

"What?"

"It's a drug. They use it to control us. It messes up your mind so bad, I won't be able to tell the truth, and I doubt Mors would be able to make any sense of what's going in my head."

"Then... then let me be your witness."

"What?"

"Let me inside your mind. Even if you're drugged, I can testify to the truth of what's happened to you."

"They'll say you're lying."

"And Professor Mors will testify that I'm not. And Pallas."

"Pallas wouldn't lift a finger to help me!"

"Pallas will do what I ask. She's my friend, even if she isn't yours." He sat on the bed next to her and put his arms around her, pulling her to him. "Please, Aer'La. Let me help. At least... let me see the truth."

"It's ugly."

"I've seen Carson naked. What could be worse?"

Despite herself, she laughed. "Carson's not hard to look at naked."

"No," Cernaq agreed. "But I'm not about to tell him that."

"All right... I wasn't going to sleep anyway... It won't do a damned bit of good, but you can see whatever it is you want to see in my mind."

"I want to see everything."

"How do we do this?"

He grinned. "First, take your clothes off."

"What?"

"If our minds are going to link, well, that's a much higher degree of intimacy than coitus," he explained.

"Co-what-us?"

"Fucking."

"Oh."

"In order for this to work, we have to create an atmosphere of complete relaxation and utter trust," he went on. As he spoke, he shed his own uniform tunic and touched the insignia-crested clasp on his belt to release it. "Phaetonians would create that atmosphere via meditation. We don't have time for me to teach you to meditate. We'll have to settle for having sex."

"Settle?"

"No offense. Sex with you is almost as good as meditation."

Cernaq stepped out of his pants and stood naked before her.

"Is something wrong?" he asked, indicating the fact that she was still clothed.

"No. I just... I wanted to look at you for a minute, that's all."

"Is it all right if I read your mind now?"

She nodded.

"You're thinking that this might be the last time you see me this way," he said.

"I don't see how it won't be." She began to slowly remove her own clothes.

"And you're thinking of Druberj."

"I always do, when I see you. Especially naked. Does that bother you?"

"No. He was the first person who was ever kind to you. I'm flattered by the comparison. But you're going to see me this way again, Aer'La. Often. I promise."

"I wish I could be sure."

"I'll make you sure. Now lie down."

Suddenly, she looked afraid. "You first. I need to be on top."

"Because you fear being under someone else's control. But you have to surrender that fear, if this is going to work. I need to guide you in this. It will be hard enough that you're not Phaetonian."

She sat on the bed, crossing her arms over her breasts. It may have been, he thought, the first time she'd ever covered her nakedness in front of anyone. "I..."

He sat next to her. "Aer'La, you taught me everything I know about sex. I was afraid, too."

"No you weren't!"

"I was. I was doing something none of my people had done for hundreds of years. I didn't even know if I was capable. I'd learned to suppress my erections before they happened. I didn't know if they could be... brought to their usual conclusion. I'd never masturbated. I was afraid nothing would do what it was supposed to, and I'd be confirming all those rumors about Phaetonians. I was afraid I'd disappoint you."

She cupped his face in one hand and kissed him. "You've never disappointed me."

"Then please trust me."

"What do I do?"

"Open yourself to me."

"That's easy."

He laughed. "On every level – not just with your legs."

"Oh."

"You can start with... the obvious, but work out from there." He took her shoulders and eased her back on the bed, saying soothingly, "Relax... and open up. Open your ears... your eyes... let everything move in freely, just like the air into your lungs..."

He moved on top of her, sensing that his weight was almost nothing to her, like a warm, comforting blanket settling over her. Meeting her eyes for consent, he arched his hips and entered her easily. With Aer'La, for him, there was never resistance. She was always ready. He began to thrust gently. She sighed against his neck.

"What if it doesn't work?" she whispered. "What if my mind won't let you in?"

"Then we'll have to keep doing this until it does," he whispered back. Then he lowered his lips to hers, gently parting them with his tongue. Neither of them spoke any more.

It took several climaxes for each of them before any level of relaxation could be achieved. Cernaq continued patiently, calling out to her with his mind, letting the feeling of his penis entering her become a metaphor for them both. He was entering her. He was inside her. He touched her deepest, most hidden places.

When it happened, they almost didn't notice. Suddenly she was thinking his thoughts, and he was thinking hers, and neither of them could have said it hadn't always been that way. He saw his face above her with her eyes. He felt his own breath, warm in her ears, his tongue and lips on her neck, as if it were his ears and neck being thus caressed. He felt his own erection throbbing within her, as if he were the one being entered.

As though I were fucking myself, he thought. *Carson would be amused.* He heard Aer'La laugh in his mind, for the sounds emitting from her body were not the sounds of laughter.

They were together. Their minds touched.

Now, Cernaq said to her, *let me see what happened...*

And she did. Her birth into slavery and her training, her first love with Druberj, his murder... all the things she'd told Atal when they'd met... and more...

Aer'La:

After Druberj died, and I killed Jin, I slept for a long time. Days, I guess. They fed me grog. I didn't care. I wanted the pain to go away. Each time I awoke, and realized that Druberj's mutilated corpse wasn't just something I'd seen in a nightmare, I promised myself that I'd find some way to end it. To kill myself. Then they'd pour grog down my throat, and I'd sleep again.

When I finally woke up, I was in the back of a truck, which was moving. I heard the rumble of an engine, and felt the jolts as the wheels hit bumps in the road. The ground vehicles in Varthan Freespace aren't like the ones you'd ride in the Inner Worlds. They still have wheels, and usually burn some kind of fuel to move.

I was naked and alone in the compartment. There was a manacle clamped around one of my ankles, and the manacle was chained to the wall of the truck. I figured I hadn't had any grog for about half a day. I could think straight, but my head hurt like hell. I guessed they were ready to put me on the auction block. They didn't grog you before a sale. They wanted you alert.

If I was about to be sold, then I must be on some other planet. I figured it was probably Den. That was the most likely place to sell slaves. Den was the seediest port in Varthan Freespace, and the most popular for all kinds of traders. It's near the Confederate border, so people of all races and all alliances pass through. I'd heard the masters say that you'd see anyone in the universe you might be looking for there, if you just waited long enough.

The truck stopped moving. I heard the canopy pop open, and at least two people get out of the front, heard the crunch of footsteps and the harsh buzz of voices as they came around to the back, where I was. The lock bleeped as someone keyed its open sequence. The cargo hatch would open next. I shut my eyes tight, pretending to be asleep.

"'S'it safe to leave her?" asked a male voice I didn't know.

"The grog'll be good for another two, three hours," said an answering voice – Master Harl's voice. "Let's go see the agent."

"I'm tellin' you, the sumbitch'll want fifteen."

"I pay ten. That's standard," said Harl. "Close the hatch."

"Gon' ask fifteen, I say," said the other, as he reached back and took a swipe at the hatch. It fell back into place, but I could tell its latch hadn't caught. He hadn't pushed hard enough for the magnets to pull it shut and the electronic lock to click.

Their argument continued and their voices faded as they walked away. I had no idea, then, what they were talking about. I only knew numbers because Dru had taught me to count to twenty or so. I realized later they were talking about a commission on my sale, and Harl didn't want to pay what the agent was asking. Their greed saved my life, I guess, that and Harl's friend being lazy with the hatch.

When it was quiet, I inched over to the hatch and urged it open, just enough to see out. The truck was parked between two buildings. I didn't hear any voices or footsteps, so I figured no one was around. There was a door a good way off, in the direction their voices had gone. That must have been where they went, I thought. I probably had five minutes, if no one else showed up. Harl thought I would still be asleep for a while, so he wasn't worried. He didn't know the grog had never knocked me out like it did the other girls. That was good.

I twisted to check out the manacle. It was an old one, as old as the truck. Harl and his bosses didn't spend money on things like hardware. The lock that held the thing clasped around my ankle was a simple one. It was enough to hold most of the girls, grogged out of their minds as they usually were, and too stupid to think about how the lock might open. I knew a little bit about locks, though. I knew that a lot of them opened to the same key, and that often the keys weren't really complex. Dru and I had practiced our lock-picking skills on the doors and cabinets in Master Hix's bed chambers. The lock that stood between me and freedom on the streets of Den was nothing compared to the lock on the hutch where Hix kept his finest wines. We'd opened that one. I could open this, and I did.

I slipped out of the hatch opening, holding it almost shut as I went, and then pushing it closed behind me. I thought for a minute that I should leave it ajar, so I could slip back in if Harl showed up early. I'd already broken the manacle's lock, though. There was no way to avoid punishment. I might as well go for broke. I ducked immediately under the wheels of the truck and lay on my naked belly on the gravel, checking out my surroundings.

At the front of the two buildings between which the truck was parked was a street. Like the alley, it was covered only with dirty gravel. Den was a backwater world. It looked like it was evening. The sky was a dark gray, with some red streaks shot through it. I later learned that it's never broad daylight on Den. It's either dark or darker. So it may have been high noon when I crawled out. I couldn't tell by the number of people, either, 'cause they say it's always busy on Den.

I didn't stop to think about where I was going to go. I didn't have time to do that. It occurred to me that everyone I saw walk by was wearing clothes, that I might stand out for being naked. I didn't know what to do about it, though. There were no clothes to be had. I wriggled out from under the front of the truck, and I ran.

I can't say I wasn't noticed, a naked girl among a bunch of fully clothed tourists. Some of them yelped as I dashed down the street, hopping and wincing as the gravel cut into my bare feet. They must have known, at least most of them must have, that I was an escaped feral slave. One or two reached out for me, but I was too quick for them, knowing I couldn't let myself be grabbed or slowed in any way.

As I ducked around people, zigging and zagging, I looked for a likely place to hide for a few minutes. I needed to rest, and I needed to deal with very important business.

Another alley between storefronts offered me some shelter. Den's biggest city is built on an old and pretty common plan – streets in a grid like cage bars, with buildings arranged in squares between them. The alley I ducked into had something else old and common – trash bins. Not the expensive kind of outdoor bins, with their own incinerators or vaporizing units, but plain, filthy trash bins. This was a poor section of a poor town on a poor planet. The money changed hands here, but it didn't stay here.

I hid behind one of the bins and kicked another over, letting everything inside spill out. I sifted through the trash quietly, searching for what I needed. I tried not to think about the sticky gunk that I got all over me as I did so. There were too many awful things it could have been. I'd worry about being clean later, if I lived.

Anything sharp would have worked. I found a glass bottle. Good enough. I smashed it against the side of the building and broke off a good, sharp chunk. Taking a deep breath and gritting my teeth, I pinched off an inch of flesh, whose location I'd memorized, on my right hip. With the other hand, I took the shard of glass and gouged into my own skin.

When the pain hit me, I shuddered and had to force myself not to cry out. My blood began to ooze purple down my leg and onto the ground. I didn't worry about it. Dru had shown me where and how to cut so it wouldn't bleed too much. So I wouldn't die from the cut. He'd shown me how to feel where they put the thing, and drawn me a picture of what it looked like. Dru had shown me so much...

I refused to let myself think about him. There'd be time, later. If I stopped now, I'd come apart, I'd get caught, and it would all be over. If I wanted to live – did I want to live? Dru would have wanted me to, I was sure. So, for him, yes, I'd live. For a while, anyway. Maybe, for him, I could get to Freedom. At least one of us would have made it.

The thing I was looking for – the thing I was cutting into my leg to get at – was an I.D. chip. I hadn't even known I had one until Dru had told me. He'd shown me the tracking system at Master Hix's house that picked up their signal. As long as you had one in you, they could use a tracker to find you, wherever you were. Any slave who wanted to escape would have to cut it out of her.

As pain goes, I guess I'd been through worse. That doesn't mean it didn't hurt, of course; but I got the damned thing out of me. It was a little, plastic square, about the size of a fingernail. I'd never have been able to find it, but it was pretty hard, and close to the surface.

I wanted to wait, to rest and get over the pain of what I'd had to do. I knew I couldn't. If Harl had a tracker – and I'm sure he did – the chip would lead him right to me. I tossed it as far as I could down the alley, and then took off running again.

Finding clothes was my next problem. On top of being a naked Inihu, I now had blood smeared all over my leg. I couldn't run as fast, because my leg hurt. Sooner or later, someone was going to catch me. Would they take me back to the auction block, hoping to get money for returning me? I couldn't take the chance of finding out. I needed clothes to disguise myself, something that would cover as much of me as possible.

A scream interrupted my thoughts, a woman's scream. It was followed by the screeching of a ground car's brakes, and screams of more people. Just up the street, a crowd of people gathered in a circle. A crowd was a good place to lose myself. I ran to them. Hiding in a forest of legs, crouching low, I saw what the screaming was about. A girl, about my age, and well-dressed, lay on the street. Her eyes were open, and looking in my direction, but they weren't seeing me. There was blood on her face, and her legs were turned in ways legs shouldn't turn. She'd been hit by the car whose tires I'd heard screeching. A man, well-dressed like she was, huddled over her, crying. A woman stood over him, screaming for help. She demanded to know where the police were.

Someone said harshly that the police were too smart to be caught out on the streets of Den. The woman cried harder, and began to shout at the sky to let her little girl live. So this was her mother? And the man must be her father. I could have told the woman she was shouting for no reason. There was no chance her little girl was going to live. I could see it in her eyes – open, but unfocused, like Jin's when I'd broken her neck.

Another man – it must have been the driver of the car – came to speak to the crying woman. She attacked him, beating on his chest, and looking like she was trying to rip out his eyes. Other people moved in to pull them apart. No one seemed to be doing anything to help the girl. She lay there, dying, if not dead already, the bags she'd been carrying laying in the street where they'd been thrown –

The bags!

No one was looking at them. They were all looking at the girl. The bags, from one of the nearby stores, lay between the feet of some onlookers. I crawled slowly toward them, hoping no one would remember or notice them before I got there. I knew what shopping bags were. The Masters often had them, and they always held new things. Food. Wine. New clothes.

Quietly, I pawed through them. Sure enough, the girl had been clothes shopping. I found what looked like a dress and a coat, grabbed them, and hugged them to me. I started to go. Then, I saw something shiny on the ground near the bags, reflecting what little sunlight there was on Den.

Den still uses cash money. I know now that not many planets do that anymore. Den had to, though, because so much of the business done there was illegal. You couldn't use credit accounts. Tourists who came to Den always carried money, as this girl and her parents must have, to go shopping. You could use credit, but the best deals were always for cash. When the car had hit her, throwing her bags far from her body, her money had gone flying with them. Slowly, quietly, I gathered it up, too.

As I got ready to slip away, I looked back at the girl's body, one last time. My heart skipped a beat. She was looking at me. For that moment, just a moment, her eyes cleared. She seemed to see me. Nothing in her face changed, except her eyes, but they told me she saw me.

Her eyes should have held questions, I thought. "What happened to me?" "Am I dying?" "Can you help me?" "Why me?"

But they didn't. I saw only... a kind of peace. It was as if she was okay with what was happening, and wanted me to know she didn't mind. It was like she was making her peace with the world. I couldn't understand. Peace with the world was something I could never imagine. I'd been at war with everything since the day I was born, and I figured I'd spend the rest of my life that way.

But this little girl had given up. She'd admitted defeat in the battle, probably just as she found out there was a battle. For just a moment, I envied her. She had found peace. Then her eyes were glassy again. Or maybe they had been all along. Maybe I'd imagined the whole thing.

I didn't have time to feel guilty that this girl's death had helped me out. I had to keep moving. I had to find a place to put the clothes on. I looked around, frantically. I saw the car which had killed the girl. The door was still open, where the driver had gotten out. I ran for it, making sure no one was looking at me. No one was. A naked girl just wasn't the free show that a dead girl was. I learned that people are funny that way.

In the passenger compartment of the car, I quickly dressed, taking the time to check the wound in my leg again. The bleeding didn't seem too bad. It should be all right until I got... wherever I was going. Where was I going? I hadn't made any kind of plan. The chance for escape had been there, I took it, and now... what? I was an escaped slave. I was wearing stolen clothes and carrying stolen money. I was hidden away in a car where I was sure I wouldn't be welcome. On the other hand, a car moved a lot faster than I could on foot. It could take me far away from the place I'd escaped, the place I'd left the tracking chip. Maybe –

"And what do you think you're doing?"

It was the driver, who'd just returned to his car. I didn't know what to say. He was a big man, and ugly. He reminded me of one of the masters. Would he be as cruel? I tried to think of a story to tell, because I knew the truth wouldn't work.

"Well?" he demanded. Then he took a good look at me, noticing my grey skin. "Ohhhh... " he said. "I see how it is. Run away from the auction block, did you?" He got in the car and pulled the hatch shut behind them. Then he keyed a button on the console. I heard clicks beside and behind me. He'd locked the car down.

"Well then, we'll go for a little ride, won't we?"

"Please..." I said dumbly. "Don't take me back."

"Sorry, darlin'. I'd keep you for myself, if I could. You'd be more trouble than I could handle, though, and the city pays a nice, fat reward for returning an escaped slave. Now, you just come along quietly, and – "

I remembered the money I'd picked up. When I'd dressed, I'd hidden it in a pocket. "How much will they pay you?" I asked.

He looked at me suspiciously. "Why is that any of your business?"

"Because I might be able to pay you more, to take me away from here." It was a bluff. I could barely count. I had no idea how money worked. Did I have more than they would pay him?

"Might you?" he asked. "And where would a feral get money to pay me?"

"What do you care, as long as you get paid?"

He nodded. "Okay. Good point. How much do you have?"

This was it. Would it work? I reached in, pulled out a few of the thin slips of plastic and, handed them to him.

"That's half of what I'll give you. You can have the rest when I get out of the car."

This was a trick I'd learned at home. The customers who came to use us often paid half up front, not handing over the rest until they knew we'd show them a good time.

He smiled. It wasn't a pleasant smile. "How'd you know I won't just take this, and add it to my reward money once I turn you in?"

"I don't," I said, swallowing hard. "But I do know that, if you try to stop at the auction block, you won't live to open the hatch." I leveled my eyes with his and glared hard. "They were gonna sell me because I killed someone with my bare hands. It wouldn't bother me to do it again, if someone did something to hurt me."

He stared back at me for a minute, then he laughed. Now his smile was kind of nice. "I like you, little girl."

"I mean it," I said. "I'd rather die than go back there, and I'd sure kill someone else, if I had to."

"I bet you do mean it," he agreed. "It's a deal, then. Half now, half on delivery. Where am I delivering you?"

"Ummm..."

"A word of advice," he said. "There's nowhere on Den that they might not find you. I'd get the hell off planet, if I could. You can work your way to just about anywhere if you get on the right ship at the spaceport." He looked me up and down and added, "And a pretty thing like you might not even have to work."

"The spaceport, then," I said. It would get me away from here. Then where would I go?

* * *

The spaceport on Den would have been exciting, if I'd had time to enjoy it. Ships from everywhere, because people come from all over to do business on Den. It's in Confederate space part of the time, in Qraitian space part of the time. It's also right at the edges of Varthan Freespace. The laws are pretty shifty, and pretty much anything goes. Anything can be bought, sold or traded. It was where the "nice" people of the Confederacy came when they wanted to do business that wasn't so nice.

There were so many people coming and going that it was easy to disappear into the crowd. It was especially easy for me, because most people are taller than I am. I can disappear behind just about anyone. I can also slip into spaces other people wouldn't fit into, and dive between a pair of legs to get away if I have to. I also had the coat I'd taken from the dead girl's bags, which hid most of my grey skin from view. It even had a hood. A coat doesn't look out of place on Den, because it pretty much rains there all the time.

I had no idea where I wanted to go. I also had no idea how to pick a ship and know where it was headed. I also couldn't just walk up to a gangway and ask to board a ship without a ticket. Even with the money I had left, they'd ask too many questions. My driver friend had told me my best bet was to sneak aboard, hide until the ship took off, and then work out a deal for passage. Most Captains, he promised me, won't put someone out an airlock unless they absolutely refuse to work, or somehow endanger a ship. "And no one would put a pretty thing like you out an airlock," he'd said.

There was a line of people waiting to board on of the big cruise ships. I joined that line. It would make me look less suspicious, if I acted like just another passenger while I figured out what was what. Bodies pressed in around me. I kept the coat pulled tightly around me, not wanting any of my skin to show. I heard some tourist boys jeering that it looked like rain. I ignored them.

At the front of the line were the scanners. They were checking tickets, asking where people were going, and searching bags for weapons. I didn't want to try to get past that, I thought. I'd just move in this line long enough to let me figure out –

Then I saw him: Master Harl.

How had he gotten here so fast, I wondered? Had the driver turned me in, after all? No. It must have just made sense that I would come here. He was searching through the crowd, stopping people and talking to them. In his hand, he carried a little holo image. I knew about holos. Many of the masters had holo projectors. This one showed an image of me.

I dove forward, between the legs of an old Quintil man who was shouting at his wife for spending too much money at the shops. He nearly tripped over me, and shouted some filthy words I didn't know as he fought to keep his balance.

I didn't stay to listen. I moved through the crowd as quickly as I could, my skin tingling and the hairs on the back of my neck rising as I imagined Harl's steely grip closing about my arms. Hardly looking where I was going, I threw myself forward. A huge shape loomed ahead, shadowing that section of the concourse. A cargo transport. Its holds stood open, yawning black holes. Robots loaded crates and flats inside, automatically scanning and verifying the contents, as a few disinterested humans sorted through lists of items that were either missing or shouldn't have been there and were.

The humans hadn't seen me. I wondered if the robots were programmed to notice intruders. I looked back. Harl was still nearby. He hadn't seen me, but was moving my way. I had little choice. I ducked past a robot's huge treads and under its pincer-like arms, and into one of the holds. It was dark inside. I moved down an aisle formed by towering stacks of crates, tied down by retaining cables and nets for zero-G travel. I crouched in an alcove between two such stacks, and I waited for the shout or the rapid footsteps which would let me know I'd been discovered.

They never came. Once, I heard Harl's voice come close, but then it drifted away again. I expected the lights to come on. They didn't. I expected a final tour of the hold by cautious, human inspectors. There wasn't one. They'd loaded the cargo in this section, and they were done. Within the hour that I crouched there, during which my legs fell completely asleep, the huge doors to the hold were closed. I was alone in the near dark. I knew that soon the cargo transport would be catapulted into atmosphere, to be caught and towed by a freight tractor. When that happened, if I wasn't secure, I would be tossed about and probably banged and bruised to death. I didn't know much about space travel, but I knew that much.

It occurred to me that the cargo within the crates, held only loosely in place by nets, was safe from collision with other objects. If I were in a crate, I should be safe too. There was only a little light – emergency cells in case the ship lost power. I used it to find my way to the top of the net closest to me. It wasn't easy. I imagine it would be impossible for most species, but our muscles are better than those of most species. That's the way we're bred. I made the top of the safety net, slithered inside, thunking my knee against a crate. I suppressed my urge to cry out at the pain.

The second crate I came across was large enough, and the latch wasn't secure. I opened it, dumped the contents – a few very expensive-looking gadgets and a lot of packing material – to the bottom of the net, and climbed in. I pulled the top shut, and, making sure it wasn't airtight, I tied it shut from within with the soft belt from my dress.

And then the loss of blood, the leftover grog in my body and the excitement of the day all caught up with me. I slept.

* * *

I woke up because someone was shaking me roughly. It was a human man. A boy, really, barely older than I was. He had bad teeth. His breath stank. A beard was starting to grow on his face, but he was so dirty all over that I couldn't tell if he was growing it on purpose, or just never bothered to shave.

"Out," he said roughly.

"Where am I?" I asked. I wasn't in the transport's hold any more. My crate had been moved while I slept. I was still in a hold, but this one was brightly lit, and much bigger.

"You ain't askin' the questions," said the boy. "How'd you get in there?"

"I – I fell asleep," I said lamely. "I... I was at the spaceport, and I got lost– "

His mouth hung open. "The spaceport? You tellin' me you rode the cargo carrier into orbit? Damn, bitch, you lucky you didn't get yer brain shook loose. How'd you know if there'd even be air?"

To tell the truth, I hadn't even thought about air. I guess there was no guarantee cargo would be kept where there was air, was there? But I wasn't going to tell this boy I'd been so careless.

"I told you I fell asleep," I said. "I didn't mean to wind up... here."

"Yer on the *Arbiter*, stupid," he told me. Then he saw the bulge in my pocket where I'd put my found money, and where some of it was sticking out into view. "And whatcha got there?" he asked, reaching his hand out toward it.

Before he could touch me, I grabbed that hand and twisted it backward at the wrist, a trick I'd learned in the barracks back home. He screamed and pulled away from me. I let him go. I figured I'd made my point. "That's mine," I said. "And call me 'bitch' or 'stupid' again, and I'll break your arm."

He shook his head. "Ask me, you's plain crazy, girl. I oughtta toss ya out the airlock."

"You can try," I said back. I sounded a lot braver than I felt.

"Too bad I can't," he said. "This here's a military ship. Captain won't let us space anyone, without his order." He looked hatefully at me. "Damn shame, too. Come with me."

"Like hell," I said.

"Look," he sighed, "If ya don't come with me, the Captain'll send an armed squad to arrest you. Or kill you. I don't care which. Prob'ly they won't, neither."

"Where do you want me to go?" I asked.

"To see the Captain."

"Can he give me a job?"

He wrinkled his nose. "A job?! He ain't gone give no job to no stow'way!"

"Then who can give me a job?" I asked.

"Nobody! I mean... If anyone's gonna give you a job, it'll be the Captain. But he won't."

"We'll see," I said. "Take me to him."

He shook his head again. "Yes, yer highness. Right this way."

* * *

The Captain's name was Joncyn Miles. He was shorter than me, but he was heavier. He looked middle-aged to old. His hair was mostly grey. I expected him to be harsh and nasty, like the masters when they caught a slave stepping out of line. He wasn't. If anything, he seemed bored. He asked me to sit down in a chair next to his desk. No man had ever asked me to sit down before.

"What's your name, girl?"

"Aer'La."

"Aer'La. Hmph. Citizenship?"

"I – what?"

"What planet are you from?" he asked, a little irritably.

"I... I don't know."

His eyes went wide.

"That is... I never knew its name. I was on Den, when I... I got into one of your carriers."

"They say you fell asleep."

"Yes."

"In a cargo crate, at a spaceport?"

"I, uh... "

"You were hiding," he said knowingly. Could he read my mind? I'd heard some people out in space could read minds. What would be the point of lying? Even if I could lie, I wasn't sure I needed to. Miles seemed reasonable enough. Maybe I could get him to help me.

"I was. There's... there's someone looking for me."

"Parent?"

"Don't have any."

"Police?"

"I don't think so."

"Have you done something wrong?"

"No," I said automatically. Then I saw Jin's lifeless eyes, looking right through me as I held her twisted neck in my hands. "I mean... that's not why they're looking for me."

"No warrants, then?"

"No what?"

He smiled. "I believe you'd know, if there were any." He slapped his knees deliberately and leaned back in his chair, stretching his spine. "Well, Aer'La, you present me with a problem."

"I do?"

"Yes. I have to decide what to do with you. I'd send you back to Den – "

"Please don't!"

"Rule one aboard ship, Aer'La: don't interrupt the Captain."

"Sorry."

"It's forgotten. At any rate, I can't put you off at Den. We made our Lindstrom jump hours ago. We're back in normal space, halfway to the next conjugate."

"I don't know what that means," I admitted.

"You really haven't done this before, have you?" he asked. "It means we can't turn back, not without a change in orders. I have rumors of a Qraitian incursion to investigate. That won't wait." He scratched his chin and looked at me thoughtfully. "Did you have any idea where you wanted to go?" he asked.

"No. I just... needed to get away."

"Well, no one rides this ship for free. *Arbiter* is a border patrol ship, not a passenger vessel. It's hazardous duty."

"It can't be more hazardous than where I've been, Captain," I said. "I'm willing to work."

"What are you trained for?" he asked.

"Ummm," I stuttered. What could I say?

He stared at me, waiting for an answer. Then he caught on. "Aer'La," he said carefully, "I'd like you to take off your coat."

"I'm cold," I said.

"No," he said gravely. "I keep it comfortably warm in this cabin, and I believe you're engineered to withstand more cold than I am... aren't you?"

I dropped the coat. He looked at me and shook his head. "A feral. Damn."

"Please, Captain, I'm not dangerous!"

He looked sad. "Yes, child, I'm afraid you are. You're stolen property."

"Nobody stole me! I ran away!"

"Nevertheless, I'd be called a thief if I let you stay."

"I... I could disguise myself!"

"I doubt it, and I can't stake my career on it."

"Can you at least put me off somewhere? I'll never tell anyone I was here!"

He was quiet for a moment. "Our next stop is a military space station. I can't leave you there. I'll... have to think about it."

I was losing the argument. I knew it. I had one last chance, while we were alone. "While you're thinking," I said casually, "is there somewhere I could take a shower or something?" I shucked off my dress as fast as I could and stood before him, naked. "It was awfully hot in that cargo bin."

Captain Miles gawked. I guessed this was the last thing he'd expected to see. Probably it was something he'd been thinking about, though, since the minute I'd stepped through the hatch to his cabin. He looked away, quickly.

"Oh, it's all right," I said, walking closer to him. "You can look. I was bred to be looked at by men."

"P-put your clothes back on, child!"

"I'm not a child," I said sweetly, taking his chin in my hand and turning his face toward mine. "I'm a big girl. All grown up." I ran the backs of my fingers from his ear to his collarbone with one hand, and began lightly rubbing the front of his thigh with the other.

"Want me to show you?"

He swallowed hard. His jaw started to tremble. He was mine.

* * *

It's funny, isn't it? I escaped slavery by becoming mistress to a Border captain. Captain Miles let me stay, of course, once I showed him what work I'd been trained for, how good I was at it, and how willing I was to work at it with him.

It wasn't that bad, really. He was no uglier than some of the masters who'd taken me. He didn't force himself on me, though I wouldn't have fought him if he had. I needed him. At least he didn't hurt me. Most of all, he gave me work to do aboard ship. I'd never held down a job before, with responsibility of my own. I was beginning to feel like a person. It wasn't much, really. I basically cleaned up and inspected equipment (once he learned I had a knack for machinery).

Then one day I interrupted two fighting crewmen. Both were casuals. They had no discipline at all. The only thing that kept them from slitting the throats of their Captain and officers was fear. And almost nothing kept them from turning on each other. These two were fighting in a corridor of the gravitied section of the ship over a bottle of illegal whiskey. The smaller one was losing badly, and in real danger of getting killed.

I stopped them. Like I said, my muscles are more than they look to be. I slipped between them – easy for me – and shoved them apart. The small one was relieved. The bigger one came after me. I broke his nose and three of his fingers in one crack. I thought sure the Captain would be furious. He showed up only moments later. He wasn't mad. He was thrilled. He'd finally found someone who knew how to handle his casuals and wasn't afraid to.

He made me his boatswain. I was practically an officer. I like to think I turned out to be good at the job. I didn't break any more bones – well, okay, a few – but I kept the boys (and the few girls pressed in) in line. Mostly I used the same weapon I'd used on the Captain. I was attractive to them. My pheromone had them all hot and bothered all the time. That made them want to make me happy, and I took major advantage of the fact. I know now that females of most human species can't play this game as well as I could. They might charm the men into following them around like puppy dogs, but if they bumped into a really hard character, they could wind up dead. There are a lot of hard characters on the Border. I didn't have to be afraid – there wasn't a one of them I couldn't take in a fair fight. Besides, I never fight fair.

There was one person aboard I *was* afraid of – Doc Faulkner. I'd had to go to her just after I'd left Captain Miles, sweating and satisfied, in his cabin that first day. I'd tried to talk him out of it, but he insisted that someone had to look at my injured leg.

I was really afraid, when I saw her. I wasn't used to old women, for starters. My kind stay teenagers for most of our lives, then age and die within a few months. I never saw one of my "sisters" grow old. I don't know if they were locked behind closed doors, or worse, but we weren't allowed to see them age. At night, with the lights out, we passed around stories about what the old looked like and scared ourselves half to death. Many of us swore we'd kill ourselves when the first gray hair appeared.

And this old woman, this doctor, was the one who got to decide if I was fit to stay aboard and keep my fancy job. For a while the Captain convinced her to leave me alone, to let me settle in. She got her way eventually, though. I think he was a little afraid of the Doc, too. I got scheduled for an examination.

I'd been in doctor's offices on Vartha. They were veterinarians, actually, and they weren't gentle. Most of them had the job because they weren't allowed to be human doctors anywhere in the Confederacy anymore. I didn't expect a Border doctor to be any better. I was really afraid she was going to make me leave the *Arbiter*.

I waited, naked, in a private examining room. I was surprised that the infirmary wasn't as cramped as the rest of *Arbiter*. I mention being naked (aren't you *usually* naked at the doctor's?) because there were these odd pictures on the walls – old men with funny headbands and some kind of goggles over their eyes, examining children with equally odd instruments. I realized these were pictures of doctor's offices from some world, and realized there was some planet where you wore clothes to see the doctor. I would have laughed at that silly idea if I hadn't been so frightened.

On one counter was a little silver box on which tiny, multi-colored lights were blinking. I wondered what it was. With nothing better to do, I went over to look at it. The lights were pretty. Was it a doctor's instrument?

Before I could touch it, a tiny voice from within it said, "Tap the green light to activate me."

I jumped and backed away. I wasn't used to talking boxes. Then I told myself to stop being silly. Space was full of these kinds of things. The ship's computer had had a voice once, someone told me, but it didn't talk any more. Still, I'd better get used to talking machines.

What would happen if I touched the green light? I was scared, but I couldn't resist. I dragged my fingernail over it. Light shot out of its center, and a tiny person appeared. He began to talk, shouting, actually, but his volume was low, because he was so small.

I bolted to the other side of the room and crouched behind the exam table. It had to be a ghost! A demon! Another late night story in the barracks had told of the Dv'Bakad, the hungry demons who came for the wicked. Was this glowing figure one of them, come to punish me for daring to escape?

Then I realized the little figure wasn't shouting anymore. It was singing. It had a nice voice, too, a young voice. A boy's voice. The song was about loving someone, and longing for them. I peered up from my hiding place. I had to be careful. The Dv'Baakd were tricky. Maybe it was trying to lure me to my death with sweet music.

Now I really saw the figure for the first time. It was a boy. He was human. He might have been a few years older than me, but not much more than that. He was on the small size, if I could judge by the tiny image. His body was almost hairless, except for his head. I could tell, because he was naked. Lights twirled around him, reflecting off his body, which seemed to be covered in glitter. Even his hair gleamed in the light, a golden color, shifting to every color in the rainbow as the lights changed. He was beautiful. Looking at him made me think of Druberj. Of course, I thought of Druberj every minute. Seeing this boy, though, was a little like seeing him again. I got up and walked back to the counter to watch him and listen to his song.

"Pretty, isn't he?" said a voice behind me.

I jumped again. I hadn't heard the door open. It was Doc Faulkner.

"I - I'm sorry!" I blurted. "Is it yours? I was just – "

"It's all right. Those damn things are too tough to break. I didn't even realize I'd left it here." She was very small. She came up to my shoulder. And she didn't carry a lot of weight, either. I probably could have lifted her with one arm. She had reddish hair, streaked with gray – and wrinkles! I'd heard of them. When she spoke, though, her voice filled a room. It was an intelligent, strong voice, one that was used to being listened to and respected.

"Who... what... is it?" I asked.

She laughed a little harshly. "I didn't think there was a girl in all the galaxy who didn't know Brand Greer."

"I don't."

"He's a singer. Not a very good one, really." She reached out and tapped the red light on the little box's front. The boy and his song faded away.

"I – I thought he had a nice voice."

"Girls your age usually do. My eldest great-granddaughter agrees with you. I bought that holo-concert for her birthday next month. One of my husbands will probably kill me for polluting our home with Inworlder culture, such as it is."

I just nodded. I didn't understand everything she was saying.

"Would you like a copy of it? Music – even hopelessly banal music – promotes mental and physical health."

"I – " I hesitated. Why was this stranger offering me a gift?

She laughed. "I didn't mean to put you on the spot. So," she said, looking at her notes on a little notepad. "you're Aer'La. I wasn't prepared for you. I'm supposed to examine everyone *before* they start work aboard *Arbiter*."

"I know. I kinda... came on at the last minute."

"And two steps ahead of the posse, judging by the condition of that leg."

She guided me onto the table and bent over my wound, prodding at it, but never hurting me. "Gods," she said at last, "who did this to you?"

"I... kinda... did it myself," I admitted.

"Why – ?!" she began. Then she seemed to catch on. "A tracking chip, was it?"

I nodded.

"So," she said, going to a cabinet and getting out supplies to treat the gouged flesh, "you're a feral... aren't you? As well as a stowaway?"

"I – "

"Don't worry. As far as stowing away goes, I don't think it's any more wrong for someone to steal passage from the Navy than it is for the Navy to blackmail people into serving."

"Huh?"

"Never mind. I have an opinion for every occasion. As to the rest, if you're worrying that I might turn you in as a fugitive, don't. I know what you're running away from. I've been to Varthan space. I've seen ferals."

"Do you think I'm dangerous?"

"Should I?"

"Captain Miles told me most humans are afraid of us. Like they're afraid of wild animals."

"I'm afraid that's true. Of course, most humans are afraid of their own shadows. We've bred so many qualities into so many different flavors of humanity, you'd think we'd get rid of bigotry and stupidity. I have to admit, though, I've seen psychopathic behavior from ferals. Some of your people are too dangerous to try to integrate into mainstream society. So far, you've showed no dangerous tendencies. At least, none more dangerous than those of the rest of the crew. If you did..."

"You'd send me back to Vartha?"

She took my hand. I wasn't prepared for it. It seemed out of character for her. But when she did it, her whole face seemed to come alive with a compassion that wasn't usually there. Or maybe it was there and just not always where you could see it. "Never that," she said. "I might arrange for you to be in protective custody, in a hospital – "

"Custody? Isn't that the word they use for what I was in back home? I'd rather die."

She looked at me a long moment. "I might make that possible, too."

"What? For me to... kill myself?"

"Yes. I believe it's a right each person has. I believe that, when there's no hope for a physical recovery, it can be something a healer should make possible."

"You're not like doctors back home," I said.

She laughed. "I'm probably not much like doctors anywhere." She finished treating my leg – I barely realized she'd started! – by spraying something sticky over the wound. It hardened immediately, making something that felt like extra skin. "All right, you can keep the leg. Now, let's get some basic information on you. How old are you?"

"I'm not sure. I mean – I haven't learned Confederate years yet."

She nodded. "I'll estimate fourteen standard years. Lie back." She began looking me over, asking me to breathe, poking and prodding and listening and looking. "You noticed my pictures?"

"Yeah. I mean yes." I was trying to learn more formal language. The Captain and the Doctor didn't speak as roughly as everyone else here. I thought I should sound more like them, so maybe they'd see me as less of an animal.

"They're archaic. From a time when the practice of medicine was mostly guesswork and something they called 'common sense.' There were some good healers, of course, some naturally empathic men and women. I like to be reminded where my profession came from – and how little it's progressed in many ways."

I nodded. I wasn't sure what I was expected to say. It took me a while to realize that Doc Faulkner just needed an audience a lot of the time. She didn't expect an answer, probably wouldn't have known what to do with one.

"I have another collection of artwork in my cubicle – " she jerked her head toward the hatch on the other side of the small examining room. "Somewhat more controversial depictions of the history of medicine: supernatural rites, human sacrifices, things we don't always like to admit contributed to our understanding of the human body. You show too much curiosity about life and death and people start to call you a Frankenstein."

"A... what?"

She chuckled. "A Terran religious fable," she said. "About a man who tried to make a human being. Some people think it really happened. I subscribe to the belief that it was fiction, written for entertainment. I'd never say that to a Terran. It would be blasphemy. He's quite the ultimate symbol of evil for the Terrans, opposed as they are to scientists playing with the makings of life."

I understood maybe every third word she was saying. "Did you know him?"

"My girl, the story dates back to the Terran year 1815." She looked at me, as if that was supposed to mean something. Then she laughed quietly. She laughed easily, this old woman. "I was just a little girl then."

"When was the year 1815?" I asked.

"Over five hundred years ago."

"You're – "

"No," she said quickly. "I'm not that old. I was making a joke."

"Oh," I said, but I didn't understand why it would be funny. I decided to ask about something else she'd said. "What are Terrans?"

She sighed. "You don't know much about life out here, do you?"

"I'm trying to learn," I said.

"I'm sure you are. You seem to learn fast, too. That's good. Terrans are the species of which all other human races are an offshoot."

"I don't understand."

"It's like this: the Terrans were first. Just born the way they are. Evolving – changing – to adapt to their environment. Then some people decided it would make more sense if humans planned their own genetic designs." She stopped, seeing I was thoroughly confused. "Um... found a way to pick things like height, and hair color, intelligence and resistance to disease."

"Isn't that a good idea?"

"Maybe. But most Terrans disagreed, so those people left Terra and came to space. Terrans stayed the way they are. They're not designed."

"Are my people designed?" I asked.

"Your people are bred, the way livestock are. A male with the right characteristics is matched with a female with the right characteristics, and a child is conceived. It's done by guesswork, largely, and an innate knowledge of what makes a good specimen for sale.

"My people are engineered," she went on. "It's a little more scientific and detailed than the process used for your people, but the end result is the same: what's deemed by someone to be a "better" specimen is conceived. My people's results are probably better. We achieve our aims a higher percentage of the time. We manipulate chromosomes in laboratories, instead of just putting the best available sperm into the best available egg. The goal is the same, though. Someone says, 'let's improve the race so that it meets our needs.'"

"It sounds like you're slaves, too," I said.

"In a way we are, I suppose. We're slaves to our need to control – people and circumstances. We've established a level of control over our destinies our ancestors couldn't have dreamed of. We're halfway to immortality. Our technology allows us to heal damned near any wound. You could lose both your legs, and I could give a perfectly matched cloned pair. We keep the clones on hand, in fact, in stasis. I'll probably grow one for you. Your decision, of course.

"But I think, in becoming such masters of our fate, we're also making ourselves victims of predictability and comfort. The greatest accomplishments of humanity have come from the malcontents and the misfits. Careful planning of human characteristics leaves little room for misfits.

"And that may be where the Terrans have an advantage over the rest of humanity. No one plans them. No one engineers them. If they want to have a baby, they have one. If the genetic pairing results in a defective or a misfit or a just plain mundane, then it does. No one's there analyzing the result, or trying to get power of veto."

"So the Terrans are... savages? Like wild animals?"

She looked at me pointedly. "That's a pretty odd comment for a Feral to make, don't you think?"

"I... I'm sorry. I just – " I looked down. I didn't know what to say. I'd made her angry, just as I thought she was beginning to like me.

Her hand cupped my chin, pulling my face gently into a line of sight with hers. "It's okay. Don't let me intimidate you, kid. I have a habit of pointing out human failings, and sometimes I'm not too nice about it."

Then I asked her, "How do you know so much?"

She laughed. "I've lived a long, long time, Aer'La."

"Will I ever know as much as you?"

"You could," she nodded. "If you pay attention to... everything. Start by reading whenever you have the chance. I can recommend some primers on the history of the Inner Worlds – "

"Um, I... can't read," I said, ashamed.

She gasped quietly. "Of course you can't! Oh, I'm an old fool!"

"You? I'm the one who can't read."

She put her arm around me. It was a good feeling. "Only because those bastards who raised you neglected you. You have nothing to be ashamed of. I'm the one who should know better than to make my patient uncomfortable. How would it be if I taught you to read?"

I almost stopped breathing. I thought again of Druberj, and those wonderful stories we'd lost ourselves in. How even being a slave hadn't been so bad, when I'd had Druberj and his books.

"Would you do that?" I asked.

"If only to make up for ruining your musical tastes by offering you a copy of that trashy holo. Which I *will* buy you a copy of. You've had few enough pleasures in life." She saw I was still hopelessly confused. She said gently, "And I'll be honored to teach you to read, Aer'La."

"What about the Captain?"

"I'm pretty sure he knows how to read."

"No, I mean – "

"I know what you meant," she said sadly. "You come from a world where those in power try to keep their subjects ignorant, so they're easier to control. I wish I could say that's very different from the rest of the universe, but it's not. Still, you are allowed to learn to read here, whether Captain Miles likes it or not. If he gives you any trouble, you just tell me. I'll handle him."

I thought she probably would do just that.

"Does this mean... I get to stay?" I asked.

"Why not? Until you prove otherwise, you're a fourteen year-old girl – not necessarily good, not necessarily bad. And you're willing to learn. I've met very few people who fit *that* description in my time. I'd be a fool to send you away, now wouldn't I?"

She extended her hand. "Welcome to hell, shipmate."

* * *

Aer'La's memories began to fade and intermingle with her dreams. Soon, she was sound asleep. Much as he would have enjoyed sharing her dreams with her, Cernaq untangled his mind from hers even as he untangled his body from hers. Quietly, and giving Aer'La a gentle command to go on sleeping, he got up from the bed.

He would not sleep tonight. He needed the time to document all that he'd seen. To prepare. When the Varthans arrived, he needed to be ready for them... whatever they tried.

Chapter Eight
Harl

It was during the following duty shift that a ship bearing Varthan registry was sighted, and maneuvered itself to a matching vector with *Titan*. After the small ship had docked, the Captain was escorted to Atal's cabin. Atal chose not to show his visitor to the promenade – that was for polite company. This person, in his opinion, was decidedly neither.

A tall man, dressed in expensive clothes, which he wore badly, and distinctive in appearance only in that he bore a nasty scar on his face, which raked through one eye, stalked arrogantly through the hatch and up to Atal's desk. Unlike Aer'La, his skin was a milky beige color, close in hue to Atal's own. The dominant race of Varthans all shared this white skin.

Atal was seated, reviewing reports on his holo display. He'd planned to be doing this when his visitor arrived, and, as he'd also planned, he continued to review them for a few moments after the visitor spoke.

"I'm Harl."

The Varthan's proximity made Atal very grateful that Inworlders like himself had the ability to deaden their olfactory senses. It meant he didn't have to smell Harl, or the less-well-dressed bodyguard who accompanied him. He felt for Metcalfe, though. The young midshipman had escorted them here, and had no such gifts. Atal could tell by his tight jaw that he was relying on military discipline to avoid showing his revulsion.

"You Captain?" the new arrival asked.

"Jan Atal," he replied, inclining his head.

"The Admiral sent me t'you."

"I see. Admiral Fournier?"

"Yeah. Practical man, that. You?"

"Am I practical? I suppose we'll find out."

"You know why I'm here."

"To claim a slave?"

Harl feigned distress at this question. "Slave? Certainly not, Captain! A Varthan national, who illegally entered your space. We're here to lawfully escort her home."

"I was told you were an investigator, come to determine the condition and value of stolen property."

Harl chuckled. "A misunderstanding, that. Forgive me saying so, Captain, but your people jump to conclusions about us Varthans. You hear one of us is wanted, you automatically cry 'slavery.' I ask you, is that fair?"

"You'll forgive our parochial bigotry."

"Well, of course... er... what?"

"I said I'd hate to judge you too quickly."

Harl grinned. "You're a gentleman, Captain. Now, if you'll just hand over the girl – "

"The girl who says she was, in fact, a slave? Sounds like the wrong party."

Harl's pretense of gentility, oafish though it was, left him. "That's a lie, Captain. Her kind is given to lies. Criminal types, all of them. That's why I need to remove her... for the protection of your crew."

"I'm not sure I can allow that," said Atal.

Harl grimaced. "You've been ordered to give her to me," he said coldly.

"I've been ordered to allow you to inspect her. I'm going to do that. You may start by meeting and questioning your... suspect – under adequate supervision, of course." Atal nodded to Metcalfe, who went to the promenade door and opened it. Doctors Mors, Pallas and Faulkner, followed by Aer'La, entered.

Atal had invited them to observe and look for weakness, as well as to detect the lies he knew would be told. He wasn't sure how this would play out, and he needed every advantage that two telepaths and the aged physician could provide. He realized that Aer'La would have preferred Cernaq be present, and Cernaq was certainly a capable telepath as well. Atal wanted to limit the contact between the Varthans and his young officers, however. They were too personally involved in this. He hadn't even really wanted Pallas here, but Mors had quietly insisted.

Aer'La's expression was guarded. Her gaze was cast at the floor, as it would have been years ago when she was a slave. When she looked up, and saw Harl, her eyes widened. Her head snapped quickly left and right, as she instinctively sought refuge.

Sabotaging Atal's intent to conduct orderly introductions, Harl advanced on her.

"Don't look to escape, girl. You're coming home." He started to reach for her. Metcalfe stepped in his way. Harl sized him up, snorting a laugh. "You'd best stay out of my way, boy. A slip of a thing like you isn't fit for combat against a white Varthan."

"Captain Harl," Atal barked, "you are a guest on my ship. I'll ask you to behave as such. My officers will be treated with respect, including those... under inquiry."

Aer'La moved around Metcalfe and drew close to Atal. The poor child was shaking. Atal had never thought he'd live to see the day. "He doesn't treat anyone with respect, Captain," she said, her voice deadly calm. "He's a slaver and a murderer."

The remark inflamed Harl. "Ye lyin' slut!" he spat. "I'll take ye apart – "

He advanced once again.

Atal was out of his chair and in front of the Bos'n in a heartbeat. He could have let Metcalfe handle all the security. He'd trained the boy in several styles of hand-to-hand combat, after all, and he was proficient. He might, in fact, have been more technically able to defend himself than his Captain; but Atal had the advantage of a physically imposing height, compared to most people. He towered over Harl.

"And you'll take me apart as well, Captain?" Atal asked pleasantly. "I need to know now so that I can postpone my dinner plans while I'm reassembled."

Harl drew a half step back. "I'll not be insulted!"

"I'm not sure you were," Atal said.

He colored. "I'm not a slaver. I'm a private detective. And I've killed no one."

"You killed Druberj, you son of a bitch!" Aer'La shrieked. She started to come around Atal toward Harl, her fear washed away in a flood of lust for revenge.

Atal put his arm out and, gently, realizing he could conceivably lose said arm, clasped Aer'La's shoulder. Thankfully, she responded to his touch, and held her place.

"She lies!" said Harl. "She's got no authority to accuse me!"

Atal turned back to him, almost whispering. "Captain, this is more than a Confederate vessel. This is my ship, and we'll do things my way. If my Bos'n says you're a murderer, then I will proceed on the assumption that you are. Watch your step."

For the next few minutes, Harl proceeded to catalog the indignities he was capable of performing on Atal's person, his vessel and his crew. The Captain let him rant. He'd learned long ago that threats were seldom backed up by actions, that a wise man acted rather than threatened, and that the unsaid was far more frightening than the explicitly stated. Simply, he knew Harl was scared as hell of him, while he feared only what Harl might do to Aer'La.

By rights – by legal rights, in the eyes of those so devoid of judgment that they needed the law to tell them what was right and what was wrong – Harl could just walk out of here with Aer'La. The odds were he was going to do just that, despite Atal's delaying tactics.

When Atal was clearly unaffected by his tirade, Harl calmed himself. "I am a law-abiding man, and wouldn't want to be accused of bein' uncivil. I'll do as you ask, Captain. And I believe you will all come to see – sadly – that her accusations are simply clever lies. A criminal trying to evade capture. You are all good people. You're not used to dealing with the type of lowlife it is my job to pursue. It's easy for you to be taken in."

"You," he said to Aer'La, "sit down."

She turned to Atal. "Sir, do I have to go through with this game? We all know what he is... "

Mors nodded gently for her to sit. "Just be calm, child. Remember, lack of self-control doesn't lend to one's believability."

Aer'La never liked being told to calm down. Her reaction to such suggestions was frequently violent. She sat, nonetheless.

Harl began to pace in front of her chair, his hands behind his back. "I know that... morals in the Confederacy are harder than in Varthan Freespace. You allow less. You judge and condemn the baser acts of living beings. I hope none of you, having been sheltered from the kind of life my people lead, will be too shocked by the things – "

"Get on with it," growled Celia Faulkner. "We're shocked by damned little."

Harl shrugged. "Girl," he said, "How did you come to be on this ship?"

"Captain Atal requested my assignment here."

"You were already one of his officers?"

"Yes. His Bos'n, anyway. A non-commissioned officer."

"And how did you come to be one of his officers?"

"He took command of my last ship."

"And how did you come to be on a Confederate Naval ship?"

"I was recruited by her previous Captain."

"You were pressed into service?"

"I... needed passage. I volunteered."

"To be the Captain's whore?"

She took a breath. "No."

"Did you have sex with him?"

"Yes."

"Would he have let you stay if you hadn't?"

"No."

"Then you were his *whore.*"

"We exchanged services."

He grinned. "Fancy term, coming from gutter trash." He raked his glance at his audience, looking for reactions. Pallas looked unsettled by the conversation. The entire subject was, essentially sacrilege on her world. She hadn't had the benefit of long years away from Phaeton, as Mors had. Sexuality would, it followed, embarrass or even enrage her, to judge by the behavior of others of her kind.

Aer'La started to rise, her muscles tightening. In a moment, without intervention, Harl would be dead. Atal was tempted to let the moment pass, but he inclined his head ever so slightly, letting her know she was to keep her place. She did. He had to give her credit. She was trusting him to bring her through this. Atal didn't know if he would have trusted another that far.

"And when Captain Atal took over, you began 'exchanging services' with him?"

She colored and looked down. "No."

Harl raised his eyebrows. "No?"

"I've never had sex with Captain Atal."

Harl looked to Atal for verification. His look raked the Captain's body and clearly suggested that his reproductive organs must be missing or defective, if he'd passed up such an opportunity.

"She's telling the truth," Atal said.

He turned back to her. "Did you offer yourself to him?"

"I did." She said it slowly.

"And he refused you?"

"Yes. No. He helped me without asking for payment."

"He gave you charity?"

For the first time, she held her head up and met his eye. "Charity is giving to those who have done nothing to earn it. Captain Atal helped a fellow being, by allowing me to stay where I was useful and to earn my keep. That's what civilized beings do."

"Oh? And since you are so civilized, do you now offer your "services" to all takers for nothing?"

"No. I offer them only when I want to."

"And if the Captain demanded that payment now? Would you refuse?"

She looked at Atal and said gently. "His kind of man would never demand that sort of payment." After a pause she added, almost muttering, "And, because of the man he is, I would not refuse him anything."

Harl looked pointedly at the others. Again his eyes locked with Pallas's, longer this time. Her jaw was tight. Harl seemed pleased. Then he returned to Aer'La, leaning close. "Are you an Inihu?"

Aer'La's face was impassive, but her eyes held panic. What was she to say? Atal answered for her.

"Of course she is. No one's denying what her species is. We're simply denying that you have any reason to take her.

"Don't I?" asked Harl. He turned back to Aer'La. "Tell me, girl, where were you when you first... *ahem*... joined this crew?"

"What difference does it make?" she asked.

Harl raised his hand as if to strike her. Aer'La bared her teeth. Metcalfe reached for his sidearm.

Atal spoke quickly to stave off violence. "Captain Harl, you will not touch her. Try that again, and I'll clap you in irons."

Their gazes met, Harl clearly assessing his ability to take Atal in a fight. His assessment must not have been favorable, for he quickly looked away.

"I need to know where she was," he muttered.

Atal nodded. "Tell him, Aer'La."

"I was on Den."

"You escaped your keeper?"

"I escaped *you*. At the auction block."

Harl looked up. "She lies again. She was... under medical care." He reached into his vest and extracted a small holo globe, the cheap kind which tourists could buy at spaceports. He tapped it on. An image of a child appeared before Aer'La, whose face paled.

"You know this girl?"

"I – "

"You should. You robbed her."

"No! It wasn't like that!"

"You also murdered her, didn't you?"

"No! She was hit by a car!"

"After you slit her throat and threw her body in the street!"

Aer'La looked frantically to her fellows. "He's lying!" she cried.

Harl shook his head. "Dishonest to the last." He put his nose almost against hers and cupped her chin. Aer'La turned her face from his breath. "Don't you think it would make you feel better to tell the truth, girl?"

Atal knew Aer'La could stand no more of this. "Captain Harl, have you quite finished your... investigation?"

"I'm satisfied that she's the one I'm after. Of course, I was satisfied of that all along."

"Then, since Bos'n Aer'La's presence is not required while we discuss terms, might I allow her to go?"

He nodded, laughing to himself. "You can let her go – *if* she's confined. But discussing terms will do you no good. I'm taking her."

"Midshipman Metcalfe will escort her to her cabin, where she'll be placed under arrest." Metcalfe held his arm out to Aer'La, who stood, and, uncharacteristically, accepted the proffered appendage.

As they moved to go, Harl added a final dig. "Doesn't it embarrass you, girl, to have manipulated your betters this way? Don't you wish you'd spared yourself the humiliation of having people," he gestured at Pallas, "like this fine lady learn what you really are? What you've done?"

She met his gaze. He waited patiently for her eyes to drop in supplication. After a few moments, she spat in his face. Celia snorted a harsh laugh. Atal had to bite his own lip. Harl, calm with the assurance that he'd already won his battle, wiped his nose with his sleeve.

"Fortunately," he said, "I've been inoculated against the diseases these creatures carry."

After Metcalfe led Aer'La away, Harl looked across to Pallas. He seemed to have zeroed in on her, having spotted weakness which he hoped to manipulate and create an ally. "You see how they behave when trapped? It's for their protection, as well as that of society, that we keep them... controlled."

"Control," said Mors, "is rarely of benefit to the controlled. Yet the benefits are often touted by those who do the controlling."

Harl started to respond. Pallas interrupted him. "Professor, I'm not sure I can agree. I've met Aer'La on several occasions. The behavior I've witnessed indicates a mind ruled by base passions, unchallenged and unsupported by intellect. Can such a creature learn to control itself? If not, should not someone control its behavior?"

Harl looked smug. Mors said, "Pallas, our people have accepted Reason as our absolute and limited our passions to those we can explain and understand, those which can be intellectually justified. But Phaeton followed a long road to its current destination. We evolved our intellects in at atmosphere of free thought. Could we have followed that road if we had walked it under a yolk?"

"I don't mean to be disrespectful, sir, but not all savages evolve into higher intellects."

"I hate to interrupt," Atal said firmly, "but this is not the time for philosophical analysis. If the rest of you will excuse us, I'll speak with Captain Harl privately."

Mors nodded deferentially. Pallas looked annoyed at the interruption. As the others left, she hung back. "Captain Atal, might I be allowed to remain?" At Mors's look of surprise, she said, "Captain Harl's methods are of interest to me, Professor. I've had no opportunity to actually interview a Varthan. I won't interfere."

"Very well," Atal sighed. "I suppose I owe it to your mentor. Captain Harl?"

"The young lady is quite perceptive. I shall enjoy her company."

Mors and Celia left, the latter rolling her eyes. Pallas seated herself in the visitor's chair opposite Atal's desk.

Atal gestured to Harl to sit. He declined, so the Captain remained standing as well.

"So... you claim she's not an escaped slave, but a murderer?"

Harl smiled too confidently. "Surely you know that tales of slavery among my people are exaggerated, Captain? There are a few practitioners who remain... stubborn. The girl is not a slave. She is a custodial ward of a Varthan citizen."

"I'm impressed. That's a very pretty euphemism. But slave-holders throughout history have claimed to be beneficent caretakers of lesser species, that the slaves must be kept in captivity for their own good."

"These are not ordinary beings, Atal. These creatures are fit for little else – that is, they're not equipped to care for themselves. They're too wild. Not everyone is meant to be free. Some just can't handle freedom."

Pallas spoke up. "If you'll excuse my interruption, Captain, that's quite true. Historically, our joint culture has recognized a criminal class, denied rights for the protection of others. "

"Thank you, Dr. Pallas. I'm sure Captain Harl appreciates your support."

"I'm merely analyzing the situation objectively, Captain. Truth does not have a political affiliation."

"I see," Atal said testily. He could not help wishing that his young guest would keep silent. While he was aware that she and Aer'La disliked each other, he did not think that her sympathies would lie with a bounder like Harl. Her "objective" analysis, however, was not helping things. What was Mors thinking, asking that she remain?

"Captain Harl, something stinks here. Even if I stipulated that Aer'La was dangerous and needed custodial care – which I do not! – "

Harl sighed and said gravely, "She *is* a murderer, Captain, and my people do not let a murderer go unpunished for *any* reason."

"She denies your charge."

"Naturally. She may not even remember committing the crime. They're not very bright creatures, you know."

Atal estimated that Harl's intellect could have fit into Aer'La's brain fifty times and left room for walk-in closets, but he let the point go. "Whom did she kill?"

"A tourist. A child. Pretty young thing," he said sadly. "I'm afraid I had to examine the body. As I said, she slit the little girl's throat in order to rob her, then pushed the body, still in its death throes, in the path of a ground car. Of course, the coroner immediately noticed that the wound to her jugular had bled like that inflicted to a living person, meaning it had caused her death, not the impact. And of course we have the girl's fingerprints on the murder weapon. A shard of glass she'd foraged from somewhere. She was foolish enough to leave it at the scene.

"Captain," Harl said with as much sympathy as he could feign, "I know you're fond of the creature. Were circumstances different, I'm sure you and I could come to, shall we say, an arrangement? But this is a capital crime, and must be dealt with. You see, you cannot deny the truth of my earlier statement. A wild animal will always be wild, and will always need to be caged. Now, I believe we were going to discuss terms?"

"We were... until you turned this from a case of recovering property into a capital case, crossing jurisdictional lines. Now I'll have to consult the Attorney General's office, of course, and launch my own investigation."

Harl colored, but kept his composure. "I believe your orders are clear, Captain. You are to surrender the girl."

"My orders *were* clear, sir. I was to surrender an escaped slave."

"But that – "

" – That was a 'misunderstanding,' yes. But it was the basis of my orders. Now, it seems, I am not harboring an escaped slave. I cannot proceed on those orders. I must proceed as I would if any other member of my crew were accused of a crime."

"You're deliberately stalling for time, Captain!"

Atal smiled. "Why, so I am. Twenty-four hours, in fact. I'll get back to you in exactly that amount of time. Until then..." He rose, once again towering over the Varthan. "Get your sorry ass off my ship."

To his surprise, Atal did not have to call security to enforce his unmannerly demand. Harl turned on his heel and left, with a brief but courteous salute to Pallas.

When the hatch closed behind Harl, Atal turned to the Phaetonian girl.

"Well, Doctor... shall I offer you a drink? Or shall we get right down to you telling me just what in hell you thought you were doing just now?"

Pallas was unflustered by his brusqueness. She sat back in her chair and clasped her hands placidly over one raised knee.

"I'll be happy to explain my behavior, Captain. I think you'll be fascinated to hear what I've learned..."

* * *

"Who was Druberj?" Metcalfe asked. They were in her cabin,

where she was nominally confined, under arrest. She sprawled on the bed, while he fetched her a cup of tea.

"Another slave," she said. "We were lovers."

"And that's his murderer they sent?"

She nodded. Metcalfe knelt on the bed, placing the steaming mug in her hands, not letting go until he was sure she had a firm grasp upon it. Her hands were still shaking.

"Are you all right?" he asked.

"Hell no. Seeing him again brings it all back."

He reached out and pulled her back against his chest, reclining himself against the headboard of her bed. She curled up against him placidly, clearly grateful for the comforting embrace.

"I never thought I'd see you afraid of anything," he said.

"We're all afraid of something, aren't we?"

"I guess."

"He... he raped me, Navy," she said quietly. "A lot of men did, over the years, but he was the first. He was our... overseer, I guess you'd say. I was just little, and he – " Her breath caught, and the rest came out in a sob. " – he enjoyed it. I could tell."

Metcalfe held her tighter, using one hand to stroke her hair.

"He'll never hurt you again, Aer'La."

"No? What are you gonna do, Navy? Kill him?"

"I will if I have to, and I'll enjoy it."

She shook her head, sadly. "You're not a killer."

"There's a first time for everything. If ever a man needed killing..."

Aer'La turned and faced him, her expression deadly serious. "Stay away from him, Navy. He's dangerous. He has dangerous friends. If he didn't someone would have killed him a long time ago. It's not worth your life – "

"You're my friend," said Metcalfe. "It damn well is worth my life. I'd be dead by now, if it weren't for you. Besides, I think we can make Harl back down – "

"Trust me," she said, "you can't. He won't give up. He's never lost a slave. He's proud of that."

"Well he's going to lose this time."

"I want to believe that. You don't know them like I do, though."

"No," he said, "but I know *us*. We don't lose. Captain Atal's brought both of us this far, hasn't he?" Metcalfe gestured around the room. "Look, Aer'La! We're on the *Titan*! We're *officers*! The Terran and the slave! Who but Captain Atal could have made that happen? You think he'll let one of us get taken into slavery?"

She stared at him for a few moments. "How do you do it?" she asked.

"Do what?"

"Keep... hoping. Keep believing you'll win in the end?"

"What else *can* you believe?"

She dropped her head. "That there's no way out."

He'd never seen her like this before. Aer'La didn't admit defeat. She spit in its eye. She was the fiercest, most determined person Metcalfe had ever met. But since Harl had shown his face, all that had changed. His presence obviously invoked all the wrong memories for her, and changed her back to what she used to be: a slave, a creature with no hope, no spirit, no sense of self.

"My people are the joke of the galaxy," Metcalfe said. "We're the evolutionary precursors to the *real* human race, at least that's the way the inworlders see it. We're something they're ashamed of, especially because they know they're really not that different than we are. A lot of my people do admit defeat. They don't believe they *can* win. I guess... I guess, in order to be one of the ones who leaves Terra, you have to believe you can win no matter what the odds. Like now – there's no way I can think of to get through this, but I still believe we'll come through."

"That's not very realistic, is it?"

"I guess not," Metcalfe admitted. "It's called faith. It's not about realism. It comes from our religious heritage. I'm afraid most of my people have abandoned it."

"I never did understand religion. What is it? No other races have it, do they?"

"Sure they do," he said. "Reason and intellect are a religion to the Phaetons. Education is a religion to the Quintils."

"But what is a religion?"

"It's... I don't know if I can explain. It's a belief that there's a higher purpose than finding food and shelter and reproducing. It's a belief that someone's watching out for you."

"Like Atal watches out for us?"

"But he's only human. I mean a superior being."

She looked at me strangely. "You're kidding, right? The Captain *is* a superior being!"

For a minute he thought she was joking. Then he realized she meant it. "You consider some people... better than others?"

"Of course. You and I are, well, we're lower life forms. I was bred for servitude. You weren't bred at all. How can we pretend to be equal to someone like Atal, with engineered intelligence and emotional training and bio-control – "

"Stop it!" he said, more forcefully than he meant to. She looked guardedly at him. "I mean... my people don't see it that way. Our beliefs teach that all humans are of equal value, with equal rights."

"That doesn't make sense," she said. "How can you believe we're equal to them? Do we have the status of a Quintil? Do we have a chance at the wealth? Well..." she grimaced at him, "...I guess you do. I don't. I'm a few levels down."

"That's not true."

"How do you know that? Who says some aren't better than others?"

"Our... creators," he muttered.

"I don't believe in any creators," said Aer'La bitterly. "Some of my people do, but I... I've fought for everything, all my life. No god ever showed up to help me. And what kind of creator would make people just to be slaves?"

"I doubt your creator intended you to be a slave, Aer'La. That's a mortal concept, slavery."

"Then why would someone create us at all? If so many bad things can happen?"

"So we'll learn and grow. We'll have experiences..."

"*Why?*"

"I don't know. My church said we go on after this life to eternal paradise. I find that hard to swallow. But I think, after we die, we go *somewhere*. This life is, well, it's sort of a testing ground, to prepare us for what comes next."

"How do you *know* that?"

"I don't. Like I said, it's about faith."

"So..." she said thoughtfully, "you really think it's not over... when it's over. When someone dies, you haven't really lost them?"

"I'd never have survived my sister's death unless I believed that," Metcalfe said. "If I didn't think I'd ever see her again, that she was here and then just... gone... it would all seem so pointless."

"But... when someone dies... they're dead... They're..."

"Their body is dead. Don't you believe in a soul, Aer'La?"

"I... I don't know. What is a soul? I always hear about them..."

"Everything that makes you who you are... except your body."

"So... where does it go? The soul? Can you see it?"

"Doc Faulkner would probably say she could, but no. I don't think so. And I don't know exactly where they go. Maybe they stay right here among us. Maybe they can see what we're doing."

"That could mean that Druberj is watching me?"

"Yes. I like to think Lydia watches me."

"Maybe Druberj is with her?"

"Maybe," he smiled.

"Do you think they would have liked each other?"

"Lydia liked everybody. She was so... kind."

"So was Dru," she said, her eyes unfocused, as if she were lost in memory. "I hope... I hope they are together... somewhere... if what you say is true. Maybe they're even lovers!"

"Uh... I don't think... that is... "

"What, can't they have sex in the after life?" Aer'La demanded. "'Cause I'm not going unless they do!"

"The Church says the soul is a spirit beyond physical pleasure."

"Ick."

"Besides," he said quietly, "Lydia never... " He couldn't bring the words out. Somehow, when talking about Lydia, who was so innocent, it didn't seem right.

"Never?" asked Aer'La, knowing what he meant anyway. "How old was she?"

"Twelve."

"Well, what was she waiting for?"

"She was only twelve! She was too young!" He saw Aer'La's surprised expression, then added, "On Terra, anyway."

Aer'La thought it over. "Wow. Never. I *hope* they're lovers."

Metcalfe decided to bring the conversation back to a serious subject. "Aer'La, how come you never mentioned Druberj before?"

She shrugged. "I - I don't know. I guess... when he and I were together, it was a secret. We couldn't tell anyone else. Having sex with someone you picked yourself, instead of someone who paid for you... that was perverted where I come from. So Dru was my... kinda my secret life. My hiding place. I guess I just got in the habit of keeping him to myself. Even after I came to the Navy, when things were bad I'd... Well, I'd think of Druberj, sometimes. Pretend he could talk to me. Pretend he could tell me that everything was all right, and that... " She stopped, embarrassed. "This is stupid, isn't it?"

"I don't think so. We all have some kind of mental retreat from the world."

"I guess I should have told you about him. He deserves to be remembered. I did tell Cernaq. He reminds me of Dru."

"That explains your amazing patience for the stubbornest member of our little clan," chuckled Metcalfe.

"I guess maybe it does. Cern's... special."

"I should call him to sit with you."

"I don't need a damned babysitter, Navy."

"Sorry. Maybe I should go."

"I didn't say I wanted you to go either." She shifted her weight harder against him, pressing him back against the wall and the headboard. "I'm comfortable."

"Okay... I was ordered to keep and eye on you. So, tell me more about Druberj. Would I have liked him?"

Her face lit up as she began to recall him. "You would have been crazy about him. I remember this one time..."

* * *

Despite Aer'La's insistence that she not be treated like an invalid, Cernaq showed up at her cabin not long after Metcalfe had brought her there. Knowing the Phaetonian's presence would be more helpful to her than his own, and feeling he really should report back to Atal, Metcalfe excused himself.

A bounce tube deposited him at a junction in the corridor just short of the captain's suite. Hearing familiar voices carrying around the corner, he stopped, keeping himself invisible from the speakers. The corridor, fortunately, was not busy. The corridors near the captain's cabin rarely were. Most members of the crew did not care to be caught by the Captain unexpectedly. It might encourage him to find them work to do.

The first voice was clearly that of Pallas. Metcalfe's pulse quickened, thinking of seeing the beautiful scientist again. Then he realized the other voice belonged to Harl. He heard Aer'La's name mentioned, and decided Pallas must be working on him for information. He waited out of sight, not wanting to interrupt if she *was* learning something useful.

"– It may just be my upbringing," Pallas was saying, "Dr. Mors has told me that Phaetonians must learn tolerance when we live among other peoples. Still, she really is the antithesis of everything my people have tried to make themselves. And I'm not jumping to conclusions. I've met her on several occasions."

"They're all like that, my dear," said Harl. "And don't judge yourself harshly. You can throw out all the philosophy you like. Me, I'm just a working man. I see it as being as simple as you being a lady with class, who's been brought up with some standard of decency. The Inihu? They're animals. Not only hasn't she been raised right, she *can't* be. Between you and me, that's *why* they're bred and trained the way they are.

"Of course, I realize that it must repulse a fine person like yourself, you bein' Phaetonian and all. But you must admit that there are... needs which must be met, among less advanced races. And it is better to have those needs met in a planned environment, by those trained to do it, rather than having their betters sullied in the act. Don't you agree?"

"I... suppose."

"I mean... I've no doubt that – someday! – we'll probably follow your people's fine example and do away with these base instincts altogether. In the meantime, though, well, the demand is there. We can't disrupt the economy of countless worlds by pulling the plug, now can we?"

"That would be disruptive, wouldn't it? But..."

"What? Don't be afraid to say anything to me. My feelings are very hard to hurt."

"Well – how do you do it? How do you work with... her kind? I mean, maybe it's easier for you, not being from Phaeton, but I can't help feeling... reviled. She... those creatures... they wallow in... *sexuality*. Even if you're not from my world, how can anyone debase herself that way?"

"They are a sad lot, aren't they? Not fit for anything else, really. And meant to be kept... within their limits."

"How old was the girl she murdered?"

"Twelve standard years. A baby. A whole life in front of her. I can't really blame the creature of course..."

"She has no concept of morality, does she? She's just... emotional reaction."

"Very true."

"Couldn't these tendencies be bred out of her race, though? I mean, I can see how, without careful planning, certain traits might reinforce themselves. They really can't be prevented without engineering, even in my own species. I don't mean to insult you, if you're not engineered, Captain. It's just that, without engineering, you don't know what you're getting. This girl is an example of the kind of sociopathic personality which often results from random breeding."

Metcalfe barely restrained his temper, which would have driven him to step round the corner. His non-engineered, Terran temper seethed to confront the ugliness that was being given voice. What Pallas had just said about Aer'La was what so many "concerned" physicians and counselors at the Academy had said about him. He desperately wished Harl had said it. He could easily have hated Harl and been done with it, but Pallas...

Pallas. How could so intelligent, sensitive, and, most importantly (to a twenty-one-year-old male) beautiful a woman say such things, not only about Aer'La in particular, but about all non-engineered humans? It was bigotry, pure and simple. A person capable of such feelings could easily distance herself from the injustice of Aer'La's situation. Such a person could certainly never really care about him. Nor could he care about her.

He was about to walk away when she called to him. He turned. She was standing right behind him. Apparently, while he was reigning in his anger, she had ended her conversation and dismissed Harl.

"I knew you were there, of course," she said. Her expression was tentative, as if she knew how angry he was, and feared he might become violent.

There's no 'as if' about it moron, Metcalfe reprimanded himself. *She's the most powerful telepath on Phaeton. Of course she knows how angry you are.*

"If you knew, then why did you say those things?" he demanded.

"They weren't meant to apply to you specifically. Don't personalize my – "

He cut her off. "I personalize everything, thank you very much. Because everything that happens in my life happens to me."

"I was merely pointing out – " she began with an even tone.

He was not calmed. "What? How much better you are than Aer'La? How well you're capable of analyzing her worth as a human being?"

"No. And she's not human, she's – "

"That's not the goddamn point!" He shouted. Then her startled expression caused him to lower his voice. "You've only met Aer'La a handful of times. I've worked with her for a year. None of the things you said about her are true. Even if they were, how dare you defend the idea that a beast like Harl could make her a slave?"

"I wasn't – "

"Do you even know what he did to her?"

"What?" she asked.

"None of your business!" Metcalfe spat.

"Well, of course, that's a logical chain of reasoning."

"Oh, why don't you just pull it out of my mind?" he said irritably.

"I already did, since you were being obtuse. So," she said thoughtfully, "Aer'La says Captain Harl is a rapist and a murderer."

"You say that like you don't believe it."

She shrugged. "He says she's the murderer, as I believe you heard. I suppose the two stories could be reconciled. They could both be guilty."

"How can you be so... so damned cold and analytical about it?"

"I've spent my life training to be this way."

"Well, congratulations then."

"It certainly allows me to accomplish more to resolve the situation than your bouts of primal rage. Did you know that your heart rate and blood pressure have increased by a factor of – ?"

"Who cares?"

"You should. It might affect your health, if you let your circulatory system rage out of control that way."

"And how the hell do you know that, anyway?"

"The data are in your mind. You just don't know how to read them. I do."

"Since you can read so much in so many minds, why can't you read whether or not Harl is lying about Aer'La being a murderer?"

"I can."

"And?"

She looked at him for too long a moment. "And I'm not ready to reveal that information."

"Why not?" asked Metcalfe. "If the murder charge is phony, then his only claim on Aer'La is that she's his property. And he's trying to pretend he's not a slaver. Proving that he's lying might just send him packing!"

Again her impassive gaze seemed to pierce through him as she considered her response. "Metcalfe, has it occurred to you that maybe Aer'La *is* lying?"

"No."

"Your confidence in her is that strong?"

"Yes."

She nodded. "I see."

And then she walked away, leaving Metcalfe alone and extremely confused.

* * *

"Investigation? I didn't authorize an investigation!"

Jan Atal sighed and poured himself his fifth cup of coffee for this shift. At this point, he would have preferred something with rum, but he was on duty. He refused to develop *that* particular filthy habit.

"I'm afraid you did, Georg," he said, leaning back in his chair and crossing his legs. He wanted to look as inappropriately comfortable as possible when his holo image reached Fournier's office. "At least, you informed me that the Varthans were sending 'an investigator.' That implies that there will, in fact, be an investigation."

"One day, Atal, your cleverness is going to be your undoing."

"Noted, Admiral."

"Well, at any rate, I assume Captain Harl has completed his... investigation?"

"If you call terrorizing an innocent child an investigation, yes. And he – naturally – came to the conclusion that Aer'La is the one he's looking for."

"Well, we knew that."

"So we did," Atal agreed. "What we did not know is that they're now claiming she's an escaped suspect in a murder investigation."

"So?" blurted Fournier. "You didn't expect them to come barging in, saying, 'hand over my fucking slave,' did you? Not everyone has your casual disrespect for political correctness."

"He's lying."

"Of course he's lying! Oh, really, Atal, you are such a child at times. I've explained to you what's at stake here. It's tragic for the girl, but we can't plunge worlds into recession and let millions starve to protect one person. The fact is, telling the truth about her background – whatever that is, for I'm sure she's a filthy liar as well – jeopardizes our economy as much as our simply refusing to cooperate would. Captain Harl's story is... expedient."

"It's bullshit."

Fournier sighed. "I assume that's another Terranism you've learned from your crew? And a vulgar one at that?"

"Only the best for you, Georg."

"Atal, you've been courting an insubordination charge since the day you came under my command. I warn you, I'm at my breaking point."

"I only need the rest of the day – "

"No, dammit! Over the course of the next twenty hours, the media could detonate this thing like a powder keg! If more than one story leaks out, public opinion will split. With the Qraitians at bay, we can't afford to weaken our public support base. We must act decisively to end this, before it becomes a discussion point for the masses!"

"So, right or wrong, you'll just hand Aer'La over," said Atal, bitterly.

"In fact..." said Fournier slowly, "that's exactly what I'm going to do. Yes. I can see from your attitude that I can't trust you to handle the task. The Lead Arbiter is issuing a statement later today, announcing the Confederacy's new zero-tolerance policy for fugitive murderers and pirates. This will be an excellent opportunity to show the Admiralty enforcing that policy."

"Meaning what?" asked Atal, his mood sinking.

"Meaning," said Fournier, "that I will be bound for *Titan* as soon as I can arrange an emergency transport. I'm going to see to it that this thing is done right."

Metcalfe's Prayer Journal

Grrrr...

I don't suppose prayers should begin with 'Grrrr,' should they?

I'm just extremely disappointed. And frustrated. Extremely frustrated.

I'm disappointed to learn that Pallas, whom I... okay, whom I worshiped... could harbor such ugly thoughts about a friend of mine. And is it only because Aer'La's a friend of mine that I'm disappointed? Would I be okay with bigotry, if it didn't apply to someone I knew? I hope not. Please don't ever let me be that way.

Kaya says it's not bigotry. We had quite an argument about it, and she seemed bound and determined to defend Pallas, no matter what I said. I accused her of taking Pallas's side because she was a fellow inworlder. She said *that* was bigotry. Maybe it was.

Anyway, Kaya said it was natural to distrust people who are different – a defense mechanism. Until you know what someone's about, being too free and easy with them could get you killed. I suppose there's some truth in that, but Pallas's obvious distaste for Aer'La didn't have much to do with physical danger. It sounded like it had a lot more to do with Phaetonian prudery, an attitude that all sexuality is backwards and dangerous.

Dangerous? Okay, maybe I see Kaya's argument about a defense mechanism. I still think it's bigoted to look at a whole race and say you disapprove of their way of life. And then to suggest that maybe they need to be "controlled." That's just too much like what a lot of inworlders have said about my own people.

And what was that "I see," foolishness when I said I believed Aer'La was innocent? What did that mean? Does she think Aer'La's guilty? Or not? There's something Pallas isn't telling me! What is she up to?

And why does my pulse still race when I'm near her, if her bigotry turns me off so much?

What's wrong with me?

Chapter Nine
Meet the Press

From the InterSpace discussion net...
OPINIONS | POLITICS | VARTHAN FREE SPACE
Topic: Titan's Refugee Bos'n

From MODERATOR - kilroy (kilroy.public.quintil)
Okay, be nice. Whom do you believe? The feral claims
she was a slave and had to escape. Bigwigs like Jan Atal
and Mors of Phaeton vouch for her. The Varthans claim
she's an escaped murderer. Bigwigs like Secretary
Fournier and all the Arbiters vouch for them. Where do
all you little people weigh in?

From titanfan (Titanfan.customers.DH)
Pretty clear where the politico's heads are. When the
Varthan slavers say jump, our elected officials say how
high. I wonder how much of a bounty Fournier will collect for handing this girl over?

From bushytail (bushytail.ephemerals.rainbowone)
Wow, titanfan, can Jan Atal do anything wrong in your
eyes? Why don't you just blow the guy? You think
Fournier's on the take? Like Atal's clean. He's heir to one
of the most shameless of the special interest cartels. The
girl's his personal fuck toy, and he just wants to keep her
in his bed. You should really be the first to want to see
her go, tf. Then *you* can volunteer to wax his blaster for
him!

From guest (nobody.centrallib.Quintil)
I'm confused. Didn't the Arbiters Council outlaw slavery in Varthan Freespace?

From titanfan (Titanfan.customers.DH)
Attn: Bushytail - As Rainbow One allows public dueling, my second and I have purchased tickets on the Douglas *Comet Cruiser* and are scheduled to arrive your space-port Monday next. I have logged my challenge with your planet's public system, and booked firing range 12B at the spaceport. I prefer privately owned facilities, but am on deadline this month, and don't wish to spend more time on this unpleasantness than necessary. Please assure your family that I will kill you quickly and cleanly, and pay twice the customary survivors' benefit. I await your reply, and request to know if there are any prior claims. I would expect there is a long line of people waiting to kill you.

From MODERATOR - kilroy (kilroy.public.quintil)
Children, please! I am tempted to suspend discussions for a day, until you can all learn to be civil. Bushytail, please log an apology to Titanfan and get this fight over with. TF is right, you shouldn't have insulted it. I'd hate to lose your lively input to the group, and TF is reputed to be a very good shot.

From TerraSucks (terrasucks.public.quintil)
Who cares what happens to the feral? They're almost as bad as the earth trash! Space 'em all!

From DATABASE-ADMINBOT
USER bushytail.ephemerals.rainbowone has dissolved its public identity. As this person no longer exists, legally, claims against it must be filed with its Escrow Trustee: Torne, Hernia, Lein & Snob, Ltd, Quintil Offices.

From bttmntz (bttmntz.nobody.nowhere)
It's a hoax! There is no Titan Feral! It's all an attempt to –

From HighpR

It's just frightening, that's what it is! Anyone could be a feral! The government needs to do something! What if – ?

"Five, can you turn that shit *down*?"

This request came from Carson, who sat one table away from Blaurich in the officers' commissary. It was one thing, after all, to surf the infonets during breakfast. Many people were prone to do so. Carson himself preferred to read Byron, Shelley, Eminem, or some other classic poetry, but people were entitled to their choice of material. The discussion groups, though, were so thoroughly annoying. Each contributor was represented by some holographic avatar it had chosen. ("It" being the pronoun of choice, as gender was not part of the public identity.) Most of these tended to be ridiculously caricaturized cartoon mammals or reptiles, with squeaky voices their owners thought were cute. With the volume at the level Five had set it, they were only vastly irritating. Besides, BushyTail's animated squirrel avatar kept leaping onto Carson's table and trying to steal his toast.

"You should try to stay informed, Carson. It behooves an officer – "

"There are going to *be hooves* up your ass, Sestus, if you don't stop lecturing everyone," said Kaya. "My hooves."

"Really, Atal," Blaurich drawled. "Your time with these ruffians has wreaked havoc with your manners." His eyes twinkled, "But anything you want to do with my backside is fine by me."

"Your levity is inappropriate, given current events, Mister Blaurich," said Cernaq.

"Why? Oh, yes, the feral."

"Her name is Aer'La," said Kaya coldly.

"It doesn't really matter what her name is, now does it? She'll soon be shipped off for trial by her own people. I'm quite confident, given her violent nature, that she's guilty – "

"Aer'La's not a murderer, Five," said Carson. "And you don't know anything about her, so why don't you shut up?"

"So, I'm to believe the creature's never killed anyone?"

"I didn't say that," said Carson. "But never without reason." He smiled coldly at Blaurich. "Your existence might be reason enough."

"I trust that I am not hearing my midshipmen... bickering?" a voice interrupted. It was Darby, who'd wandered up behind them.

"Why no, Captain," said Blaurich quickly. "In fact, we were discussing some news items that pertain to the *Titan*."

"Indeed?" asked Darby. "I'm afraid the Captain has had me rather busy. I haven't caught the news."

"Aer'La's all over it," said Kaya.

"Well, that's to be expected, isn't it?" asked Darby. He pulled up a chair and joined them at their table. Five also wandered over, afraid, no doubt, of missing an opportunity to shine ever brighter in the Deputy Captain's eyes. "The thing we need to do," Darby went on, "is be sure that we take every opportunity to maintain our ship's stalwart reputation while the attention is on us."

"Which will make for many opportunities," observed Cernaq dryly, "since the media are already on board."

"Good point, Mister Cernaq." Darby looked suddenly alarmed. "Er... I trust... none of you have... spoken to them? Since the news broke?"

"I'm sure we haven't, sir," said Five. "Though I, myself, have had to turn down six interviews which were attempted via... private channels."

"Good for you, Mister Blaurich. We can't be too careful, especially since public opinion is so squarely directed against a nominal member of our crew."

"Actually," said Cernaq, "that may be changing."

"Eh?"

"It seems the Confederate Civil Liberties Fellowship – "

"That pack of trouble makers?" Darby interrupted.

"The very pack," agreed Cernaq. "They've filed a brief with the Arbiters' Council. The Confederate Charter guarantees that, in matters of interspace commerce and law, every reasonable effort shall be made to guarantee that due process of law is executed. A fair trial – "

"We can't force the Varthans to follow our trial practices! The Charter wasn't meant to interfere with the rights of sovereign worlds to deal with their citizens."

"Ah, but she's not a citizen," said Kaya.

Darby shook his head. "Those troublemakers are going to make the Varthans angry!"

"And after they bought those lovely sconces for the Arbiters' Hall," quipped Carson.

"Mister Carson," said Darby through his teeth, "you will learn in the course of your career that it doesn't do to insult or bully influential allies. Especially after the Arbiters' Council has taken such a firm stand against suspect who attempt to flee their planets' justice."

"Not so firm a stand, I'm afraid," said Cernaq.

"What?"

"The Arbiters' Council has... amended their statement in Aer'La's case. They insist she surrender herself, but they feel some attempt should be made to ensure that a thorough investigation is conducted. They are, therefore, asking that Admiral Fournier pick one of his executive staff to accompany Aer'La to Varthan Freespace, and observe the proceedings."

"Well," sighed Darby, "that's not so bad, is it? It maintains cordial relations with the Varthans, while providing – "

" – While providing the impression that the Confederacy gives a damn," finished Carson.

"Yes. What? No! Really, Mister Carson! I'll not have that disrespectful tone directed at the Council or the Admiralty by one of my officers!"

"Captain," Five said gently, "if I may?"

"Yes, Mister Blaurich? Some courteous, military decorum would be welcome."

"Only it seems to me that, with the media already here, you have an excellent opportunity to bolster both our ship's public image, and the Council's."

Darby clapped him on the shoulder. "Quite right, Sestus!" He wagged a finger at the other three midshipmen. "You young people are wanting some decisive action taken in this case, of course. Well, I'm going to show you action, yes I am."

Kaya wrinkled her brow skeptically. "Really?"

"Really, Mister Atal. I," he finished ceremoniously, "am going to call a press conference."

* * *

Atal stood with Mors, Celia Faulkner and Darby by the dais Darby had erected for launch day. For his press conference, the Deputy Captain had had Blaurich scramble some of the casuals to reassemble it.

"Are you sure you don't wish to address them yourself, sir?" Darby asked Atal, for what must have been the sixth time. "It is Captain's privilege."

Atal smiled beneficently.   Darby did protest too much, he thought to himself. The man was clearly dying for this latest opportunity to jump before the holo cameras, and was terrified his Captain would take it away at the last minute.

"I've no desire to address them, Mister Darby. I am delegating that unpleasant task to you. *That* is Captain's privilege."

"You're very droll, Captain, really. I am honored."

While Darby ascended the dais, Celia leaned into Atal and whispered. "Is he really as dumb as he pretends to be?"

"Dumber, I think," replied Atal. "But, if you mean, 'does he really think I'm doing him a favor,' I doubt it. He's too shrewd."

"Really, Captain, why are you allowing this? You were wise to keep these paparazzi locked out of the military areas – and out of the loop on Aer'La's case. Why this reversal?"

"Because they're going to publish 'news' whether we give statements or not. It's better if we do. We stand a chance of some kernel of truth getting through that way."

Celia gave a derisive snort. "I doubt it. Not even the slightest kernel of truth slips by these carrion. They eat it all and then vomit out raw sewage."

"Agreed. But this circus sideshow is what they came for. I can't deny them outright. So I feed them Darby, whom they adore."

"Yet you refuse to speak yourself."

"Because I know a better man for the job." He pointed to Mors.

"I'd deny it," said Mors without looking back at them – of course he knew everything they were saying – "but I despise false modesty. Besides, you'd know I was lying."

While Darby made his opening remarks to the throng of eager reporters gathered about him, a decidedly non-journalistic onlooker appeared at the other side of the dais. It was Harl, grinning obsequiously at them.

"What the devil is *he* doing here?" Celia demanded.

"I'm not altogether sure," said Atal. "And I thought you didn't believe in the devil."

"I didn't, till I met *him*."

Harl appeared to listen with decided interest while Darby finished his opening remarks. Then the Deputy Captain descended to stand next to the Varthan. This pairing made Atal's blood run cold.

It was Mors's turn next to speak. After Darby had introduced him, a hush fell over the crowd. Normally, they would applaud any dignitary, but people seemed to know instinctively that the elder Phaetonian would value silent reverence more.

Mors smiled genially at his audience, adding a pleasant "Good afternoon." Then he folded his hands in front of him as though meditating, and said, "Captain Darby has already issued a statement on behalf of Captain Atal and the *Titan*. It outlines the facts in Aer'La's case. Since you're all still standing here, however, I assume you want to know more. As a scholar – and longtime partici-pant – in Confederate history, it would seem I am in a position to provide insight." He spread his hands. "What would you like to know?"

"It there still slavery in Varthan Freespace?" called out the clear-est voice.

Mors nodded. "I believe we must admit there is. In addition to the testimony of Master Aer'La, there have been several incidents on the Varthan border in which Confederate nationals have been impli-cated in abducting Confederate children for the Varthan slave mar-ket. I know that Captain Atal's crew on the *Arbiter* personally han-dled one such case. There are others."

"Then why is the Arbiters' Council denying slavery exists?" called another voice.

"I don't believe they have denied it. They've simply remained silent while the Varthan Trade Union has denied it. And that, my young friends, is the darker side of politics."

"Professor Mors, you've met the girl. Have you questioned her?"

"I've spoken with her."

"Is she a murderer?"

"She says not."

"Is she lying? I mean, come on, sir, you would know."

"I believe I would, yes. And my scans of her thoughts indicate that she believes what she is saying."

"Yes," said an impatient voice, "but isn't it also true that these creatures minds work differently than ours? And that they can make themselves believe what they want to?"

Mors frowned. Not an angry or displeased frown, but a contem-plative one. It suggested he was giving ample consideration to the question. More than it deserved, perhaps. This was the expression he often assumed when another person said something blatantly stupid or offensive. Atal knew it well. He had, more than once in his youth, said something Mors had found blatantly stupid or offensive.

"To say that one mind 'works differently' than another is to make a statement which does not contain much actual information," said Mors. "Each individual mind is unique, and thus 'works differently' from others. Some minds are more logical, some more artistic, some more literal..."

"Yes, but you know what I mean," said the reporter.

Mors shook his head sadly. "No, I really don't. Even a telepath can't know what you don't know yourself. You have a loose understanding of how your mind works, and you believe Aer'La's doesn't meet those parameters. You have no idea what those parameters are. You are relying on a feeling that she is a lesser life form than yourself, more bestial, less ethical – "

"Are you calling me a racist, professor?"

"I do not label any person. I am attempting to explain to you your own thought process. If you find it racist, then you have passed judgment on yourself." He paused and directed himself to the entire assemblage. "These... creatures... parallel humanity in every way that counts. Varthans are humanoid, if not human. Anyone can be conditioned to believe something that isn't true. Even a Phaetonian. If this is the case with Aer'La – "

"I'm afraid, sir, that it is the case."

The assembled heads turned to the source of the voice. Harl stood, looking up at Mors, his body poised in a confrontational stance.

"Captain Harl," said Mors softly. "Perhaps you'd like the opportunity to explain that statement."

"I would very much," said Harl. Not awaiting further invitation, he stepped up beside Mors on the Dais. It was a tableau of striking contrasts, the Varthan trader, resplendent in his leathers and silks, swaggering, against the old scholar, plainly garbed and unassuming in manner.

The Varthan faced his audience and bowed low.

"Oh, give me a break," muttered Celia.

"My good people," said Harl, "I am not so eloquent a speaker as your professor here. I am a simple businessman, a private detective. It should not be my place to dispute the word of so grand a gentleman as Professor Mors."

Harl bowed again, this time to Mors.

"But," he went on, "I feel I must bring the truth to light. The feral – Aer'La – is lying. I know this to be true, for I have seen the evidence with these – my own eyes – of the grisly thing she did." Here he pointed to his eyes, as thought there might exist some doubt on the part of the audience as to where the eyes were, and to whom they belonged.

As he had in Atal's office the day before, Harl produced his hologram of the alleged murder victim. At the touch of a button, her sweet, innocent face looked out at the crowd. Harl took a moment to enlarge the image and chase it upward, so that it was visible to all, floating over his head.

"I ask you to gaze for a moment at this beautiful face," Harl said sadly. "Her name was Treva Maklyn. She came to Den two days before her fourteenth birthday. She didn't live to see it. She bled to death on a street in Den's market district, her throat cut. As an additional indignity, her dying body was hurled into the path of an oncoming car.

"She came to Den with her biological mother and her mother's lover. They wanted to do some shopping before her birthday party. Wanted to buy a pretty dress for her to wear when she celebrated her first public coupling with a boy she'd promised the honor to. The dress she picked was too expensive, but it was her big day. Her mother couldn't say no to her. She was so young, and life needed to be perfect for just a little longer...

Harl stopped and dabbed at his eye with a gloved hand. "Imagine," he lamented, "imagine this fragile blossom, come to buy some trinkets to make her party special." He waved his hand over the crowd of young and beautiful inworlders. "Coulda been any of you here. Sweet, unsuspecting child. And everything woulda been all right, if only she hadn't had the misfortune to meet up with a born killer. A predator. A psychopath who preys on innocence.

"I speak of the animal that claims to be bos'n of this very ship in which we now stand. Aer'La, she calls herself." His eyes darkened, his voice lowered. His audience listened, enraptured. "Understand, my good people, that whether you or I like it or not, there are those who are dealt a bad hand in the game of life. Those who cannot rule their own instincts, cannot conquer their own fears. It's not their fault. It's fate which called the dance in which they spin uncontrolled, a dance of lust, murder and self-destruction."

"Oh my gods!" Celia whispered. "The bastard is a rhetorical genius!"

"Most con men are," observed Atal.

"The creature has misled these worthies aboard your grand ship, the *Titan*. They believe she is their friend. Like the decent folk they are, they stand by her as a comrade, little suspecting... the horror of which she is capable. I wish I could tell them it was all all right. I can't. I can only show holographs of a murdered child, her jugular vein slashed by a fragment of glass which the feral rooted out of the garbage. A coroner's report, testifying that the wound was made and began bleeding before the body was struck by the car, and that the wound in the throat was the cause of death. Genetic test results which show the feral's blood on the glass shard – put there as it cut her own hands while she cut the child's throat. That blood mixed with the innocent blood of her victim on the fatal glass.

"And I can share with you the testimony of one Captain Miles of your own Confederate Navy. Once master of the good ship *Arbiter*. His words describe the feral when she was found, stowed away in the hold of his ship, still wearing the tatters of the delicate, pink frock Treva Maklyn was to gently lift from her tender flesh to offer herself to her boy. 'Twas for the dress, and the remaining money she'd carried when she'd bought it, that the creature Aer'La killed Treva Maklyn."

Celia hung her head. "Oh sweet goddess... safeguard this poor child from the evil of this world."

Atal placed a supportive arm about the physician's shoulders. For one of the few times in his life, he wished his own path had led him to the faith Celia could muster in the existence of better beings, and of their willingness to visit justice and healing on a suffering humanity. He wished he could bring himself to believe, as she could, that such divine intervention was possible for Aer'La. He could tell that Harl's words had moved this crowd of jaded reporters to a near righteous frenzy. They wanted Aer'La brought to justice, or they wanted her dead. They wanted vengeance for the killing of one of their own. And they would visit that feeling onto the public which consumed their words and images so eagerly. That public would also lust for action against this evil.

It would be as if the very stars themselves cried out for Aer'La's blood.

Chapter Ten
Arrested

Atal and a team of his officers – Metcalfe, Cernaq, Carson and Kaya – waited on the boat deck for the arrival of Admiral Fournier's party, a grudging honor guard. Atal had left Darby and Blaurich standing watch on the command deck. He couldn't stomach their privileged, inworlder snobbery just now. Metcalfe piped the Admiral aboard. Ordinarily, this would be the bos'n's duty, but Aer'La was still confined. It had been all Atal could do to keep Harl away from her until Fournier arrived.

The official pleasantries of requesting and granting permission to board were exchanged, and then Fournier clapped Atal on the shoulder formally.

"Captain Atal, as senior ranking officer present, I am informing you that I am assuming command of this vessel. You and your officers will stand down until further notice."

Before Atal could reply, Fournier turned and called up the gangway to his ship, "Sergeant of the guard, commence lockdown!"

Two dozen Confederate Marines, encased in full, obsidian battle armor, each wielding a pulse rifle, cascaded down the gangplank two by two. The first six broke formation, one coming before Fournier and saluting, the others going to stand, one for one, before Atal and his officers. The remaining marines stood at attention.

The marine in front of Atal stiffly transferred his rifle to one hand, saluted, and then held out his hand to the Captain. "Your sidearm, sir."

Atal looked to Fournier. "What is the meaning of this?"

"Sergeant," said Fournier, "time is of the essence. We'll omit the formalities."

The Sergeant nodded to his troops, who seized the pistol grips on each of the pulse guns which hung, holstered, on the hips of each of *Titan's* officers, and extracted them. Only Metcalfe attempted to resist, shooting a hand out to grip his weapon before the marine did. Impassive, the soldier seized the midshipman's hand and wrenched it painfully backward.

Fournier stalked over. "Stand down, Mister Metcalfe, or he *will* break your arm."

Metcalfe relaxed his arm in the marine's grip. The man let it go and claimed his weapon. "Admiral Fournier, I protest your treating my officers in this manner!" Atal barked.

The Admiral moved to him, motioning the marines back into formation. "I am now commanding this vessel, Atal. This is an emergency situation. I am here to take a fugitive into custody. Because your crew has behaved downright mutinously in this matter, they have been labeled potential sympathizers with a hostile. I am therefore not bound by the ordinary restrictions.

He turned to the other officers. "The marines are authorized to use maximum force in securing the prisoner. Resistance – any resistance – will be dealt with with extreme prejudice. If any of you attempt further violence or active resistance, no questions will be asked about the force used against you." He leveled his eyes with Metcalfe's. "Nor will these soldiers hesitate to kill."

"Admiral," said Atal stiffly, "be advised, per section thirteen, article 27 of the Navy Code, that a grievance will be – "

"The Arbiters Council is expecting your grievance, Atal. In fact, I believe they've already completed their response to it. Your border patrol heroics end now, ladies and gentlemen. You are officers in the Confederate Navy, and it's high time you started behaving as such." He turned back to his entourage. "Seal all sections and place guards at every main bulkhead. No casual traffic will be allowed. Normal ship's business will be conducted only with the explicit, documented authorization of Captain Atal, who will serve as operational deputy. All personnel will be required to carry their orders with them. Any violators will be arrested and held indefinitely, pending court martial."

At the sergeant's call, dozens more marines in formation flooded the boat deck, fanning out to seize and hold *Titan*.

"You and your officers," Fournier said to Atal, "will accompany me."

* * *

Aer'La lay on her bunk, attempting to watch a holo. Doc Faulkner had told her that, above all, she must stay relaxed. Aer'La had never known how to relax. If she wasn't working, she was engaging in active recreation with a shipmate. Her fellow Arbiters had stayed with her pretty much since her confinement began, but now were required to meet Admiral Fournier's party.

Fournier was here to take her off *Titan*, and back home... back to Varthan Freespace. An ironic name, she thought, since a large number of the Varthan population who lived there were not free. Nor would she be free, but maybe for a few more hours. She was a realist. There was nothing the Captain or Mors would be able to do, no matter the faith Metcalfe and Cernaq might have in them. Nor would Cernaq's grand plan to witness for her amount to anything. The masters had the power, as they always had. Right or wrong were not at issue. Only power mattered.

She tried once again to clear her mind and focus on the holo drama she'd downloaded. At any other time, she might have enjoyed it. Now...

The hatch to her cabin opened quickly. Any welcome visitor would have knocked. Aer'La suspected this visitor would be anything but welcome. She jumped up from her bunk and poised herself for action, the bunk between herself and the entrance.

Heavy boots thudded hard against the deck as two armored marines entered, one with pulse rifle raised and seeking a target, the other holding a pair of handcuffs at the ready.

"Your name is Aer'La?" asked the woman with the rifle.

Aer'La did not answer. The woman's companion punched up an image from his palm implant. He studied it, compared it to his victim, and nodded. "That's her."

"I.D. confirmed," the female marine said into her wrist comm unit. With the rifle trained on Aer'La's heart, she and her companion advanced.

The male held out the cuffs. "We're taking you into protective custody. Do not attempt to resist."

The idiot obviously hadn't done his homework. "Do not attempt to resist" was a null phrase to Aer'La. Hooking a foot under her mattress, she sent it flying into the faces of the two marines. A human of Aer'La's size and shape wouldn't have been able to lift the mattress this way, much less throw it so far. It caught her assailants by surprise, though they managed not to be knocked off their feet by the weight which struck them.

Aer'La leapt up using the remaining bed frame as a spring board, pulled herself into a ball, somersaulted, and made a three point landing on the mattress, forcing it down and further knocking the marines off balance. She was now closer to the hatch than they. She made for it frantically.

She was aware that the female raised her pulse rifle. Then she heard the male shout, "No! Don't kill her!" just before he propelled himself through the air towards Aer'La, grabbing her ankle as he landed.

She kicked at his helmeted head, then clawed at his wrist with her upper hand. Neither attack accomplished anything. He was too well armored. If she was to gain any ground, she would have to be able to handle his entire weight, and throw him. She vaulted herself up with her lower arm, using her strength to turn while still in his grasp and land on top of him. She aimed a driving fist at his neck, where the helmet ended and the collar of his vest began, hoping to inflict enough damage to distract him.

Distract him she did, but there was still the female. She'd come up from behind while Aer'La grappled with her partner. Raising the pulse rifle over her shoulder, she brought its butt down hard on Aer'La's skull. Pulse rifles were mostly plastic and titanium in construction, and so did not have the heft of a more ancient firearm. The blow was enough to disorient Aer'La, however. Then the female marine seized her by the shoulders and hurled her bodily across the cabin. She landed on her back across her desk. There was a shattering sound, and then the sharp burst of pain as shards of crystal drove themselves into the flesh of her back. She'd landed on a crystal statue of the hunt goddess, Diana, a recent birthday gift from Celia Faulkner.

Before she could get up, the female marine was on her, pinning her legs against the desk, and yanking her upper body forward so her partner could place the cuffs around Aer'La's wrists.

The woman looked at Aer'La, her eyes cold. "You stupid little bitch. Did you really think you could get away from us?"

Aer'La spat in her face.

They led her out of the cabin and into the corridor. There a new indignity confronted her. On either side of the hatch, two lines of people stood at attention. The line on the left was headed by Admiral Fournier. Beside him, their faces set in masks of stone, were Atal, Faulkner and her fellow Arbiters, plus Blaurich and Flynn. Darby stood at the front of the line on the right, which included most of the casual crew. Seeing Aer'La bound and bloodied, Felicity Shan let out a whoop of delight. Darby called out for silence in the ranks, but not before Ceres Smith very quietly placed her boot heel on top of the younger woman's instep and shifted her weight onto it. Shan gasped, hopped gently on her non-injured foot, and allowed her eyes to warn Smith that they would take up this matter later.

Fournier called the assembly to attention. Aer'La was held upright by a marine at each arm, facing the Admiral. "The officers and crew of the *Titan* have been assembled at my order to witness the arrest of Aer'La, formerly Bos'n of this vessel. Let this serve as an example to each and every one of you of the futility of attempting to take lightly the discipline of the service, or to play fast and loose with Navy regulations."

He looked Aer'La up and down. "I can see from this outburst that we can expect trouble from the prisoner. The reports of her savagery are clearly not exaggerations. Ship's Physician?"

Flynn briskly stepped out of the line and saluted.

"You will see to it that the prisoner is taken to the infirmary, and the medications prescribed by the Varthan investigator are administered."

Celia Faulkner's eyebrows shot up. "Admiral, I protest – "

"Captain Atal, you will maintain discipline among your personal staff!" Fournier snapped, cutting her off. "Please remind non-essential personnel that their opinions are neither relevant, nor are they welcome."

"Admiral – " Atal began.

"There will be no further discussion, Captain."

Celia's face, like those of the former officers of the *Arbiter*, was a study in self-control battling with humiliation and anger. On most of the faces, self control was not faring well.

Aer'La's own self-control, what little there was of it, was exhausted. She jerked forward in the grasp of the marines, as though she might launch herself on the pompous figure of the Admiral. "You son of a bitch!" she roared at him. "It's not enough to do this to me! You have to bring my friends into it!" She pulled hard against the restraints and screamed until her throat hurt from the effort. "If I can get away from them, I swear I'll kill you!"

"Remove the prisoner," Fournier said tightly.

As they dragged her down the corridor, Aer'La called over her shoulder. "Do you hear me, Fournier? You better hope they kill me, or someday I'll rip your fucking throat out!"

Her female escort lifted her rifle and once again clouted her behind the ear with its butt. This time it had the desired effect. After an initial burst of light shone before her eyes, blackness descended, and Aer'La passed out.

* * *

On orders from Fournier, Atal left his officers and reported to the infirmary to witness the administration of the "prescribed medication" to Aer'La. The medication, of course, was the sedative cocktail Aer'La called grog. He was not ordered to bring Faulkner, and he knew Fournier would object to her presence. That was only a side benefit to her being there, in Atal's eyes. He also wanted his own medical observer present.

Atal knew that his young officers needed him, as well. They were angry, hurt, very probably considering resigning from the service. Indeed, if he thought, as most of them did, that this matter was closed, he might join them in abandoning ship. Atal knew, however, that the matter wasn't closed – not quite. Keeping close watch on what happened to Aer'La was priority one right now. Much as he wished he could counsel his proteges, they would have to wait.

Flynn had selected one of the *Titan* infirmary's many private examining rooms for the administration of the drug. Arriving there, Atal and Faulkner found a man and a woman with holo cameras waiting impatiently at the door. Their eyes lit when they saw Atal, and both bolted to intercept him.

"Captain Atal, can you confirm – "

Atal raised his hand. "Please. This is... a bad time for my crew." He looked around him. "How did you even get in here?"

"Admiral Fournier authorized it. Captain Darby selected two of us by lots to – "

Atal nodded impatiently. "I see. I take it you've been instructed to wait here?"

"Yes. But will you go on record as objecting to – "

"I will not go on record at all," said Atal. "At the moment, I don't speak for this ship. My private opinions, like the events transpiring today, are none of the public's damn business." Gesturing to Celia to follow him, he shouldered past them and entered the examining room. Aer'La lay, still groggy, on the table. Flynn fussed over a nurse as he prepared the injection. Mors, Fournier and the two marines stood to the side.

"Nicely put, Jan," said Mors, "if inaccurate. This is very much the public's business. Their money is funding these obscene proceedings."

"Professor," said Fournier, "I allowed you to be here as a courtesy. Please don't abuse the privilege."

"You're a fine one to talk of abuse, Fournier," said Celia.

"What is she doing here?" Fournier demanded.

"I believe I am allowed to bring members of my staff along when their skill sets are relevant to the business at hand," said Atal. "Or have I lost all of the privileges to which a captain is entitled?"

Fournier sighed roughly. "I don't really care, Atal. Let's just get this done."

"First things first," said Atal. "Celia, check Aer'La for injuries. When this is over, the Admiralty will answer for any damage that female orangutan has done."

"Absolutely not!" said Fournier. "Your spiritual guru has no business examining this patient!"

"How would you like to spend the rest of your days eating flies on a lily pad, Admiral Fournier?" asked Celia.

Atal suppressed a smile. "Not yet, Doctor. Georg, a prisoner undergoing treatment is entitle to third party assessment of her condition, as is a prisoner against whom physical force has been applied. You can dance around the issue all you want... but I *will* repeat my request in front of those two reporters, if you refuse it now."

"You're nothing but a jailhouse lawyer, Atal. All right, dammit. Make it quick!"

While Celia moved to look over Aer'La, Atal asked, "And what the hell are the media doing here?"

"We're going to do this above board, Atal," Fournier almost sneered. "There's been too much secrecy in the handling of this matter already, and secrecy is bad press for the Navy. The public is terrified of these ferals – "

"Because the media has been spreading lies and hysteria!" said

Celia.

"That's their job, Doctor. Our job is to calm the public's fears. Not just to make them actually safe, but to make them *feel* they are safe. By capturing this escaped feral, we've shown them that their military *can* protect them."

"And who protects them from the military?"

"Doctor, that's hardly an appropriate question," said Fournier.

"I believe it's *the* appropriate question," interjected Atal. "When you send your storm troopers to brutalize a woman who has yet to be convicted of a crime, when no warrant has been issued for her arrest – "

"The Arbiters' Council instructed that she was to be released into the custody of – "

"But there were no grounds for taking her into custody to begin with!" insisted Atal. "Only a murder charge made by a charlatan, who claims he has evidence, but has not turned it over to any – "

"I refuse to entertain this discussion!"

"Aer'La has a mild concussion," Celia announced. "In addition, there's a great deal of bruising, and several lacerations to the skin of her lower back. All courtesy of your attempts to protect the public, Admiral."

"The Varthans will treat her, I'm sure," said Fournier.

"I want to make some holos for the record."

Fournier stalked towards her. "This has gone far enough! I've allowed your examination, and you said there's nothing wrong with her. I won't – "

"I said no such thing!" Celia shot back. "I said she's been injured. Her injuries are not life threatening, and no permanent physical damage has been sustained. That doesn't mean she hasn't been assaulted. There should be a record – "

"Why?" Fournier demanded. "So she can file a lawsuit?"

Celia drew herself up and set her chin firmly. "It's possible."

"This is ridiculous!"

"Georg," said Mors quietly, "I'm afraid you have to admit that your arresting officers went overboard. And there were quite a few witnesses."

"Professor, pardon me if the situation makes me speak bluntly, but your people's pacifist beliefs don't always fit reality. Government can't always do things nicely and politely."

"Phaetonians are not exactly pacifists," Mors said mildly. "We believe that the concept of the marketplace is applicable in all arenas. Free and fair trade relies on people giving kind for kind, and that requires honesty and respect for the rights of all. Violence necessarily negates – "

"This is not a classroom, Professor," Fournier said sharply. He turned to Celia. "You may have all the holos you want, *after* this animal is sedated. And now, all further discussion is closed. Corporal, invite the reporters in."

* * *

Vixyn Tantacles was everyone's favorite human news reporter. Her publicist said so, anyway. Vixyn believed a disturbingly high percentage of what her publicist told her, just as a disturbingly high percentage of the public believed what Vixyn told them.

Vixyn was a staggering beauty in a culture of staggering beauty. She never appeared in public clothed. She order destroyed any holos or representations of herself clothed in anything other than body glitter and holo jewelry. A niche industry had grown in Confederate space, selling holos of Vixyn wearing clothes. Her lawyers attempted to stamp out such illegal trade, but were no more effective than any celebrity's lawyers had even been at stopping her fans from getting what they wanted.

Today, Vixyn's broadcast of *The Naked Truth* covered a topic that titillated viewers even more than Vixyn's own mammalian endowments did: the capture of the escaped Varthan Feral aboard the *Titan*. Appearing in living rooms, bedrooms, passenger lounges, on sidewalks, beaches, and floating overhead at sports arenas, Vixyn related the gruesome details of the latest episode...

"Naval authorities today successfully arrested Aer'La, the Varthan feral who escaped medical treatment on Den nearly three years ago. She's been masquerading as a human ever since, and had worked her way up to become bos'n of the *Titan*, the Confederacy's flagship.

"Authorities say Aer'La resisted, leading to a dangerous battle, in which arresting officers barely escaped with their lives. After the feral was subdued, she was taken to the ship's hospital, where, as you see in the companion holo to my right, she was given the medication she's so badly needed, all these years.

"Here, Dr. Romney Flynn administers the injection of what he describes as a complex of psychotropic drugs, including sedatives, antidepressants and antipsychotics. Without them, a feral's natural tendency towards homicidal rage is curbed only by her own intelligence and capacity for self control. Experts assure us that neither commodity is present to any degree in members of this species. Given her behavior today, clearly, Aer'La isn't long on self-control.

"Dr. Flynn explains that the drugs will give Aer'La a sense of well-being, something she's always lacked without them. He says that her psychological history, taken by Dr. Celia Faulkner, who apparently helped Aer'La hide her inhumanity, shows a past riddled with paranoid delusions, feelings of rejection, and nymphomaniac tendencies.

"You'll notice here that Aer'La appears to relax as the drugs take hold.

"Aer'La will now be taken to Varthan Freespace, accompanied by a Confederate representative. There, she will stand trial for the crime of murder."

"Coming up next: talking to kids about Masquerading Feral Anxiety, and an exclusive interview with *Titan* midshipman (and Quintil's heartthrob) sexy Sestus Blaurich. Sorry, boys and girls, he kept his clothes on during the interview."

* * *

The main hatch to the infirmary opened, rousing the Arbiters, who had sunken, silent and foreboding, each into his or her own thoughts. Two marines led Aer'La out. She appeared to be walking under her own power, but her eyes gazed blindly forward, registering nothing.

Cernaq stepped into their path. Both guards went rigid at first. Then, seeing the slim form which posed them no threat, halted for a moment.

"Aer'La?" said Cernaq quietly. He lifted her face with one finger. She had dropped her eyes to the ground when he'd appeared before her. Now, looking at him, her eyes attempted to focus. She blinked, trying to help them. It was clear, though, that it wasn't working. She shook her head, vacantly.

"Aer'La," he said again. "Did they hurt you?"

"I... I don't know," she mumbled. "I... I don't know you, master."

They led her on down the hall. Cernaq didn't watch them go, his own face now pointed at the deck at their feet.

"Cernaq?" asked Metcalfe. "Did you pick anything up? In her mind? Is she – ?"

Metcalfe broke off, for Cernaq had looked up at him. Neither he, Carson nor Kaya had ever seen the Phaetonian cry. Now the glistening, yellow eyes which looked at them leaked silent tears.

Yes, he had touched Aer'La's mind. And there, he'd found nothing familiar.

Chapter Eleven
Quicker than the Eye

"I want to see her," said Celia Faulkner, in a tone which brooked no argument. "In fact, I demand to see her. She's my patient, dammit!"

Georg Fournier studied her, the only sign of stress on him the slow, rhythmic tapping of two knuckles against the side of his leg. He was a cool one, all right. No doubt the result of having his conscience removed several years back, thought Atal. The century-old matron of a Wiccan coven was not an easy woman to ignore. She carried an air of wisdom, confidence and subtle malice about her. She inspired in even the bravest officer fear that, if crossed, she just might turn the object of her pique into a small, semiaquatic salamander. Currently, she was also giving the Secretary of the Navy the withering, disapproving gaze that her young shipmates referred to, simply and in tones of reverence, as "The Look."

He was only phased enough to eschew his accustomed rudeness. "I'm sorry," he said. "It's impossible. Dr. Flynn will provide medical supervision until the transfer – "

"No!" insisted Celia.

Fournier suddenly looked very tired. "Doctor... this is a difficult situation. You're only making it worse. There's nothing you can do for the girl, anyway."

They were on Atal's promenade – the Captain, Celia, Fournier and Mors. The impromptu meeting had been called at Mors's suggestion when Celia had very nearly been arrested trying to enter Aer'La's quarters.

"Tell me Georg," Mors now said, "what exactly is supposed to be happening?"

"The girl will be transferred to Captain Harl's ship."

"And why hasn't that been done? You have her drugged."

"The Judge Advocate General's office insisted on reviewing Harl's evidence prior to transfer."

"Then there's still a chance Aer'La won't be extradited to them," said Celia.

"No, Doctor, there is not," Fournier replied. "This is merely a formality which is being observed. When the evidence is confirmed – "

"What if it isn't?" Celia demanded. "What if it doesn't hold up?"

"It will," said Fournier quietly.

Celia nodded impatiently. "You've seen to that, I suppose? How much of the budget have you spent on making sure that – ?"

Fournier bolted up from his semi-seated position against Atal's desk. He towered over the small figure of the Doctor and bellowed, "That is enough!"

Celia held her ground. "Do you deny it? Do you deny that it would be politically embarrassing to the Council if the murder charge against Aer'La were dropped or disproven? Do you deny that steps might be taken to assure it won't be?"

Gritting his teeth, Fournier answered, "Even if the evidence is not sufficient for a conviction or arrest by traditional Confederate law, by Varthan law, she must still stand trial. They are members of the Confederacy, but they have their own ways. As a citizen of Varthan Freespace, Aer'La must be governed – "

"She's not a citizen, dammit, she's a slave!"

"She is a subject. The law applies. The J.A.G. is merely reviewing the case to determine if it falls under its jurisdiction. Now, Doctor, you will show proper decorum, or I will have you confined."

"Georg," said Mors, clearly trying to draw the Admiral's attention away from Celia, "don't you think the girl should be monitored? Jan's people have suggested she might be suicidal. If she kills herself, wouldn't matters become... unfortunately complicated?"

Atal suppressed a smile, despite the gravity of the subject. Mors, even after a century or more away from home, was still Phaetonian where it counted. Use self-interest to appeal to your opponent, and you'll stand a far better chance of swaying him. Never mind Aer'La's welfare, Mors knew that her death would be an inconvenience to Fournier. That would make him want to protect Aer'La, where human decency and compassion might not.

"Dr. Flynn is keeping watch."

"Dr. Flynn has many patients to worry about. There's a more efficient method of guaranteeing her safety."

"And that is?"

"A telepathic scan, of course."

Fournier looked as though he'd been expecting that answer. "And I suppose you're volunteering?"

"Actually," said Mors, "I believe young Mr. Cernaq is more suited to the task. He is... familiar with Aer'La's psyche."

"You mean he's sleeping with her. My god, are they *all* sleeping with her?"

"Is there something wrong with that?" Celia muttered.

Mors, for his part, allowed himself to look uncomfortable with the question. "I am not... conversant... in such practices. Nor would it be seemly of me to attempt to discover – "

"I don't think it's a good idea," said Fournier.

"Because you're afraid of exposing Aer'La to... rogue influences... That might suggest you're trying to hide something, Georg."

"I'm just trying to get this over with! I have an entire Navy to run!"

"And Aer'La," said Mors gently, "has a right to adequate care, and to visitors. Unless proven dangerous, the accused is allowed – "

"She is proven dangerous!"

"Not since you sedated her," Celia shot back.

"And I don't trust telepaths around a prisoner!"

Mors raised his eyebrows, but said nothing.

"That is," stumbled Fournier, "the boy has a personal relationship. It's not advisable to have him... too close."

"As a telepath, he can tap into her mind from anywhere on the ship," said Atal. "So it doesn't help you to keep him away."

"Nor does keeping him away prevent him from scanning her. So why allow him into the room with her?"

"Because physical access will make it easier for him to scan, and easier for him to take steps to prevent her from... creating complications," finished Mors.

Fournier looked defeated. "You're all so damned clever, aren't you? All right, dammit. Let him see her. But he'll have an armed escort!"

Mors smiled graciously. "Of course. If it gives you peace of mind, Georg."

"Nothing," sighed Fournier, "can give me peace of mind when

I'm dealing with this crew."

* * *

Cernaq entered the darkened cabin, calling out to the A.I. to activate some lights. Of course, Aer'La hadn't turned the lights on. She was too incoherent to care about light, and the marines had been standing watch in the corridor, till now. Now, one of the armed guards walked at Cernaq's heel, his weapon raised.

"You can put that down," Cernaq told him, checking the man's peripheral emotions to be sure that his own tone was as disdainful as others had often told him it could be. It was. "She's in no condition to fight you."

"Orders," muttered the guard.

"She's not even capable of coherent thought," Cernaq added. *Which makes you about even,* he said to himself.

"Just the same," said the guard.

The light bathing the room revealed Aer'La to be asleep on the deck. She hadn't even attempted to get into bed, and Cernaq doubted anyone had thought to help her. Putting the guard out of his mind, he went to crouch beside her. She was in a deep slumber. He brushed the hair away from her face, and called out to her telepathically.

She moaned quietly, and rolled onto her back, looking up at him, squinting against the light. "Dru?" she muttered.

A wash of guilt that he didn't quite understand passed over Cernaq. She thought he was the dead boy, Druberj. Traumatized, muddled by drugs, her mind was retreating into the past. Her training as a slave, so brutally imprinted on her psyche, was driving all her responses.

"No," he whispered. "It's Cernaq."

She looked blankly at him. "Master? I - I'm sorry, Master." She started to rise, he caught her with his hand and gently held her down.

"You need to rest. Don't be afraid."

She shook her head. "I should have been ready for you, Master. I... I didn't mean to fall asleep." She reached up and placed her hands on his chest, sitting despite his resistance. She kissed him repeatedly on the cheeks, her hands playing at the fastenings of his tunic, slipping beneath the folds of his uniform to caress the flesh beneath.

"Aer'La, no – "

"No, please, Master! Don't reject me! I can make you happy! After you've punished me – I know you have to punish me – but after. I'll make you feel so good..." Her hand strayed to his crotch, where she raked the backs of her fingernails over him.

"Aer'La – "

There was a snort of laughter from behind him. "Go ahead," said the guard. "Might as well get some while ya can, kid. Don't mind me if I watch."

"Shut up," Cernaq spat back, then, clinically deciding more invective was required, added, "you fucking asshole."

Not bothering to notice if he'd offended the guard, he turned back to Aer'La. He gently removed her hands from him and wrapped his arms around her, rocking her gently. "You don't have to do that," he whispered. In her mind, he added, *There'll be plenty of time for that when you're well.*

Her eyes, still unfocused, nonetheless tried to train themselves on him. "Y - you talked... in my head..." she said wonderingly.

He nodded. "Don't let it frighten you."

"Hey," snapped the guard, "no funny stuff."

"Making telepathic contact is what I came here for," said Cernaq. "Right now I'm just trying to calm her."

Aer'La registered the guard's presence. "Is he to have me first, Master?" she asked.

"Not if I can help it," Cernaq muttered. Then the thought occurred to him that the guards might just try something like that. He would have to maintain constant contact with Aer'La. He wouldn't allow her to be used in this condition.

Aer'La, he called out again, *try to remember. You're not a slave. We're on the Titan. My name is Cernaq.*

Quiet. And then, not words, nor any symbol that might represent complex thought, but an image... an image of Aer'La and himself...

Yes, he encouraged her. *That's right. You know me. We're friends. You've been drugged. Try to resist it. Focus on my mental presence.*

More images, of herself, of Cernaq, of Metcalfe, Carson, Kaya... of Atal and Celia...

That's very good, Aer'La. Remember...

Cernaq?

Yes, Aer'La. His own laughter, nervous and relieved, echoed through their minds. The thought-formation of his own name had never before held such meaning.

Thank you, her mind said to him. *I was... lost... in there.*

You're safe now.

No. I'm not. Help me, Cernaq, please.

Any way I can, Aer'La. You know that.

Stop my heart.

What? No!

Yes. You can do it. Please, Cernaq... kill me.

No!

I'd rather die in your arms, with someone I... I love... than go back there. Please, Cernaq.

You're not going back there. Captain Atal has a plan. I know he does.

You're lying. I can see that, in here. You're lying to me.

No! I'm sure he has a plan. I just don't know –

He'd have told you by now, if he knew a way out. They're going to come for me soon. Please let me die in peace.

Fighting the upsurge of despair that threatened to engulf him, Cernaq reigned in his feelings, as he'd been taught to do so many years ago on Phaeton. He couldn't let emotion interfere with his reasoning. Seeing Aer'La like this, touching her mind, desperate and frightened as it was, brought out so many feelings he wasn't accustomed to, in such depth as he'd never experienced. He couldn't even begin to identify...

He cleared his mind, the first step in Phaetonian discipline, to establish the dominance of Reason over all. He asserted his sense of self, the second step. He carefully tagged and identified all feelings and impulses of which he did not understand the intellectual root. He set them aside for later study.

Now, he was prepared. His reasoning mind could function, free of interference. Aer'La wanted to commit suicide. That, of course, was not a viable alternative. He had to convince her of that. Her mind was in no shape for reasonable dialogue, however. Aer'La's was a primal, emotionally reactive mind, lacking training, its sense of identity maimed by years of negative reinforcement, of exposure to the poisonous teachings that the individual is the rightful property of others. He could not quickly correct the damage. He also could not stay with Aer'La continuously. The guards would not allow it. Yet, if he were to leave her, she might find some way to accomplish herself the grim task she'd asked him to carry out. She might take her own life. He had to prevent that. Metcalfe had been right. Confronted with a mind unable to help itself in the here and now, Cernaq had no rational choice but to buy time, so that he could help her later.

Go to sleep, Aer'La, he said to her mind. At the same time, he used his interface with her nervous system to cause her heart to slow its beat, her mind to allow itself to sleep. It was not the drug-induced sleep, full of nightmare visions as it was, that he allowed to return. It was the true sleep the body craved, and which he needed Aer'La to have, while he decided what to do next.

"Hey!" a voice called out to him, intruding on the hypnotic peace of their joined minds. It was the guard. Cernaq allowed his attention to return to the physical world.

"What's the matter with you?" the man demanded. "Can't you hear your goddamn radio going off?"

Indeed, his personal radio was signaling for his attention, on the *Titan* officers' channel. He keyed the microphone. "Cernaq here."

"Mr. Cernaq," said Atal's voice, "I'm sorry to bother you. Is Aer'La... stable?"

"She's in no immediate danger, sir. I've put her to sleep."

"Good. Conference in my office. Ten minutes. I'm afraid it's bad news..."

* * *

When Cernaq arrived, his three fellow Arbiters, Celia Faulkner, and Professor Mors were already present. "Thank you for coming so quickly, Cernaq," the Captain said. "I've received word back from Headquarters... from the Judge Advocate General's office."

"Where's Admiral Fournier?" asked Metcalfe, his tone colored with irony. "He's in command, after all."

"This is not a command conference," said Atal. "This is... a private meeting. I felt that Aer'La's friends deserved to know, before the media and the crew." Atal sighed and rubbed the bridge of his nose with steepled fingers. "I have a friend at J.A.G., who's one of the principal defense attorneys. He let me know in advance that they've decided Aer'La's case falls outside their jurisdiction. She was never, legally, a member of the crew, so – "

"That's bullshit!" spat Metcalfe.

The situation was far too serious for the Captain to correct anyone's manners. He merely nodded in agreement with Metcalfe's outburst.

"There's more, isn't there?" asked Celia.

Atal nodded gravely. "With the question of jurisdiction decided, Aer'La is now to be remanded to the custody of the Varthan investigator. Captain Harl is coming to claim her within the hour."

A chorus of objections sounded, but Atal held up his hands to still them. "I'm well aware of everyone's personal feelings in this case. I trust you are all equally aware of mine. I wanted to be the one to tell you, however, that we've exhausted our legal options up to this point. Aer'La must be turned over to the Varthans. From there... You're all aware that the Council has asked Admiral Fournier to appoint an executive staff member to accompany Aer'La. I have filed an official request that I be given that appointment."

"You're leaving *Titan*?" asked Kaya. "For how long?"

"For as long as it takes. Until Aer'La's... trial... is over."

Kaya started to speak. Atal cut her off. "No volunteers. I will not be taking a staff, assuming I'm given the job." He surveyed the occupants of the room with his eyes. "I want you all to know how... how sorry I am, for what that's worth." His tone became firm. "But I also want you to know that you are still officers aboard my ship. I expect you to follow my orders. You are to take no actions that I have not authorized. Clear?"

The four midshipman nodded, as did Celia. Mors watched with a bemused expression.

"I swear to you," Atal finished, "that I haven't given up yet."

He dismissed them, and they dispersed. Cernaq walked aimlessly in the general direction of his cabin. His duty shift was over, and he needed time, to digest what was happening. He needed to decide if he'd done the right thing in sedating Aer'La so she wouldn't kill herself. So buried was he in concentration that he didn't hear Metcalfe come up behind him until the other man had taken him by the elbow.

"We need to talk."

"Not now, Terry. I... am in no condition..."

"Cernaq," Metcalfe said urgently, taking his friend's hand and pressing it into his own, "you have to listen. We have work to do."

At the firm touch, Metcalfe's thoughts tickled the edge of Cernaq's mind, inviting him to explore further. He did, and he was ready to listen.

* * *

"I thought you were done here," the guard complained as he accompanied Cernaq back into Aer'La's cabin.

"As you so delicately pointed out," said Cernaq, "I was interrupted by a signal from my Captain. I was forced to put my work on hold."

"Yeah," the guard observed. "You put her on hold, all right. She ain't moved since you left."

"Indeed not," agreed Cernaq. "I can be very persuasive. It takes only the gentlest suggestion, sometimes, to push a mind in the desired direction."

"Just make sure you don't go pushing my mind."

Cernaq smiled. "I'd have to find it first."

The guard missed the insult. "You mean you can't work that stuff on me? Like, I'm immune?"

"Utterly," said Cernaq with a straight face.

This pleased the idiot. He shook a meaty finger at Cernaq. "See, you people aren't as smart as you think you are."

"I can only imagine. Now, if you'll be quiet, I'll complete my scan and report back to the Captain."

"Better hurry. She's bein' transferred as soon as the Varthans get here."

Cernaq grunted understanding and set to work. He had no time to be subtle. A psychic jab roused Aer'La. Despite the affects of the drug, she awoke and sat up, recognition on her face. "Cernaq?" she muttered.

Don't talk, he said in her mind. *It makes it harder to maintain the illusion.*

Huh?

Never mind. Just come with me, and be very quiet.

She accepted his hand and got up.

Stay beside me. Don't react to anyone, or to anything I say out loud.

She did as she was told.

Cernaq walked toward the guard. "That will be sufficient."

"You're done?" he asked. "That was quick."

"I just needed a final scan to complete my report."

He moved past the guard, Aer'La following him, looking quizzically as she did. The guard, rather than watching them, was staring thoughtfully at the spot where she had lain before.

"How long she gonna sleep?" he asked.

"Oh, some hours," said Cernaq. In the man's mind, he could see the unimaginative carnal fantasies forming, what he could do to amuse himself with the sleeping woman, before the Varthans arrived. Cernaq could see just as clearly the image in the guard's mind of Aer'La, still asleep, still lying on the floor. It was, in fact, a subtle push from Cernaq which inflamed the guard's desire for her, allowing the illusion to work more effectively. He was seeing what he wanted to see. It made it easy to obscure the message his eyes were sending to his mind – the picture of Aer'La, conscious, about to leave the room with Cernaq.

"You coming?" Cernaq asked him.

"Uh," said the guard, "you go ahead. I wanna... keep an eye on her, for a minute."

"As you wish," said Cernaq. Boldly, he took Aer'La's hand and led her into the corridor.

He didn't see me? Aer'La wondered.

In fact, he did. But I kept the information from registering. When he is told what happened, he will, no doubt, remember seeing you.

Where are we going? What are you doing?

I believe Metcalfe said something about a 'laundry truck.'

He led Aer'La down the corridor, his telepathic sense probing ahead, to be ready to work his power of suggestion on any passersby.

Neither of them noticed the telltale red signal which flashed at the opposite end of the corridor, nor the floating security camera to which it was attached. Security cameras were not standard aboard *Titan*, and they had no idea one had been installed here. Of course, they had no idea it had recorded their exit from the room, for a holo camera's optics could not be bypassed by Phaetonian telepathy.

* * *

"Okay," said Metcalfe, "we've done it. Now what?"

They were in Metcalfe's cabin. Aer'La, still seeing through a haze of grog, had been hidden away for safe keeping. Afterwards, Metcalfe and Cernaq had gathered their allies and told them what they'd done.

"We need to get her off the ship," said Kaya.

"Obviously," agreed Carson. "But how? There are storm troopers on every exit, and reporters behind the storm troopers."

"And where," wondered Cernaq, "do we take her, even if we can get past them?"

"I think I can help there," said Celia Faulkner. Inviting her had been Kaya's idea. Metcalfe and Carson had been skeptical about taking the plot beyond their inner circle. Kaya had put her foot down, however. They needed someone with contacts, the kind of contacts that took the better part of a lifetime to cultivate. Since her father, for obvious reasons, couldn't be asked to help with their mutinous scheme, that left Celia. Aside from the utter soundness of the argument, the two Terrans found it hard to disagree when Kaya put her foot down.

"I believe my family will take in Aer'La," Celia went on. "I've discussed it with my senior husband, and he's going to bring it before the family."

"Hecate is still a member world. Won't there be... repercussions?" asked Cernaq.

"Possibly," agreed Celia. "But imagine, Mr. Cernaq, what would happen if a company like, say, Douglas Holdings were to find itself at odds with the Council."

"A deadlock," said Cernaq. "Military force would likely not be used, because of the political and economic power D.H. commands."

"Precisely," she said. "And my world also commands a great deal of economic power. We're a major food supplier, one of the breadbasket worlds of the Confederacy."

"Would your whole world come to bat, if your family decided to take Aer'La?" asked Carson.

"My eldest husband commands great respect among our people. Hecate is a tightly knit colony. If Kelby advocates taking a stand, they'll take it."

"You brought up another point, Doctor," said Metcalfe. "Douglas Holdings has the kind of power that Aer'La needs. What if we got them on our side?"

"Douglas Holdings has become a very large bureaucracy over the past few decades. Getting it to take notice of your problem requires a great deal of creativity and no small amount of time. While they have their charitable operations arm, and," she looked over the assembled Arbiters and smiled proudly, "we have a great deal of creativity at our disposal... we do not have time on our side."

"All right," said Metcalfe. "Hecate it is. Now, how do we – ?"

The door to Metcalfe's cabin opened suddenly. Atal stepped in, followed closely by Darby and Five. The Captain's expression was unreadable. Darby was angry, almost purple with agitation. Five... Five was trying not to smile.

They knew.

"Well, this is a pretty lot," said Darby, surveying the room. "I can't say I'm surprised, but I must say – "

"Not now, Mr. Darby," said Atal. He looked at Metcalfe, no one else.

"I was hoping we'd be done with this before you found out," Metcalfe asked quietly.

"Then this was your idea," asked Atal, "as I expected?"

"It was *our* idea, dammit," protested Kaya. "We all – "

"Shut up, Kaya," said Metcalfe. He held Atal's gaze. "I formulated the plan. They didn't know anything about it, until Cernaq and I brought Aer'La here."

"That won't prevent any of your standing before a court martial," said Darby.

"Quiet!" Atal barked. Then, forced to agree, he said, "You will all answer for your parts in this, but I've no doubt who the ringleader was. Mr. Metcalfe, you'll come with me for questioning. The rest of you are confined to quarters until further notice."

"What about the feral?" demanded Five. "Where are they hiding her?"

"No one knows that but me," said Metcalfe. "And I won't be telling."

"We should commence a search," said Five.

"All in good time, Mr. Blaurich. First..."

Five, his face awash in eagerness asked, "Shall I take Metcalfe into custody, sir?"

Atal looked darkly at his executive officer. "He'll answer some questions first. After that, barring any surprises... You've left me few options, Mr. Metcalfe."

* * *

Georg Fournier was waiting for them on the promenade. He

looked disheveled, something that didn't seem possible, given his public image. His face was alive with agitation when Atal brought Metcalfe in.

"What the hell is going on here, Atal?" he demanded. "I'm hearing rumors that the prisoner has escaped!" His eyes locked on Metcalfe, and his expression became sickly. He swallowed hard, shaking his head in disbelief. "Oh, no... don't tell me..."

"Mr. Metcalfe arranged for Midshipman Cernaq to remove Aer'La from custody," Atal said matter-of-factly.

The Captain keyed his data implant. A hologram fizzled to life over his desk. It showed a view of the corridor outside Aer'La's cabin, showed Cernaq calmly exiting, Aer'La at his side... showed the guard, just standing there.

"What the hell?" Fournier demanded.

"That was caught by the security cameras you ordered me to install," said Atal.

"And a damned good thing I did! And you thought – oh never mind! How did they do that?"

Atal looked to Metcalfe. "The Admiral asked a question, Mister."

"Cernaq used his ability to impede the function of optic nerve transmissions to the guard's brain. He made the guard believe that a latent image of Aer'La, still in the cabin, was what he was seeing, while he suppressed – "

"I knew Phaetonians in the service would come to no good!" Fournier snarled.

"He was following my orders, sir," said Metcalfe.

"You have no authority to give orders to another midshipman!"

"I... I have some influence, sir, I..."

"Are you saying you threatened him?"

Metcalfe swallowed. "I refuse to answer that question on the grounds that the answer might serve to incriminate me," he said stiffly.

"Just as I thought. It will do you no good. There'll be evidence enough, I'm sure... For now..." He stepped close to Metcalfe. "Where is she?"

Metcalfe was silent.

"Don't toy with me, Midshipman!" Fournier growled. "I know you know where she is."

"Yes, sir, I do."

"Then you will take me to her, right now."

"No sir, I won't."

"Mr. Metcalfe," Fournier said in a low, dangerous tone, "you have already ended your career in the Navy. If you remain uncooperative, I will see to it that you spend your life in prison as well."

"I can't cooperate, Admiral. What you're ordering me to do is wrong, and I won't be party to it. Aer'La is a free citizen – "

"Quiet!" snapped Fournier. "Mister, you may believe that you are a freedom fighter on a holy crusade, but I'm afraid you are misguided. And your error in judgment is going to be very costly to you. The girl is not a free citizen, she is a fugitive from justice. She is being sought on charges of murder, charges which her state can support with overwhelming evidence, I might add. You, by harboring her, are not only interfering with an officer of Varthan law in the performance of his duties, you are making yourself an accomplice after the fact in murder – the murder of a Confederate citizen."

"Yes sir," Metcalfe said quietly. He was rarely quiet. Clearly, Fournier hated it when he was. It upset his status quo.

"Dammit, man, you can – and will! – be court martialled! You could also be extradited to the Varthan government, and made to stand trial there. Do you realize you're taking your life in your hands?"

"Do you realize you're taking Aer'La's?" Metcalfe demanded, unable to maintain the pretense of calm any longer.

Fournier shook his head. "Atal, your officer is disobeying a direct order."

The Captain looked squarely at Metcalfe. "You have received your orders."

"Yes sir."

"Well?" Atal asked quietly. "What are you going to do?"

"I can only do what I know to be right, sir."

"Despite the consequences?"

"Yes sir."

The Captain looked back to Fournier. "I have given him his orders, Admiral. There's little else I can do."

Fournier looked away. "Lock him up. And get me the Phaetonian boy."

"Cernaq doesn't know where she is, Admiral. I'm the only one. I wouldn't let him share the blame."

"He's a telepath! Of course he knows!"

"No, Admiral," said Atal. "Not if he deliberately refuses to seek out the information. And I'm confident he would, in this case."

"Fine," said Fournier. "Then we'll have one of the other Phaetonians pull it out of Metcalfe's mind."

Atal shook his head. "That's against their code of ethics. They won't do it."

"Code of ethics!" Fournier spat. "High-handed morality! Doesn't anybody give a damn about the security of the Confederacy? You can't eat your ethics, Atal! And they won't protect you against the Qraitians!" He regained his composure. "Begin a search for the girl. And I still want to question the others."

"I take full responsibility for their actions, Admiral," said Metcalfe. "I will accept the penalty."

"Oh yes," agreed Fournier. "You will."

He went to the door, opened it, and motioned into the hallway for someone to enter. Darby strode in, accompanied by Sestus Blaurich. Clearly, judging by the self-satisfied expressions on both their faces, they'd been allowed to listen in on Fournier's questioning of Metcalfe.

"Mr. Blaurich," said Fournier, "Mr. Metcalfe is to be placed under arrest, pending court martial. The charge is mutiny. You will escort him to the brig."

Five smiled triumphantly and snapped off a brisk, "Yes, sir!" He came over and clapped a hand on Metcalfe's shoulder. "Please," he whispered, "try to fight me."

"I'll come quietly," said Metcalfe in his iciest tone. He could tell that Five was disappointed.

"Mr. Darby," Fournier went on, "Midshipman Cernaq is to be kept confined in his quarters. A hearing will determine if he, too will stand trial. You may release the others, but inform them they will be questioned, and a disciplinary review conducted against them all."

Darby nodded and began to leave. Mors entered, looking, for once, to be in a hurry.

"Jan, what's happening?" he asked.

"An arrest is happening, Professor," Fournier said before Atal could respond. "And I'm afraid I must ask you not to interfere. I'd hate to have to remind you that you have no authority in this matter. You are not a commissioned officer, no matter your status at the Academy."

"Who's being arrested?" Mors demanded.

"Mr. Metcalfe," Fournier said tightly. "He has released the prisoner, and sequestered her in a location he refuses to divulge."

Mors nodded understanding and looked calmly at Metcalfe. "You realize the consequences for your actions could be grave, Mr. Metcalfe."

"I do, sir. The consequences for correcting authority when it's wrong usually are."

"So they are," agreed Mors. "Of course, I'll do all I can to assist in your defense."

"What you will do, Professor," said Fournier, "is use your telepathic abilities to help us find the fugitive. Failure to surrender her to the Varthan officers could create an embarrassing incident. Your intervention can prevent that."

Mors shook his head with a small frown. "No. I'm afraid I can't do that."

"What?" Fournier demanded. "You're obstructing justice! I don't care what your standing is with the Council, I'll have you charged – "

"As you yourself pointed out, Georg, I have no military capacity. I am a private citizen. I am under no obligation to obey military authority, nor to assist in a military effort, unless I so choose." He smiled, "And, even if you manage to instate emergency conscription, I think you'll find I'm far too old to be drafted."

"But," Fournier sputtered. "You're allowing a disaster to occur!"

"Possibly I am. The choice, it seems, is between an embarrassing interstellar incident, and an injustice against sentient rights. In this case, I applaud Mr. Metcalfe's moral stand, agree totally with his actions, and will not lift a finger to impede his progress."

"Professor," said Atal, "I'm afraid you're fighting a losing battle."

Mors smiled. "It's the kind I enjoy fighting best, Jan." His face darkened. "Though I must say it saddens me that my elder student doesn't seem to possess the courage of his protege. I thought I'd taught you better than that, old friend."

Metcalfe's Prayer Journal...

What's that old saying? "It never rains but it pours?"

And your kind used to be believed to control the weather, so I think it's appropriate here. First I discover that the most beautiful woman I've ever met is a flaming bigot. Then, I'm tossed in the brig, and before I even have a chance to lick my wounds, you send Carson after me. I wasn't up for round three-million-sixty-two in our on-going fight, but he pulled me right on into it.

You know I didn't mean the things I said about him. You know I'm sorry. Now, could I be so presumptuous as to ask the strength to tell him? And does he feel this guilty when he's raked my ass over the coals?

No? Of course not. Why did I ask?

He's right, of course. I am holding out information, and it isn't fair to him, or to any of my friends. I loathe secrecy. Why can't I tell them the truth? Carson and Kaya? They care as much as I do. They want to help as much as I do. Shouldn't they know, if only to spare them the pain they've felt? And the even greater pain that's coming?

When all is said and done, they're going to hate my guts, aren't they?

Carson always thought I considered myself better than everyone else. Okay... that's actually fair. I do consider myself better than most. If that's a sin, I don't know what to do about it. I can only judge by observation, and what I observe in the rest of the race – all branches of it – is a lot of arrogance (the unfounded kind – I know I'm arrogant), a lot of stupidity, a lot of incompetence...

But I don't think I'm better than him... do I?

"Listen, Universe," he'd howled, when I told him that the Captain's plans were 'need-to-know,' "Terence Metcalfe is superior! He's a better kind of human being!"

Do I really believe that? Do I really come off that way?

He said all I cared about was my rank and my career. That people mean nothing to me. That it would be my fault if anything happened to Aer'La. Then he got really pissed and started shoving me.

I wanted to slug him, but I knew he was right. If I were him, I'd say the same things. All this business of keeping secrets – what does it get us?

If I'm right, Aer'La's life.

If I'm wrong...

Either way, they'll hate my guts.

Just like I guess Pallas already does. Did from the moment she saw me. Just like I... wish I could hate her. She's a bigot. She hates me for where I'm from, not what I am. She's the lowest form of human life.

So why does it hurt so much that she's angry at me?

Chapter Twelve
Inner Voices

Cernaq? You seem... distressed.

I'm confined to my quarters, Pallas, for helping Aer'La escape custody.

What? Cernaq, have you considered the consequences of such an act? You could be charged as an accessory to murder.

So I could. But Aer'La cannot be returned to slavery.

Where are you, anyway?

I'm on the Varthan ship. Captain Harl invited me for a tour.

I can't say I approve –

Don't abandon your objectivity, Cernaq. I've learned quite a bit by coming here.

Is that why you went? To learn?

That's why I do everything I do. How much do you know about the Varthans?

I only know Aer'La. I don't believe she's typical.

I won't speak to that belief. They're almost our polar opposites. Passion-driven. Uneducated. Their self-interest is highly developed, at least among the ruling classes. It's perverted, though. They strive for their own wealth and physical comfort, but have no regard for their principles. They would happily commit an immoral act for financial gain. They would, similarly, sacrifice their own dignity.

Cultures built on slavery are always disgustingly opportunistic.

It's hard for me to be here. They're so... low. All of them. It's almost like they're not completely sentient. I wonder if it's genetic?

I don't believe so. Aer'La is completely sentient.

You must see qualities in her that I don't. I find her fairly well-suited to this environment. She has her people's tendency to use force to achieve her desired ends, without regard for the rights of others.

She was raised in that environment. She is becoming more enlightened.

Your emotions may be clouding your judgment. Does that always happen, when one has had sex with another person?

I don't believe my judgment is clouded. As to the rest, perhaps you should have sex and find out.

I intend to. It's on my list.

Be careful, Pallas. Terry Metcalfe is not someone to be used as a research project. He's not someone to be used at all. If he is intimate with you, he will form an emotional attachment –

I have no intention of causing him distress. Besides, I don't believe I'll be having sex with him. He's extremely upset by my association with Captain Harl.

It is... a disturbing development. You realize that his intentions –

Oh, don't worry! Harl tried to get me in his cabin as soon as we got here. I gave him a gentle push to want to show me the ship instead. I may be a virgin, but I'm not hopelessly naive. I certainly wouldn't want to experiment sexually with him.

I'm glad. And I'm sorry that you've alienated Terry.

So am I. It was necessary, though.

Meaning?

You really should study my memories of this ship and its crew, Cernaq. There is no military discipline, nor any understanding of the importance of one's assigned work. There are no shared goals, no mutually beneficial outcome for which they all strive. The strong rule the weak, and fear is ruthlessly maintained.

Harl nearly killed a man not long after we came aboard. He beat him almost to death with a chain. Apparently, the victim had forgotten to complete maintenance tasks Harl had assigned. I don't believe he'd actually understood Harl's instructions. The error was correctable; the man could have learned from his mistake... I suggested this to Harl. He didn't understand me.

I attempted to apply first aid to the man. He was a bloody pulp. Harl stopped me. He said their own medics would keep him alive, and, later, Harl himself would decide if the man should live, or be finally beaten to death.

There is still blood on my hands. They have no personal cleaning facilities for the crew. I would have to go to Harl's cabin to wash.

You need to get out of there. It's not safe.

Harl has an overwhelming desire to protect me. He understands that, if I am his ally, he stands to gain much. I am perfectly safe, as long as I remain with him and continue to cool his sexual ardor with my mental skills. If he stays in command –

Is he likely to lose command?

At any moment. His hold over his crew is tenuous. If he were to reveal a moment's weakness – if an opponent were to best him physically – I've no doubt he would be brutally and immediately slaughtered.

And his killer would assume command?

Undoubtedly.

I was also able to observe a number of Inihu under Harl's care.

Ironic that he says he's not a slaver – with slaves on his ship.

He says they are not slaves.

'Custodial wards,' or some such nonsense?

Are you sure it's nonsense, Cernaq?

What do you mean?

The animals – ferals – I saw... I know they were drugged, but... when I tried to touch their minds, it was like... touching an animal. No coherent thought. Primal emotion... chaotic. And, physically... some of them soiled themselves and didn't realize it... several masturbated the entire time I observed them... When the crew would come to... use them... some didn't even notice. Some seemed to enjoy the experience only if pain was inflicted on them... One woman's arm was broken during the sex act. A compound fracture, with bone protruding... she didn't acknowledge it.

As you say, they were drugged.

But Aer'La's mind, when not drugged, is similarly chaotic.

It is not as well-ordered as a Phaetonian mind, I grant you.

Nor a Terran, even. Metcalfe's mind –

Metcalfe's mind is unusual among his people. Even among Inworlders. He is more devoted to rational thought than the average individual.

Still, you see the difference. Aer'La is a creature of passions. In that way, she is characteristic of her race.

And... you would see her... enslaved? Like those women you saw?

...

Pallas?

Not all people – all sentients – have equal faculties. The idea that we are all basically intelligent, moral, capable of deciding what's best for our own welfare – just a legal fiction. Pretty words in our founding documents, meant to make everyone feel secure and entitled. Meant to artificially elevate those with lesser gifts to the status of those with greater gifts, so that envy doesn't bring about revolution and social collapse.

It's true legal equality is more of a guiding principle than a reality...

But is it even a valid guiding principle? Are there not some people who need to have their decisions made for them, their actions curbed, their freedoms inhibited, lest they harm others through their own moral or intellectual incompetence?

There are individuals of whom that's true –

And what if there were an entire species of whom it was true?

You're espousing racism, Pallas.

'Racism' is only a word. Like all words, it means nothing out of context. If one species is, in fact, inferior in every way to another, is it so wrong to simply admit that fact?

It's... dangerous. Aer'La's case is a prime example. Those who don't know her assume she's dangerous and unstable, because she's an Inihu. They haven't taken time to collect the facts about her as an individual.

And you have, but don't you understand...? She's not dangerous to you, because you've befriended her. Many people in the Inner Worlds and on Terra keep pets – animals who would be dangerous in the wild, but have been tamed.

I don't see –

Those animals would not likely harm the humans to which they have bonded, because they recognize those humans as the alpha member of their own pack. They might, however, harm other humans. There is legal precedent –

– Cernaq!

What?

You are... angry.

I suppose I am.

At me?

Yes, Pallas.

Why? Is it...? You believe you are in love with Aer'La.

I don't know what that term means, precisely. I know that Aer'La is extremely important to me. Her welfare is as important to me as my own.

Perhaps more. Your comparison of her to a domesticated beast angers me. If that is love –

Love is the recognition of one's own moral ideals realized in another.

Perhaps that's a pretty fiction, Pallas.

You are not the Phaetonian you once were, Cernaq.

No. I'm not.

Cernaq... what if Aer'La *is* a murderer?

I do not believe it. I have seen the truth in her mind.

Harl says the ferals have such strong emotions, such a capacity for self-delusion, that they might even fool a telepath. She might have made you see lies as truth.

Pallas, although you see that I've changed, I am still a Phaetonian. My rational capacity is my very identity. If I stop trusting my own judgment, I may as well stop living. I believe Aer'La is innocent. I believe her people are unfairly enslaved. All of my actions will proceed from that premise.

Then I hope you are correct, Cernaq. Harl has learned what you and Metcalfe have done. He's on his way to see Atal and Fournier now. Whether you're right or wrong, I'm afraid things are going to go very badly for you and your friends.

* * *

"Show Captain Harl in. We're ready for him."

The order was given by Fournier to Sestus Blaurich. With the arrests of both the Bos'n and the executive officer, the Prince of Quintil Industry had been assigned by Darby to head security for the duration of the shake-up.

The Varthan captain shoved his way past Blaurich and stormed inside. He may have been drunk. His body language bespoke a lack of control. Maybe he was just that mad.

"I've waited long enough, Admiral! Where is my prisoner?"

"*Captain* Harl – " Atal began.

Fournier held up a hand, silencing him. It was damned rude, on Atal's own ship, but that was Fournier's style, to take liberties. "Captain Harl, I apologize for the delay. It seems that..." He glared sidelong at Atal. "... Errors have been made. I am now in full control of the situation, and promise you that I shall correct – "

"Where's my prisoner?"

"Well, as I was explaining – "

"Where is the bitch?"

Fournier actually looked taken aback by Harl's outburst. Atal found it refreshing to see. The Admiral maintained his diplomatic calm, however. "She has – temporarily! – broken custody."

"That's what I'd heard. Thought it was a joke. You've *lost* her!"

"That is essentially the case. You see – "

"You genetically degenerated *fuck!*"

Fournier went crimson. His jaw clenched. His fists clenched. For a moment, he seemed to be debating between unleashing one of his celebrated fits of intimidation, or just decking the bastard. Then he regained himself.

"Captain Harl," his tone was shriveling. "I fully respect your authority in this matter, and intend to lend you every possible cooperation; but I must insist you remember that I am Admiral of Confederate Navy, and entitled to a certain level of respect."

"You've lost my prisoner."

"As I said, mistakes were made."

"Who made mistakes, Admiral?"

"That... is unimportant now. What is important is that we correct the mistakes. We're going to. The girl cannot have left the ship, and I am organizing search parties – "

"Not good enough."

"I beg your pardon?"

"Admiral, your people lost the girl. Why should I trust them to find her?"

"What are you suggesting?"

"I want ship's schematics. I'll conduct the search with my own people."

Unnoticed, Atal shook his head in wonder at the nerve of the man. Surely not even Fournier wasn't stupid enough to fall for that. Give classified information on ship's design to the Varthans? He couldn't possibly –

"Done," said Fournier.

"What?" Atal demanded.

Fournier glared at him, speaking as if this glaring tactical error were the obvious next step to take. "Give Captain Harl ship's schematics, and order your security teams to assist him and his people in searching the *Titan*."

"Sir..." Atal stammered, suppressing several of the choicest Terran profanities Metcalfe had taught him. "Ship's schematics are not for general release – "

"Not for release to the enemy, no. Are you suggesting that our Varthan allies are not to be trusted, Atal?"

Atal knew better than to answer. He just looked at Harl and said tightly. "I consider it unwise to release ship's schematics, sir."

"Your objection is noted. Give him the schematics. I want the prisoner found. I still have at least one of your officers to court martial, Atal, and I don't have all year to spend correcting your mistakes."

* * *

"Am I... disturbing you?"

Metcalfe looked up. On the other side of the transparency which formed the front wall of his cell, her voice carried to him over an intercom, Pallas stood, observing him.

"You would know, wouldn't you?" he asked, not looking up. He lay casually on one of four bunks in the cell.

"Why does that bother you? You've worked with telepaths for years. I suppose it's just me you object to?"

He hesitated. He really didn't know how he'd felt about her. Since coming to the cell, there'd been plenty of time to think; but all of his thoughts had been about Aer'La.

"I couldn't say." After a moment, he asked, "Why did you come here, anyway?"

"I heard what happened. I was... sorry."

"Why? I'm in a cage, like the rest of the animals. Like Aer'La, whom you clearly hold in such contempt."

"You're very bitter. I suppose you feel betrayed, that I haven't simply dismissed Captain Harl, the way you have. I believe you'd call it 'fraternizing with the enemy?'"

"Something like that."

"Has it occurred to you that I might simply be seeking further information?"

"It's occurred to me that you were being awfully chummy with a slaver."

"I could hardly gather information from him by being belligerent. If you'd put your baser emotions aside, long enough to – "

"'Baser emotions?' You know, Doctor, I don't know if it's Aer'La you hold in contempt... or all of us."

Pallas was silent for a moment. She actually looked hurt. The mildest pang of regret tapped at Metcalfe's conscience. He *was* speaking in extreme anger. When he did that, he often treated people as if they were invulnerable. He also had a habit of assuming Phaetonians were invulnerable. He knew it wasn't true. Perhaps he should back off.

"So," Pallas said icily, "You approve of Aer'La's crimes?"

Maybe not.

"You mean, do I approve of escaping slavery? Hell yeah, I approve. My kind have this historical aversion to captivity. We've lived through a lot of it these past few centuries."

"Terra was liberated decades ago."

"Terra was reclaimed decades ago, *Doctor*, by your people, not by mine. If you believe we're a free world, I've some prime real estate on Hestia's dark side you might be interested in."

"I wasn't impugning Terrans when you were eavesdropping on my conversation with Captain Harl," she said, and tried to keep an even tone. "I merely – "

"You impugn all humanity by even implying that a slaver's opinion is worth considering. I can't believe you'd suck up to a... a – !"

"Has it occurred to you that this... woman you're protecting might actually be guilty of murder?"

"It has not."

"Why? How long have you known her? How can you be so sure?"

"Because I *do* know her. She's vicious and hot-tempered, but she's not a murderer. She'd kill in a second to protect one of her own – and by her own I mean her shipmates. She's been at my back in more than one fight, and I know I can trust her. And she knows she can trust me, no matter what the evidence says."

He stood, crossing to face her through the transparency. In retrospect, he would realize that his anger over Aer'La's fate drove him harder than he should have let it. That didn't stop him, at that moment, from saying, "If you can't see that Aer'La is what she is, and that Harl is a chronic liar and a manipulator, then maybe Phaetonians don't have the enhanced brain power everyone says they do, or maybe someone slipped up on your gene chart, Doctor. Even so, I can't believe Professor Mors hasn't taught you to think any better than you are right now."

Pallas drew herself up. "He taught me to think for myself. Just because I disagree with you, does that say to you that I'm not thinking? Are all Terrans such incredible egotists, to believe that conscious thought is defined as that which most closely resembles what's happening in their own minds?"

"Bigotry is not part of real thought, and what you were spouting to Harl was nothing but bigotry. It really *gets* to you, doesn't it, the idea that some of us 'creatures' engage in sex – even *enjoy* it! That's so far from your experience, your narrow, Phaetonian way of viewing the universe, that you just can't stand it, can you? Well, I'm sorry that the rest of humanity isn't the collection of high-minded eunuchs your people are, but does that entitle you to advocate selling us into slavery?"

For just a moment, he thought her control might lapse, her face begin to color. "I think perhaps sex is the issue here, Midshipman. I think your inability to control your own sexual needs causes you to be unable to think clearly about Aer'La. I think her pheromones have taken hold of your glands to the point that your brain is no longer part of the equation."

"And maybe," he shot back, "you're jealous that no one looks at you the way they do Aer'La?"

"And maybe you're nothing but a degenerate sensualist, like all of – " She broke off, took a long breath. "Mister Metcalfe, I don't believe this conversation is productive any longer."

"I don't understand why you came here in the first place," he said.

She shook her head. "No. Neither do I."

She walked away without another word. He stood there, not knowing what to do next, in silence. He didn't know how long it was before Kaya came along. She studied his face closely, and grinned a pixieish grin.

"You all right?"

He shrugged.

"Want to tell me about it?"

"No."

"Pallas was just here."

"I know."

"She looked mad."

"I know."

"Your technique must be improving."

"Leave me alone," he said, and started to turn away.

She pulled up a chair to the transparent wall and settled down, leaning against it. She grinned again. "Never."

* * *

Carson and Celia Faulkner had, independently, decided to visit Cernaq in his own, less uncomfortable confinement. The Doctor was now reclining in his desk chair, a cup of tea perched atop her hands, which were folded over her chest. Carson sprawled on the floor across from her.

"Damned shame we couldn't have moved fast enough to get the child to Hecate," Celia observed.

"Then we all would have been up on charges, Doc," said Carson.

"I'm not sure we all won't be anyway, when Fournier is finished here," said Cernaq. "Though, granted, imprisoning Metcalfe removes a sizeable thorn from the Admiral's side."

"Shouldn't we be checking on Aer'La?" Faulkner wondered. "Since Metcalfe is confined, he can't go to her – "

"He has indicated that he will divulge her location, should the need arise," Cernaq replied. "In addition, I am in constant contact with Aer'La as we speak. She is in no physical danger."

"Then you already know where she is?" asked Carson.

"I am carefully avoiding that bit of information. Our contact is limited to my providing updates, and reassurance. She knows that Metcalfe has been arrested. I have been trying to calm her feelings of – "

The hatch opened suddenly. Sestus Blaurich stood in the opening, looking expectant and accusing.

"Hello, Five," said Carson.

"Haven't you heard of knocking, Mr. Blaurich?" asked Celia.

Five smirked. "Courtesy is not strictly required in an emergency situation, nor when dealing with a prisoner."

She bristled. "Courtesy is always required, young man."

Five ignored her. "I've been placed in charge of security by Captain Darby. Until the prisoner is secured – "

"You haven't secured her?" Carson interrupted. "Now, here I thought you were omnipotent, Five. Couldn't Mummy's money buy enough bloodhounds?"

"Quiet!" snapped Blaurich. "This assembly is improper. Until we have established the whereabouts of the fugitive Varthan, I cannot allow any opportunities for conspiracy to foment."

Faulkner stood and approached him. "This has gone far enough, you little miscreant. I'm going to see the Captain – "

He blocked her path. "No, Doctor. You'll have to wait until I can escort you. First, I'm going to – "

He broke off as Cernaq bolted up off his bunk, his face ashen.

"Gods, Cernaq, what's wrong?" demanded Celia, moving to him.

"Aer'La," he muttered distractedly. "I can't..."

"What kind of game is this?" spat Five. "Cernaq, sit back – "

"Shut up!" hissed Carson, who had also gone to Cernaq's side. "What about Aer'La?"

"I've lost contact with her... Can't feel her conscious mind... There was a surge of pain... and then..."

"What does that mean?" wondered Celia.

Instead of answering, Cernaq leaped toward the open hatch and the corridor beyond. Five jumped to block him.

"Oh no! You're staying right here!"

"You don't understand," Cernaq said weakly. "She's – "

"I understand that you're confined to quarters, Mister! Now get back, or I'll be forced to restrain you."

Sestus Blaurich was noted for his athletic prowess. Against as small and waif-like an opponent as Cernaq, anyone would have expected him to easily triumph in a fight. He was supremely confident that he could incapacitate the Phaetonian with one blow.

It came as a great surprise to him when Cernaq decked him. He rebounded off the corridor bulkhead opposite the entrance to Cernaq's cabin, and lay, his breath knocked out, his pride wounded, watching his unlikely attacker disappear around the curve of the ship's hull.

* * *

Aer'La was secreted away in a storage locker in one of the ship's holds. Cernaq had indelicately snatched the information from Metcalfe's mind the second he'd lost contact with her. He had run as fast as he could, his energies focused on re-establishing contact with Aer'La's mind. Only to cloud the minds of onlookers, to slow any pursuit, did he allow himself to be distracted. He could not render himself invisible to a crowd, the way he had befuddled the guard in

Aer'La's cabin. That would have required contact with each and every mind. The effort would have exhausted or even killed him.

But he could cause a mild disorientation, a sense of doubt. People would see him running, but not be sure it was Cernaq they saw. It would slow them down, anyway. Time. He needed time. Seconds counted.

The hold was not staffed. The cargo here had been marked for long-term storage. Most of the bins contained supplies the *Titan* would need during the course of her travels. In Metcalfe's mind, he saw the locker where Aer'La was hiding. Roughly he extracted the combination and keyed it, grateful it wasn't counter-secured with a DNA scan.

The latch released, and the container front popped loose. Cernaq flung it open. The space inside was small, just enough for an average-sized person to recline somewhat comfortably. It was tall enough for even the tallest person to stand inside. Tall enough for a few feet of clearance between the head and the ceiling of the bin. Tall enough for a few feet of clearance between the toes and the floor, if a person were to suspend herself from the ceiling...

Tall enough for a noose, improvised from the legs of Aer'La's coverall, to have clearance to be looped around a cargo hook in the ceiling. Tall enough for her feet to clear the floor as she hung...

Cernaq, suppressing a decided urge to vomit, leaped into the bin and caught Aer'La around the middle, lifting her frame to relieve the pressure of the noose around her neck. He registered the heat of her body, the faint pulse of her heart as he pressed his head against her chest. Her consciousness was too far submerged for him to tap her mind for life signs, even in these close quarters. With a human it might have been possible. Aer'La was not human.

The tension on the noose relieved, he was able to slip it free of the cargo hook, and Aer'La's weight descended onto his shoulders. *Dead weight*, came the words, unbidden, to his mind.

He heaved her quickly to the deck outside, placing her on her back. As his hands began to prepare her for CPR, his mind called out desperately to Celia Faulkner, beckoning her to join him here, transmitting the sense of emergency. He felt her presence far away. The ability of a non-Phaetonian mind to respond was limited, especially at a distance. Celia was trained in opening her mind at other levels, however. He detected her acknowledgement, her understanding of the situation.

As he brought his lips to Aer'La's to force air into her lungs, he also desperately, irrationally wished that Metcalfe had taught him to pray...

* * *

That the man was a born thief should have surprised no one. Leaning over Atal's desk with one hand behind his back, like some ancient general planning a campaign, Harl had perused the schematics Atal had supplied. As quickly as any professional might case a prospective victim's home, he'd stabbed a finger at the screen and exclaimed, "There!"

He'd indicated the full-G cargo holds, which he'd pronounced the most likely place for a fugitive to hide. He'd tried to insist on going alone, to avoid interference. Fournier had almost let him, but Atal had put his foot down – the risk to ship's property was too great. Harl would certainly not be careful to avoid damaging cargo and containers in his search. Atal, Mors and Fournier wound up accompanying him. Mors had insisted on Pallas as well. When she joined them in the hold, Atal thought something seemed amiss with the young doctor. She was sullen. Her eyes lacked the sparkle, however mild, that he was accustomed to seeing in them. Fournier had insisted on having Metcalfe brought in as well, to witness his defeat at the hands of the Varthan Captain. As two of Fournier's marines lead him into the hold, his wrists cuffed behind him, he noted the boy's defiant glare at the Admiral, followed by a sympathetic glance from Mors, and Pallas's gaze going to the floor.

Ah well, Atal thought, *time to sort that out later.*

Fournier opened his mouth, no doubt to bait Metcalfe, but was interrupted by a shout from the corridor. Darby came in, leading a limping Sestus Blaurich, who also sported a very black eye.

"Captain! We have a situation!"

"Darby," snapped Fournier, "we're dealing with a situation here, as well. Get the boy to medical... and for all our sakes, don't let the cameras see the state he's in!"

It gave Atal selfish pleasure to see that some things weighed heavily enough to make Fournier cease fawning over the little prince.

"B-but sir," blustered Darby, "Blaurich was injured during an escape! By Midshipman Cernaq!"

"Cernaq... did that?" Atal wondered.

"He... he just went crazy," said Blaurich.

Fournier rolled his eyes. "What next?" he demanded.

"Where is Cernaq now?" asked Atal.

Darby shook his head. "No idea, sir. I expect he'll be with the feral – "

Harl, while they spoke, had been opening and examining the various bins, opening every storage locker, poking and prodding every suspension net, trying to force the lids off containers. As Darby spoke, he called out, "Who had the combination to these?"

He was standing before a bank of storage lockers designed for dry goods and other non-perishables. They were kept locked to prevent the crew helping themselves. Only the quartermaster normally maintained the combinations. Atal crossed to Harl.

"That is an airtight container. I doubt the girl has evaded your clutches only to suffocate herself."

"Ye'd be amazed at what I seen in my line of work, Atal. These ferals will try anything. This case fr'instance," he gestured at the secured door. "With a portable oxygen supply, a good-sized man or woman can last hours inside. 'Course a lot of 'em go crazy from bein' locked in the dark. And some of 'em do suffocate. I've retrieved a dead body or two."

"Get him the damned combinations, Atal," said Fournier.

Atal keyed his data implant, accessed the quartermaster files, and selected the combination key chart. Numerals appeared in the air before him, and he shoved them roughly toward Harl. The holographs glided obediently into place

"I'd appreciate it," Atal said, "if you'd exercise appropriate care. All of this cargo is valuable, and much of it will be destroyed if you tamper with it."

He bowed. "As you say, Captain." With a sideways glance, he began keying combinations in, opening doors, shining his hand torch inside. When he reached the third door, the punched combination resulted, not in the satisfying click of an opening latch, but the jarring buzz of an entry error. Harl tried the combination again, only to receive the same rude noise. He turned to Atal. "Combination's wrong for this one."

"It's been changed," Darby postulated.

Fournier turned on Metcalfe. "Well?"

Metcalfe swallowed. "Well what?"

"Don't toy with me, Mr. Metcalfe! You're practically convicted already! You'd best cooperate."

Metcalfe looked to Atal. "Captain, this is ridiculous! He just wants to rifle through our cargo and identify what we have. If he sends word to his raider friends – "

Harl flushed, turning his attention away from the door. The insinuation that, because he was Varthan, he was in league with raiders and pirates was blatantly insulting. All Varthans reacted badly to the suggestion that they participated in this kind of activity, because most of them *did* participate in this kind of activity.

Atal started to speak, to stem off yet another physical confrontation, but Fournier beat him to it. "Mr. Metcalfe, please remember you're here as a prisoner, to witness the discovery of evidence which will no doubt lead to your conviction and imprisonment. It is not your place to insult an investigator performing his lawful duties. Now sir, the combination."

"Captain – " Metcalfe barked again, almost desperately.

"Give it to him," Atal said quietly.

Sneering, almost choking on the words, Metcalfe recited a string of alphanumerics. Harl keyed the combination, and the door flipped obediently open.

And an arm flipped suddenly out. Aer'La's arm.

Mors was at her side first, cradling the body, which fell limply and sickeningly against him, a scrap of torn fabric tied at its throat.

As often as Atal had seen death, nothing prepared him for the sight of Aer'La's body, the swollen tongue, the shock white of the skin in death, the agony etched on the once beautiful face, bespeaking the pain of Aer'La's final, tortured moments of life.

Mors said quietly, "No life signs. It's been here for a few hours."

Harl's fists shook in frustration. Cheated of his victory, he looked as if he might easily kill them all.

"There will be restitution for this, Atal."

"Do I understand that you expect a cash settlement?" Mors asked slowly, still holding the body in his arms. "For the loss of your property?"

"We..." Harl sputtered, caught off guard. "Justice was to have been done. There was to have been a trial. She was a murderer!"

"If she was, then justice has been done," Mors said. "In our space, Captain, suicide is the right of the accused. We believe a person has the right to first judge herself. Obviously, Aer'La did."

Harl almost spat. "We have no such 'rights' in Varthan space. You have cheated us – "

"Not us," Atal said. He turned to Metcalfe, whose face was ashen. He looked close to tears.

"Captain, I'm – " he began.

"Did you hide her here?" Atal demanded.

"Yes, sir."

"I knew it," said Fournier.

Atal ignored him. "What did you hope to accomplish?"

"I didn't want them to take her," he replied, with no inflection. His voice was dead. His eyes were dead. As dead as Aer'La's body just yards away.

"So you left her alone in the hold, knowing she was terrified, knowing she was desperate. If you hadn't acted like an imbecile, she'd still be alive."

Metcalfe bit back a sob. "I'm sorry," he muttered.

"You're... you're sorry?" Atal said it again, shouting, "You're *sorry*?" With no warning, he drove his fist into the boy's jaw. Metcalfe fell hard and didn't get up. Fournier jumped backward from where he'd been standing a proprietary watch beside his prisoner.

"Gods, Atal!" he snapped, more surprised than anything else.

"Your apology can't raise the dead," the Captain said to the quivering body on the floor. To the two marines he snapped, "Get him out of here."

Fournier recovered himself and turned his diplomatic charms on Harl. "Captain, I cannot say how much I regret this unfortunate situation, and you understand that I speak for the Admiralty. I assure you, we shall meet with your government to negotiate a – "

"Shut up," Harl said quietly, menacingly.

"I – Captain, please – !"

"I said 'shut up,' you mincing prick!"

Fournier blanched.

Harl went on. "I'm tired of listening to you, Fournier. I was the moment you opened your mouth, and now you've nothing to offer me, I don't have to listen anymore."

He stalked away down the corridor. It was clear that, having seen Aer'La's corpse, he'd lost all interest in the others. It almost seemed he was pretending not to care. Perhaps he had to. Aer'La had defeated him once and for all, in his eyes. She'd cheated him of the opportunity to take possession of her, which was clearly what he wanted in this matter.

As Harl left, Pallas watched him a moment, then bolted after him. Metcalfe, still on the deck, watched her go, burying his face in his hands.

Chapter Thirteen
Revelations

Two hours later, Atal was back in his office with Fournier, Mors and Metcalfe. Metcalfe had been returned to his cell and given a chance to clean up. He still looked disheveled and somber, of course. The mood among the ship's officers was grim. Atal had not ordered a search for Cernaq. There would be time for that. Feeling a complete bastard, he'd also avoided seeing Kaya. He knew she needed him now, but he simply could not see her. He hoped, eventually, she would forgive his callousness.

Metcalfe slumped on Atal's office couch, listening dumbly to Fournier. He almost appeared drugged, his reactions were so limited.

"The court martial will begin at ship's time 0700 tomorrow," Fournier announced. "I will chair the court martial board, Mr. Metcalfe, and I think it fair to warn you that I intend you to spend the rest of your life in prison. Even if I wanted to be charitable, I can't afford to be. You've gone too far over the line. You've made a mockery of the discipline of the service, and you must be brought down hard."

Was this mugging, painting as bleak a picture as he could for the boy, so Metcalfe would confess, accept a lighter sentence, and make Fournier's life easier? Or was it just the Admiral's need to flex his muscles, even before a defenseless opponent? It was hard to know with Fournier.

"You've done your people little good," he went on. "You've only confirmed the stereotypes you claim you want to disprove. You can't expect the government of Terra to come to your defense, either."

It was true that, at Metcalfe's last court martial, the Terran government had issued a statement, asking for lenience. Citing anti-Terran bigotry in the mass media, and the many cases of unprovoked violence against Terran nationals throughout Confederate space, it was easy to see how a Terran could be driven to feel persecuted, and perhaps react violently.

Clearly, it still galled Fournier that Metcalfe had received such support. Unfortunately, Atal thought, he was probably right that no one from Terra would stick his neck out in such a manner twice.

Fortunately, it wasn't left to a Terran official to stick his neck out this time. Atal cleared his throat.

Fournier looked at him. "Something the matter, Atal?"

"I'm afraid you'll find it difficult to convict Midshipman Metcalfe, sir," he said. "You see, insubordination usually involves disobeying orders."

"And he has!"

"No, sir, I'm afraid he hasn't. I ordered him to hide Aer'La."

"But – " Fournier's eyes went wide. No doubt, he was at once outraged at this confession and thrilled by the prospect of finally hauling Atal up on charges. Then his eyes narrowed. "You're making that up! You're just trying to – "

"I have a witness."

Atal nodded at Mors, who smiled and inclined his head.

"I heard Jan give the order, in this very room."

Fournier shrugged. "Well, maybe Metcalfe obeyed your orders, but he certainly disobeyed mine, and – "

"Again, under my orders, sir. I specifically ordered him to refuse to cooperate with you. So, your charge of insubordination must be leveled against me."

"Huh! Well – " He sputtered for a moment, mulling over his options.

Mors said gently, "Before you make any decisions, Admiral, I think you should wait and hear how the Captain has spared the Navy considerable embarrassment."

The door from the Promenade opened. Pallas stepped in, now looking far more collected than she had in the hold. She nodded graciously to Fournier and stood expectantly before the door as it slid shut.

"Oh, great," Metcalfe muttered. "The witness for the persecution."

Pallas didn't react. Of course, she probably already knew anything Metcalfe had to say about her.

"Stand down, Mr. Metcalfe," said Atal.

"This," Pallas said formally, holding up a small silver shaft about the size of a grape, "is a standard issue audio recorder and DNA verifier. I'm sure Admiral Fournier is familiar with their use."

Fournier grunted. He would be familiar with such things, of course. The recorders had defeated the age-old argument that voice and image captures could be faked, and thus were not admissible as evidence in courts of law. By capturing a DNA sample from the saliva or skin of the speaker and coding the sample to the recording, it verified the identity of the speaker, and verified, legally, that they had said what they had said. It could be faked, of course, but so could signatures and fingerprints. This was actually a more reliable verification.

"You'll hear my voice first. The other belongs to Captain Harl." She slid the cylinder into the interface port on Atal's desk terminal, and the voices played back on the office speakers.

"Captain Harl!"

"Oh... Hello, Doctor."

"Are you leaving?"

"Not much point in me staying, is there?"

"I see that you're frustrated. I imagine you wanted to see the girl stand trial."

"That, uh... Well, she's escaped her just comeuppance, I must say."

"I sense loss, Captain, if you'll forgive my being so bold. She meant more to you than you've told the others. She represented more..."

"Well, that... "

"You needn't be reticent with me, Captain. Since touring your ship, I've seen what savages the creatures are. Aer'La... she often threatened me with physical violence. Such dangerous elements must be... controlled."

"You're very understanding, milady. Perhaps it's true that Phaetonians are a cut above the rest of the humans."

"I believe we are. There should be no stigma associated with admitting that which is supported by evidence."

"Yes. You are... quite a superior woman."

"Thank you, Captain. I'm glad you see that. You also see, I would think, how I might be able to... help you?"

"Eh?"

"Let us be honest, Harl. May I call you Harl?"

"Milady... please."

"We both know that there's more to this than having the girl stand trial. What she represents to your people... to her people... is a symbol of possible escape. Even though she died, she escaped your care, and successfully evaded you for some years. If you do not return her alive... her symbol remains. She is a martyr to her cause. Now other Inihu might hear of her, and also dream of escape..."

"Yes..."

"And – since you were unsuccessful in perpetuating the belief that no Inihu escapes – there will be those who will ... behave unjustly toward you."

"I will be ready for them!"

"Oh, I've no doubt you will; but couldn't a telepath be of some assistance to you?"

"Well... now... maybe. I mean... would you... consider that?"

"I might. You know, Phaetonians are not merely detached intellectuals. We strongly believe in the Free Market. Your business is profitable, no doubt?"

"I could give you anything you dream of, Milady."

"I don't want to be given things, Harl. I want to earn them. That's the way of my people. In exchange for assisting you, I'd like a share in your business. Is that possible?"

"I would imagine..."

"For instance, how much might Aer'La have fetched on the market, if she hadn't escaped you?"

"Oh, that would have been a lucrative deal. You see, many of the slaves I sell, I only act as agent. Aer'La, well she was from a lot that I'd invested my own money in. Raised her myself. The syndicate still backed me, of course, but I owned sixty per cent interest in her and her sisters."

"Stop," said Atal. Pallas paused the playback. Atal turned to Fournier. "Well, Georg? He admitted he's a slaver."

Fournier's expression drooped. "All right... yes. He did not, however, disavow the murder charge, so our actions – "

"Actually, Admiral, he did," said Pallas. She keyed the player again, searching for a timestamp. "I'll spare you the interim conversation..."

"I lied, good lady. I hope that does not lessen your opinion of me? I acted with the interests of my people as my overriding priority. I manufactured the evidence that the slave had killed the girl so that your people would not take some sort of silly, moral stand. I believe in this case, how

does your saying have it? Ah, the end justifies the means? You under-
stand? Desperate times call for desperate measures."

With a look of vague disgust, Pallas clicked the cylinder out of
the playback slot. "I trust that is sufficient to prove that Aer'La was
not a murderer?"

"Not that it matters," Fournier muttered.

Atal clasped Pallas's shoulder gently. "That couldn't have been
easy for you. You did an excellent job."

"I told you she would," Mors said, with evident pride. "You deaf
mutes think that, just because we're intellectuals, we Phaetonians
can't be excellent spies – we can."

Mors delighted in calling non-Phaetonians "deaf mutes," since
they could neither read nor broadcast their thoughts. For his people's purposes, they couldn't hear or speak. He knew it annoyed the
hell out of Atal when he said it. At the moment, however, Atal did-
n't have time to play.

"The Captain felt someone should be in Harl's confidence," Pallas
explained calmly, "for the purpose of gathering information. My intent was to secure just such a confession."

She didn't meet Metcalfe's eyes as she said it. He was watching
her, though, the expression on his face one of uncertainty, and perhaps regret. Atal knew that giving Pallas this mission risked forming a breech between her and his officers. They would not take
kindly to someone who appeared to line up with the Varthans
against their friend. She was aware of this risk, however, and had
chosen to take it. It had been Aer'La's only chance.

Atal was particularly sorry to have seen the glow of puppy love
fade in Metcalfe's eyes. Such love often didn't last anyway, but to
kill it deliberately was tantamount to spraying weed killer on the
first flowers of spring. He probably owed Metcalfe an apology for
not cluing him in to this part of the plan, but he had to trust these
two to work out their differences on their own. If they couldn't...
Atal had been known to compromise his principle of live and let
live.

"Dr. Mors felt Dr. Pallas was the right candidate to get information from Harl," Atal explained to Fournier. "She played on his van-
ity while appearing to be above such nasty dealings as espionage."

"I believe the art of seduction has a time-honored place in espionage," said Mors. "There was a figure in Terran history named
Mata Hari, who – "

"I would hardly claim to be versed in the art of seduction, Professor," Pallas interjected.

"The lady doth protest too much," observed Metcalfe.

Mors went on. "At any rate, Georg, had you allowed Harl to take the girl on this trumped-up charge, and then evidence had been found and circulated that he'd lied – "

"And it would have circulated," Atal assured Fournier.

" – It would have been quite embarrassing to ConfNav, and the scandal would have damaged relations with the Varthan free worlds. Now, the whole matter is a proven embarrassment, which the Varthan cartels will be only too happy to see swept under the rug."

Fournier looked non-plussed in the extreme by the whole line of conversation. He shook his head impatiently. "But the girl is still dead!"

The signal from Atal's outer door bleeped angrily. On Atal's desk, the miniature figure of Carson appeared. "Captain, Dr. Flynn is urgently requesting to – " it began.

The corridor door opened, and Flynn stomped in.

" – see you," finished the tiny holo. Having done its job, and its sender knowing that it had arrived a bit too late, it vanished.

"Yes, Doctor," said Atal, "please come in."

"I won't have it, Captain!" Flynn blustered.

"And 'it' would be...?"

"That... *woman!* Seizing medical supplies! Misusing my facilities! Violation of genetic protocols – "

"Breathe, Dr. Flynn," Atal reminded him, for it truly seemed he needed reminding. "I assume by 'that woman,' you mean Dr. Faulkner?"

"I do, sir!"

"How has she... displeased you?"

"She – she – "

"She activated a brain dead clone of an individual who had not given consent for its use," said Celia Faulkner's voice, from behind Atal. She had entered through the promenade door, as Pallas had. She stepped between Flynn and the Captain and said pleasantly, "I'm perfectly willing to pay any damages the donor asks. I won't even take it to court."

Flynn beat at sides with his hands. "You know perfectly well that the donor is dead!"

"I'm afraid it's true, Captain. At the time I quickened the clone, the donor was dead."

"Well, then," Flynn began, "I demand – "

"Clinically dead," Celia interrupted.

"What?" demanded Flynn and Fournier. Realization dawned in the eyes of the latter.

"Clinically dead. That means no pulse. The heart had stopped. Respiration – "

"I know what clinical death is, *Doctor.* It's an outmoded term, you know that. Brainwave activity is the final measure of legal death. If that hasn't ceased – " He broke off, his face going white. "Then the patient... can be revived."

"There just might be hope for you after all, Romney," said Celia. "In this case – well, I'll let you see for yourselves. Mr. Cernaq!" she called through the open door.

Cernaq walked in, escorting a pale and tired, but decidedly alive, Aer'La.

"Atal," Fournier said in his most dangerous voice, "I'd... like an explanation..."

"Naturally, Admiral." Atal nodded to Celia. "The good physician will be happy to explain. It was, after all, her brilliant handiwork."

"Hardly what I'd call brilliant, Captain. Any first-year resident worth her salt can quicken a clone sans a sentient brain, stabilize it, and reproduce the symptoms of death by – "

"You *faked* that?" This from Fournier.

"On my order, of course." Atal said.

"And you didn't tell me?"

"Well, for one thing," said Atal, "there wasn't time. Cernaq, following his... sudden departure from his cabin, found Aer'La. She had hanged herself with a makeshift noose, as you saw. He summoned Dr. Faulkner, who intervened. He then informed Mors, who transmitted my orders. We had to act quickly to plant the fake corpse."

"You knew I would never have allowed it!"

"In your position, you scarcely *could* have allowed such an action, Georg,"said Mors. "That is why I suggested you be excluded from the list of those who knew of the plan. This was best carried out by those... less bound by their diplomatic obligations. You are, of course, free to take disciplinary action against us all, if you feel it appropriate – "

Mors' great popularity and influence in the Navy was due in part to the fact that he could say such absurd things with a straight face. A political opportunist like Fournier would hardly take action against him. If he did, he might suddenly find himself requested to accept a special ops assignment on the Border.

"But it would seem to me," Mors continued. "that Captain Atal and his officers have used unorthodox methods to bring about an equitable solution for all concerned. Except for Harl, of course, but nature will no doubt equalize him one way or another."

* * *

In fact, it was not long before Mors's prediction came true. While the assembled group was still reviewing the day's events, Pallas announced that Harl was approaching Atal's office, his mind on demanding restitution. Atal ushered Aer'La, with Cernaq, back to the promenade.

Harl arrived, accompanied by his omnipresent first mate.

"Atal," he announced, "I'm prepared to depart. I feel, however, that some – er – compensation is due me and my crew."

"Really?" asked Atal politely. "How do you figure?"

"Well, my reputation as a – er – private investigator has been compromised by the mutinous actions of your officers. My livelihood depends on credibility, y'understand, Captain." He reached into his coat pocket. "I've worked up an estimate of the lost revenue – "

"Which, coincidentally, comes to the amount for which you believed you could have sold Aer'La," said Pallas. "Thus covering your financial losses, and saving face for you before your crew."

Harl's jaw dropped. His mate eyed him closely.

"Milady?" he wondered. "Surely you're forgetting – "

"I forget very little, Captain Harl. I certainly haven't forgotten the dubious pleasure of having to be in your presence these past few days. I imagine it will take a great deal of bathing to reduce the ill effects of the experience."

Harl was dumbstruck. "B-but... you said – "

Pallas allowed herself a slight smile. "I lied, my good Captain. 'Desperate times call for desperate measures.'"

Harl's mouth moved. For quite a few seconds, no sound came

out to accompany the moving of his lips. Any number of profanities seemed to flit through his mind, ultimately escaping him. Then he stepped toward Pallas, his fists raised, shrieking, "You *bitch!*"

Atal interposed himself between them. "Captain Harl, don't forget I can have you arrested if you become violent."

Harl snorted. "Your security couldn't take me down, Atal."

"I could," said a voice behind the Captain, and Harl's eyes, already livid with rage, nearly popped from their sockets.

"Aer'La," said Atal to the new arrival in the doorway, "you were supposed to stay out of sight."

Aer'La shook her head and stepped forward. "No," she said quietly. "I've hidden enough. I've run away enough." She leveled her gaze at Harl, who actually drew back as she advanced on him. "I won't hide anymore. I won't run anymore. I won't try to take my own life." She looked in turns at Cernaq, Celia, Atal and Metcalfe, "because it's a life worth living."

"Now look here, girl – " Harl began.

"No," she said, her voice trembling. "You look here, you demented fuck. I let you scare me. I let you do things to me that no one should ever," she inhaled sharply, trying hard to maintain control, "*ever* have done to them against their will. I let you think you owned my body. I believed you owned my body." She stepped in until her face was an inch from his. "You don't. And if you try to touch me – or anyone here – again, I'll kill you. You might be lucky enough to kill me first, but I doubt it. My life is mine. You'll never control it again."

Harl swallowed. "Well. I don't think it'll... do any good for anyone to be... killed." He looked to his mate for reassurance. He received none. The man's eyes were cold and questioning. "Atal," he said. "Since the girl is alive..." He looked to Pallas. "Since you clearly know some of the... more expedient fictions I was forced to... well, I've lost money, haven't I? But I think payment for my loss, at double the market value, for damages, should – "

"You expect them to pay you?" Aer'La demanded. She seized Harl's collar and lifted him off his feet, arching her back, as he was significantly taller than she.

"I believe I deserve some compensation..."

Aer'La closed her eyes and held her breath for a long moment. Then she said, "Yes. You do have some compensation coming."

In an instant, her calm was gone. She lifted Harl higher and threw him bodily against the nearby wall. He lay, stunned. Aer'La allowed him no recovery time. She leapt on him and pummeled his face and chest savagely. The Varthan Captain's blood spattered her face and arms, and began to ooze on the deck beneath him.

Once the initial shock had dissipated, it was Cernaq who came forward. He made no move to touch or restrain her. He merely called her name softly.

Her hands now at her victim's throat, she rasped, "No, Cernaq. Don't even ask. I'm going to kill the son of a bitch! It's what he deserves!"

"Yes," said Cernaq gently. "I believe it is. Only please, Aer'La... don't be the one to do it. They'll arrest you. They'll charge you. You'll lose your commission." He knelt beside her and held out his hand. "And we'll lose you. None of us want that."

Aer'La paused, her hands still at Harl's throat. Tears of frustration formed in her eyes and ran down her cheeks. "Cernaq, please... he murdered Druberj! I can't let him live!"

"Then," said Cernaq quietly, "let me do it."

"What? No!"

"Yes. I can kill him easily. I don't even have to touch him, just stop his heart." He reached out and stroked her face with his fingertips. "Let me face the charges. Let me go to prison, or mental reconditioning. You've suffered enough."

"I can't do that. I can't lose you, too. But I can't let him... don't you understand, Cernaq? For Dru's memory, I can't..."

"Would you trade my life for Druberj's memory?" he asked.

She couldn't speak. She merely shook her head.

"Then don't ask me to trade yours. For Druberj's memory, Aer'La, do what he would want you to do. Go on living. Be loved. Live... in Freedom."

Aer'La took her hands from Harl and brought them to her eyelids, pushing hard to staunch the tears. "Freedom," she whispered.

"You've found it," said Cernaq. "Would Dru have wanted you to let it go? For him?"

In answer, she fell against his chest and buried her face in the warm folds of his tunic.

Behind them, Atal stepped up to Harl's mate. "You have five minutes to take your Captain and get off my ship."

"There is still the matter of remuneration," said the mate.

Before Atal could reply, Mors said, "He's right."

"What?" Atal demanded.

Mors looked at Harl and frowned. "There's nothing more dangerous than a wounded animal. Or a man who thinks he's been cheated of what's rightfully his. I believe it would be safer to give Harl his money and send him on his way."

"I will take the money," said the mate. "We will decide, later, who will keep it."

"Meaning you'll kill him," said Pallas, nodding to Harl.

"That's not our business," said Atal coldly.

Fournier stepped forward. "Professor... there's sense in what you say. Sir," he said to the mate, "are you willing to let this matter drop, if they pay you?"

"I would consider our business closed, were I paid for the slave."

Fournier said to Atal, "It could never be known, you realize. The press would have a field day." He sighed. "But it would eliminate a very large headache for the Council and the Admiralty."

"Yes," agreed Atal. "Pay the man."

"What?" blurted Fournier. "Me? It was Mors's idea!"

"Oh," said Mors, "I'll be happy to – "

"No," said Atal firmly. "It's Fournier's headache to cure. It's his secret to keep. Let him do the deed."

"See here, Atal – "

"You were willing to hand Aer'La over to slavers when you thought it was expedient. What's expedient now? And it is, by the way, my condition for not talking to the media." Atal smiled.

Fournier gritted his teeth. "You're nothing but an extortionist, Atal."

Atal nodded. "It's probably in my genes."

"I don't care," said the mate, "as long as I get paid."

"Blackmail," said Fournier when the mate was given his money and had dragged the barely conscious Harl from the room, "Absolute blackmail. Of me, of the Varthan... of the whole damned Navy. You're all just a.... a pack of criminals."

"Crime is relative, Admiral," said Mors. "After all, what is a crime, but a violation of a law? And what is a law, but that which politicians – called by some the most persistent criminal class in human society – have found to be politically expedient to introduce as a set of guidelines? There was a time when human sacrifice was legal, as was child molestation, spousal assault – "

"We're not in one of your lectures, Professor," Fournier interrupted. "And I'm well aware that you all believe you did the right thing, but – "

"And what do you believe, Admiral?" asked Atal.

"I believe, Atal, that I have more pressing matters to which to attend than the supervision of a pack of delinquents. If you will have my ship readied, I will be returning to Quintil within the hour." He left the room with what failing dignity he could muster.

Atal looked after him. "That," he said, "is the best news I've had in quite some time."

"Sir," said Cernaq, who still cradled Aer'La, "I regret to inform you that, in the course of rescuing Aer'La, I struck a fellow officer."

"I know," said Atal. He grinned. "Quite a shiner you gave him."

"I submit myself for disciplinary action, Captain," said Cernaq. "I regret my failure to conform to regulations."

Atal nodded. "I know you do. I only wish I did. Well, Cernaq, if your fellow midshipman can forgive an equally inappropriate attack by his Captain – "

He looked to Metcalfe, who smiled. "I rolled with it, sir. You really telegraph a punch, you know."

"If I ever really hit you, you'll never see it coming," said Atal. "Don't worry about it, Cernaq. Regulations only kick in if Five – er – Mr. Blaurich – wants to press charges. I believe I can safely say that... he's going to find it to his advantage not to."

"I don't understand, Captain," said Cernaq.

"Don't worry. I'll handle it."

"Thank you sir," said Cernaq. He looked at Aer'La, for once, content to be quiet in his arms. "For everything."

* * *

Some time later, Metcalfe and Cernaq coaxed Aer'La up to go and share their good news with Kaya and Carson. Atal and Mors were deep in conversation with Celia, and Pallas hung nearby, looking a trifle uncomfortable. Surprising both Metcalfe and Cernaq, Aer'La went to her and invited her to join them for a drink.

Pallas, though clearly stunned, said, "Thank you... I'd like that very much."

"You know, Doctor," said Aer'La, "I have to tell you I never had much use for Phaetonians. I mean – "

Pallas smiled at her, very tenderly. "I understand. Our peoples are pretty much diametrically opposed."

Aer'La nodded. "But you went out on a limb for me. I won't forget it."

Pallas shrugged. "It was the least I could do for anyone in your situation. And... " she grinned mischievously, "it was kind of fun."

They said their goodbyes to their elders, and went out into the corridor. Pallas fell into step beside Metcalfe. He looked at her warily, wondering what she could possibly say after all they'd said.

"I'm sorry," she said simply.

"You? But I – "

She smiled. "You are a 'mean-spirited, bigoted, jack-ass,' yes."

"I... I... "

"Well, you said it."

"I *thought* it. There's a difference."

"Not on my world."

"Well, there is here. And you're right. I mean I'm right, I am."

"No you're not. I lied to you. I wouldn't blame you if you never spoke to me again."

"I know you were just acting."

"Partly," she said seriously. "Some of the anger, well..."

"Well?"

"You... you hurt my feelings."

"But you knew I was just... I mean... you can read minds!"

"That doesn't really make it hurt less when you're insulted by someone who... "

"Someone who what?"

There was a long pause, during which Metcalfe thought how unfair it was that one of them could read minds and the other couldn't.

"Someone who really knows how to insult a girl."

"I really am sorry."

They walked another moment in silence. Aer'La and Cernaq were engrossed in a quiet conversation of their own.

"If you don't mind my asking – " Metcalfe said after a moment.

"– yes?"

" – how *did* you get that recorder close enough to Harl's mouth to get a sample?"

Pallas chuckled and walked on ahead.

Epilogue

"... and welcome back to The Naked Truth's weekend edition. Joining me in the nude is yummy John Smith, CEO of Concubines Limited! What's new, John?"

"Well, Vixyn, it sounds like Bos'n Aer'La's troubles are over. The investigators from Varthan Freespace have cleared her of all charges in relation to the murder of young Treva Maklyn and – "

"I'm sorry, John, should I know that name? Erla?"

"Aer'La, Vixyn."

"Right. Who?"

"The escaped Varthan feral who's bos'n on the *Titan*. She was all over the news – ?"

"Great! I'm sure someone somewhere remembers. So. She died?"

"No, she's free. Cleared of all charges. Allowed to stay aboard the *Titan* and keep her commission."

"Hadn't there been some talk of making her return to Varthan Freespace?"

"There had, but, since she hasn't committed a crime, the Varthan government isn't going to force her to come home. If she doesn't want them, they don't want her. They're reasonable people, after all. It's not like Aer'La's a slave..."

"Slave! Hah! That's a good one, John. Slavery in this day and age. Moving back to the real world, let's talk about the ugliness surrounding Brand Greer's penile replacement surgery."

"Oh, let's not! The footage of the accident at his concert was too much for those of use with everything to lose..."

* * *

"It's customary to ask for the doctor's bill plus two-hundred per cent," said Darby. "Of course, one can always add pain and suffering."

"As if that spindly gelding could cause me pain," spat Five. "But there is my reputation to consider. I can't base it on the doctor's bill, since Dr. Flynn didn't charge me. The Navy paid for the corrective treatment." He brushed his fingers over the skin under his eye, where, until this morning, there had been a large, purplish bruise. The bruise was gone now, the perfection of his face restored.

"Market price can still be established. I'll instruct Romney to work up a properly inflated estimate – "

"Do you think he has any money? Don't those intellectual types all cast their fortunes on the star winds?"

"Hey, Sestus, how's your eye?" It was Kaya. She floated towards them, pulling herself along the Command Deck's handholds until she was an arm's length away. Carson was with her.

"Hardly. Phaetonians prize wealth. I believe you'll find – "

"My eye is on your lovely backside, as always, Atal."

"I hear you were jumped by at least six strapping men," said Kaya in wonder. "It's a miracle you're still alive."

"I don't know where that story started."

"You mean you don't know where you were when you started it?" asked Carson.

"Laugh all you will, Carson. I'm thinking of naming you as a party in the lawsuit. It's the atmosphere of hostility created by yourself and Metcalfe that caused Cernaq to attack me."

"It was your own stupid fault for standing in his way," said Kaya. "I'm sure any trial board would understand that there was a life at stake, anyway. But it won't be going to trial."

"You mean Mr. Cernaq is going to settle?" said Darby. "Extremely wise of him."

"Perhaps, Captain," said Five. "Depends on what he's offering."

"Cernaq isn't offering anything," said Kaya. "But you might want to check your mail. I believe you'll be hearing from your family attorney."

"Wha –?" Sestus grunted. He tapped his palm and scrolled through the illuminated characters of his mailbox menu. There was, indeed, a note from his father's attorney. He read it quickly, then spat out a stream of expletives. "Problem?" wondered Kaya.

"What have they done now?" demanded Darby.

"It seems," said Sestus through his teeth, "that Atal Holdings has awarded a lucrative pharmaceutical contract to one of my family's subsidiaries."

"Damned nice of them, too," said Kaya. "Your people did not have the lowest bid. Guess your service is just better."

"Our service! Listen to this: 'In light of this lucrative award, it would be in the best interests of corporate goodwill if no claims were made against Atal Holdings or its interests at this time. Contract signatures are dependent on the signed release of all – ' Perfect!"

"Meaning you'd better not sue Cernaq, if you know what's good for you."

"How," Five demanded, "is Cernaq considered an interest of Atal Holdings?"

"He's being represented by our defense team," said Kaya. "As a favor to Dad."

"I don't believe this!" hissed Darby.

"Buck up, Five," said Carson. "Won't this increase the value of your shares in your family's company?"

"But Cernaq doesn't have to pay!"

"I dunno," said Kaya. "He still has to look at you every day. Isn't that payment?"

"If you and your family weren't so... shifty – "

"Shifty!"

" – he and his friends wouldn't be here to look at me!"

"Well, get used to us, Five," Carson smiled. "We're going to be here to annoy you for some time to come."

"Shifty, Mr. Blaurich? Who's shifty?"

"Captain!"

"Apparently, we are, Daddy."

"That's Captain Daddy. Care to rephrase that assertion, Mr. Blaurich?"

"Well, y-yes, sir, I... uh... "

"I thought so. Thank you for the effort. Save it. I don't care."

"Captain, I'm sure Mr. Blaurich didn't intend – "

"I'm sure he didn't intend to damage his promotional chances either, Mr. Darby; and I did not ask your opinion."

"Captain! I protest! I should be at liberty to offer my opinion. I am your Deputy."

"So you are. As Deputy, then, would you arrange for the casuals to assemble for a formal transfer of command ceremony at 0800? If it's convenient for Bos'n Aer'La, of course."

"Bos'n Aer'La!"

"Yes, after her ordeal, and the embarrassment caused by a disgusting public arrest, I feel we offer her a firm show of support. Agreed?"

"Well... I'd rather assumed that... that is... Bos'n Aer'La is innocent of murder. I'm sure I speak for everyone when I say we're all thrilled at that news. But... she's still..."

"A feral?"

"A non-citizen, sir."

"Hardly. You see, Bos'n Aer'La was never a slave in Varthan Freespace. There is no slavery in Varthan Freespace."

"I'm glad to hear that!"

"Don't be. It's a lie. But it's a politically convenient lie. And we've made it convenient to us. The Varthans argue that the Inihu in 'medical custody' are mentally incompetent. That is their excuse for denying them citizenship in the Varthan Alliance. Legally, if an Inihu is mentally competent, she is ergo a Varthan citizen, and thus, a citizen of the Confederacy. Correct?"

"Sir, how do you propose to prove Aer'La competent?"

"By using the oldest defense in the book, Darby. We're going to do nothing."

"Eh?"

"Burden of proof of mental incompetence is on those who claim the individual is not competent. No one has to prove himself sane to enjoy his rights. Someone else must prove him sane to deny them. Or we'd all be institutionalized. So, until some court rules otherwise, Aer'La is sane and a citizen."

"I – I see..."

"So," Atal said, as if speaking to an idiot child, "she's staying."

"I'd already drafted her discharge orders – "

"That's why they call them drafts, Darby. Because they're not final until I say so. I don't say so. So, toss your discharge orders in the trash, get down to the hold, and do your damndest to make my Bos'n feel that she's the best thing to hit Confederate space since the stellar fusion."

"I – I – "

"Blaurich, you go help him."

"Aye... sir..."

"And make it a big show, boys. Music would be nice. Canned if you can't line up an honor guard. And maybe a citation for courage in time of adversity."

"And flowers," added Kaya. "Women love flowers."

"Aer'La doesn't," said Carson. "Unless they're edible."

"No flowers," said Atal. "Candy. Nice box of candy. You can afford that, right Darby? Not that it's an order, of course."

Darby sighed. "Oh, of course, sir. Come on, Sestus. We're going shopping."

* * *

"She's gonna fuckin' kill you, Shan. You know she is!"

"If I were you, I'd get offa this ship!"

"Too bad there ain't no way off this ship! We're in deep space."

"'Cept to jump out an airlock!"

"Hell, I'd jump out an airlock, if I was you, Shan. Be a less painful way to go."

"I hear the dry good bins ain't a bad place to hole up, if ya – "

"Shut up!" screamed Felicity Shan. "All of you just shut the fuck up!"

"Ungallant behavior's what I'd call it," said Volster. "Turnin' on the poor girl, just 'cause them two perfumed ponces handed her a medal and some chocolates! She's still nuthin' but a – "

"I think you'd all better be quiet," advised Ceres Smith. "Looks like the little hallway confab is about over." She looked with no pity at Felicity Shan. It was true enough that, until yesterday, they'd all been on her side. Until yesterday, the Bos'n wasn't coming back. Sadly for Felicity Shan, this was today. That was the way of it, when you rode public opinion and stuck your neck out, as she had. When self-interest caused the tide of public opinion to turn, your neck was still out, but no one would intercede if an axe came toward it.

Well, thought Smith, the silly little bitch should have kept quiet during the arrest. Whatever she thought of Aer'La, no one deserved to be treated that way. She'd had no business trying to play the cheerleader. Smith might have written her lack of discretion off to youth, but she suspected stupidity was the more likely cause.

Aer'La re-entered the hold, carrying her clipboard, not looking up from it.

"Okay," she said crisply, "I think some of you missed the zero-G training. And I see you haven't signed up for make-up training. I was serious about docking pay, people. Your checks are gonna be smaller than you wanted."

"Now, Bos'n," Volster sighed heavily, "you should be forgiving. See, we thought that order no longer stood."

Aer'La smiled dangerously. "Did you? I guess that makes sense. You thought you were going to have a new Bos'n, who did things the way you're used to?"

"Well, no ma'am, we – "

"Don't lie to me, Volster. I hate liars. Worse than I hate people who don't take their work seriously. Got me?"

"Aye... sir."

"Make-up training. Here. Tomorrow. Oh-six-hundred. Miss it, and I'll put you off the ship without a suit."

"I'll be there, Bos'n."

"Good." Aer'La walked past him and stood before Shan. For a moment she stopped and glared at the other woman. Shan shifted uncomfortably on her feet. "Ms. Shan," Aer'La said finally.

Felicity Shan swallowed. "Bos'n?"

"You be there too."

"Wha – I mean – I – "

"Something wrong with you, Shan?"

"No ma'am. I – no."

Aer'La stepped closer. "You expected something else? A few loose teeth for that little cheer you gave the other day? Believe me, I thought about it. You thought it was funny to see me in irons like that, huh?"

"N – no."

"Yeah you did. But see, I think you've changed your mind. There was a time when I thought I only wanted to see the people I hated hurt. Thought nothing could make me happier. I changed my mind. I don't think it's funny to see anyone humiliated. I bet you've changed your mind, too?" She cupped the girl's chin in her hand. Both of them were aware that the simplest squeeze would shatter her jaw. "Haven't you, Shan?"

"Y – yes, Bos'n."

"Good. Don't forget it. And don't any of you think of ignoring one of my orders again. I'm here to stay."

* * *

"So, you don't object, Professor?" asked Pallas.

"Object? It's rather what I was hoping for. You know I don't approve of the cloistered life for a truly gifted student."

"But I won't be available to help you in your work – "

"You will be helping me, child. My current research project will attempt to tie together many social and political factors, to develop an historical mapping of the future of humanity itself. Almost any data is potentially valuable. And what could be more valuable than data collected by an operative in one of the nerve centers of Confederate power, the *Titan* herself?"

In a rare gesture of familiarity, he placed his hands on her shoulders. "These young people, these Arbiters, can teach you a great deal. And you can be an asset to them, as well."

"I hope I won't be an imposition."

"I know Jan Atal. He wouldn't allow you to stay, if he didn't think his crew would benefit." Mors winked. "Some more than others, eh? I read that you're back on speaking terms with young Metcalfe. Planning on doing a little field work on those Terran mating customs you were so – "

"Professor!"

"Come now, Pallas. Prudery doesn't become a Phaetonian."

"Neither does being a... dirty old man," she said teasingly.

"Dirty old man? Terran expression no doubt." He grinned. "I rather like that. Yes."

"If you're so curious about their mating habits, you should do your own field work."

He nodded thoughtfully. "Oh yes. Someday I will. Time enough for that, though. Honestly, I'm only a little over two-hundred!"

* * *

Her diminutive form outlined by the pure white of her cloak against the ebon black of space, Celia Faulkner held out her hands for silence. Standing before the windows of the Captain's promenade was the closest one could come to being outdoors in space. Really, it wasn't that different from being enshrouded by the protective atmosphere of a planet. In fact, the view was slightly better, without the many layers of atmospheric gases in the way. If one had some imagination and wasn't too much of a purist, it was an ideal setting in which to feel the spiritual presence of nature.

Ordinarily, she would have led this service sky-clad, but, while these young people were no doubt comfortable being naked in each others' presence, she doubted they were ready for her to parade around in the altogether. The cloak brought a bit more dignity to the proceedings, and dignity was what was called for.

After a sufficient time of silence had passed, giving each person time to reach out – or in – to the infinite, she raised her hands up high. "Goddess," she intoned. "Time has passed since this, our brother, departed this plane of existence; but time is daunting only to us, with our limited capacity to understand. His spirit is in your care, as is each of ours."

She looked to the mourners. Aer'La stood between Metcalfe and Cernaq, on one side of a table which has been dressed as a sacred space. On it stood a crystal bowl and a lone candle, for there was no body, no artifact, to represent the honored dead. On the other side of the table stood Atal, Carson and Kaya. Each held a goblet of wine.

"The spirit remains. It is tied to the body. It begs release. The tie to the flesh can be painful. Often the parting is traumatic. The living must ease this departure. If the spirit is tied to another spirit, as this one is, it can be torn between its own body, and that other spirit.

"Aer'La," said Celia gently, "speak to your dead. He is here. He could not leave without your release. Tell him what you need to tell him. Help him on his passage."

Aer'La stepped forward, looking uncertain. She took Cernaq and Metcalfe's hands and squeezed them, possibly harder than she meant to. Neither complained. Falteringly, her voice rough from holding back tears, she said:

"Druberj... I... want to thank you... for loving me. I didn't know people could be happy. You taught me that. I think... you could have taught me so much more. For years now, I've remembered your death. I've thought about the person who caused it. I've want-ed to kill him..." She paused. Beyond her control, the tears began to slide down her cheeks. She ignored them. "I had that chance yester-day...

"But I know it wouldn't have brought you back. Revenge... I thought that's what you deserved. But... see, you gave me a gift. Freedom. Without you, I wouldn't have it. If I'd killed Harl, I'd have given it up. I think... I think that's not what you would have wanted. I think you would have wanted to know, Dru... I've found Freedom. It's real. It's full of people that... that I love..." Her chest heaved. She choked down a sob. "... like I love you. I always will, and..."

After a time, Celia thought it was clear Aer'La would say no more. She spoke the closing words:

"Journey on now, Druberj. We will follow you, in time. Although we didn't know you in this life, you are now our loved one, our dead, as you are Aer'La's. For she is ours. You will be born again. We ask that it be in the same time and place as those who now stand to ease your passing. We wish to know you. We wish to love you again."

She picked up her goblet from a side table. As previously instructed, each of the Arbiters in turn raised theirs to their lips, drank, and poured the remainder into the bowl on the table. Celia did this last, then set down her goblet and went to take Aer'La's hands.

"He is free now. In a way we don't understand, he will at once be with you, and beyond. He feels no pain, but he does feel your love."

Aer'La nodded and squeezed Celia's hand. Cernaq led her off the promenade, into the Captain's office.

"So," Atal said quietly. "That's your people's funeral service."

"Not really. Mr. Metcalfe and I adapted it. This was all his idea."

"No one should die without a funeral," Metcalfe said. "It's inhuman."

"Well, non-sentient, anyway," said Celia. "Come, now. We'll have a meal, and share stories. We didn't know Druberj, but it's appropriate to remember those who touched our lives, as he touched Aer'La's." She stopped and lit the candle. "It burns as we leave the sacred space. The wine remains to represent the nourishment the departed spirit receives from our spirits. The flame lingers, as the spirit does. One more light, burning amongst all the lights in space."

"And standing on its own," observed Atal. "Burning unhidden and unafraid."

"Why, Captain! How poetic."

Atal cleared his throat.

"He used to write sonnets to my mother," said Kaya in a stage whisper. "I've saved copies."

"Demon child," Atal muttered. "I should have drowned you at birth."

"You'd have died of boredom, Daddy, and you know it."

"There are worse fates."

"Speaking of worse fates," said Metcalfe, "do you suppose Harl's finally met his by now?"

"By rights – and Varthan tradition – he should have been killed by now," said Atal. "Crafty as he is though, he may have found a way to survive. I don't think he'll bother us, though. Aer'La will make short work of him if he does. I don't have time to care about him, though. It's more important to me that we're all alive, and, finally, we're all free."

www.ingramcontent.com/pod-product-compliance
Lightning Source LLC
Chambersburg PA
CBHW020822260626
47169CB00003B/794